THE RENOUNCED

ALSO BY LOGAN YOUNG

THE POWER OF PRINCIRUM SERIES:

THE VANQUISHER OF WATER
THE TRIALS OF THE FAVORED
THE ETERNITY OF THED

THE RENOUNCED SERIES:

THE RENOUNCED

COMING SOON

THE RENOUNCED, BOOK 2

THE CLASH OF ELEMENTS, BOOK 1

THE RENOUNCED

LOGAN YOUNG

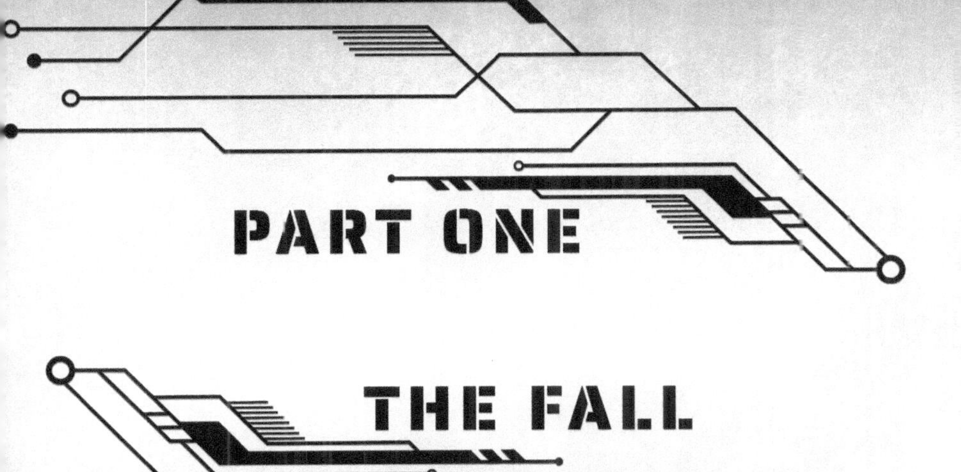

PART ONE

THE FALL

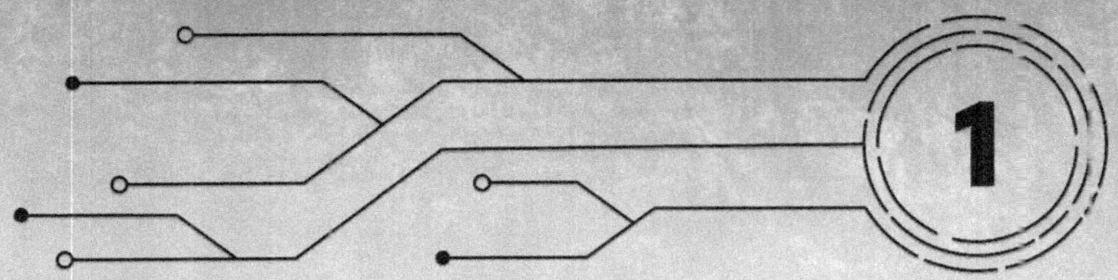

1

I DON'T REMEMBER FALLING asleep. I'm not entirely sure I did. I lie in bed, the silk sheets twisting around me like a vise. No matter what I do, it's like ice inching up my skin. A shudder runs down my spine, and I sit up, gasping as I clench the supple cloth between my fingers.

I'm not normally like this. In fact, I usually like mornings. My servants wake me, and the room is full of warm light, with a fire dancing in the marble hearth. But today, there's only a chill darkness in my room. I guess it's fitting; today isn't exactly a happy day. I'm going to a funeral, after all.

I shiver as my feet hit the icy floor. Taking a deep breath, I slowly make my way across the pitch-black room. My palms sweep blindly in front of me, searching for the handle of my closet door. This is ridiculous. I don't have much time, and I'm wasting it stumbling through the dark. I'd be better off pulling my robe over my head. Why does my father have to be so uptight? Was it necessary for him to—

"Ouch!" I can't stop myself from crying out as pain shoots through my leg. I hop in place, grabbing my pulsating shin as I fight the urge to shout again. If I could see my face, I know it would probably be bright red. This is so stupid. Why am I fumbling around in the dark, trying to find my closet like an idiot? This is precisely why I wanted Lysander and the rest of my servants here. They know where the furniture and light switches are better than I do.

But of course, my father has forbidden the whole family from attending the funeral. I know he's the new head of our family, but what right does he have to order *my* servants around? Besides, all I want to do is honor my grandmother on my family's land. It's not like I'm trying to sneak into Midtown, or giving money to some filthy Slummer.

My shin is still throbbing when I reach the closet. I pull the doors open, and automatically, soft, gentle light illuminates above the cabinets. I sigh, the pounding in my ears subsiding now that I can finally see, and toss my robe on the now velvet-carpeted floor. On the small couch at the back of the closet sits a perfectly folded stack of clothes. The corners of my mouth twitch. Lysander's been my valet since I was twelve. I doubt he knows I'm planning on attending the funeral, but at least he knows what outfit to pick for a somber day. I should find a way to thank him when I get back. If nothing else, it'll drive my father crazy. He hates it when I'm kind to the servants.

The fitted black silk suit, hemmed with swirls of golden thread, slips over me like water. The black diamond buttons are cool against my shaking fingers. I inhale deeply, and the chill morning air steadies my hands. Walking over to the full-length mirror, I take in my handiwork, and sigh. "It'll have to do," I mutter, running my fingers through the brown waves over my forehead. Honestly, it doesn't do much, but at least it's not hanging in my eyes anymore. It's the best I can do on my own. I guess I really do need to thank Lysander when I get back.

I walk through the empty halls and down the servants' stairs to the back door. Since our family has so many servants, this door is never wired into the security system. The back lawn glitters with dew. I rush across the grass, my heart thudding against my ribs. I can't be late. I've wasted so much time already.

Gram had always been there for me. Once, when I was about five, my father went ballistic when he caught me helping a servant clean up my room. He was about to lock me in there for the rest of the day, until Gram found out. She'd had my back ever since.

So, today, no matter what, I will be there for her.

Besides, the service shouldn't be long. Gram hated long, drawn-out, or over-the-top affairs. I'll be back before Lysander even comes to wake me up. My father will never know.

The grassy meadow lies below the lawn, its vibrant pink, blue, and yellow flowers swaying in the breeze. Their sweet scent tickles my nose, and my pulse slows a little. A small white stone building stands alone in the center of the meadow. No one is there.

I wish I could say I'm surprised, but I'm not. Gram was a little quirky—but then, who's grandmother isn't? Most people in Newtown think she lost her mind decades ago, given her "unnatural preoccupation with the undeserving" in life. My stomach twists into a massive knot as my hands tighten into fists. Gram may have been strange, but that doesn't excuse my father for banning the whole family from attending her funeral. She spent a small fortune on her personal mausoleum; someone in the family should see it.

I bite my lip and take a shaky breath. I don't have time to be angry. Not when I'm the only one here to remember Gram.

Suddenly, through the fading darkness, a faint orange glow blooms behind the mausoleum. The muscles in my face relax as it bobs slowly around the side of the building. Someone's lit a torch; someone else is here to bury my grandmother.

"See, Ezariah," I mutter, a smile spreading across my lips, "Dad can't scare everyone off."

When I reach the bottom of the hill, I find not one, but three men standing silently in the torchlight. They're all a little older than me, but not by much. My mouth falls open, and the hairs on my arms stand on end as I take in their tattered, stained overalls. Drones. The pungent aroma of sweat, factory smoke, and oil drifting off them is a dead giveaway. But that makes no sense; leaving your assigned residence zone is illegal. Enforcers have hunted people down for less. So, how'd these drones make it from Midtown to Newtown—and why are they at my grandmother's funeral? It's not like these drones knew Gram. Not like I did.

Warm light seeps over the horizon. I raise my hand, shielding my eyes as tears stream down my cheeks. A low, hypnotic chanting fills my ears, making my bones shake. Next comes a strange smell, like jasmine and sandalwood, stinging my nose, and I fight the urge to sneeze. I blink several times to clear my vision. Several men in black robes are walking down the hill towards us, supporting a dark brown casket. The man at the front carries a smoldering box swinging from a golden chain covered in glittering red gems. I can't help but smile; it just screams Gram.

The men don't make a sound as they carry Gram's coffin into the mausoleum. They place her on a raised marble pedestal before backing down the sweeping steps. Tears burn my eyes as the last one closes the ornate wooden doors, emblazoned with a fox seated before a gilded tower. Gram's crest.

I want there to be more, but I know there won't be. This was what Gram wanted, after all. My father is wrong, and I don't care if he freaks out when he finds out I was here. This is where I should be. This is my chance to say goodbye.

The man who carried the incense steps forward and starts to sing. I don't know the song, or even the language, but I understand its meaning almost instantly: he's saying goodbye. The melody winds around me like a breeze, and I sigh. I can almost picture Gram humming along, nestled in her favorite armchair, while my little brothers, Theron and Callias, play at her feet. Another flood of tears burns my eyes, and I wipe them away. It's strange, perhaps, but it's a perfect send-off for her.

"Arrest the nonconformists!"

I spin around, nearly slipping on the dew-slick ground. A pack of Enforcers are marching down the hill, the gold buttons on their dark uniforms glinting like stars. The Midtown drones scatter, running off in every direction. Several Enforcers race after them, their batons crackling with electricity.

I shake my head. What did they expect? I knew those drones must have snuck out of Midtown to be here. With any luck, the Enforcers will take them back there, where their kind belongs, and I can say goodbye to Gram in peace.

Two Enforcers continue on their path—but it's not toward the drones. They're approaching me. My insides turn to ice, my breath freezing in my lungs. Why are they coming for me? I'm not a nonconformist. I'm Ezariah Malkin, grandson of Lady Malkin. I'm attending a funeral on my family's own land, which we've held since the Great Fall. I've broken no laws. I have every right to be here. So why are they drawing their batons?

My feet move before I can think, breaking into a run, but rough hands grab me from behind. I gasp as steely fingers dig into my skin, pinning my arms painfully against my sides. I struggle to pull away. The air crackles, and pain explodes through my thigh.

"No!" I gasp as the Enforcer raises his baton again. "Don't you know who I am?"

I pull against the Enforcers' grip, fear and desperation clawing at my insides. I can't breathe as they half guide, half drag me from the mausoleum. At the top of the hill, the other Enforcers shove the captured Midtown drones into the back of an armored car.

But this isn't right. Why am *I* being treated like a criminal? These filthy drones clearly broke the law by coming into Newtown. But I've done nothing wrong. All I wanted was to say goodbye to Gram, and I didn't even get to do that.

"Where are you taking me?" I demand. The Enforcers remain silent as we speed across the grass. "Why are you on my family's estate?"

"Quiet!"

My hands tremble as the car rushes over the uneven ground. I've heard what happens to people in the Department of Correction. Nonconformists are beaten, and some even do hard labor. If someone really messes up, the department can even revoke their residency status.

But this is crazy! They can't be taking me there. The Department of Correction is for criminals, like the filthy Slummers, or these drones who snuck out of Midtown. I try to breathe, but it's like there's a massive weight on my chest. This is a mistake. It has to be.

The car turns sharply, and my head slams into the window. Who taught these idiots how to drive? At this rate, I won't even make it wherever we're going in one piece. Fuming, my head pounding, I look out through the thick, tinted glass. We're driving down a long, narrow road lined with trees. A massive white marble building sits at the end of the graveled drive, its tall windows reflecting the bright sunlight. My heart pounds like a drum, drowning out all other noise as it sinks in: we're not at the Department of Corrections. We're at my house.

The transport screeches to a halt, and I nearly collide with the window again. An Enforcer pulls me from my seat and marches me up the marble stairs, my legs wobbling beneath me. The two massive metal doors swing open when we reach the landing, revealing the wide-eyed face of our head housekeeper.

"Wh-what's going on?" Mrs. Thistlea stammers, her alarmed gaze falling on me. "Mister Ezariah! Is everything—"

"Where's Mr. Malkin?" one Enforcer says coldly, cutting her off. "We need to speak with him immediately."

I look from Mrs. Thistlea to the Enforcers, my stomach twisting into a knot. Why would they want to see my father? He's never broken a law in his life. I'm the one they've arrested for doing nothing wrong. Maybe they're here to apologize for the misunderstanding? I doubt it. Based on my treatment so far, these Enforcers don't seem like the apologizing type.

"Of course." Mrs. Thistlea nods. "Right this way."

She leads us through the vast halls as the Enforcers drag me along, their hands squeezing my upper arms. Mrs. Thistlea opens the dining room door, and my heart sinks. At the other end of the long table, my parents, Aunt Elara, and Uncle Galen fall silent. Even from the other side of the room, I see their eyes dart between Mrs. Thistlea, the Enforcers, and me.

I can't bring myself to look at any of them, so I stare at my shiny black shoes. I know I'm in for it. The Enforcers will tell my father where I was. He'll probably revoke my credit privileges for a month, at least.

"Mr. Malkin," one of the Enforcers barks, addressing my father. "We'd like a word."

"What's going on?"

My mother's quiet voice makes me look up. She's on her feet, her wide eyes glistening, and she takes a few tentative steps toward me, still wedged between two Enforcers. My heart races as I look into her eyes. She's afraid. But why? I don't understand what the big deal is; all I did was attend Gram's funeral. Last I checked, that wasn't illegal.

"What is the meaning of this?!" my father demands, also getting to his feet. His narrow eyes lock onto me. "Release my son at once! You have no right to—"

"According to the data you submitted to the Department of Order, Lady Malkin's funeral was likely to attract several nonconformists," one of the Enforcers says, her voice low and gravelly.

The words bounce around the inside of my skull. No. It can't be true. My father sent the Enforcers to Gram's funeral!

My stomach lurches, and I fight the urge to vomit. I know my father and Gram disagreed on a lot of things, but why would he tell the Enforcers to go to her funeral? Did he hate her that much? But why? She was such a sweet old lady.

"That doesn't explain why you're holding him," my father says, his eyes falling on me again.

"This man was at the service, sir. He claimed that this is his family's estate," the Enforcer says. "I take it this information is correct?"

My father's face turns beat red, and his eyes wider as he

turns to me. I think they might pop out of his head. I want to look away, but find myself unable to move or even speak. My arms tremble as I silently plead for him to understand. Gram was always there for me. How was I supposed to know he'd told the Enforcers that nonconformists would be at her funeral?

But I know better. My father has never understood me.

"There must be some mistake," my mother says, her voice little more than a whisper.

"No mistake, ma'am," the Enforcer says.

I glance at the man holding me. Through the slit in his helmet, I can see his face. Narrow eyes. Pinched nose. It's like he's smelled something rotten.

My face grows hot. What right does he have to judge us? He's an Enforcer—probably a Midtowner at best. Our family's been in Newtown since the Great Fall. He should be grateful to even be standing in a house like ours.

"If you have nothing else to add, we'll begin documenting all known nonconformists—including this one," the lead Enforcer says, nodding at me. "And we'll begin investigating their families."

"Wait," my father says, his voice cracking like a whip.

I expect to see anger burning in his eyes. Instead, his face is white, and his eyes are like dinner plates. He's afraid. The sight is enough to make me want to run from the room. Why is he scared? The Enforcers are here because of him!

"Sir, the system must account for all known nonconformists," the lead Enforcer says.

"I understand," my father says quickly. "And have no desire to disrupt AURA's system. But it was my information that resulted in the arrest of the nonconformists. All I'm asking for is five minutes."

The Enforcers glance at each other, and the one in front gives the smallest of nods. The grip on my arm loosens, and I stumble forward, momentarily caught off guard. The pounding in my ears slows, but my father's worried expression makes me pause.

Why is everyone making all this fuss over me going to a funeral? I get it: being caught by Enforcers isn't a good look for the family. But I'm not a nonconformist, so I don't see the problem here.

"The study," my father says, taking hold of my still-throbbing arm. "Now."

I do as he says, stumbling out of the dining room after my mother, aunt, and uncle, my father's hand like a brand on my upper arm. I try to shake him off, but he digs his fingers in, sending stabs of pain through my already sore shoulder. I don't have to see his face to know my father is furious. He probably blames me for bringing the Enforcers to our door. But he's the one who told the Enforcers to go to Gram's funeral, so this is just as much his fault as it is mine—maybe even more so. But I doubt he'll see it that way.

Uncle Galen opens the study door. It's small, the walls lined with hundreds of old, dusty books that I've never bothered to read. An ornate desk sits in front of the stained glass window, a large throne-like chair positioned behind it. Several plush chairs are arranged in front of the desk, along with a simple wooden one.

"Sit," my father says brusquely. He pushes me into the rickety wooden chair. A lump forms in my throat as my father joins my mother, Aunt Elara, and Uncle Galen on the other side of the desk. They all look worried. But right now, I don't care. Why is my family treating me like a criminal? All I did was disobey my father. That's not against the law.

"What's going on, Elias?" Uncle Galen demands, looking at my father. "Why would you send Enforcers to Mother's funeral?"

"You know why, Galen," my father snaps, and I can see his nostrils flaring. "Our mother never held Nomisman's laws in high regard. After she died, the Department of Order called me in for questioning."

Uncle Galen's eyes widen, and my mom and Aunt Elara

gasp. My father's words hang heavy in the air, and my heart pounds against my chest. So, my father had to go to the Department of Order. But why? My father has never broken a rule in his life.

"What did they want?" Aunt Elara asks.

"To know if I was as nonconforming as her," my father says. "I assured them of our loyalty to Nomisman and AURA, and to maintaining AURA's Laws of Economic Stability. But they wanted more."

"So, you confirmed that Mother was a nonconformist?" Uncle Galen asks.

"Of course not. That would put us all at risk. Besides, the old bat was good at covering her tracks. I told the Enforcers that any attendants at her funeral were likely to hold nonconformist beliefs."

"That's why you forbid us from going?"

The words leave my lips before I can stop them. My father turns his gaze to me, his eyes narrowing to slits. I can practically feel the heat radiating off of him. I press my back into the stiff chair. Is he going to hit me? But he just takes a shaky breath.

"So, what does this mean?" my mother asks tremulously. "Ezariah was there, with the nonconformists. Do they think—"

"Of course they do, Aelia," Uncle Galen says, cutting my mother off.

"The Enforcers could question the whole family, thanks to Ezariah," Aunt Elara says, shooting me a look. "Your other sons, Theron and Callias. Me and Galen's daughters. We're all at risk now."

Clearly, they're all afraid. But why am I getting all the blame? It was my father who sent the Enforcers to the funeral, and he did it to get them off his own back. They should be just as mad at him.

And Gram being a nonconformist? I knew she was different. She had her way of doing things that rubbed people like my father the wrong way. She hated it when people talked down to Midtowners or Slummers. I always just assumed she was compassionate. But Gram, a traitor to Nomisman? There's no way.

"I told you not to go to that stupid funeral."

For some reason, the anger in my father's voice doesn't send my heart racing. I shift uncomfortably in my chair, take a breath, and stare right at him. He's sitting in the throne-like chair behind the desk, his cold eyes glaring at me.

"There was no reason for you to go. But like always, you disobeyed—"

"There was a reason," I cut in, my voice shaking with suppressed anger.

"What did you say?" His voice is deadly quiet, which makes me shudder.

"I know you hated Gram," I say, "but you had no right to send Enforcers to her—"

"I had no *right*? I have every right," my father says slowly, emphasizing every word. "I'm the head of this family now. Maintaining and elevating our position is my sole purpose. My mother didn't hold Nomisman's ideals in high enough esteem. She should have been bettering the Malkins. Instead, she spent her life worrying about the thieves and animals in the Slum. She let our family become a subject of gossip."

"The rest of Newtown already thinks we're like her," Uncle Galen hisses. "If AURA found out, we could lose everything."

"You were supposed to fix this, Elias," Aunt Elara says. "We've waited years for Lady Malkin to die, and for you to take control of this family. But now—"

"I *am* fixing it," my father cuts in, and I see the veins protruding on his forehead. "Any association with her, or her backward way of thinking, won't be tolerated in this family."

"Gram wasn't backward. She was kind!" The words tumble from my mouth before I can think better of it. My arms shake as an eerie silence falls over the room. I turn to my mother who stares at my father, her eyes wide with alarm. This time, I know I've gone too far.

But I don't care. Why should I? According to my father, I'm always crossing some line. This is no different than any of our other arguments, and nothing ever happens in the end.

No, not nothing ever happens; *happened*. Nothing ever happened, because when I crossed the line, Gram saved me. She always saved me. But now, Gram's gone, and there's no one standing between me and my father's fury.

"I won't let our family lose everything because of you," my father says, his cool voice turning icy.

"Elias, please." My mother's voice is hushed, but it's like she's standing right next to me. "Ezariah's only sixteen. He's just a boy."

"A boy who needed to learn this lesson long ago," my father says, his voice shaking slightly. "His complete disregard for Nomisman's laws brought the Enforcers to our door. Remember the Corvuses? They lost everything—their estate, their wealth, their standing—all because they went against AURA and failed to maintain the Laws of Economic Stability. I won't let anything like that happen to our family. No. For the Malkins to survive, Ezariah needs to be removed."

It's like I'm listening to my father speak from a mile away. I need to be removed? Where would I be if I weren't here, in my family's home? I have nowhere else to go.

But that's not true… There is one place I could go.

I shake my head, as though that simple gesture could make it untrue. My father can't mean there. He wouldn't do that to me. He couldn't. Not his eldest son.

"Ezariah Malkin," my father says, "I Renounce you as my son and as a member of the Malkin family."

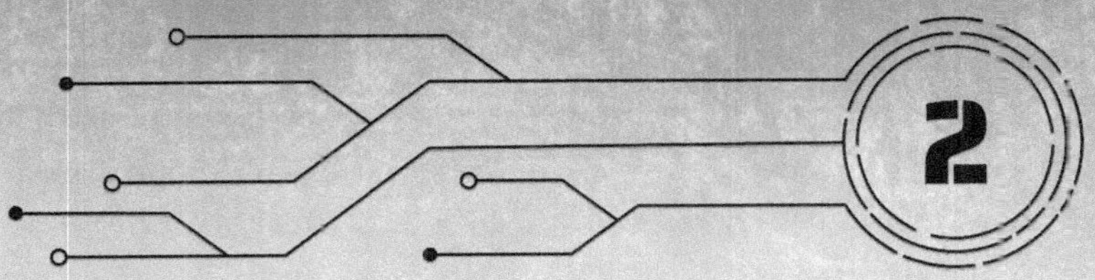

I WANT TO MOVE, to scream, to do something. Instead, I shake so violently that I almost fall off my chair. I try to look at my father, but he doesn't meet my gaze. Seconds pass, but it feels like years as my whole world implodes around me. I struggle to breathe. I messed up. I know that now. Going to Gram's funeral was a mistake. But does he need to Renounce me for it?

Renouncing isn't a rare punishment in Newtown. If someone's actions threatens a family's social standing, the head of that family has the right to cast them out. And that's just the beginning. It's not like the Renounced are sent to Midtown to live with the workers and entertainers. No, the Renounced are sent to Lowtown: the heart of the city. Everyone calls it the Slum. Of course, I've never been there, but I've seen pictures of it in school. There people have nothing, living like the animals they are in a misery of their own making.

And that's where my father is sending me.

"You need to leave. Now." My father's voice jerks me out of my stupor. "You have no place in my family's house."

I stare at my father, but it's like I'm looking at him through the wrong end of a telescope. The room spins around me, but I still see him sitting on his throne-like chair, surrounded by my family.

No—my former family. I stopped being a Malkin ten seconds ago.

My legs are still quivering, but somehow, I manage to stand. I stumble for the door, my trembling hands barely able to turn the knob. I shut it a little more forcibly than I intended to, the sound echoing down the empty hall.

Somehow, I make it back to my rooms. I reach out to open the door, but it flies open before I even touch it. Lysander slips past me, his brown eyes trained on the gold-and-silver pattern crisscrossing the carpet.

It's like I've been punched in the gut all over again. Not only will my family no longer acknowledge my existence, but neither will anyone who works for them. But that doesn't explain how the servants already know my father Renounced me. Were they listening at the study? I wouldn't put it past them. The servants always know everything around here. So if he already knows I'm Renounced, why was Lysander here?

The answer is waiting for me in the middle of the room: a pile of my travel bags.

The tightness in my chest lessens slightly. I want to thank Lysander, especially since I have no idea where he keeps the bags when I'm not traveling. He could lose his job if my father finds out he helped me—or worse. But I can't acknowledge this favor; I don't know how long I have before my father drags me out of the house.

Grabbing the largest bag from the pile, I run into the closet and stuff in whatever clothes I can reach. A shimmering white shirt made of diamond thread. A pair of pants studded with sapphires. In no time at all, the bag is ready to burst at the seams. I try to close it, but my hands are so unsteady that I only pull the zipper halfway down the bag. I close my eyes, and my chest feel like it's going to burst.

"Get it together," I say, taking a shaky breath. I can't lose it. Not now.

Suddenly, the door bursts open. I jump violently, slipping off the slick velvet couch. My heart races as I look up. There's an Enforcer in my doorway. I might be a little short for my age, but this Enforcer is massive; his helmeted head nearly hits the top of the doorframe. Through the slit in his helmet, I can see his eyes darting between me and the half-open bag between my legs.

My heart stops. No doubt my father sent him to make me leave his home. What am I supposed to do now? I'm not ready!

With a huff, he steps into the closet, picks up the only bag I managed to pack, and zips it with one hand. Then he hoists me to my feet like I'm no more than a rag doll. I stare at him, fighting the urge to recoil. He *touched* me. What gives him the right to touch…?

The fire inside me dies as quickly as it appeared. Of course this Enforcer can touch me now; I'm Renounced. I'm probably worth less than the mud on his boots.

I follow the Enforcer into the hall. In no time, we're descending the curved staircase to the entryway. Of course, my family is there, standing by the double doors. I look at my mother, but she just stares intently at the space above my shoulder. Even from this far away, I see the tracks her tears have carved through her makeup. Aunt Elara and Uncle Galen stand beside my father, my little brothers held between them.

My insides writhe and I want to spit fire. My aunt and uncle hold Theron and Callias's little shoulders, but they're struggling to shake them off. I look to my father, who of course doesn't look at me. Why would he have my brothers here? Probably, in his twisted mind, he's trying to prove a point. But why? Theron is nine, and little Callias is only seven.

My father nods to the Enforcer as we walk past. I might as well be invisible.

There's a new armored car waiting at the bottom of the front steps. The one that brought me here is long gone, as are the drones from Gram's funeral. I sigh shakily. At least I won't be stuck in a car with the drones. Maybe I can use the ride to figure out what—

"No!"

The high-pitched yell pierces me like a knife. I turn around, yanking my arm free from the Enforcer's grip. Theron is running down the sweeping marble steps, Callias right on his heels. My aunt and uncle stand in the doorway, their faces a mixture of terror and shock.

But their shock is nothing compared to mine. What are Theron and Callias thinking? They need to go back—right now.

"You can't go!" Callias says, his little fingers twisting around mine.

"This isn't fair!" says Theron, taking my other hand.

But he's not speaking to me. Theron's eyes narrow as he stares back the way he came. My father stands in the massive doorway, flanked by Uncle Galen and Aunt Elara.

"Why does Ezariah have to go?"

Even from down here, I see my father's shoulders shake. The hairs on my arms stand on end, and suddenly, I've forgotten how to breathe. I try to shake my brothers from me, but it's no use. Their hands are like vises around my own.

"Master Malkin," the Enforcer says to my father, "you allow citizens under your charge to fraternize with Renounced?"

"I... Of course not," my father says. "Members of my family adhere to AURA's laws."

"Elias, please." I hear my mother's feeble voice from somewhere behind my father. "They're so little. You can't—"

"Disobedience will not be tolerated." My father cuts my mother off like a freight train. "I Renounce them all. Take them, Commander. Now!"

"No!"

Anger fills me like fire, and it feels like I'm vibrating. I'm propelled forward, and all I can see is my father. He can't do this! Sure, Renounce me; he's always hated me. But Theron and Callias? They've never done anything wrong. They don't deserve—

"Stop!"

My side sears with pain, and the crackle of electricity fills my ears as I collapse to my knees. The Enforcer hoists me to my feet and pushes my little brothers and me into the car. I try to say something, but my mouth won't form the words. Slowly, almost in a daze, I turn in my seat. My father is pulling my mom back into the house by her arm. We roll down the graveled drive, my mother's wail piercing the thick car windows, tears shining on her face.

My brothers bounce up and down on either side of me as the car turns onto the street. I wish they'd sit still. On the outside, I fight to keep my face blank. But inside, it's like someone is squeezing my heart in their hand. My brothers stood up to my father, just like I did—and he Renounced them for it.

But why would they do it? They must have known what would happen. Well, Callias may not have known. But Theron should have.

I open my mouth, but something in their faces stops me from speaking. In them, I see none of the fear or dread that's coursing through my own veins like acid. In fact, there's a light in Theron's eyes that I've never seen before.

I fall back in my seat, staring at the dark roof of the car. What am I supposed to do now? I have no plan and no idea of where to start with one. Everything has happened so fast, I've barely had a moment to think. And that was fine when I was Renounced alone and only had to worry about myself. Now, I have two kids to think about. And they're just sitting here, acting like we're going on a grand adventure. How am I supposed to break the news to them? Don't they know where we're going and how dangerous it is?

"Lookie!" Callias yells, his face pressed against the window.

Through the thick, tinted glass, I see two fifty-foot black metal pillars: the barrier. Of course, I've never been to the barrier in my life; why would a Newtowner want to cross into a lower residency zone? But I've seen pictures of it in school. The teachers always show them during the weekly history lecture.

During the Great Fall, the country called America lapsed into economic and social chaos. When all the senseless fighting over resources finally stopped, the founders of Nomisman vowed to reestablish order. They created the Advanced Unification & Regulatory Algorithm to unify the country and stabilize the economic flow. AURA also wrote the Laws of Economic Stability to prevent another Great Fall from ever happening again.

What was left of the country was divided into twenty circular cities, all designed to be economically efficient. The smallest urban zone, Lowtown, is located in the center of each city. That's where the government provides free housing to those with no money. The next biggest is Midtown, then finally Newtown. Newtown is the largest, since its residents possess the most wealth and influence. Metal pillars ring each section, a deadly invisible current flowing between them to keep citizens from changing zones without proper clearance. Workers like our servants and government officials like Uncle Galen can move between zones if they have the proper work clearance, but they are required to return to their assigned zone by the end of the day.

The car stops a few feet from the barrier, and the Enforcer climbs out of the vehicle. I glance out the window. This isn't the Slum; we haven't even left Newtown yet. Why have we stopped?

The Enforcer opens the back door, and I instantly recoil. Callias stops moving as I press him into the opposite door. No matter how hard I try, I can't stop my body from shaking.

"Get out." The Enforcer's large hand wraps around my arm. "I don't have all day."

Pain shoots through my shoulder as the Enforcer pulls me from the car. Fuming, my face hot, I barely manage to land on my feet. I want to say something, but I stop myself as Theron and Callias join me. I take a deep breath. I need to keep it together.

We're escorted into a building near one of the pillars. It's small and could easily fit in my closet. My stomach tightens. No, not my closet; my former closet.

"Sit." The Enforcer points to a long wooden bench. I take a seat, and so do Callias and Theron.

"You are Renounced, making each of you your own entity in AURA's system." The Enforcer pulls a large black case out from behind a counter. "So, you will be given an ID tag. It stores your identification documents, residency clearance, and financial information."

The Enforcer steps out from behind the counter. In one hand, he holds a small cracked tablet. In the other is a giant syringe filled with bright blue liquid.

I cross my shaking arms, instinctively grasping my forearms. No. This isn't right. We don't get tagged until we're eighteen. That's the law.

The sight of the massive needle sends a shiver down my spine. I want to run, to get as far away from here as possible. But where would I go? Home? That's the first place I think of. But of course, I can't go there ever again; I'm Renounced. They'd slam the door in my face before I even made it up the steps. Besides, the feeling is mutual. If I never see my father's face again for the rest of my life, that's quite alright with me.

"Ow!"

Theron's cry pulls me back to reality. The Enforcer bends over him, the needle stuck deep into my brother's skin. The Enforcer plunges the bright blue liquid into Theron's arm, removes the needle, and holds the tablet over the injection site. The scratched screen turns green, and the Enforcer returns to the counter, leaving Theron with tears brimming in his bright green eyes. He slides across the bench, pressing his tiny body into my side. I look at him, and all the feeling drains out of me. What is wrong with me? How, at the first thought of escape, could I forget I'm not alone? How could I forget my brothers?

According to the law, we may not be a family anymore, but I don't care. I'm the oldest; Callias and Theron are my responsibility now. I can't just think about myself. After all, I'm the reason their perfect lives will never be the same. It's now my job to make sure they're okay.

The Enforcer returns with another injection, and this time, he grabs my arm. I brace myself as the needle enters my skin. I don't want to scream—not in front of Theron and Callias. But as the Enforcer pushes the plunger, I can't stop myself. The blue liquid is like fire and ice in my veins all at once. The Enforcer quickly confirms my ID tag with the tablet. It's a struggle to keep my face calm as I rub the spot with my thumb. It throbs like a nasty bug bite, and I think I feel something hard deep beneath my skin.

"I don't want one," Callias says, his voice shaking.

"Um…"

Callias's eyes are wide, and he's shaking so badly that it's making the bench we're sitting on vibrate. What am I supposed to say? The Enforcer is going to give Callias a tag whether he wants it or not. I feel like someone has kicked me in the stomach. Callias's excitement from the car ride is completely gone. But I still don't think he understands everything that's happening. I think his sole concern is the pain of the injection.

"Wait!"

The Enforcer stops, his hand inches from Callias's arm.

"I… Can you… It'll hurt him," is all I can string together.

The Enforcer must have something to numb Callias's arm before injecting the tag. I've seen other kids get their ID tags on their eighteenth birthdays. They do it at school. And they always say it's painless.

I want to stand, to do something. Doesn't this Enforcer care about hurting a little kid? Callias is only seven. This man should be protecting him.

The Enforcer shoves the needle into Callias's arm before I can open my mouth. My little brother screams. I wrap my arms around him, trying to give him some comfort. I want to do more, but what can I do now that it's over? So, I just sit, watching the Enforcer confirm the new tag in Callias's arm.

"Alright," he says, stowing the case behind the counter. "Let's go. Now!"

As Theron follows the Enforcer out the door, I pick up Callias, who is still whimpering, and catch them as Theron enters the car. I want to put Callias down; he's heavier than he looks. But his unhurt arm is wrapped tightly around my neck. So, I try to strap myself in with Callias sitting on my lap.

The Enforcer turns and hits several buttons on the dashboard computer. It's like he's set my tag on fire. Theron and Callias cry out, and I bite my cheek, determined not to make a sound. After a few moments, the pain subsides to a dull throbbing.

"Your tags are now active and integrated with your nervous system," the Enforcer informs us impassively. "Lowtown is your assigned residential zone. If you cross the barrier and leave your residential zone without proper clearance, you will be stunned, and the Enforcers will be notified. Your tags will be inactive while inside any Enforcer vehicle."

The Enforcer drives straight through the barrier into Midtown. I look out the window, hoping to distract myself, but the car is moving too fast for me to see anything worthwhile. From what I can tell, Midtown looks like a smaller, less shiny version of Newtown.

My leg slowly grows numb beneath Callias as the car winds through the streets. After a while, he loosens his grip on my neck and slides off my lap to press his nose to the window. Without warning, the Enforcer turns every few seconds, barely missing a collision with several buildings. My head stomach lurches, and I close my eyes, trying to breathe through my nose. Are all Enforcers terrible drivers?

Finally, the car slams to a stop. I barely manage to stay in my seat as the Enforcer climbs out and opens our door. "Get out," he barks.

I stumble from the car, and can't stop my mouth from falling open. It's like we've gone back in time. The street is uneven and bumpy. It's nothing like Newtown's pristine roads, which glow when it's dark. Several of the grimy buildings look like they're leaning on one another for support. I bite my lip. This area looks like it's on the verge of collapse. I breathe in to steady myself, and the air feels thick and heavy. I gag as the foul taste hits my tongue. I can't name it, and I don't want to. How can anyone live in a place like this?

My bag lands in a heap at my feet. I glare at the Enforcer, who is already back in his car. Doesn't he know how valuable this bag is? Everything I now own is inside it.

My feet carry me to the Enforcer's car. I grab the window as it rolls up, my heartbeat growing faster by the second. Through the slit in his visor, I see the Enforcer's eyes narrow. Is he going to force me off his car? He has every right to now.

"I … I need help," I stammer. My grip on the window tightens, and my knuckles turn white. A faint buzzing fills my ears as I stare at the Enforcer. Now that I'm here, the reality of the Slum is all too visceral. How are we going to survive this place? "What am I supposed to do?"

The Enforcer just stares at me. Then his eyes shift to Callias, who is holding tightly to my free hand, and Theron, standing beside me. I didn't even realize they had followed me to the car.

"Kid, I gotta go," he finally says. "Good luck."

I begrudgingly let go just before the Enforcer's car speeds off between the nearest ramshackle brown buildings. I want to throw something after him. What is wrong with that guy? I thought he was going to help us. But now, aside from my brothers, I'm really on my own.

We seem to be standing in some kind of town square. What must pass for shops around here fills the lower levels of the surrounding buildings. Little tables and makeshift stalls pepper the open cobblestone square. Heaps of blackened, ripped clothes lie against the buildings. Clearly, no one is willing to wear them. I don't blame them. Who would want to wear frayed clothes full of holes, covered in more stains than I care to count? Don't people wash their clothes here? I shudder at the thought.

No, wait… Taking a step closer to the filthy piles, the hairs on my arms stand on end. Clothes don't move, or stretch out an arm as someone walks past.

They're people.

"C'mon," I mutter to my brothers, picking up my bag with my free hand as one of the beggars eyes it greedily.

"So… Do you have a plan?" Theron asks.

"Um…"

Until now, it's taken all my willpower not to freak out. How am I supposed to come up with a plan when we literally have nothing? Nowhere to live, no idea of what to do, and no one to help us. Is this what our lives will become—reduced to begging on the side of the road?

I know we can't just stand in this square forever, but I can't seem to move my feet. Everywhere looks a million times worse than where we are.

"Well…" Theron shrugs. "I'm gonna look around."

"Wait, Theron!"

But he's gone before I can take a step. Every thought of planning our next move vanishes. What the hell is he thinking? I tighten my grip on Callias and my bag and run into the square. "Theron!" My strangled cry barely rises above the busy hum of the Slummers. Some vendors hold up their wares as I pass, but I hear nothing. I don't care about their Slum garbage. I need to find Theron. I cannot lose him now.

It's then that I see him as his mop of dark brown hair disappears down a narrow side street. I race to catch up with him, dragging Callias behind me. We finally reach Theron as he peers down another alley.

"We need to … stay together," I pant, letting go of Callias to clutch the stitch in my side. "You can't just run off like that!"

"Sorry." Theron shrugs. "I just wanted to explore."

"Me, too!" Callias pipes up. "I wanna explore, Ezariah!"

I press my palms into my eyes. This isn't fair. How can I tell them no when they both just want to look around? This place is our new home, after all—but it's more dangerous than I ever imagined. Can't Callias and Theron see that?

Of course not. We don't learn about the Slum in school until we're thirteen. But I've only been here five minutes, and I already know it's no place for little kids to run around. The Slummers are savages. They have no morals and no sense of Nomisman's values. Who else would live in a place like this?

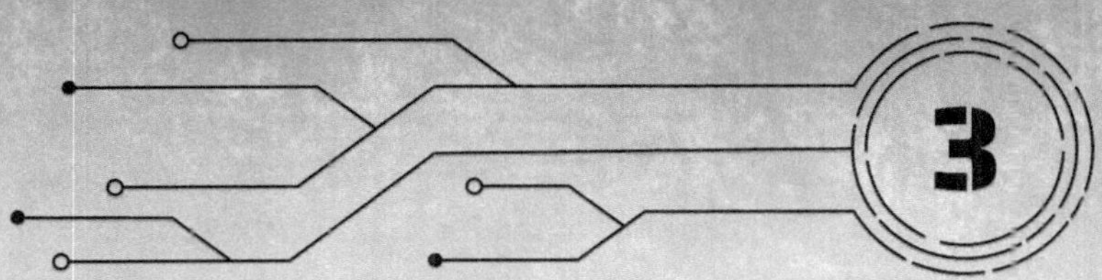

EVEN THOUGH IT'S still the middle of the day, the world feels darker with every step I take. Behind me, the square looks like the bright light at the end of a dark tunnel. I sigh and instantly gag, tears welling up in my eyes. Even the air in this disgusting alley is worse than in the square.

Of course, Theron and Callias don't notice. They're a few yards ahead of me, looking down streets and peering through boarded-up windows. I want to call them back, but stop myself. How are they not freaking out right now? I'm barely keeping it together as it is.

Theron walks past a pile of overturned bins, and a hand darts out of the darkness.

"That's a pretty thing." A man emerges from the shadows, his blackened fingers twisted into Theron's shimmering gold shirt.

My muscles tense as my heart pounds against my ribs. I tighten my grip on my bag. The man's hair hangs in a tangled mess around his face, his tattered clothes billowing around him. He can't be older than our father, but he's easily thinner than even Theron. I've never seen anyone look so crazed.

"Hey! Let me go!" Theron struggles against his grip, but it's no good.

I trip over my feet, trying to place myself between this man and Callias. Theron pulls against the man's skeletal arms, but it's useless. Shaking, I grab Theron's hand and pull with all the strength I can muster. I can't let this madman take my brother.

Theron screams, the sound of ripping fabric fills the air, and he falls into my arms.

"Run!"

Theron and Callias don't need me to tell them twice. They sprint back to the square, and I hurry behind them, my bag swinging wildly. The slapping of my feet against the ground fills the air. Is the man following us? I don't dare to look back.

The foul air sticks in my throat, but I don't stop until we reach the square. I barrel right past the boys, grabbing Callias's flailing arm in my free hand. We need to hide—now. There are abandoned shops all around the square, and we sprint through the door of the nearest one. It swings open so quickly that we topple to the floor in a heap.

Panting, my side searing, I push myself up. I can see the alley through the broken blinds. It looks completely deserted. I press my forehead against the dusty glass and try to catch my breath. This place is insane.

"Are you okay?" I grab Theron's shoulders, looking him up and down. Besides the tear down the left side of his shirt, he seems fine. I breathe deeply, trying to stop my hands from shaking.

"I'm okay. Promise," Theron says. He peers around me, no doubt trying to see if the man followed us. I'm not surprised; Theron's probably even more rattled by this than I am.

"Who was that?" Callias asks. "He smelled funny."

"Does it matter?" How am I supposed to know who that guy is? "We're never going down there again."

"Why not?" Theron asks. "Just because—"

"Because I said so."

I press my palms into my eyes. My heart is still hammering in my ears. What is wrong with my brothers? Don't they see how dangerous this place is? That man attacked Theron just to steal his shirt. I doubt he even knows how valuable the shirt is. From the looks of him, he wouldn't know class if it bit him.

"Whoa," Callias says, his voice full of wonder.

I turn from the window. What I thought was a deserted shop is actually stocked with the oddest assortment of items I've ever seen. Counters line the walls, stacked high with what I can only call junk. An old, frayed cloth, a spool of rusty wire, and a set of chipped plates all sit on the shelf nearest the door. I furrow my brow. What kind of a store sells trash?

"Let's look around," Theron says, his eyes widening.

"Really?" My little brother grew up with literally everything he could ever want. What's so exciting about an abandoned store full of junk?

Theron disappears into the clutter, and I grab Callias's hand before he can run off too. I can't lose sight of both of them in this dark shop. What if we're not alone? The hairs on my arms stand on end.

Why does Theron keep running off? He should be terrified after what our father did. I know I am. Now that I'm still, I can't stop my arms from shaking. I guess running after Theron and Callias was good for something, but I can't chase after them forever.

"Didn't expect customers today."

I jump, letting go of Callias's hand, and lose my footing. Pushing myself up, I see a man emerge from behind one of the counters. He's short, with thinning black hair, and a head that looks a little too large for his body. His clothes are ragged and dirty, like the rest of the people I've seen here. As he draws nearer, a foul smell enters my nose, like food gone bad.

"Wha...?" I cough, trying not to breathe too deeply.

"You 'ere to make a deal?" The man's voice is rough, like he's speaking through a mouthful of dirt. "If not, get out. I'm not givin' handouts."

"A deal? Like, buy something?" I eye the shelves of broken plates and patchy, stained clothes. Who in their right mind would buy any of this crap?

"I wanna buy something!" Theron materializes from a few rows down. "At least a new shirt."

"Um…"

To be fair, Theron's shirt is ruined. He'll need a new one sooner than later. But everything here looks like it's had at least four owners before landing on these shelves. I can't imagine buying any of it. We'd be better off finding a proper clothing shop.

"What's in there?" The man nods to my bag sitting on the floor.

"Just clothes," I say, picking it up. What does he care? Clearly, this bag isn't from his shop. My insides turn to ice. That man in the alley wanted to rip Theron's shirt right off of him. What's this guy willing to do to see everything in my bag?

"Open it," the man says, his voice stern as he steps towards my brothers and me. "Or I'll call the Enforcers."

It feels like someone is squeezing my lungs. Why would this guy call the Enforcers? I've done nothing wrong.

My eyes automatically travel to my forearm. Pain radiates from my new ID tag, where the skin is already turning blue. I look up and see the man's narrowed eyes darting between my new tag and my brothers.

"Hey, you two take a look around," he says to Theron and Callias, his voice a little softer. "But don't break nothin'."

As Callias and Theron disappear between the shelves, the man points me to the counter. I breathe a little easier, placing my bag onto the rough wood. Maybe I misjudged him. He was nice enough to Theron and Callias.

The man empties my bag, tossing its contents into careless piles, rubbing each fabric slowly between his gnarled fingers. I want to say something, but bite my tongue. I wish he'd be more careful. Seeing my clothes piled up on the counter is strange. They're all I have.

"This stuff isn't half bad," the man says, his thumb caressing the glittering ruby button of one of my old evening shirts.

"Really?"

"Really," the man says, finally tearing his eyes away from my clothes. "It's quality stuff. Don' see much like it down 'ere."

I try not to smirk. Judging by the contents of the shelves, my clothes are the nicest things to ever enter this shop.

"I'll take it all."

"Uh, what?" I must have misheard him. I thought he was checking to see if I stole anything from his miserable store.

"I'll take it all," the man says again. "Give you a fair price for the lot."

"I'm not selling my clothes."

This guy is clearly trying to take advantage of me. I'm still wearing my funeral garb; I must look like an easy target. But I can't sell my clothes. What would I wear tomorrow?

"You got credits, kid?"

"Credits?"

"Money," the man says slowly.

"Um, no… But—"

"How you gonna eat without money?" The man cuts past me. "How you gonna care for little ones without money?"

"I … um…" The thought hadn't yet entered my mind. The words bounce around my head, and I feel empty. Of course we need money. How else are we supposed to buy things? Why'd I spend all that time at home packing a bag? Why didn't I think about money?

The answer hits me like a cane to the gut. I've never had money before; minors can't hold currency in Nomisman. Whenever I wanted to buy something, I just gave them Gram's name and didn't have to worry about it. In fact, the only money I ever saw in my house—my former house—was on credit drives, and my father never let me anywhere near those.

"Exactly," the man says, like he knows what I'm thinking. "I'll give you three hundred ten phys for the lot of it."

"What?" I may have never held money before, but I've never

even heard of phys. Back in Newtown, we pay for everything with credits.

"It's about seventy-seven credits."

I sputter out a laugh. "You're joking, right?" Just one of my shirts costs at least five times that.

"'Fraid it's the best I can do," says the man with a shrug. "Gotta stay under the radar. Take it or leave it, kid."

I bite my lip. I know we need the money. But is it enough to cover us in the Slum? Based on the contents of this shop, nothing here must be very expensive. Maybe it'll be enough for us to get by until I can figure something else out.

"I'll take it."

"Smart move."

The man disappears into the back room, taking my clothes and bag with him. He returns with a small leather satchel and slides it across the counter. I pick it up, and it's surprisingly light. I peer inside. The bag is full of odd square coins of varying sizes. I furrow my brow. This is money? It looks like a child made it.

I find Theron and Callias near the back of the shop. They're bent over a dusty display, examining what looks like a selection of old teeth. I clamp my mouth shut as my stomach lurches.

"C'mon," I say, trying to take my brothers' hands. I grab Callias, but Theron slips through my fingers like water.

"I want a new shirt," Theron says, playing with the tear in his golden shirt. "There's some over there."

The clothes are on a small rack at the front of the shop. They're by far some of the dirtiest clothes I've ever seen, all dark grey, although I doubt any of them started that way. Theron tries one on, and the frayed hem easily reaches his knees. I rub the sleeve between my fingers. It feels like unpolished wood. I look around. This can't be all there is.

"Wait here."

I return to the counter, but there's no one there. I open my mouth to call for the man, but stop myself. I don't know his name. Luckily, he must've heard my strangled cry, and he shuffles out of the back room seconds later.

"Yeah?"

"Um... I... Sorry. I don't know your name."

"It's Bart."

"Right. Bart. My brother needs a new shirt. His got ripped.'

"Clothes are up front."

"Um, don't you have anything ... else?" I barely stop myself from saying *"better."*

"It's the best selection in the square," Bart says, his puffy eyes narrowing. "They're thirteen phys each."

"What?!" I don't think I can take much more of this. There's no way a raggedy shirt is worth that much, especially given how little he gave me for the quality stuff I had. "I'm not paying that!"

"Hmm...." Bart looks me up and down, and the hairs on the back of my neck stand on end. "Tell you what. You and your brothers give me your clothes. I'll give you twenty phys and let you each pick out new clothes at no cost."

The thought of that rough cloth touching my skin makes me cringe. I'm not selling my last set of decent clothes just to wear rags. Before long, Bart's probably going to offer to buy our hair. I may be Renounced, but I still have my dignity.

"I'll just pay for the shirt." I pull out my leather money bag and pour the contents back onto the counter. I feel a twinge as Bart takes a handful of medium and smaller coins. I may be overpaying for the shirt, but at least Theron's not wearing a ripped one anymore. I try to focus on that.

"Lemme guess." Bart speaks so low that I have to lean in to hear. "You're Renounced?"

"I... Um... We... It's..." is all I can string together. We obviously stand out here.

"Figured. You Newtowners don' blend in here. Don' usually see any that young." He jerks his head, and I turn to see my brothers picking up a lumpy old ball. "What'd they do?"

"They … didn't want me to go." Saying the words makes me want to crumple to the floor. My brothers are in this place because of me. They did nothing wrong, but now they're stuck in the Slum for the rest of their lives. Why couldn't they have just stayed quiet? If they had, they'd still be home. At least there, they'd be safe.

"Well, 'ats a shame."

"Why?"

"This," Bart says, his voice a mere whisper as his eyes dart towards the front door, "is no place for little ones."

The sun is setting behind the crumbling buildings as we step back into the square. Shadows stretch over the uneven cobblestones, and figures seem to bloom from the darkness. I toss Theron's worthless old shirt into a bin and grab his and Callias's hands. I need to get us out of here before anything else goes wrong.

All of the streets leading out of the square look identical. People could be lurking down any one of them, just like last time. My eyes dart around, searching for anything that might indicate a safe path out of here. But all the filthy streets look the same to me. So, I take a deep breath and pick one at random. Hopefully, the closer we get to the border between the Slum and Midtown, the better things will be.

"Where are we going?" Theron asks.

"We need to find a place to sleep."

"But I'm not tired," Callias says, and yawns.

"Yes, you are," Theron sneers.

"Am not!"

"Knock it off," I hiss, my heart pounding in my ears. I can't have these two drawing attention to us. I already feel like someone's watching us.

How anyone gets around here is a mystery to me. Even though the sun hasn't set yet, the shadows cast by the misshapen buildings shroud the streets in darkness. I try to lead us in what I think is a straight line, but after the third turn, I have absolutely no idea where we are.

A cat appears out of nowhere, streaking across the road in front of us. I jump, letting go of Theron's hand.

"Where are you running off to?" Theron calls, chasing after it.

"Theron!" I race after him, hoisting a dazed Callias into my arms. Why won't he just stay with us? "We need to stick together," I pant, grabbing his hand as the cat vanishes through a crack in an old door.

"Why?" he asks.

"Because…" Do I tell him that our new home is also home to the worst people in the city? I decide against it; there's no point in freaking him out now. Besides, what can I do about it? It's not like we can go back to Newtown. My chest tightens, and tears sting my eyes. I blink them away. I need to keep it together.

"Because it'll be dark soon," I finally say, "and I just don't wanna lose you."

"Sorry," Theron sighs. "I just wanna look around."

"I know. Tell you what," I add, forcing my face into a smile. "I wanna find the border of Midtown. Can you get us there?"

I doubt Theron will be much help. He knows no more than I do about this place. But maybe this will keep him from running off every five seconds.

"Yeah!" Theron takes off, pulling me along behind him. I keep glancing over my shoulder every few steps. I can't shake this feeling that someone's watching us, lurking just out of sight. But every time I look around, the street's deserted.

I take a deep breath and cough on the musty air. I need to get a grip. I've had a long day; my legs and arms feel like lead, and stars pop in my eyes every time I blink. I shake my head, hoping to wake myself up. Instead, a dull throbbing begins behind my forehead. Great. That's just what I need: a headache on top of everything else. We'd better make it to the border soon.

The sky turns from pink to indigo as we round what must be our hundredth corner. About fifty yards ahead of us, the leaning buildings of the Slum stop. I see those tall black pillars: the barrier to Midtown. A squad of Enforcers stands outside a large Midtown building, made of red brick, with large towers belching clouds of thick black smoke. I exhale, and my muscles relax a fraction. We made it.

Suddenly, a bell rings, and people start streaming out of the building. The waiting Enforcers surround them and escort the workers to the barrier. One by one, the workers place their arms into a hole in one of the pillars. Even from far away, I see their ID tags glow green beneath their skin as they step across the barrier and into the Slum.

My eyes widen as the realization hits me. These Slummers are allowed to work in Midtown. But why? What did they have to do to earn their daily freedom from this hellish place?

I set Callias down and double my grip on Theron's hand as we walk through the growing crowd. I can't have him running off here. Now that we're at the edge of the Slum, I don't know what to do. Surely, one of these buildings is the free Slum housing I've heard about. But which one? None of them look fit for anyone to live in.

"Excuse me!" I shout, my heart racing slightly. I hurry toward one of the workers as she climbs the steps of the nearest building. "Do ... do you live here?"

"Who wants to know?" the woman demands, her voice rough and gravelly.

"We're ... um ... new. Is there a place open?"

"Do I look like the manager?"

The woman skulks inside before I can respond. I hurry after her, practically dragging Callias and Theron behind me. Luckily, I stick my foot out and catch the door before it closes. Ignoring the pain in my toe, I pull it open.

The room is small and bare, save for a counter topped with a rusty bell. The boys slide down the bare wall, their eyes puffy. I'm not much better. My head's pounding, and my insides feel like they're tied in knots.

I ring the bell. Nothing happens. I ring it again, and the sound makes the throbbing in my head double. I shut my eyes. The darkness helps, but not much.

"You need somethin'?"

My eyes flick open. I take several steps back, trip over my feet, and fall to the floor. A short woman with thinning brown hair stands hunched behind the counter.

"Sorry," I stammer, scrambling to my feet. "I was wondering… Do you have any… Can we live here?"

"'We'?" The woman narrows her eyes, looking me up and down.

"Me and my brothers." I step aside, showing her Theron and Callias. They look exactly how I feel, slumped against the wall, their eyes half closed.

"ID?" She looks bored.

Reluctantly, I extend my arm as the woman pulls out a beat-up scanner from behind the counter. She holds it over my forearm, now a patchwork of blues and purples. The scanner beeps, and I see the screen flash green.

"Fresh in, I see," she says, her bony fingers typing something into the scanner.

"Um … yeah."

"Well, lucky for you, I have an opening. Just became available this afternoon. Woulda been gone if you came tomorrow." She holds the scanner over my tag again and presses something. "It's on the top floor. 708."

I have to try several times to get the boys' attention. Callias stands after a couple of prods, his eyes half open. But I can tell from the look on Theron's face that he will need a bit more convincing.

"Time for bed," I whisper.

"I'm tired."

"I know." Why did I let him run around so much? "Don't worry, we got a place upstairs."

My legs feel like they're on fire as we mount the endless

stairs. My body aches, and the foul, thick air burns in my throat. More than anything, I want to fall onto my bed, burrow beneath the covers, and never come out again. Maybe if I did, this nightmare would be over.

About halfway up the stairs, I scoop Callias into my arms. My back feels like it's splitting in two and my legs feel like they're filled with fire, but I ignore it. I'm relieved when we finally step onto the top floor. When we reach door 708, Theron's eyes are half shut, and Callias's head is nestled into my shoulder.

I wave my tag over the scanner where the knob should be. The door clicks, but doesn't move. It seems slightly too large for its frame. I jam my hip into the wood, and it bursts open.

As we step into our new home, my first impulse is to roll my eyes. The main room is the largest, with two smaller ones on either side. Except for two brown mats on the floor of the smaller rooms, the apartment is completely empty. My expectations were already low, but this must be some sort of joke. How can anyone live in a place this small? The whole thing could easily fit in my closet back in Newtown.

"Where's all the stuff?" Theron asks thickly as I hit the light switch near the door.

"It's…" What am I supposed to say? This place is a dumpster fire.

"Where's the rest?" Callias's head bobs to either side as he looks around.

"This is it, Cal," I say, trying to sound more optimistic than I feel.

"This can't be all there is." Theron frowns, his eyes widening.

My head feels like it's going to explode. Don't they understand that this empty apartment is all we have now? I'm tired, everything hurts, and I can't spend the rest of the night explaining our circumstances. I'm barely holding it together as it is.

"Why don't you guys pick out your room?" I say, trying my best to make it sound fun.

"I don't wanna share," Callias moans.

"We've never had to share before," Theron says.

"Oh. Um…" Of course they don't want to share. We've never had to share anything in our lives. "I thought you guys would like to have a sleepover for our first night."

Luckily, Theron and Callias are exhausted enough to fall for it. I let them pick which room they want, but both are basically identical. Callias's eyes droop the second his head hits the sleeping mat. Theron lies down, too, and I'm almost out the door when his voice stops me.

"Where's the blanket?"

Seriously? All I need is for them to go to sleep. I take a breath, but it does little to calm my fried nerves. I can't get mad at him. It won't do either of us any good. Until today, everything Theron's ever wanted has been at his fingertips. He'll probably lose it if I tell him the truth. He's just a little kid, after all. I can't tell him tonight.

"I'll try and find one," I say, shutting off the bedroom light. "But I don't know where anything is. Try to sleep. I'll bring one in once I find it."

I hear my brothers' slow, heavy breathing a few seconds after I shut the thin door. I press my forehead against the rough wood and breathe for what feels like the first time since I left for Gram's funeral. Hot tears well up in my eyes, and I blink furiously, trying to push them away. This can't happen. Not where they can hear.

I crumple to the floor in my own dark room, my face landing on the stiff brown mat. It stinks; I'm obviously not the first person to use it. Tears slide down my face as everything I've pushed down claws its way to the surface.

Gram's gone. I'm Renounced. And because of me, my brothers are Renounced too. We've been injected, chased, and frightened. I've sold everything we had. Everything I know is gone. How could anyone think that my Gram cared about any of the savages in this dismal place? After what I've seen today, none of them are worth saving.

After a while, my tears stop falling, and the aches and pains of the day fade. Now I'm hollow; there's nothing left but emptiness. We have to survive in the Slum, a place that's even worse than my darkest nightmares. And I have no idea how we're going to do it.

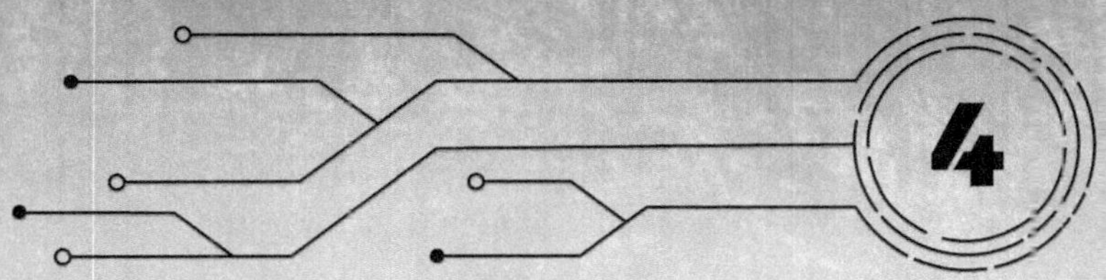

THE WARM LIGHT of sunrise seeps through my eyelids. I want to savor this—my brief moment of peace. Between all the screaming and shouting I heard last night, I barely got any sleep. I roll onto my side, turning away from the light, and it's like someone's driving a nail into my skull.

Wincing, I bury my face in my mat. The nasty smell burns my nose. Even after sleeping on it all night, I'm still not used to it. Why won't it all just go away—the smells, the pain, everything? Maybe this is all a bad dream, and it will all vanish when I open my eyes. If so, I'd like to wake up now.

Slowly, I open my eyes. I'm still lying on a filthy sleeping mat in an empty room. My arms and back shake as my muscles twitch sporadically. To top it off, the throbbing in my head doesn't stop.

"So much for wishing," I murmur.

I sit up. The grey walls sway back and forth as stars pop in my eyes. My stomach jumps into my throat, and I can't keep myself upright. I fall sideways, and my head smacks onto the concrete floor. The pounding in my skull doubles, and I lie frozen, sprawled halfway off my mat. What do I do? I need to get up, but I don't want to move again. It just makes everything worse. And that was just from sitting up. What will happen if I stand, or try to walk? I could fall, or worse. I've never felt this horrible in my life.

Every time I try to stand, the room reels around me. I take it slow, first propping myself up on one elbow, focusing on my breathing while trying not to choke on the thick air. But even that barely helps; my stomach still lurches with the slightest movement. I clamp my mouth shut. I can barely stand the smell in here as it is; filling the room with even worse smells won't make things better.

Eventually, I manage to get to my feet. My legs still wobble precariously, but at least the walls have stopped swaying. Slowly, I make my way to the main room. I feel disgusting. The last time I showered was the night before Gram's funeral. I need to find the bathroom. Last night, I was so focused on getting the boys to bed that I didn't have the energy to look.

There's just one problem: I can't find it anywhere.

"Seriously?" I grumble. How can this apartment not have a bathroom? This place just keeps getting worse.

I spot a small nook that I didn't notice when we arrived. I open the few cupboards, but they're as bare as the rest of the apartment. There aren't even any plates or cutlery. There is a small sink, but that doesn't help with my current situation. In the few minutes it's taken me to look around, my desire for the bathroom has doubled.

I rub my face, which doesn't help my pounding head. This apartment is entirely useless. I need to find a toilet. There has to be one somewhere in the building. Where else are people supposed to relieve themselves, or bathe? Outside? Is that why it always smells? My spine shudders, and I shake my head. Even this place can't be that bad.

My feet are so stiff that I have to try a few times to jam them into my shoes. I try opening the front door quietly, but it doesn't budge. I have to ram it with my shoulder several times before it finally opens. Pain spreads down my arm to the rest of my body like wildfire, filling me with a dull ache.

In the hall, I'm not really sure what to look for. The apartments are all numbered, so maybe the bathroom won't be? There are two unmarked doors at the end of the hall. The one on the left reveals a mostly empty closet except for an old broom, a rusted bucket, and a can full of thick white powder. I open the right-hand door and step into what must be the bathroom, though I wouldn't dream of calling it that. An old, cracked mirror hangs above a dirt-colored sink. A beaten-up toilet sits just beside the sink, smudged with large black and brown specks. There's a small excuse for a tub wedged into the other side of the room, entirely coated in grey grime.

My stomach lurches, and my hand flies to my mouth. I cannot go to the bathroom in here. It's disgusting. I could pick up any number of diseases in a filthy place like this. But my need to relieve myself easily outweighs any discomfort I may have. Besides, it's not like I have any other options.

I raise the toilet seat with my foot. I don't want to look down, but for some insane reason, I can't help myself. The small amount of urine I produce in the black bowl is dark yellow. That's not right; isn't it always supposed to be clear? I can't deny it anymore: less than one day in the Slum and I've already picked up some strange illness.

Back in the apartment, I hear sounds coming from the boys' room. I rub my face. Naturally, our crappy lodging doesn't have a clock, but I know this is the earliest my brothers have ever woken up. Maybe if I'm really quiet, they'll go back to sleep? After what I just endured in the bathroom, I need a moment of peace before facing them. But the noises don't stop, only getting louder.

"You guys okay?" I stick my head into their room.

Theron and Callias lie on their mats, curled up into little balls. They squeeze their eyes shut like they've dared each other to make their faces as small as possible. Callias clutches his stomach, while Theron holds his head in his hands. They look miserable.

"My tummy hurts," Callias whimpers, staring up at me.

"So does my head," Theron says, his voice barely more than a whisper.

"I'm sure it's not too bad," I say, my own throbbing temples as I kneel between their two mats. Crap. I could handle feeling sick when it was just me, but now Callias and Theron feel bad too. What am I supposed to do? Back in Newtown, Gram sent servants to fetch the doctor whenever we got sick. Their medicines could fix anything in a matter of hours. But here? Do they even have medicine in this godforsaken place?

But it doesn't make any sense. We've been in the Slum for less than twenty-four hours. How could we all get sick that fast?

"Make it stop," Callias says, his eyes the tiniest of slits. "You can fix it. Right?"

"Um…"

"Please, Ezariah," Theron groans. "My head feels like it's gonna explode, and my mouth's really dry."

I wish I could let them just go back to sleep. That's all I want to do. But I have no idea what's wrong with us. Given how disgusting the Slum is, each of us could have something different. This is officially beyond what I can manage. I need to find us a doctor. There has to be one somewhere in this hellhole.

I have both boys dressed and out the door in five minutes. I don't bother mentioning the bathroom. Luckily, walking down the hall takes all their focus. I'm grateful. I don't think I can face that disgusting place again—especially now.

Maneuvering down the stairs is the most challenging thing I've ever done. My legs shake on every step, and the pounding in my head only grows. About halfway down, I have to pick up Callias, which doesn't help. I try to keep my face neutral; I don't want them to see how miserable I am. It'll just make everything worse.

In the dull morning light, the area outside our building is a ghost town. I pause, looking out at the emptiness. What am I supposed to do? My immediate thought is to move outward; that's how I found our apartment. But we're already at the edge of the Slum; the barrier is twenty feet away. There's nowhere we can go.

But that's not true. I turn and see the shadowy street that brought us here. We could go back in. A shiver runs down my spine, which quickly becomes a dull throbbing all over my body. It's the last thing I want to do. But what other option is there? My insides gurgle, and it feels like someone is squeezing my stomach from the inside.

"C'mon," I say, gritting my teeth as I take a tentative step. "Let's go this way."

My eyes dart in every direction, expecting to encounter the horrors we endured yesterday. But we never do. In fact, the narrow streets are transformed. The buildings, all covered in large, worn posters and fliers I didn't notice yesterday, no longer fill me with a sense of doom.

A few streets in, other people start descending from the buildings. I instinctively grab Theron and Callias's hands. I can't have them running off again; I'm so shaky that I doubt I'd be able to catch them even if my life depended on it. Of course, in their current state, they'd probably only make it ten feet before collapsing. Either way, it's best to keep them close.

"Excuse me," I pant, trying to grab the attention of a tall, thin man a few feet in front of us. He begins to turn his head, but for some reason, he quickly turns away.

"Hey!" Anger burns away some of my pain. I know he heard me. "We need help. We're sick."

The man shakes his head and walks away without saying a word. And he's not the only one. I try to ask everyone we pass, but they turn their heads and go on with their business like I'm not even there. I even see a few roll their eyes as they walk away, muttering under their breath.

I want to scream, to throw something, but I doubt I could even manage it right now. Why won't these people help three sick kids? Okay, I know I'm not really a kid, but Theron and Callias certainly are. Regardless, we clearly need help.

The deeper into the Slum we go, the more people pile into the streets. I try to steer us away from the Slummers, to the side of the road where we aren't so close to them. But there are so many people, we have no choice but to follow the crowd. I doubt I could push our way out, even if I weren't sick. There are just so many people. I always knew the Slum was packed with disgusting beggars, but seeing it in person is very different.

We don't stop until we're right back where we started: the square where the Enforcer dropped us off. People weave between the many carts and stalls, and all the shops have their doors open—even Bart's.

I grit my teeth, tightening my grip on Theron and Callias. There has to be someone here who can help us. But where do I start? Where would a doctor be in a place like this?

"You boys new 'round here?" an old woman asks, looking us up and down with narrowed eyes. "You don't look so good."

"We're sick." I wince as my head gives a nasty throb. "We got here yesterday, and now we need medicine."

"I see." The woman chuckles.

"Can you help us or not? We need a doctor," I snap, unable to mask my desperation. I don't see what's so funny about sick kids.

"Of course I can help." She smiles. "I have just what you need in my cart."

My eyes narrow as I follow the woman through the rows of makeshift tables and stalls. She's a good foot shorter than me, her back stooped with age. She's so thin that a decent wind would probably knock her right over. What kind of a doctor is she?

The woman's cart turns out to be piled high with small, wrinkly balls, all in various shades of brown. I stare at them, dumbfounded. Whatever they are, I know they're not medicine. I grab Callias and Theron. This is a waste of time. This woman is no doctor.

"'Ere you are," the woman says, handing a withered ball to each of us. "These should fix you right up."

I hold the ball up to my stinging eyes. It's so tiny, I could easily hold five in one hand. I squeeze it, and the soft surface gives slightly. The hairs on my arm stand on end. How is this squishy ball supposed to fix us?

"No." I put the ball back on the cart. "We don't need these. We need medicine. We're sick."

"You're not sick, you stupid boy." The woman shoves the ball back in my hand, and a deep brown liquid oozes from it. "You're hungry."

"Hungry?" That can't be right. I shake my head, trying to think back. When was the last time I even ate? Of course, I got up too early for the funeral to eat yesterday, and with everything that happened afterward, I didn't even think about food. The last time I actually remember eating was dinner the night before last, when my father announced that none of the family were to attend Gram's funeral.

My jaw drops as my stomach tightens again. I've never gone so long without eating.

"It's seven phys for the apples."

Apples. So, what I thought were grotesque little balls are actually apples. They must be different from the ones we had at home. With shaking hands, I pull my money bag from my pocket and fish out seven of the smallest square coins. The old woman smiles, stowing the coins in a large metal tin before turning to serve another Slummer.

Saliva floods my mouth as I stare at the wrinkly little apple. Tentatively, I take a bite. The apple is so mushy that I don't even need to chew it. Somehow, it tastes sour and stale at the same time. My stomach lurches, and I want to spit the rotten thing out. It's by far the most disgusting thing I've ever tasted.

"How is it?" Theron asks, eyeing his apple like it's an alien.

"It's…" Even though I want to vomit, I force myself to swallow. I blink rapidly, trying to keep the tears from my eyes. If that woman's right, these disgusting apples will make us feel better. "It's good," I lie and force myself to take another bite. It tastes even worse the second time.

"Ezariah, it looks funny," Callias says, wrinkling his little nose.

"Aren't we looking for a doctor?" Theron asks. "Shouldn't we be—"

"Look, we don't need a doctor." I kneel on the cobblestones and look Theron and Callias each in the eyes. "I was wrong, okay? We're not sick; we're just hungry. We haven't eaten in over a day. That's why we feel like this. This food will make us feel better."

Callias licks his lips as his eyes fall to his apple. Slowly, I raise mine, and we each take a bite. Callias squeezes his eyes shut, pursing his lips, but he doesn't spit it out. For me, the third bite isn't any worse than the second.

"Ezariah, I really don't want—" Theron begins.

"Will you just eat it?!" I snap, unable to take it anymore. "It'll make you feel better."

Theron steps back, looking like I hit him in the face. My insides twist uncomfortably, but I ignore it. I didn't mean to shout at him, but I need Theron to understand that this is our life now. Things aren't going to be like they were back in Newtown.

"Theron," I say, making a real effort to keep my voice calm, "you need to eat it. We're... We live here now. And this is what the food is like."

"It's not *too* yucky," Callias says, taking another bite of his apple. "It kinda tastes like applesauce."

I'm not sure if it's Callias's goofy grin that does the trick, but Theron finally takes a bite. I sigh and force down the last squishy piece of my apple. I hope this works. If not, I'm not sure what else I can do.

It takes Theron and Callias a while to choke down their apples. Callias finishes his first, and we sit on the front steps of a building while Theron continues to eat. After a while, the pounding in my head fades, and my stomach no longer feels like someone's tied it in a knot. My muscles even relax a little, and

I'm not sure if I'm more surprised or relieved. The disgusting apples actually worked.

Even Theron starts to look a little better. He's still pale, but he no longer looks like he's about to collapse. "I wanna look around," he says, throwing the brown core of his apple into the nearest pile of garbage.

"Why?" Clearly, Theron is feeling more like himself again. All I want is to go back to our little apartment and hide. We've spent too much time out here today for my liking.

"Why not?" Theron shrugs. "Don't you want to know more about this place?"

Honestly, I don't. I've already seen enough of the Slum to know all I need to know. It's filthy, cramped, and full of dangerous people who eat and sell garbage. Doesn't Theron realize that AURA created the Slum to keep all the sketchy, radical people away from the civilized ones?

Theron plops down beside me. "Please, Ezariah?" His eyes are wide, and his bottom lip is quivering. "I promise I won t run off or be crazy."

Ouch. Am I really that easy to read?

"C'mon, Ezariah," Callias says, pulling on my arm. "It'll be fun."

"Okay, fine." I chuckle, unable to stop myself. Besides, it's not like we have a whole lot to do for the rest of the day. At least this little excursion will keep Theron and Callias busy. "We can look around. But only for a little while."

"Yes!" Theron jumps up, punching the air.

My brothers lead the way out of the square. I stay right on their heels. I know Theron said he wouldn't run off, but I want to be close, just in case.

I don't see why my brothers are so interested in this place. All of the buildings are identical: stone or brick ground levels, topped with wooden upper floors. A good wind could probably knock them all down. Is that why several look like they're leaning on each other?

Curling posters cover nearly all the available wall space. As we pass what must be the tenth in a row, I realize they're all the same. I stop, taking a closer look. The Nomisman seal is stamped on the bottom corner of the poster, which is covered in large, bold writing.

BY DECREE OF THE GOVERNMENT OF NOMISMAN:

PER THE LAWS OF ECONOMIC STABILITY ESTABLISHED BY AURA, RESIDENTS OF LOWTOWN MUST PRESENT THEMSELVES IN THE TOWN SQUARE ON OCTOBER 15 AT NOON FOR THE CULLING. THE WINNER WILL RECEIVE NEW RESIDENCY STATUS, INCLUDING ALL IMMEDIATE FAMILY MEMBERS, PERMITTING RELOCATION TO SELECT PARTS OF MIDTOWN.

ATTENDANCE IS MANDATORY.
IN AURA WE TRUST.

I read the poster two more times, sure that I must have misread it. But there it is, plastered all over the walls of the Slum. There's some kind of lottery—and the winner gets to leave this hellhole.

I wrack my brain, trying to remember my teachers' words. We learn about the Laws of Economic Stability in school, but I can't remember anyone ever mentioning a Slum lottery. That's a detail I doubt I would have forgotten.

Or would I? Before yesterday, I couldn't have cared less about what happens in the Slum. But now, I do, in a way I would have never dreamed possible. Warmth spreads through me as I stare at the yellowed, weather-torn poster. I can't stop the smile from growing on my lips.

A few blocks from our apartment, Theron finds several shops at the bottom of a building. The first is filled with rolls of fabric. Callias immediately asks for a blanket. I stare down at my shoes; I completely forgot to look for blankets in our apartment. So, I let him pick out a piece of fabric he likes and have the man behind the counter cut enough for two blankets.

Theron and Callias run into the next store, their new blankets draped over their shoulders like capes. A sweet smell, quite different from the rest of the Slum, hits my nose as soon as I step inside. Saliva floods my mouth as I stare at the shelves, covered with loaves of bread, muffins, rolls, and pastries.

I grab Callias and Theron as we walk the aisles, but it's not to keep them from running off. My stomach gives an uncomfortable lurch as the warm scents fill me up. I double my grip on my brothers, desperate to keep my hands occupied. Now this is how to deal with hunger.

"That all?" a young woman asks as I place a bag of fluffy rolls on the counter. "Eight and a half credits."

"Okay," I say, pulling out my leather money bag and staring and the strange assortment of coins.

"Or it's thirty-four phys if you're low on credits."

Back at our apartment, we're barely make it over the threshold before Theron rips the bag open. The rolls are bigger than my fist and covered in a thick layer of cheese, leaving cur fingers covered in grease. I search the cupboards more thoroughly than I did this morning and find two chipped cups. I fill them with water from the sink. It's a light brown color and leaves a metallic taste in my mouth, but it's better than nothing.

When I send the boys to bed, each wrapped in their new blankets, I feel like I'm about to collapse. I can't believe we did it. I got us through our first day in the Slum. No one attacked us. We even found food that doesn't look or taste like garbage

And maybe, just maybe, I may have found a way to get us out of here. I lie on my sleeping mat, staring up at the dark ceiling. The Culling is our ticket out of the Slum, and it's only a few weeks away. The thought brings a smile to my face. Once I win the lottery, we'll never see this horrible place again.

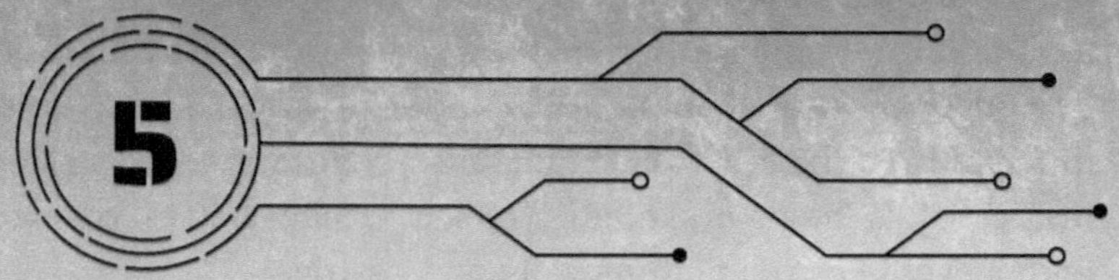

IF I SLEPT LAST NIGHT, it wasn't for long. It's still dark out, and the chill in the air stings my skin, but I don't care. Even as I lie on this filthy sleeping may, I'm practically humming with anticipation. Today's the day of the Culling. After surviving nearly a month in the Slum, I'm finally going to get us out of this miserable place.

How long will it take before we're in our new home in Midtown? I assure myself that we'll be there by the end of the day. Finally, Callias, Theron, and I won't have to live on top of each other like animals. The thought warms my insides, and my lips stretch into a smile. It's a strange feeling—almost foreign. After everything we've endured in the Slum, we deserve so much more.

When I can't stand waiting anymore, I figure I might as well get up. I pull on my black suit jacket, which is unrecognizable after almost four weeks of constant wear. The golden trim is nearly gone, the edges are fraying, and after not washing it since Gram's funeral, the smell brings tears to my eyes. I can't wait to buy new clothes once we're safely in Midtown. Hopefully, we'll get to go shopping before moving into our new home. Yet another reason to get out of this hellhole.

Theron and Callias are dead to the world, curled up under their thin blankets. I can't help but stare at them. They look so small. A small part of me doesn't want to wake them. At least when they're asleep I don't have to worry about them.

"Time to get up," I say, shaking Callias's slight shoulder.

He lifts his head a fraction before it falls back to the sleeping mat. I bite my lip and shake him a bit more forcefully. Callias rolls onto his side, pulling his blanket over his head.

I'm not as gentle with Theron. Instead of trying to rouse him, I simply grab a fistful of his blanket and pull.

"Hey!" Theron whines, his tangled hair hanging over his eyes.

I stifle a groan. Don't they realize how important today is? It's Culling day—our last day in the Slum. They should be excitedly running around or bouncing off the walls. It's taking all I have to keep myself calm.

"What's for breakfast?" Callias asks, finally sitting up.

"Um…" I didn't think about breakfast. Of course we need to eat something before the Culling. I'm not sure how long it will take, and there certainly won't be any food worth eating there.

In the tiny kitchen, I split the last of our loaf of bread three ways. I try to take my time, but I eat my piece in two bites. Saliva floods my mouth, and tiny bumps rise all over my arms. As always, I crave more the instant it's gone. I force myself to drink the metallic water from the tap to fill my stomach. After today, I won't have to drink anything so awful ever again.

We leave as soon as the boys finish eating. I contemplate packing our things before realizing all we own are the blankets I bought Theron and Callias, and the worn clothes on our backs. I don't bother bringing the blankets. They're filthy now, and maybe someone else will find a use for them.

"Why are we goin' so early?" Theron asks, and I hear the annoyance in his voice. "Doesn't the lottery thing start at noon. What's the rush?"

I bite my tongue, stopping myself from saying something stupid. Why can't Theron see the magnitude of today? But if I'm being honest, I'm not sure I want him to. We've barely survived the Slum. The sooner I win the Culling and leave this place, the better off we'll be.

The street outside our building is already packed. People are making their way toward the center of the Slum, to the square. I instantly take Theron and Callias's hands, trying not to smile. It's hard to keep the smugness from my face. *See, Theron? We're not the only ones going to the Culling early.*

We step into the crowd, and my brothers' hands slip out of mine. I look down, my heart pounding, expecting to see them standing beside me. But they're not there.

"Theron! Callias!" I push through the mass of people, barely able to breathe. Where are they? How did they manage to vanish in a second?

I reach Callias first, who's stopped at the entrance to one of the many alleys. He's bent over, gently calling to what must be the ugliest dog I've ever seen. It's small, with matted brown fur and a crooked tail. Even from several feet away, I can see its ribs pressed against its skin.

I retake his hand and brace myself for the struggle. But Callias doesn't pull away.

"Bye!" Callias smiles, waving to the dog as I lead him away. "He's so cute."

I clamp my mouth shut, breathing deeply through my nose to try and calm myself. That mutt is the opposite of cute. Why would Callias want to touch it? It's filthy, and probably just begging for scraps.

Finding Theron is a whole other issue. More people have filled the streets in the time it took me to retrieve Callias, and now it's a sea of bodies. I look around, searching for some sign of Theron's dark hair. My pulse races as I drag Callias along, clinging to his little fingers for dear life. Where could Theron be?

"Do you see him?" I ask Callias, hoping he's spotted something I've missed.

"Nope," Callias says, sounding completely uninterested.

"We need to find him," I say, my panic rising. "If we're late... We can't miss the Culling."

I shake my head. I can't let myself think like that. There's no way I'm missing the Culling. My whole future, our freedom from the Slum, depends on it.

"Should we check his hiding spots?" Callias asks.

"What hiding spots?"

Callias pulls my arm, steering me not toward the square, but down one of the dark, winding side streets.

I never come down here if I can help it. Old sheets and torn pieces of cloth hang over slack lines, while piles of discarded junk, trash, and people sit in the shadows, barely distinguishable from one another in the darkness.

"Let's go back," I say, trying to hide the panic in my voice. Out of the corner of my eye, I see heads peeking out of the shadows, no doubt roused by our voices. "This place... It's not safe."

"Theron's always exploring down here," Callias says, pulling harder on my arm.

My heart races even faster as sweat coats my palms. Why would Theron explore here? Doesn't he know how dangerous it is? I need to find him before something terrible happens.

"Theron!" I shout, unable to think of anything better. "Theron! Where are you?"

"What?"

The knot in my chest relaxes as Theron's voice hits my ears. He almost blooms out of the blackness, running toward Callias and me with a wide smile. I hurry to meet him, dragging Callias behind me. As soon as he's close enough, I grab Theron's wrist. Before he can say anything, I turn on my heel and march back toward the main street, my heart thundering in my ears.

"Why'd you run off?" I demand once we're safely back on the main road. "What's wrong with you?"

"What?" Theron shrugs, trying to pull his wrist free. "I thought we were going to the square for the Culling?"

"We are," I say firmly as we rejoin the crowd.

"But..." Theron stammers, fighting to free his arm from my grip. "That street's faster. We can cut around and—"

"No." It's a struggle to keep my anger in check. I can't believe Theron would be so reckless. I don't care how much faster he thinks his shortcut is; it's not worth him getting attacked in a dark alley. Doesn't he remember what happened our first day here? But all Theron wants to do is run around and explore. This is precisely why I need to get us to Midtown, where it's safe.

The deeper we move into the Slum, the more packed the streets become. I jump whenever someone bumps into me, which happens way more often than I'd like. People press in around us, and I fight the urge to gag. The odor burning my nose is a new level of awful.

But even as the crowd swells, it somehow maintains an air of calm. They, like me, must be excited for the Culling. But the closer I look at them, the less excited they seem. In fact, they look almost annoyed.

It's then that I see the Enforcers. They stand on the stoops, batons at the ready, watching over the crowd. The sight of the Enforcers calms me more than the inaction of the crowd. For the first time since arriving in the Slum, I actually feel safe. No one would dare try anything with all these Enforcers here.

The crowd slows to a crawl as we approach the square. After nearly an hour, it's fair to say I'm irritable. I stand on my tiptoes, trying to see ahead as even more people press against me. What's taking so long?

The square is unrecognizable. Several long tables have been set up, each manned by multiple Enforcers. I watch one hold a small device over the forearm of an elderly woman. My pulse quickens. This is it: the Culling sign-in. I tighten my hold on Theron and Callias. I can't have them running off again.

"Arm," an older Enforcer barks, waving me forward.

I step up, and the Enforcer grabs my arm.

"Hey!" I gasp, unable to stop myself as she presses on the hard lump of my ID tag with her thumb.

"Hold still," the Enforcer snaps, not taking her eyes off my arm. I try not to move as she waves her scanner over my tag. The scanner lights up green, as does the tag under my skin. She lets me go, and I gently rub my throbbing forearm. Did she need to be so rough? I'm not like the rest of these Slummers; I actually want to be here.

"You're cleared for one entry in the lottery," the Enforcer drones, examining her scanner. "You may purchase additional entries for eight credits each."

I freeze, my foot halfway to the ground. Additional entries? I assumed each person in the Slum only got one—so, between Theron, Callias, and me, we were sure to win. But this changes everything. With more entries available, there's no way we won't escape this hellhole.

"How many will this get us?" I ask, pulling out my money bag and dumping the contents on the table.

The Enforcer blinks several times, her eyes darting between me and the coins. I try to keep my face neutral. Why is she so surprised? She's the one who offered to sell me more entries.

"Umm … alright," the Enforcer mumbles.

Another Enforcer scans Callias and Theron while the first counts the largest of my coins. I don't dare breathe as the stack of coins grows higher. How many entries will it get me? Ten? Twenty?

"These'll get you three entries," the Enforcer says, sweeping several of the largest coins into a metal box. "Keep the rest, kid."

Three entries. I stare at the remaining coins. Why won't she take them? I don't know how many phys are in a credit, but there must be enough for at least four more entries. I want to argue, but I can feel people behind me starting to stare.

"Your arm," the Enforcer says after typing something into her scanner. She scans my tag again. It flashes green for a second time, and she gestures me forward. My heart races as I take my brothers' hands. Theron keeps shooting me strange looks, which doesn't help.

"What?!" I snap.

"Nothin'." Theron shrugs. "That was a lot of money."

"It's fine," I say, shaking my head. Since when does Theron care about money? It's not his job to keep track of it. Besides, we won't need to worry about money once we win the Culling. After today, we'll actually have a decent place to live. It will all have been worth it.

It doesn't take us long to reach the square, which is already packed with people. I recognize some of them from the market stalls and the bakery, and those who beg at the barrier near our apartment. I give them a wide berth and find a spot near one of the surrounding buildings. I crane my neck, trying to see the center of the square over the hundreds of heads. It's at least fifty yards away. A dull throbbing fills my head. We'd probably be at the front if Theron and Callias hadn't needed breakfast, or run off earlier. It'll take forever to push through all of these people when we win. We're already shoulder to shoulder, and more people keep coming. Hopefully, they'll all step aside to make room for us when the time comes. I can barely stomach the few bumping into me now.

Several chairs and a long table draped in a crisp, white cloth are arranged on the enormous stage in the middle of the square. Massive screens flank the stage, streaming the activity in the square for all to see. I wrinkle my nose at the mass of grey projected there. The Slum looks even more disgusting on screen than in person.

Finally, after nearly an hour, a few figures step up onto the stage. I know right away that these people aren't Slummers. Their vibrant, glittering clothes practically glow against the sea of poverty all around them. I fight the urge to roll my eyes. The lack of proper finery screams Midtown. They're always trying to live up to Newtown fashion, but they lack the sophistication. But even these lackluster outfits make my heart race.

However, the last person to take the stage catches my eye. Her clothes are much subtler and hang loosely on her thin frame. She looks so out of place next to the Midtowners that I want to laugh. Who is she?

"Welcome," a man says from the podium, his cheery amplified voice echoing around the square. "It's time for the Culling to begin!"

I raise my hands to clap, but quickly stop myself. I barely have room to breathe, let alone applaud. But no one around me is paying any attention to the man speaking; they just keep talking amongst themselves. I roll my eyes. After today, I won't have to put up with this anymore.

"Per the Laws of Economic Stability, established by AURA after the Great Fall, the government of Nomisman declared that the residents of Lowtown will present themselves four times a year for the Culling," the man continues, practically yelling over the chattering crowd. "The winner will be granted relocation clearance to Midtown, as well as for immediate family."

Images flash across the massive screens, accompanied by an upbeat musical track. I watch the smiling people, their faces and bodies clean, their eyes clear and calm. My breath catches in my throat. That's all I want: to be happy, safe, and clean. Did all of those people really get out of the Slum?

"Now," the man says once the video concludes, "let the Culling commence! It is my honor to present the last winner, Thea Frazier."

The man claps enthusiastically as he steps aside, making room for the woman in the ill-fitting clothes. My eyes widen as Thea takes the podium, her yellow dress moving a little too freely around her narrow waist. I guess months of living a care-free life in Midtown cannot undo years of neglect in the Slum.

"Let Ms. Frazier serve as a shining example to you all," the man says, smiling widely as he grabs Thea's shoulder. "Since being culled, she's worked tirelessly at a refinery. And now, it is her honor to cull the next citizen to enjoy Nomisman's generosity. In AURA we trust."

The man holds up a tablet, and the hairs on the back of my neck stand on end. This is it! Any second now, I'm going to win the lottery and get us out of this place. We're finally going to be free.

"In AURA we trust," Thea echoes flatly, then taps the tablet.

Without warning, pain sears through my forearm. I gasp and look down, my heart racing. My tag slowly pulses bright red as other shouts of pain rise around me. I look up. Everyone is examining their tags, which are all flashing red. The red pulsing increases, and I grit my teeth. Of course—this must be how they pick the winner. That's why they scanned us coming in. But why does it have to hurt?

The massive screens show a wide shot of the square, and I struggle to keep the pain from my face. No doubt they'll zoom in on me when I win. The last thing I need is to look like an idiot in front of everyone.

But it's not my face I see on the screens. Instead, it's a woman who looks like she hasn't bathed in three weeks. I want to scream, but when I open my mouth, no sound comes out. Besides, no one would hear me; the fanfare blaring from the speakers is so loud that it drowns out the crowd.

My stomach feels oddly hollow as I watch the woman mount the stage to join Thea. The smiling man says something into the microphone—probably the winner's name. But all I hear is a dull roar. How could I have lost? I did everything right—I even bought extra entries! I deserve to be on that stage, getting ready to go to Midtown while the people cheer for me. Sending this woman to Midtown is a waste; she's a Slummer through and through.

The crowd disperses the moment the gaudy Midtowners escort the new winner from the stage. I blindly follow the mass of people, paying no attention to where I'm going. What does it matter? I lost the Culling. Now, we're stuck in this miserable, disgusting place. What am I supposed to do? The Culling was my—our—chance to escape. I haven't felt this trapped since the day my father Renounced me.

"Ezariah." Theron's voice reaches me from a mile away.

My stomach twists uncomfortably. I'd completely forgotten about Theron and Callias. But there they are, staring up at me like I have all the answers. I simultaneously want to hide and to hit something. How can I tell them that our only chance to escape is gone?

"What?" I say tentatively.

"I'm just hungry." Theron shrugs, and I'm shocked to see him smiling.

"Me, too," Callias says. "Can we grab something on our way home."

"From the good bakery," Theron adds, stepping ahead of me and Callias. "C'mon. It's this way."

I don't know which is worse: Callias calling our crappy apartment "home," or Theron referring to any bakery in this filthy place as "good." Either way, it makes my blood boil.

I grab Theron's wrist before he runs off like an idiot again and pull him and Callias from the crowded street. Several people shout as we bump into them, but I barely hear them. I've put up with Theron and Callias's crazy behavior since we arrived, but that was because I thought we had a way out. Now it needs to stop.

"Listen," I snap once we're off the street. "This place isn't our home. We don't belong here, do you understand? We're not Slummers."

Tears well up in Callias's eyes as Theron stares at me with his mouth wide open. For the first time since our Renouncement, both my brothers are still. The sight drives away my anger, and I feel hollow. I didn't mean to shout at them. Well, not out of anger, at least.

But I am angry. Why are they both okay with being stuck here? Ever since we arrived, my sole focus has been on getting us out of the Slum. Don't they want to escape this place as badly as I do? Why aren't they more upset?

"Sorry." Callias sniffs, tears sliding down his face.

"I... I didn't... I'm not angry at you," I finally manage to say.

"I know," Theron says, wrapping an arm around Callias, a

cool bite to his voice. "You're mad that you lost the stupid Culling. I'm not an idiot, Ezariah."

"Can we still get food?" Callias asks, wrapping his thin arms around my waist.

I can't help but laugh. These two are handling this way better than I am. I'm the oldest; I'm supposed to take care of them, not the other way around.

We buy more cheese rolls and a bag of apples at the bakery by our apartment. I consider getting more, but I doubt it will last long enough for us to eat it. I don't even know how long food lasts; we usually eat everything we have within a day or two. After that, the flavor is drastically worse. I'd rather come back every day than eat old food.

The sun is already sinking behind the buildings when we climb the stairs to our apartment. I feel like I've run a marathon, even though I spent most of the day just standing in a crowd. My feet grow heavier with every step. When we get to the apartment, I just want to lock myself in my room. I don't even care that my stomach is growling louder than it has in days; I just need this horrible day to end. I don't want to think about it ever again.

"Where are you going?" Theron asks when I make a beeline for my room.

I reluctantly join Theron and Callias on the living room floor. Theron has laid out the food, and the sight drives the sleep from my brain as saliva floods my mouth. I try to pace myself, but I eat three rolls and two apples in less than five minutes. I guess my hunger is stronger than I thought.

Suddenly, pounding explodes from the door. I jump, dropping my roll as my pulse skyrockets. I stare at the door, not daring to move. No one's knocked on it since we moved in. Who could it be?

More knocks sound, and my heart pounds so hard that I can feel it in my ears. I stand, and even though every instinct is screaming at me to run and hide, I open the door.

"Took you long enough."

It's the woman from the front desk. I haven't seen her since the first night when we arrived. She has an old piece of paper clenched in her fist. It's completely covered in writing that's been crossed out and written over at least twelve times. I wrinkle my nose. Even the paper in this place is disgusting.

"Sorry," I say, my pulse slowing. "What is it?"

"I'm 'ere to collect for the month," the woman says, staring at me like I've asked her a ridiculous question. She squints down at her list, no doubt struggling to decipher the many smudges and cross-outs. "You owe five credits."

"What?!" My mind is racing. There has to be some mistake. "I thought Slu— I mean, Lowtown housing is free."

"It is." The woman rolls her eyes at my idiocy. "But electricity isn't. Like I said, five credits … or twenty phys."

Somehow, I feel even more cheated than I did at the Culling. Why didn't she tell me when we moved in that I had to pay for electricity? Isn't it a basic service that's included with housing? Reluctantly, I pull my money bag from my pocket. I give the woman the coins, and she dumps them into her bag, then marches off down the hall without another word.

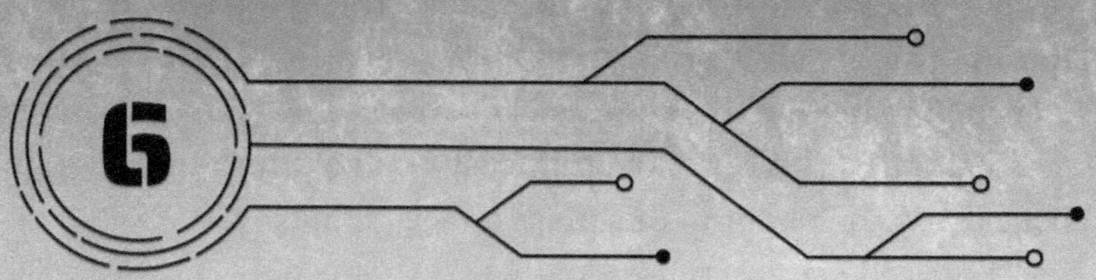

"I WANNA GO IN."

"Dude, he's probably asleep. Leave him alone."

"Don't tell me what to do, Theron."

I press my face into my smelly sleeping mat. All I want is a little peace before reality hits me over the head. Why won't Theron and Callias just let me sleep?

My bedroom door bangs open violently, and I roll sideways off my sleeping mat. "What?" I groan, the room spinning around me. "Why are you two so loud?"

"We're hungry," Callias says. He plops down beside me, grinning from ear to ear. "But there's no food."

"What?" I ask groggily. Callias's words sound like a jumbled mess. We can't be out of food already. "I just got some yesterday!"

"You mean three days ago," Theron says, sitting beside me. Unlike Callias, he's not smiling. "Remember, we ate the last of it last night?"

"Oh." I slump back, shaking my head. Why hadn't I realized we're out of food? I push myself up and blink several times, trying to wipe the sleep from my eyes. Through my tiny bedroom window I can barely see the first faint rays of morning light.

"How early is it?" I ask, trying not to sound too annoyed.

Theron and Callias shrug. I sigh and walk into the living room. Compared to when we first moved in the place is a bomb scene. Paper bags litter the otherwise bare floor, and the old dented trashcan Theron found in the street is overflowing with stale rolls and browning fruit. And there's an odd, sour smell that won't go away. How'd it get so bad in just a few weeks?

"Well, the bakery doesn't open for a bit." I yawn, my stomach growling loudly.

"What are you talking about?" Theron asks, his eyes narrowing. It's like he's trying to see into my brain or something. "It opens before sunrise."

I bite my lip. Theron really is too observant for his own good. Yes, I do know that the bakery opens before sunrise. But I don't like leaving our building when it's still dark, if I can help it. The Slum is scary enough with all the people lurking around every corner—and that's during the day. I don't want to imagine what goes on out there when it's dark. Probably people fighting in the streets over literal rags.

"We'll … go in a bit," I say, thinking fast. "I wanna clean up first."

I try to ignore Theron's shocked expression as his jaw drops to the floor. When did my brother become so judgmental? Is it so hard to believe that I want to clean? Sure, I haven't done it since we arrived… But the apartment is really filthy. We'll have to start cleaning it at some point, and right now, I need something to kill time.

I bend over and grab one of the brown papers the bakery uses to wrap the rolls. Something cold and slimy touches my fingers, and I freeze. My stomach lurches, and I know I'm going to vomit. Even though I don't want to, I examine the bag more closely. Something shiny coats the paper, and I know it wasn't there last night. I want to let go, but I can't make myself move my fingers.

"This is just sad." Theron shakes his head. He swipes the paper out of my hand before I can think.

"Don't touch it!" Who knows what could have grown on that paper since last night?

"Ezariah, it's just grease," Theron says, picking up handfuls of the shiny paper and throwing them into the already over-flowing trash can.

My face turns hot, and I quickly look away. Why didn't I realize the papers were covered with grease? My hands are coated with the stuff every time I eat the rolls. I collect as many papers as I can. My hair still stands on end, but Theron stops staring at me like I'm an idiot, so I guess it's a win.

Between Theron and me, it doesn't take long for us to clean the tiny apartment. Callias tries to help, but mostly, he just runs around. The apartment is so small that there's not much else to do once all the garbage is picked up. I stare at the overflowing trash can. Back in Newtown, Lysander emptied my garbage every day. I never even had to think about it. But now ... where am I supposed to put it? I can't keep it in the apartment.

"There's a garbage chute at the end of the hall by the stairs," Theron huffs.

I shake my head. Sometimes it's like he can read my mind. But how does he know about the garbage chute? I've never seen it before.

"C'mon." Callias smiles, pushing open the door.

Holding my breath, I grab the trash can and follow. When I catch them at the end of the hall, Theron is holding open a square metal hatch in the wall. I wrinkle my nose as the acrid air hits my nose. Clamping my mouth shut, I dump the trash as quickly as possible.

With the apartment clean, I'm forced to admit two things. One: I'm out of ways to kill time. Two: I'm actually hungry. So, even though I'd prefer to wait until later, I tell my brothers we can leave.

"Yeah!" Callias yells, pumping his fist in the air.

"Finally," Theron says. "I thought you were gonna come up with another lame excuse."

"I was not," I lie. He really is too smart for his own good.

The street is full of people walking toward the barrier. The sight takes me by surprise. I didn't expect to see this many people up this early. But of course, it makes sense: these are the Slummers who managed to get jobs in Midtown. Where do they work that needs them to be there this early?

Theron and Callias are gone before I can blink. I race after them, my heart pounding. Why do they have to run off every time we step outside? I finally catch them as they round the corner near the bakery, grabbing their wrists, but all they do is laugh. I want to tell them off, but the stitch in my side stops me. I know they're probably bored out of their minds, but what choice do we have? Until I find a way to get us out of the Slum, I need to keep them safe. I'll talk to them when we're back at the apartment. It's time I finally set some ground rules. No more running off. No more talking to strangers. And absolutely no going out after dark.

The bakery is packed, so of course, my first impulse is not to go in. I don't want to be around all of those Slummers. Anything could happen with so many of them in such a tight space. But my rumbling stomach and Callias and Theron practically ripping off my arms persuades me otherwise.

Inside, a strange aroma of delicious baked goods mixed with something sour stings in my nose. I ignore it and follow Theron down the narrow aisles, Callias's hand still held firmly in mine.

"Can we get these?" Theron is holding a large bag of rolls— larger than any I've seen in here before.

"What's wrong with them?" I ask. There has to be something wrong with them. Why else would there be so many in one bag? "Where'd you find those?"

Theron points to the shelf behind him, which is covered with similar bags of rolls, bagels, and pastries. I read the sign posted beneath them, and my heart sinks.

"They're old," I say, pointing at the DAY OLD sign. "Why would we buy old food?"

"Because there's lots of it." Theron shrugs, peering into the bag. "They look normal to me."

"Let's get these!" Callias says, examining a bag of what looks like fruit tarts.

I barely manage to suppress my groan. Have we really fallen this far? Reduced to buying old food? For as long as I can remember, no one in my family would touch any food unless the chef had made it fresh that day. My father once made the staff prepare a whole new meal when we returned home an hour later than expected.

My insides burn, and I shake my head. Why would I think about him now? I haven't thought about my father since we arrived in the Slum. It's taken all my brain power just to keep us going. And it's not like my father is a shining example of Nomisman's best; he Renounced his own kids to save his own skin.

"You know what?" I say, making up my mind on the spot. "Get them. You're right. They don't look too bad."

And with that, I let the boys go. I hear them running around, shouting at each other between the aisles. Meanwhile, I wander around and actually look at the shelves. There's a lot more than the bread and apples we usually get. There's even thinly sliced meat on the small counter near the back. Saliva floods my mouth, and I grab the smallest pack I can. The boys and I can split it tonight.

We join the line to pay, our arms loaded with the day-old rolls and pastries, fresh cheese buns, a bag of apples, and dried meat. It's the most food I've seen since my Renouncement. My stomach rumbles loudly, and I stand on my tiptoes. What's taking so long? I knew we should have waited to come in later. The line is never this long then.

"What are you doing?" Theron asks.

I look down. Callias crams one of the day-old tarts into his mouth. I want to tell him off, but my stomach rumbles again, and I give in. Before Theron can say anything, I grab two tarts, shove one into his hand, and take a bite of the other. The bread is definitely dry, but the bright red jelly in the middle is so sweet that it makes my teeth hurt. The entire thing is gone in a matter of seconds.

"Should we be eating these?" Theron asks, eying his tart warily. "We haven't even bought them yet."

"It's fine." I shrug, pulling out one of the old rolls. "I'm paying for it. Didn't you say you were hungry?"

For being so adventurous, Theron sure worries a lot. I don't see what the big deal is. We're going to buy this stuff regardless. There's no harm in eating a little of it while we wait. Besides, at least three people are doing the same thing in front of us. If the Slummers are doing it, I don't see why we can't.

It takes an eternity and a half for us to reach the rough counter. I hold my third roll with my teeth while I help Theron and Callias pile our haul in front of the baker. The sheer size of everything sitting on the counter is a little shocking. It's easily the biggest purchase out of anyone waiting in line. How long will it last? Maybe if we're careful, we can make it last until the end of the week.

"This it?" the baker asks dryly.

"Yeah," I say, pulling out my money bag. "We ate some of the rolls and tarts while we waited."

"I can see that."

While the baker inspects our pile, I continue to munch on my roll. Slum or not, it's good. For the first time in days, my stomach isn't quivering, and the mere sight of food doesn't drive every thought from my mind. Why didn't I let us get this much food sooner? I know I was suspicious of the food when we first arrived, but Theron is right—even though I'd never admit that to him. This bakery is quality. Even the Slummers in here look more put together than others we've come across. At the very least, they look like they've slept indoors. From now on, I'll let the boys pick one extra thing every time we come. That should make things easier.

"Fifty-seven phys," the baker says.

I pour the contents of my money bag onto the counter. I stare at the small pile of medium and small coins—there's less than ten of them. My heart thunders against my ribs. This can't be all there is. I know for a fact that I had at least twice this amount last week. I shove my fingers into the pouch, desperately searching for any remaining coins, but the bag is empty.

"Umm…" I mutter. "I don't think I have enough."

"No, you don't," the baker says, his eyes narrowing.

"Uh…" I say, trying to think fast. "I guess… Could we…?"

"Look, kid," the man huffs, "if you don't have enough money, get out. I've got other customers who can actually pay. But you still gotta pay for what you ate."

"Okay." I nod. The last thing I want to do is get on this guy's bad side.

My hands tremble as I return the apples, the cheese buns, and the dried meat to the shelves. My face grows hot as I slink back to the counter. Why didn't I realize we were running low on money? I'm always telling Theron not to worry about it. But I pull out that money bag at least once a day. I should've known. From now on, I'm going to start really paying attention.

"I guess we're just getting these," I say, pointing to the bags of old rolls and stale tarts.

"That's eighteen phys, kid," the baker says. "Pay up."

I quickly count out the coins: two medium, five small. My heart falls. I've been here long enough to know that only eleven phys.

"I … I don't have enough," I say, my voice shaking just as badly as my arms.

"You gotta pay," the baker growls, his eyes narrowing. "Or there'll be trouble."

"But this is all I have," I say lamely, holding up the handful of coins, my blood boiling. Why doesn't this man get it? "I can't pay eighteen phys."

"You ate them already," the man says accusingly as he steps out from behind the counter.

"Yes, but—"

"But you can't pay for what you ate?"

"I didn't... That's not what I said," I bleat. I don't know how much clearer I can be. It's not like I planned to not pay; I didn't realize what little money I had. I'm sure this can't be the first time this has happened. This is the Slum, after all. Why is this guy making such a big deal about it?

"What's goin' on?" Callias asks, tugging at my sleeve. "Are you in trouble?"

"No," I lie, trying to make my voice reassuring while my brain scrambles for a solution. "Everything's fine."

"The hell it is!" the man says. He reaches behind the counter and pulls out a wooden club.

I stumble back, and it's like someone has turned the sound off. I'm short a few coins; does that mean he needs to threaten my brothers and me? I thought this bakery was one of the few decent places in this hellhole. I guess I was wrong about that.

"You owe me for what you ate," the baker growls, pointing his club at my chest. "How're you gonna pay for it?"

How am I supposed to pay when I don't have the money? It's not like I can go somewhere to get more. I sold everything valuable that I had when we got here, and that money was supposed to last us until I found a way out of here. Back in Newtown, I never worried about how much things cost. If I wanted something, I gave Gram's name and it was mine. The money was always there. But here in the Slum, the small amount I managed to get barely lasted a month.

"I don't want any trouble," I say, placing my meager stack of coins on the counter as I step back. "This is all I have. Take it."

"How you gonna pay for the rest?" the man demands.

"I ... I don't know," I say honestly as I continue to back up, pushing Theron and Callias behind me.

The man's eyes narrow as my foot hits the worn doorjamb. I stumble into the street, trying not to fall over my brothers as they shout behind me. More than anything, I need to keep them safe.

They're not the ones who didn't bother to keep track of the money, or who got on the wrong side of a very angry baker. This is all on me.

"Thief!"

With that single word, the world explodes. People in the street take off in every direction, scattering like leaves in the wind. My mind urges me to run, to move, to do something. But I'm as still as a statue. I can vaguely hear Theron and Callias yelling, but their words sound funny, like they're underwater.

I shake my head. This doesn't make sense. I'm not a thief. I've never stolen anything in my life—at least, not on purpose.

Then something very hard rams into my chest. My legs give out, and my head slams into the uneven street pavers. Lights explode in my eyes as I try to sit up, a metallic taste washing over my tongue. I raise a shaking hand to my lips. When I pull it away, it's smeared with blood. My heart pounds against my ribs as I stagger to my feet. What hit me?

I see the narrow bakery door, several faces peering out from it, before I see the baker. Like me, he's pushing himself up from the ground. But why? Whoever hit me must have hit him too.

The baker raises his club, and several muffled yells reach my ears. Fear burns through me like fire as I see the tip of the club pointing at my chest. I try to run, but my legs are like marble. The club catches me in the stomach. I wheeze and double over, blood spraying from my lips. I open my mouth, desperate for air, but it's like I've forgotten how to breathe. Inside, I feel oddly cold and hollow. I look up just in time to see the club descending again. Pain radiates through my back as I collapse, curling into a ball to protect what little of my body I can.

I lift my head, which feels like a boulder. I try to find Theron or Callias, but my vision is all blurry. I can only make out several pairs of sterile white boots drawing closer. They're vaguely familiar, but right now, I can't place them.

"Help!" I sputter, forcing myself up on trembling arms. "Please. You … need to help…"

I need to get somewhere safe. But where can I go that's safe in the Slum?

Something hard slams into the back of my head. My arms give out, and everything goes black.

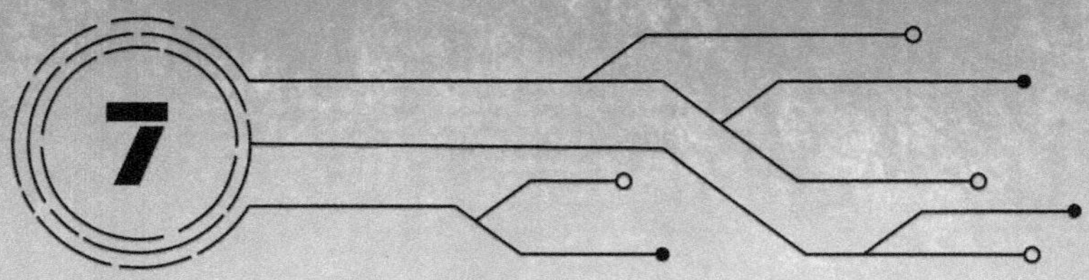

WHEN I COME TO, it's like someone is pounding the inside of my skull with a mallet. The air is damp and cold, and a foul and rotten smell fills my nose, like something nearby died recently.

I open my eyes, and tiny lights pop and flash wherever I look. Where am I? In every direction, all I see is blackness. But even through the gloom, I know I don't recognize this place. I try to focus, which is difficult, given the pounding in my head. The last thing I remember is taking Callias and Theron out to get food.

I sit bolt upright, but the sudden movement is too much. My stomach lurches, and vomit sears up my throat. Some of it lands on the floor, but most of it falls into my lap. It smells horrible, like food gone sour. The odor alone is enough to make me gag, but the warm liquid seeping through my clothes is the final straw. I retch again, and this time, I'm lucky enough to land it all on the floor.

The room is spinning, and I don't dare move again. I wrap my shaking arms around my vomit-soaked knees, trying not to inhale. The rancid smell still stings my nose. I close my eyes and focus on slowing my racing heart. Cautiously, I get to my feet. The room is not as wobbly, but I don't push my luck. I don't need something else from inside me to make an appearance.

I find a spot as far away from the pool of sick as I can. Granted, it's not far—maybe a few yards. The room is no bigger than my bedroom in the apartment. But at least I'm not sitting on top of my mess.

With my mind slightly clearer, I try to remember how I got here. But my pounding head makes that challenging. I feel certain that I've never been in this dark room before. All I know for sure is that I'm alone. If I weren't, someone surely would've said something when I threw up on the floor.

That's when it hits me, like someone has flipped a switch in my brain. If I'm all alone here, where are Theron and Callias? My chest tightens, which only makes my head feel worse. I need to find my brothers, to make sure they're safe. But how can I do that when I don't know where I am or how I got here? For all I know, they could be...

No. I shake my head, which doesn't help the throbbing. I can't let myself think that—not even for a moment. Theron and Callias are fine. They have to be. I refuse to accept any other option. And I'm going to find them.

My eyes finally adjust to the dark, and I can barely make out a barred door. I stagger over to it, grasping the bars as my legs tremble violently. I push my face as far as I can between the rough metal. The hall outside is just as dark as this room and looks just as empty.

"H-hello?" I call, my raw voice echoing back at me. "Where am I? What's going on?"

"Quiet!"

Blinding light blasts my face. I raise my hands, shielding my stinging eyes. I try to lower them, but the light is too bright. But as tears stream down my face, something strange occurs to me: I haven't seen light this bright since I left Newtown. There's nothing like it in the Slum, where all the lights flicker the same dim orange color. Am I even in the Slum at all?

"Where am I?" I repeat stupidly.

"Where all the scum from this place end up," the same voice says. "Welcome to Lockup."

"Lockup?" I shake my pounding head—and instantly regret it.. "No... This is a mistake. I'm not supposed to be here!"

"Shut up, kid. And sit down," the voice says. "You've got sentencing in five."

"No," I repeat, shaking my head between the bars. This is some sort of sick joke. It has to be! "What about my brothers? Where are they?"

The lights go out, and darkness swallows me again. My hands slide down the bars, and I step back, my mind strangely numb. There has to be some mistake. I'm not a Slummer. Why would I need sentencing? I've never done anything wrong!

I take another step back and slip on the forgotten puddle of my vomit. My knee slams painfully into the hard floor and I roll to the side. The foul smell burns my nose as the cold wetness seeps through my clothes. I shudder, my eyes growing hot as tears stream down my cheeks. But the pain seems to exist in some distant part of my brain, almost like an echo. Theron and Callias's sweet faces flash through my mind, and my stomach contorts. If I'm in Lockup, where are they? Surely, they're not still at the bakery. Did we even make it there…?

The thought of the bakery triggers something in my sluggish memory. I can see us standing in line, eating the old rolls. Then me being unable to pay. I see the baker pulling out a club and yelling *"Thief!"* for the whole street to hear. I can almost feel the blow that struck me on the head.

My heart sinks like a stone. Did Theron and Callias see what happened? I've tried so hard to keep them safe from the horrors of the Slum. But now, they know the true barbarism of this place firsthand.

But I have no idea where they are. Did they make it back to the apartment? Theron could probably find his way back there with his eyes closed. He'd have gotten Callias to the apartment, where it's safe. They'll wait for me there … right?

"What am I thinking?" I whisper. Theron is nine. I doubt he truly understands what's happening, even with how smart he thinks he is. And Callias is no better. It's my job to take care of them, and now they're all alone—probably starving. And I'm stuck in here, covered in my own vomit. To be honest, I'd rather be in their shoes right about now.

"On your feet," the guard says as the lights turn back on. "It's time for your sentencing."

I move without question to the door, squinting in the bright light, trying to see anything out in the hall. My hands shake at my sides as sweat coats my palms.

Sure, I made a mistake at the bakery. Even I know that. But it wasn't the worst thing I've seen Slummers do. Whoever's doing the sentencing will understand once I explain what happened. I never meant to do anything wrong.

The barred door slides open, and I step into the hall. My eyes finally adjust, and I see a narrow concrete passageway, lined with barred cell doors just like mine. A low, pained chorus rises from several of them. The sound makes my skin crawl. Who else is in here, and what did they do?

"Move."

I jump as the guard pushes on the small of my back, and I stagger down the hall to a different door, which isn't barred like the rest. It's solid metal, and it would probably take three grown men to move it even an inch. My heart races even faster. This can't be where I'm going. There has to be a mistake. This door is clearly for locking up hardened criminals. That's not me. My only crime was running out of money.

The guard pounds his fist on the door, and I hold my breath, waiting for something to happen. Metallic grinding fills my ears, sending a shiver down my spine. The door opens with a loud creak, like it hasn't been used for years. I fight the impulse to shake my head. It turns out that Lockup is just as run-down as the rest of the Slum. This place really is a shit hole.

Two things stand out to me as I step into the next room. The first is that it's the smallest courtroom I've ever seen. Back in Newtown, I saw courtrooms on TV all the time. They're typically huge, round marble chambers filled with benches, with a raised platform for the judge. But this room is downright tiny by comparison, holding only one long, thin table and a row of chairs beside the door. The second thing I realize is that aside from me and the guard, there's only one other person in the room.

"Case 172248."

The woman at the narrow table doesn't even bother to look up from her tablet as she points to one of the cold metal chairs. I sit, trying to hide my indignation. She could at least look at me.

When she finally does, she wrinkles her nose as her eyes narrow to slits. I shift uncomfortably in my chair. I know the horrendous smell in the room is coming from me. I haven't had clean clothes for weeks, and I just fell in a puddle of my own sick. But I'm not a Slummer, and she could stop looking at me like I am.

"Right. Let's get going. I've got a full caseload to process today," the woman says dryly, glancing down at her tablet. "The report indicates theft of goods and attempting to flee the scene of a crime. Is that accurate, Enforcer Tycho?"

"It is," says the Enforcer who brought me in.

My blood feels like acid burning through my veins. That's not what happened—at least, not all of it. Sure, I ate some food and couldn't pay for it. But I wanted to pay—I just didn't have enough money. And I didn't flee the scene, or even attempt to; the baker threatened me with a club and beat the crap out of me. But the baker's not here getting sentenced for that. The injustice of the whole situation makes me want to scream.

"I arrived at the scene after hearing a disturbance," Enforcer Tycho continues. "The suspect was subdued when I arrived. The victim, the owner of the shop, told me the suspect ate food before paying for it, and then informed the victim that he couldn't pay for what was eaten. The victim demanded proper payment, and the suspect attempted to flee."

I clench my jaw so tightly I'm surprised I don't break a tooth. That's not what happened! Okay, yes, I ate food before paying, and I did run when the baker demanded I make up the difference. But I only ran because the baker threatened me. He's the one who pulled out a club. He's not the victim; I am. The baker beat me in the middle of a filthy street.

"That all lines up here," the woman with the tablet says, her eyes darting back and forth. "Let's see what judgment AURA deems worthy."

"What?!" I say as the woman stands. I can't stop myself. This can't be it. I have to be able to defend myself. "But that's not what happened! I—"

"Save it," the woman snaps, pulling a small handheld device from the table. She walks toward me, and Enforcer Tycho grabs my left arm. Instinctively, I try to wrestle it free, but Tycho pulls so hard that it feels like he's trying to rip it off. What are they doing? I thought this was a sentencing! Why are they surrounding me like I'm some wild animal? Or worse, a Slummer.

The woman waves her device over my forearm, and it burns as the screen lights up.

"Ezariah," the woman says, sounding almost bored. "Age sixteen. Legal adult due to familial Renouncement. No priors. Is that true?"

I stare at the woman. Of course it's true. Why wouldn't it be? At the very least, it adds up with what the Enforcer who collected us from Newtown said. So, I nod.

"Good," the woman says, returning to her table and typing something into her tablet. "AURA should have all it needs now."

The woman turns to the wall behind her as Tycho lets go of my arm. I cradle my throbbing wrist, looking at the wall—and I realize it's not a wall at all. It's a giant screen, like the ones they had in the square for the Culling. But instead of displaying video, this one is covered in text. Two lines on the far left side are highlighted. I try to read what they say, but the text is so tiny that I can't make it out.

A flat female voice emanates from the speakers around the screen. *"With no priors, the current sentence for these crimes is twenty-four hours in the Department of Correction, and twenty-four hours of hard labor. Sentences will be served consecutively, resulting in two nights and two days in the Department of Corrections."*

I cannot stop my mouth from falling open. There's no judge. In fact, there's no person deciding my fate at all. It's being decided by AURA, the artificial intelligence that runs Nomisman. But Tycho and this woman didn't even give AURA all the facts. How can it fairly judge me when it doesn't have all the information? AURA is just a computer program, after all.

I gasp as the inside of my forearm turns hot. I look down. My tag flashes red beneath my skin, and my heart sinks. Somehow, I understand that AURA has already uploaded my sentence to my ID tag. Even if I could have changed AURA's mind, that chance is gone now.

"Let's go." Tycho hoists me to my feet by my armpit before I can open my mouth. But I don't resist. What's the point? There's no going back from this now. The Enforcer already uploaded my so-called crime to AURA; there's nothing I can do now. In school, every day after assembly, the students sing the Nomisman anthem and declare, *"In AURA we trust."* But how can I trust AURA when it doesn't know all the facts?

And it's not like the Enforcers care about the truth. If they did, and they truly wanted to keep people safe, they'd allow me to tell my side of the story and let me go after hearing what really happened. I'm not the one who should be in the Department of Corrections for two days. That baker is.

I expect Tycho to take me back to my cell. Instead, he leads me through a different door beside the AURA wall screen. The next room is full of metal shelves covered in dark grey jumpsuits. I wrinkle my nose as I look at the thin, ragged clothes—if you could call them that. These look like disgusting old sacks with arm and leg holes cut in them.

"Change," Tycho orders, throwing one of the grey jumpsuits and a pair of thin shoes at me.

I catch them, and the hairs on my arms stand on end. The

fabric is itchy, like it's made of plastic, and extremely heavy for its size. And the smell... Thankfully, it's not foul, like most everything else in the Slum, but there's something chemical about it that tickles my throat.

"You're not... I can't wear... Can't I just keep—"

"Get moving," Tycho barks, pulling his baton from his belt, "before I lose my patience."

I take a deep breath and do as Tycho says. I peel off my suit jacket, which is fraying at the seams. The once-pristine fabric is rough and scratchy against my dry skin. Several diamond buttons are missing, and the elbows are worn and discolored. Gram was so proud when we bought it for my sixteenth birth-day. She insisted it was a symbol of our family's prestige. But now, it's just a reminder of how far I've fallen.

The rest of my old clothes aren't much better. My shirt feels like sandpaper, and the golden embroidery unraveled off my pants weeks ago. My shoes are basically worthless, with several small holes in each sole. Gram always said shoes speak volumes about a person. But here in the Slum, appearances don't mean anything.

A shudder runs over me, and goose bumps rise all over my arms. Enforcer Tycho stares at a spot a few feet above my head, his face blank. Does he have to stare? He could at least turn around. I'm already in Lockup; haven't I suffered enough?

I try to stay positive as I pull on the grey jumpsuit. Hopefully, the burning chemical smell means it's clean, at least. And unlike my old clothes, the jumpsuit isn't soaked in vomit.

"Move." Tycho grabs a fistful of my jumpsuit and leads me through another door. This hall is just like the one with the cells, except the walls are completely bare. I breathe through my nose, trying to make myself relax. Panicking isn't going to make things any easier in here. If I do, it's going to be a long two days.

Tycho pushes me through yet another door, and bright daylight floods my eyes. I blink several times, and see what looks like an outdoor dining area. Round metal tables sit in neat rows, surrounded on all sides by fencing topped with jagged coils of wire. Through the chain link, I can see several levels of cells forming a box around the dining area.

We move up to the second story. "This is you," Tycho says, shoving me into one of the cells. "Be gentle," he adds as the barred door slides shut behind him. "This one's fresh."

I stare after Tycho. Why would he tell me to be gentle? And I'm no expert, but I know there's nothing "fresh" about this place. It looks like it's been around since the Great Fall and could probably survive a bomb blast.

Suddenly, I hear a noise behind me. I spin around, my heart racing so fast that I think it might burst. Two men stand on the other side of the cell. Their jumpsuits hang loosely on their gaunt frames, their faces drawn and lined, and dark circles frame their sunken eyes. Their hair is unkempt and greasy, falling into their tired faces—the standard Slum look.

"Whatcha in for?" the taller of the two asks.

The two men look at me expectantly, and for a moment, I just stand there, unsure of what to say. They both seem genuinely interested in talking to me. But why? They're Slummers. Why do they even care why I'm here?

"I was just taken," I mutter, instinctively crossing my arms over my chest.

The taller man nods sympathetically. "We've all been there," he says with a sad smile. "I'm Marcus, and this is Orris."

I nod, but don't offer my name. I'm not here to make friends, after all. I'm only in here for two days. The less people know about me, the better.

Marcus leans against the wall, his eyes narrow. "So, what were you taken for? Theft? Assault? Possession?"

I shrug, struggling to conceal my irritation. I already refused to answer that question once. Why doesn't this guy get the hint? Or do all Slummers need to know every crime committed by the random strangers they meet in the Department of Corrections?

"It's okay if you don't want to share," Orris says kindly. "We understand how it feels."

I glance at him, my anger bubbling beneath the surface. How could he possibly understand how I feel? They're Slummers. They have no idea what I'm going through.

But something about Orris's words seems genuine. It's like he actually wants to help me. But I know better now; no one in the Slum is going to help me. The only person I can rely on here is myself.

"Thanks," I say. I hope it's enough to keep them off my back.

Marcus and Orris continue talking amongst themselves while I scope out the cell. There are two bunk beds, one on either wall. I pick the one on the left, since I can tell from the disheveled sheets and pillows that the right-hand one is in use. It's bad enough that I'm being locked up for something I didn't do, but now I have to share a cell with Slummers. They're probably in here for doing something horrible—like actually robbing someone, or beating a person to death. I'm not like them, and I never will be.

It doesn't take long before the dinner bell sounds. I follow Marcus and Orris into the crowd, descending the stairs into the yard. People talk as the line snakes down, and I'm struck by how happy they all sound. I'm so unsettled I can barely bring myself to look up. These people don't sound like they're in Lockup. In fact, they sound like nothing is wrong with being a convicted criminal in the Department of Corrections. Do they even care? I shudder at the thought.

After getting my tray of food, I find a secluded table. I lift a spoonful to my mouth—and immediately gag. There's a metallic taste to it, and it's so grey that I can't even tell what it is. But after all the vomiting, my stomach growls so loudly that I'm surprised others don't hear it. I need to eat, and this is the closest thing to food I'll probably get in here. So, I dutifully force myself to clean my tray.

We return to our cells after dinner. A single light I didn't notice when I arrived flickers and hums as the open courtyard grows darker. I stay in my bunk, trying to ignore the noises outside our cell, but I can't block them out. Fighting, screaming, and raucous laughter fill my ears like buzzing bees. I pull the thin sheet full of holes over my head, but it does nothing to block out the sound. What would anyone laugh about in here?

But through the darkness, I see a glimmer of hope. My sentence is only for two nights and two days. After this, I'll only have one night left.

That is, if I make it to morning.

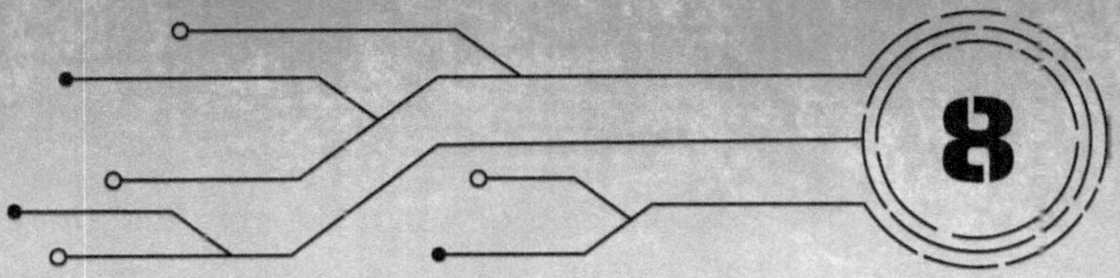

"HOW'D YOU SLEEP?"

"You know, it's not that bad once you get used to it."

I stifle a groan as I follow Marcus and Orris down to the courtyard. They've been at it all morning, trying to get me to talk. Honestly, the constant stream of fake curiosity is getting on my nerves. Why won't they take the hint? I haven't spoken to either of them all morning. But these Slummers aren't Newtowners. We may be stuck up, but at least we know when to shut up.

Breakfast is a bowl of mush I can only describe as brown. When we finish, I expect the Enforcers to return us to our cells. Instead, at least twenty of them appear in the courtyard. I haven't seen any Enforcers since Tycho dropped me off. Oddly, the sight of them makes my muscles relax. At least with the Enforcers around, there won't be any fighting like there was last night. I heard at least ten different ones break out before I fell asleep.

"Morning assignments. Quarry," says an Enforcer carrying a tablet. He types something into it, and all around me, I hear sharp intakes of breath. I look around, half expecting another fight. Instead, I see Orris's ID tag glowing green beneath his pale skin. And Orris isn't the only one. Enforcers quickly pull those with glowing tags from the crowd and lead them out of the courtyard.

I shift around uncomfortably, absentmindedly grabbing my left forearm. I'd almost forgotten the second part of my sentence from AURA: hard labor. But what does "quarry" mean? Whatever it is, I don't like the sound of it. The word itself sounds hard.

I let out a small sigh, and my muscles relax slightly. At least I'm not in that group.

"Smith."

A smaller group of inmates is rounded up this time, including Marcus. They're all at least a foot taller than me and, and a few of them look like they could easily lift me over their heads.

"Sanitation."

Another group steps forward, and my tag still doesn't glow. This group is by far the largest, mostly older men and women. I try to count the Enforcers surrounding the group, but lose track as they march out.

Sweat coats my palms as the crowd of inmates dwindles. Maybe since I didn't get into trouble yesterday, I won't have to do any work today? I was about the only one who didn't get into a fight, after all.

"Debris refinement."

I gasp as my ID tag burns beneath my skin, then snap my mouth shut as I feel several pairs of eyes lock onto me. Do they have to stare? I'm not the only one who made a noise when my tag lit up. Sure, I was louder than most, but I'm not used to the tiny device burning in my arm. I doubt these criminals even notice it anymore, if they can feel pain at all.

I join the rest of those selected for debris refinement, trying to keep my disappointment from my face. I guess being well behaved in here isn't enough to get me out of work.

My group is small, with less than twenty inmates and only three Enforcers. We're led out of the courtyard and through several concrete hallways before reaching a thick metal door. An Enforcer opens it, and a wave of heat hits me in the face. Sweat immediately trickles down my back as I step inside, and for some reason, I have trouble catching my breath. The massive room contains several large, metal domes, each topped with a thick tube connected to the ceiling. The inside of the domes glow bright orange, and even in the semidarkness, I can see the heat rising off of them in waves.

"Get to it," one of the Enforcers snaps. "All quotas will be met before you're released for lunch."

My stomach squirms uncomfortably. I'm not sure using the food here as an incentive is as enticing as the Enforcer thinks. I doubt the Enforcers even eat here; if they did, they'd think of some other way to motivate us. But I don't care about the disgusting, shapeless food. All I care about is getting out of this boiling room.

While the rest of the inmates get to work immediately, I stay back and watch, trying to understand what we're supposed to do. Clearly, nearly all of them have worked debris retirement before. There's a massive pit in the middle of the room, packed to the brim with what I can only call trash. Half-eaten food. Old clothes. Broken pieces of furniture. Discarded toys. Outdated tech. Using their bare hands, the inmates carry the garbage to the metal domes and toss it into the fires inside.

"Hurry up," an inmate hisses at me, her arms full of old clothes. "If we're fast, we'll get an extra-long lunch before the second shift."

Slowly, I step forward. How is this even legal? This stuff is trash, and they're making us handle it. I don't want to go anywhere near the stinking pile of junk. The closer I get, the more the odor of rotten food and old clothes blends with the acrid smell of burning garbage. It's hard not to vomit on the spot. Is this why the Slum always reeks? Have I been breathing in burning trash ever since I got to this dump?

I try to find the cleanest trash I can. After locating a large piece of cloth, which looks like an old bedsheet covered with faded yellow stains, I pile as much trash as I can into the center of it. Once the sheet is stuffed, I drag it to the nearest furnace. My arms feel like they've been set on fire, and I throw my trash in as quickly as I can.

The distinct smell of burning hair mixes with the already horrid assault on my nose. I examine my arms, and my mouth falls open. Nearly all my arm hair has burned away.

We work for what feels like hours. My newly bare arms shine with sweat, and after a while, there's a tickle in my throat that won't go away. I try to ignore the ash swirling in the air. Instead, I focus on the discarded clothes I find. Delicate tailoring and exquisite needlework. Cracked gems glittering in the light of the furnaces. There's no mistaking where they're from: Newtown. Burning these fine, almost clean clothes is torture. I guess a talented valet could have fixed these garments, but why would Newtowners bother? There are always new fashions to try, after all, and an abundance of credits to spend.

The Enforcers release us for lunch when the trash pit is finally empty. We return to the bright courtyard, and I hold up my hands, shielding my eyes. I can barely stop myself from gagging. The layer of ash on my hands and arms is so thick that I can't see my skin. It's like I'm wearing full-length black gloves.

We sit according to our work assignments. I try to find a place on my own, but of course, there aren't any free tables. So, I join a table with four others. One look at the food, which is an unpleasant grey-green, and what little appetite I've worked up vanishes.

It doesn't stop the others at my table, who eat and chat contentedly. I shake my head. Don't they realize we've spent the whole morning handling and burning literal trash? I look at my ash-covered arms again, and the hairs on the back of my neck stand on end. I've never felt more disgusting in my life. I dip the corner of my paper napkin into my cup.

"What are you doing?" the woman beside me asks.

"What?" I say, rubbing the wet, sandpaper-like napkin over my hands. It does an okay job of cutting through the grime. I can at least see my skin now, although it looks unhealthily grey.

"I wanna … I can't stand … the dirt" is all I manage to say.

"Okay," the woman says, laughing softly. "You know, we

shower after our labor shifts. You should just eat. You'll need your strength."

I stare at the woman. Clearly, she's trying to make me feel better, but she's doing an awful job of it. Even if I wanted to eat, how can I when my hands are so disgusting? They're literally covered in a layer of burned garbage. The last thing I want is for that to go anywhere near my mouth.

A bell signals the end of lunch, and I wait for the Enforcer with the tablet to return. I hope I get assigned a better job this time. Anything is better than handling things other people threw out.

But he never does. Instead, the debris refinement Enforcers come back. The long looks on their faces mirror my own. How are the Enforcers assigned to guard us? After all, who would choose to stand in a furnace, watching inmates burn trash? The Enforcers' heavy uniforms have to make it unbearable for them; I can barely stand it even in my thin jumpsuit.

There's more trash piled in the pit when we return, but thankfully, it's not nearly as high. But the room is hotter. The furnace doors are all open, filling the dark room with warm light. Sweat instantly coats my face and back. What idiot left all the doors open? It was hot enough in here to begin with, but now it's like we're standing in an oven.

"You five are on the pile," one Enforcer says, pointing to the five largest inmates in the group. "The rest of you, grab a shovel and start cleaning."

A shovel? I look around and see a line of wide shovels held in brackets on the wall. They're made of the same dark metal as the rest of the room, so they blend in perfectly. I grab one, but I'm not really sure what I'm supposed to do with it. If the five big guys are at the pit, sorting the trash, what are the shovels for? And why didn't we use them earlier? I wouldn't have had to spend all morning touching trash with my bare hands. At least my hands would be cleaner.

However, the other shovelers don't head for the trash pit.

Instead, they walk over to the open furnaces, their free arms shielding their faces. I stare after them, my mouth falling open. The Enforcers don't expect us to go inside the furnaces, do they? I've already lost all my arm hair! And unless burning us alive is their plan, I see no reason why anyone would go in there.

The shovelers emerge, covered head to toe in ash and grime. They take shovelfuls of soot and dump them into small holes on either side of the furnaces.

Now I understand. The furnaces were almost full before lunch. Now, the Enforcers expect us to empty them before the big guys put more trash inside.

"Move!" the Enforcer closest to me steps forward and jabs her baton into the small of my back.

"I'm goin'," I say, stumbling on the ash-slick floor.

I join the other shovelers in the furnaces. It's the most intense heat I've ever experienced, but thankfully, it's not as bad as I feared. For one thing, the furnaces are actually turned off. And with the doors open wide, they're actually getting cooler. I feel like an idiot for thinking we were going inside them while they were on.

Piles of ash taller than me sit inside each furnace. It's so light that it doesn't stay on the shovels long before drifting off. Once we've cleared most of the ash from one furnace, we move to the next one. One or two inmates stay back, using brooms to sweep up the last fine layer that we left behind.

"Are you done yet?" an inmate from the pit calls, his voice low and gruff.

None of us answer.

"Hey! How much longer? We're dyin' of old age over here!" he shouts, although he doesn't sound angry.

"We're nearly done, Jackson," the woman who sat beside me at lunch says. Her voice is stern, like a mother speaking to a misbehaving child.

I want to yell back, but stop myself as my frustration mounts. Doesn't he see that we're working as fast as we can? It's not like shoveling mountains of ash is easy. And if he wants us to move faster, he could help instead of yelling. There are enough shovels for everyone after all.

"Well, let's get a move on!" Jackson yells, hanging over the pit railing. "I wanna finish before dinnertime."

"What a prick," I whisper to myself. Jackson should do us all a favor and just shut up. My hands hurt. I'm tired. And all I want is to leave this boiling room. This is more work than I've ever done in my life. Being caged up in my cell would be better than this. But no, I'm stuck in a furnace full of criminals, and one of them won't stop complaining.

"What's that, Hoarder?"

I feel several pairs of eyes looking at me. No one has ever called me a Hoarder before. I have no idea what it means, but I don't like the sound of it.

Jackson hops over the pit rail and lumbers over to me. I try to act tough, but that's hard to pull off when the guy marching toward me is at least a foot taller than me, with arms nearly as thick as my head.

Jackson's got my hand before I can move. I try to pull it back, my heart thundering in my ears, but he's stronger than he looks, if that's even possible. He opens his mouth, and my insides freeze. What's he going to do? Bite my fingers off? I expect nothing less from the Slummers locked up in here. Instead, he spits directly onto my palm.

"What the hell?!" I demand, my skin crawling as I try to free my arm.

"Well, well," Jackson says, wiping his spit all over my hand. "Smooth hands. I know a Hoarder when I see one."

"Get off me!" I push with all the strength I have, but Jackson doesn't budge. He grins at me, and the anger inside me burns hotter. Why is this Slummer calling me names? He's the one who spit on me. I've put up with too much in this place.

"Hey! Break it up!"

I barely hear the Enforcer over the cries of the other inmates. I raise my shovel, my free arm quivering, and Jackson shakes his head. He reaches out and grabs the neck of the shovel. I pull back, but Jackson's grip is like stone.

"Ghah!" There's a crackle of electricity, quickly followed by an intense pain in my back. My arms go limp, and I fall to my knees.

Above me, I see Jackson raise my shovel threateningly as the Enforcers approach, but they have him on his knees before he can take a swing. One pulls the shovel from Jackson's limp hand while the other places her boot on his chest.

"Threatening an Enforcer," she says grimly. "Nonconformity at its worst."

"I didn't do nothin'!" Jackson shouts as the two Enforcers hoist him to his feet.

"Save it," the other says as they drag him off. "We'll see what AURA has to say about this."

"No, wait!" Jackson cries, and I hear an edge of panic in his voice. "My time's almost up! I was gonna get…"

The doors close behind Jackson and the Enforcers. I hear the unmistakable sounds of heavy boots, followed by heavy breathing.

"Back to work," the last Enforcer barks. "Now!"

I push myself up onto my hands and knees. All around me, the other inmates scatter, their eyes narrowed. Why are they looking at me like this is *my* fault? Jackson started it when he called me a Hoarder. I still don't even know what that means. If they all want to be angry, they should be angry at Jackson.

"C'mon." The woman from lunch offers me her hand. I consider grabbing it, but it's covered in ash and a shiny layer of something I cannot name. I already have Jackson's spit on my own hand; I'd rather not touch anything else unless I know what it is. I get to my feet, not even bothering to look at her. She marches off, and I distinctly hear her mutter "Hoarder" as she joins one of the other inmates.

When the Enforcers release us for dinner, I'm exhausted. No

one spoke to me during the rest of our shift, but that doesn't bother me in the slightest. Why would I talk to people who shoot me dirty looks and whisper behind my back? The sooner I get away from them, the better.

Back in the yard, I once again try to find a spot by myself. There's an open table near one of the corners, and I take it before anyone else can. Clearly, news of what happened must have already traveled through the prison. People I've never seen walk past me with their eyes narrowed, dark looks on their faces.

I take a deep breath, fighting to keep my face calm. Why is everyone in this place glaring at me? I'm not the one who did something wrong. Jackson attacked *me*. But from the way people look at me, you'd think it was the other way around.

I focus on my food, but no matter how hard I try, I cannot make a tray of grey mush, a thin, dry slice of bread, and stale water appealing. I consider not eating it, but my groaning stomach convinces me otherwise. I take a bite, trying not to think too hard about what it might be. All I have to do is make it one more night. Soon, I'll be free from this place and all the crazy Slummers too.

I'm not sure when the others start gathering around me. All I know is that once I finish eating, five people are standing around my table. My throat tightens as I look up at them. They just stand there, their arms folded across their chests. I want to tell them to leave me alone, but they all have the same thick build as Jackson. So, I keep my mouth shut and try to focus on anything else. But that's kind of hard to do when I can feel them all staring at me.

Instinctively, I stand up. Where are the Enforcers? Aren't they supposed to be stationed in the yard in case something happens? Well, something's happening right now, and I need to get out of here.

"Sit down."

One of the thugs pushes my shoulder so forcefully that I slam back down onto the metal bench. My legs are throbbing, and my eyes dart wildly around as the others close in. Why are they even bothering with me? I don't know any of them, and why would I? I'm not a Slummer like them.

"What's going on?" a voice says from behind the wall of muscle.

The inmate before me steps aside, and I can't stop my jaw from dropping. A man at least a foot shorter than me steps through the gap. He's bald, with thin-rimmed glasses and a long white scar across his eyebrow. I'd have guessed the thugs could kick him around like a ball, but clearly they're listening to him. Why?

"May I sit, Ezariah?"

I struggle to find my words, and the thin man sits beside me before I can make a sound. He's even thinner than I thought. His jumpsuit hangs loosely around him, and his face is so gaunt that I can see his cheekbones. But it's not his build that makes my heart race. He knows my name. How? I've barely said two words to anyone since arriving in Lockup. And if he knows my name, what else does he know about me?

"I have a problem, Ezariah," the thin man says, leaning on his knees while looking up at me. "And if there's one thing I don't want, it's a problem."

"Who are you?" I say, trying not to sound scared.

"Oh, sorry." He chuckles. "I forgot you're new here. I'm Cassian. Everyone in here knows me."

I swallow. The way Cassian talks about being in Lockup doesn't sit right with me. He's so casual about it, like being locked up for committing crimes is no big deal. But there's something else: everyone in Lockup knows him. How long has this guy been in here? What did he do to get himself locked up for so long?

"Like I said, I have a problem," Cassian says. "And I'd really appreciate your help in fixing it."

"What?" I say blankly, trying to look around the wall of goons. Surely, an Enforcer sees what's happening. But all the

Enforcers have their backs to us. I swallow hard. They're not coming to help.

"Oh, yes." Cassian nods, sitting upright. "Sadly, *you* are the cause of my problem."

Now I'm really confused. When did I cause a problem for Cassian? Before two minutes ago, I didn't even know he existed.

"Jackson's part of the crew. And thanks to you, his sentence has been extended."

"He *attacked* me," I stammer, looking desperately from Cassian to his guys. They have to believe me.

"Oh, I know." Cassian nods again, his tone surprisingly gentle. "Jackson isn't the brightest, picking a fight where the Enforcers can see. But he does a decent enough job for the crew."

"Crew?" I look at the assorted criminals standing around me. Not one of them looks like they're fit together in any way And what job could Cassian be talking about? They're all in Lockup in the Slum. Who in their right mind would give any of them jobs?

"Yes." Cassian nods gently. "And the crew looks out for each other. Jackson was supposed to get out in three days. But now, because of you, he's here for another two months."

For some reason, I feel bad for Cassian. He genuinely seems to care about Jackson. But I still don't see how Jackson getting himself into trouble is my fault. He insulted me, not the other way around. Then he threatened me and almost attacked the Enforcers. From where I'm sitting, I'm blameless. But I don't think Cassian sees it that way.

"The boss expected Jackson back at work," Cassian says. "It's gonna be a shock when he doesn't turn up."

At the word "boss," it's like something clicks in my brain. These people are part of some crime family. Didn't my teachers once say there could be any number of them in each Slum; there's no way for the Enforcers, or even AURA, to know for sure. That's why everyone in here seems to know each other.

And in their eyes, I'm the reason one of their own isn't getting out.

"I … I'm sorry," I stammer. "It … it wasn't…"

"I know, you didn't mean it," Cassian says, now sounding a little impatient. "But what's done is done. But the boss is owed a debt, which needs paying."

"A debt?" It's like my lungs are empty. I can't pay off any kind of debt. After all, not having enough money is what landed me in Lockup in the first place. And how can Cassian's boss, whoever he is, know that?

"A debt." Cassian nods. "You lost us a runner. And that's a problem the boss can't have."

I don't have time to wonder what a runner is. Cassian stands, and for some reason, I do too. My legs shake so violently that I'm surprised I don't fall over. Cassian pats me on the shoulder. It's an odd gesture—one I'd expect after a good conversation with someone I look up to.

"The boss'll be in touch after your release tomorrow." Cassian grins. "And Ezariah … don't bother hiding. Our eyes are everywhere, inside and outside these walls. Don't worry. We'll find you."

With that, Cassian walks off, his goons lumbering behind him. I stay where I am, frozen like a statue, my mind buzzing. This can't be happening. How did I, after one day in Lockup, get myself indebted to the mob?

I've been wrong about the Slum. I always thought it was a lawless place, full of grimy, useless beggars. But it's not. It's much, much worse.

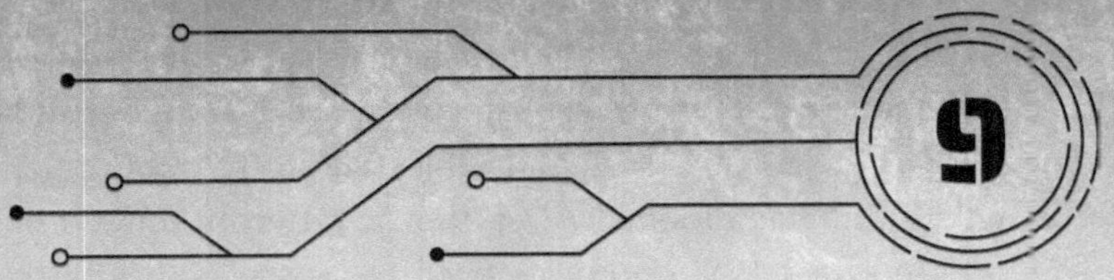

I'M NOT EXACTLY sure when I left the yard, or how I got back to my cell. One second, I was standing at my table, unable to move while my life somehow went from bad to worse. Next thing I know, I'm lying in my bunk as an Enforcer calls lights out. The whole conversation with Cassian feels like a dream, like it didn't really happen.

But as I stare into the darkness, the memory becomes sharper. After a couple days in Lockup, I was supposed to be free. But now, when I get out of here tomorrow, I won't be free at all. A cold sweat coats my forehead as my muscles quiver. Will I ever feel free again?

Images flash through my mind whenever I close my eyes, keeping sleep at bay. What will Cassian's boss do when he realizes I can't pay the debt Cassian says I owe? And I still don't understand why I'm the one paying when this whole mess is Jackson's fault. I sold everything I owned to that shopkeeper, Bart, when I first got to the Slum. How am I supposed to get more money in a place like this?

"Maybe it'll be fine?" I whisper into my smelly, shapeless pillow.

Of course, no one answers.

Come breakfast, Cassian and his goons are everywhere I look in the yard. They keep their distance, but I feel them staring as I eat and then join the other inmates for labor assignments. I'm so busy worrying about those guys that I barely notice my new assignment: sanitation duty. Luckily, the inmate beside me is also assigned sanitation, and he drags me forward to join the group.

As luck would have it, the last inmates to join us are three of Cassian's guys. I wish I could say I'm shocked, but I'm not.

While the other inmates leave for their assignments, sanitation cleans the rest of Lockup. We start in the yard, spraying and wiping down the metal chairs and tables before scrubbing the floor with industrial brooms. After the first two minutes I'm covered with sweat. The chemicals from the spray bottles burn my nose, and my skin starts to sting after doing a few tables. The only good thing about sanitation duty is that it forces me to stop worrying about what might happen when I get out. Who can think about the future when they're stuck scrubbing floors?

After our work in the yard is inspected by an Enforcer, we start cleaning the stairs. My knees throb as I kneel on the thick concrete steps, pushing my heavy brush over them again and again. It takes a long time to scrub the grime away. The sight of the thick black coating makes my stomach lurch. "Disgusting," I mutter, but I make a point to keep my commentary to myself. As far as I can tell, the sanitation crew scrubs the common areas daily, but I guess the people in Lockup are so disgusting that it's dirty again in less than a day. Even after everyone has showered, they still manage to make a mess. This place, like the rest of the Slum, seems determined to be filthy.

We move on to the cells once the stairs are deemed clean. Enforcers divide us into pairs, with one Enforcer supervising every ten pairs. Somehow, stepping into a cell that's not my own feels strange. It's like I'm violating someone else's space. Someone sleeps here. Like my bunk, this little space is someone else's escape. But all the cells are identical to mine, from the thin, ragged blankets down to the dirty clothes at the foot of each bed. If I didn't know better, I'd mistake any one of them for my own cell.

"You gonna help, or what?" my partner snaps, tossing the old sheets on the floor before she puts new ones on the bottom bunk. "We're gonna get in trouble if you don't get a move on."

Okay, now I feel a little bad. Sure, I can manage picking up trash and scrubbing floors, but I have no idea how to make a bed —probably because I've never had to. Lysander always did it for me back in Newtown. Since arriving in the Slum, all I've had to sleep with is the old sleeping mat in my room. Making a bed has been the very last thing on my mind. But clearly, there are higher standards here. I watch as my partner pulls the sheets and blanket taut, places the pillow on the right-hand corner, and clears the floor of any debris.

I strip the other bottom bunk, then start putting on the clean sheets—and nearly throw them after about three seconds. Every time I secure one corner, the opposite one slides off. My face grows hot as my hands ball into fists. This is impossible.

"You're useless," my partner mutters. Her tiny hands move so fast that she finishes my in no time.

"I'm trying," I snap, struggling to keep my frustration in check. What right does she have to boss me around? She's a Slummer. I don't care if she can make a bed in ten seconds flat. I deserve to be treated with respect.

"Get your act together," she hisses, throwing the dirty clothes from the cell into my arms. "We'll miss lunch if we fall behind."

I follow her out of the cell, trying not to breathe in the rancid smell of the sweaty clothes. We get clean jumpsuits every morning; how do these people manage to make things so disgusting in such a short amount of time?

My partner, Osanna, and me work all morning to clean the rest of our cells. We're assigned ten of them, and when we finally finish, my arms feel like they're going to fall off. Honestly, Osanna did most of the work, but I try my best to help, and at least by the end, she's stopped shooting me dirty looks. I guess it's better than nothing.

I practically run to the yard when an Enforcer finally inspects our last cell, my stomach growling loudly. I heard people in the yard at least fifteen minutes ago. I'm not exactly sure why I want to get there; it's not like the food is appealing. Maybe it's the thought that it's my last meal in this place?

When will they actually let me out? AURA said I had to do two nights in lock up and two days of hard labor. Hopefully, it won't be long now.

Afternoon assignments are doled out after lunch. I get sanitation again, but I'm not surprised; I worked debris refinement all day yesterday. We spend the afternoon laundering the dirty clothes, dumping sweaty jumpsuits and sheets into vats of steaming water. Only there's something else in there; it burns my eyes, and the water hisses whenever we toss in more clothes. Once all the dirty laundry is in, we use old wooden paddles to stir the cloudy mixture like a soup.

Somehow, this turns out to be the hardest thing I've done since arriving here. The wash mixture is oddly thick, and as I struggle to swirl the paddle through the sodden clothes, my muscles feel like splintering wood. But I've learned my lesson. This time, I keep my mouth shut, not letting myself make a sound. Instead, I try to focus on what I'll do when I'm finally out of here. First, I need to find Theron and Callias. I hope they're okay; I've been worried sick about them. And once we're together, we'll go somewhere Cassian's boss can't find us.

The afternoon's work goes much faster than the morning shift. In what feels like no time, we've drained the tubs, rinsed the clothes with icy water, loaded them into industrial dryers that could easily hold four people, and then folded them. Most of the sanitation crew seem to know each other. They talk the whole time, and some even sing songs. I try not to roll my eyes. How are these people so happy? Don't they care where we are?

Folding laundry, as it turns out, is my personal hell. The rest of the inmates get their jumpsuits into thin, neat squares. Mine look more like oblique grey lumps. But the Enforcer overseeing my work doesn't tell me to start over, so I don't bother. I don't even care when I hear the other inmates' whispers. I don't catch all of it, but I distinctly hear the word "Hoarder" again. Why do they keep calling me that?

We return to the yard for dinner once the Enforcers say the

work is finally done. The food is exceptionally gross tonight: semi-solid globs in varying shades of brown. I force myself to eat, but that doesn't stop me from gagging on nearly every bite. How is the food here getting even worse?

All through dinner, the hairs on the back of my neck stand on end. I try to ignore it. I don't have to think too hard to know what's causing it; Cassian's thugs aren't exactly discrete. They lumber around like mountains of muscle with feet, always slowing down when they get close to me. Thankfully, they don't sit at my table, or even speak. All the same, I know they're there, and I think that's the point.

My heart races a little faster as we line up after dinner. This is it: I'm finally getting out of Lockup. I've slept two nights in this dungeon, and busted my ass for two days doing the most horrendous jobs known to man. But now it's all over.

Something pushes gently into my side as I follow the crowd out of the yard. I start and nearly lose my footing on the concrete steps. I barely catch the railing, my heart racing as I whip around.

Cassian stands beside me with two of his goons, a gentle smile on his face. "Why so jumpy?" he asks, sounding so genuine that it actually puts me at ease. "This is a big day for you, my boy. You're getting released tonight."

I want to say, *"Not soon enough,"* but I bite my tongue. I don't want any more trouble with Cassian and his crew before getting out of here. They already expect me to pay some debt because Jackson is staying in here longer. Who knows what these crazy people could do?

"Yeah" is all I manage, my voice shaking slightly.

"You never forget your first release," Cassian says. He pats me gently on the shoulder and steps past me. "Remember, Ezariah, we have eyes everywhere," he calls casually over his shoulder. "Oh, and be sure to say hi to Theron and Callias for me."

Whatever excitement I feel about getting out tonight vanishes in a flash. Fear races through me as cold sweat coats my neck. How the hell does Cassian know Theron and Callias's names? I've barely spoken to anyone since getting into Lockup, and I'm not stupid enough to mention my brothers. Someone must have told him about them. But who? A pit grows in the bottom of my stomach. Cassian wasn't lying; he really does know what's happening outside of Lockup. How am I supposed to hide from his boss if they already know everything about me?

In a daze, I walk back into my cell, too consumed with my fears to realize what I'm doing. I climb into my bunk like it's just another night. It's only when the barred metal door starts to close that my brain snaps out of whatever funk it's in.

"No, wait!" I jump out of bed and bolt to the door, but it's too late. It slides shut with a loud clang, and I hear something heavy latch inside it. I reach blindly through the bars. All I know is that something's gone horribly wrong. I've served my time. I'm not supposed to be here anymore.

"Help!" I call through the bars. Hopefully, there's an Enforcer close by. "I'm supposed to get out!"

"Shut up!" Marcus hisses behind me.

"You're gonna get us in trouble," Orris warns.

I ignore them. They don't get it. AURA sentenced me to two nights here and two days of labor, and I've served all of it. I'm supposed to be released now. Why aren't they letting me out?!

"There's been a mistake!" I call, pressing my face between the rough bars. "I'm supposed to be released. Something's wrong!"

No one answers. My heart races, and even though I'm breathing, I can't feel any air in my lungs. This can't be happening! I don't belong here. I'm not a criminal like Cassian, or Jackson, or even Marcus and Orris. Sure, I made a mistake, but that doesn't mean I should be locked up forever!

I close my eyes, and I can see Theron and Callias's faces. They've been on their own for two whole days. There's no way they can survive the Slum without me. I need to get to them, no matter what. They're trapped in this horrible place because of me. I won't let anything happen to them. But I can't do anything while I'm stuck in this cell.

"Let me out!" I yell hysterically.

"Back up!" a rough female voice shouts from outside the cell.

I step back as quickly as I can. The Enforcer approaches the bars, eyes narrowed, brow furrowed. An odd mixture of frustration and relief rushes through me. Why is she so annoyed? I'm not the one who made this mistake.

"Against the wall! Now!"

Marcus, Orris, and I do as she says, and the Enforcer opens the door. She walks in, but she's not looking at me. Instead, she's examining a small screen built into her cuff.

I bite my lip. She must be looking me up in the system. Thank goodness—AURA will tell her that I'm supposed to be released. The Enforcers may not trust me, but in AURA we all trust. I wonder if the Enforcer will apologize. After all I've experienced, I deserve a lot more than that.

Suddenly, the inside of my left arm grows hot. I gasp, and so do my cellmates. My ID tag pulses bright red beneath my skin, while Marcus's and Orris's flash green.

All feeling vanishes from my legs. This isn't right. *I'm* the one getting out. Why is my tag red?

"Come here," the Enforcer orders.

I don't know why, but instead of following her instructions, I step back, running into the wall. The Enforcer lunges forward and grabs my arm. My feet slide out from beneath me, and my face and knees break my fall onto the concrete floor. Stars explode in my eyes as the Enforcer pulls me to my feet. The metallic taste of blood fills my mouth. I try to move my arms, but all that gets me is a sharp blow in the side. I cough, and a mixture of blood and saliva flies from my lips. That doesn't stop the Enforcer from dragging me from my cell.

"Where are you taking me?" I ask dazedly.

The Enforcer doesn't answer, and my mind races. She's taking me somewhere. Why? To punish me? All I did was ask to be released, like I'm supposed to be! Why am I being punished for speaking up?

After she leads me down several walkways and past many doors, we arrive in a room I haven't seen before. It's so bright compared to the dim, flickering light in the rest of Lockup that my eyes water. It's pure white, with a full ceiling of light panels. Aside from the square grates in the floor and ceiling, it's empty.

"Strip," the Enforcer orders, pushing me into the middle of the room.

"Wh-what?" I stammer, as if I could have heard her wrong.

"Take your clothes off."

A small part of me wants to refuse, but the Enforcer pulls out her baton, and I swallow my words. I do as instructed, although it's harder than I thought; the slightest movement sends a throbbing pain through my head and legs. I throw my jumpsuit and thin shoes on the shiny white floor. I try to cover myself as best I can, but the Enforcer isn't even looking at me. She picks up my uniform with her baton and throws it down a chute that opens and closes seamlessly in the white wall. She then backs silently out of the room, leaving me completely naked and alone.

I just stand there shivering. What am I supposed to do? As far as I can tell, there's no way out of this room. The door blends into the wall seamlessly just like the clothing chute; I doubt I could find it if I tried. Why would she leave me naked in an empty room?

But no, it's not entirely true; there are those grates in the middle of the room. I stand on one grate and look up at the smaller one in the ceiling.

"Gah!"

Scalding water hits me in the face, and I immediately want to turn away. There's something else in the water, and my skin stings like it's on fire, like the water is made of razor blades. I want to retreat, but I've learned enough about Lockup to know that the water won't stop until the Enforcer makes it. So, I stand over the drain while the water washes over me, waiting for the searing shower to end.

And eventually it does. The stinging water drips down my raw skin, and I look around helplessly for a towel. Instead, the door opens, and the Enforcer returns, a black bag in her hand. I turn away, trying not to slip while I frantically try to cover myself.

"Here," she says, dropping the bag on the floor and shoving it toward me with her foot. She doesn't even look at me; her eyes are glued to the back wall like she's memorizing it. I open the bag. I'm not sure what I was expecting—a towel, of course, maybe soap or a toothbrush, and something to run through my tangled mess of hair. Instead, I find a pair of faded blue pants and a grey shirt. Both look very shabby, like they're at least thirty years old. There's also a pair of shoes, so thin that they may as well be socks. They remind me of the prison uniform shoes. Are they made in the same place?

"Um ... what are these?" I haven't seen any other inmates dressed in clothes like these.

"They're clothes," the Enforcer says flatly, as if explaining something very simple to a toddler. "Kind of a requirement in the civilized world."

It's like her words ignite something in my mind. I *am* getting released! Relief washes over me, and my whole body relaxes. I reexamine the clothes. They have holes in several places and are at least four sizes too big for me.

"These aren't mine...?" I say to the Enforcer uncertainly.

"Inmate clothes are taken to debris refinement after sentencing," the Enforcer explains.

Anger erupts inside me like fire as my hands tighten around the thin shirt. Those clothes were all I had left from my old life. Even in their soiled state, they were still worth a lot more than these rags. And they just threw them out? What is *wrong* with these people? Why are they throwing away perfectly good things?

"Look, Hoarder," the Enforcer snaps, and the word makes my skin crawl. "Put them on. Or don't. Makes no difference to me. Just know that AURA's penalty for public nudity is one day and night in Lockup. Your choice."

Even though my hands shake, I do as the Enforcer says. The last thing I need is to get thrown back in here the second I leave. The clothes are so rough that I want to rip them from my body. The shoes aren't much better. My feet slide around in them, and they don't grip the floor at all, but I guess they're better than nothing. At least I won't have to walk around barefoot.

Once I'm dressed, the Enforcer leads me through another concealed door. The next room is large, with raised desks on one wall and rows of benches in the middle. It looks like some kind of lobby or waiting room. It's mostly empty, with just a few people sitting on the benches or speaking to the Enforcers at the desks.

I don't know why, but I expect people to stare as I walk by. Everyone else has ever since I got to Lockup. But no one even gives me a glance. For some reason, I feel a little let down. I'm being released from the Department of Corrections. Don't these people want to know why? Probably not. This is the Slum, after all. People leaving Lockup must be a regular thing.

"There it is—the civilized world," the Enforcer says with a tired smile, holding open the front doors.

I step over the threshold, trying not to cough on the thick, musty air. This is what the Enforcer calls "civilized"? It's the Slum. But at least it's better than Lockup. I barely made it out of there in one piece.

"Oh, and Ezariah."

I turn around. The Enforcer is still standing in the open doorway.

"Don't worry, we'll be in touch soon. The boss can't wait to meet you."

The Enforcer vanishes inside before I can open my mouth. What little joy I felt over being released vanishes, replaced with a pulsing dread in the pit of my stomach. I thought only criminals worked for Cassian's boss, but no; they've got Enforcers working for them too. Just when I thought the Slum couldn't get any worse, it finds a way.

As I eagerly put distance between me and Lockup, I realize I don't recognize the buildings, or even what street I'm on. But that's not surprising; the dilapidated buildings all look the same to me, and honestly, I've never paid that much attention before. But I need to find my way back to the apartment. Surely, Theron and Callias will be there. But how do I get there?

"Ezariah!" an excited high-pitched voice shouts from behind me.

I whirl around and something tiny slams into my stomach. I gasp, the wind knocked out of me, and stagger back. Callias's tiny arms wrap so tightly around my waist, it's like he's trying to break me in two. I doubt I'll be able to pry him off for several hours. But I don't care. The mere sight of him drives my fear to some distant part of my brain.

"Hey, Cal," I breathe, wrapping my arms around him as I fall awkwardly to my knees. "I missed you."

"What happened?" Theron appears so fast, it's like he popped up right out of the ground.

My smile could split my face, I'm so relieved. They're both here, and they look perfectly fine. Sure, they're dirtier than they were two days ago, but I'll take that over the alternative. I have to force them to bathe on a good day. It's alright. We're together again. We're all going to be okay.

"Where're your clothes?" Theron asks, raising an eyebrow.

"Um…" I can't tell them what happened in Lockup. I don't want to frighten them by recounting the horrors in there. So, I decide to lie.

"They got all ripped and dirty," I say, putting on my best smile. "So, the Enforcers gave me these instead."

"Mm-hmm," Theron huffs. "What happened in there?"

I know he's looking at me, so I bury my face in Callias's

shoulder. Why does Theron have to be so smart? I'm sure he knows there's more to the story. Should I tell him? If I do, he'll tell Callias, or Callias would insist that Theron tell him. It's best if I keep my mouth shut. Better for Theron to be suspicious than for both of them to know the ugly truth.

"I wanna know how you guys have been," I say, trying to change the subject. "I was so worried. I want to know everything that happened while I was away. How'd you even know I was getting out today?"

"Don't worry," a voice says kindly behind Theron. "They're fine. I looked after them."

I was so relieved to see Callias and Theron, I hadn't realized they weren't alone. I look up, eager to thank this stranger for their help. I can't bring myself to think what could've happened if the boys had been left on their own in the Slum.

I'm not sure what I was expecting, but this girl isn't even close. Her face is soft, but covered in black smudges. Her dark, greasy hair is pulled into a ponytail that reaches her back. But it's not her filth that I find off-putting; sadly, I'm getting used to the grime of the Slum. It's that she's wearing what looks like a thin dark purple sheet. It's wrapped around her chest and tied behind her neck to make it appear like some sort of dress. A ratty black scarf wrapped around her waist holds the sheet in place. If you ask me, the whole thing looks like it's on the verge of falling apart. But that's not the worst of it: she's not even wearing shoes, and her bare feet are so black that they're barely distinguishable from the grimy cobblestones.

I stand up, unable to look away from this strange girl. She's clearly a Slummer; one look at her tells me that much. She must be near my age. And apparently, she cared for my brothers while I was locked up. But why? She doesn't know us. It hardly matters though; I'll never be able to repay her for what she's done.

"Hey," she says, holding out her hand, which I take. "I'm Sera."

PART TWO

THE WINTER

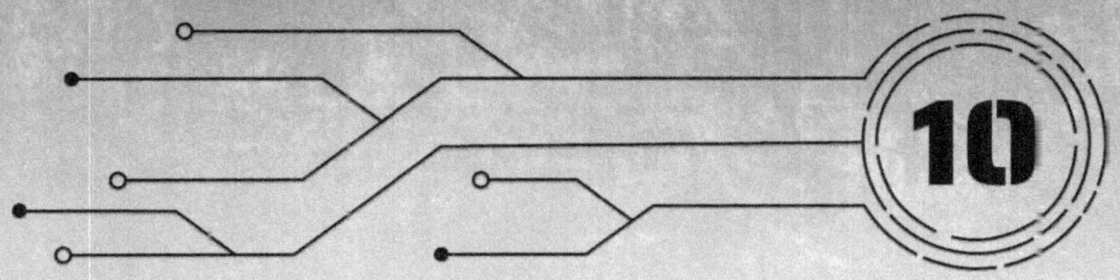

"NOT TO BE RUDE," Sera says, eyeing me up and down, "but you look like shit."

That's a lot, coming from her. "Thanks," I say slowly, trying not to sound too offended.

But I am. I know I probably look like crap. I can't remember the last time I saw my reflection. My arms ache, and there's a dull throbbing in my left temple. But what right does this Slummer have to judge me? At least I'm wearing real clothes.

"I'm confused," I say, turning to Theron and Callias. "How'd you know I was getting out today?"

"It was all Sera," Theron says, turning around and flashing her a smile that makes my insides squirm slightly. "After the Enforcers took you, Callias and I ran. We didn't even make it around the corner before Sera caught us."

"She's really nice!" Callias bounces up and down, his arms still wrapped around my middle. "She took us back to her place, gave us food, and let us sleep there."

"That was … kind of her," I say slowly, looking at Sera.

She stares back, the faintest trace of a smile on her thin lips. She's really the strangest girl I've ever seen, and that's after living in the Slum for over a month. And it's not just her sheet-dress or lack of shoes that's so off-putting. Why would she take Theron and Callias in? Kindness isn't exactly something Slummers are known for, and they don't have the resources to be generous. She must want something from me. But what? It's not like I have anything of value anymore.

"Well, I'd better get going," Sera says.

"You're leaving?" Theron asks, and the devastation in his voice is unmistakable. I try to ignore the way it set my teeth on edge.

"Yeah." Sera smiles, kneeling in front of Theron. "And your brother needs to get home. He probably needs rest after... You just take good care of him. Okay?"

"We will." Theron nods.

Sera's eyes narrow as they fall back on me. I fight to keep my face blank, but it's a struggle. Clearly, she knows much more than she's letting on. Has she ever been in Lockup? She must have. Given the state of her clothes, she seems like the type who'd get in trouble a lot.

Sera turns to leave, and my legs moves before I can think. I rush forward and grab her wrist. She whips around, her eyes wide and jaw set. Beneath my fingers, I feel her muscles tighten. I half expect her to hit me. Instead, she just stares, her large blue eyes full of questions.

"Thank you," I say, quickly letting her go. "I just wanted to say thank you."

"You're welcome," she says slowly. She has this strange look on her face, like I'm a puzzle she needs to solve. I feel the same way; she's the first Slummer I've met who actually seems like a somewhat normal person. It seems she's genuinely kind and not just looking out for herself. But I still can't help but wonder why.

Before I can ask, Sera is gone, vanishing around the nearest corner.

"Don't worry." Callias smiles, grabbing my hand. "We'll see her again."

"We will?" How can he possibly know that? Odds are that we'll never see Sera again.

"Yeah," Theron agrees, leading the way down the street. "She's always around. That's how she found us."

I want to ask what Theron means, but Sera being "always around" is the least of my worries. My stomach rumbles loudly. It's been two days since I ate a decent meal. But first, I need to get us back to our apartment. By some miracle, Theron and Callias are safe. But now, I have bigger problems to deal with. We have no money, and I'm starving. How are we supposed to get anything to eat? My stomach rumbles loudly again. After the ghastly food in Lockup, anything sounds appealing. But I try to ignore my writhing insides. First, we get to the apartment. At least there, nearer to Midtown, we'll be safer than we are here.

Theron leads us through the maze of streets, and in no time, we're back at the Slum's edge. I'm not sure what time it is. All I know is that it's late enough for the sun to disappear behind the buildings. There are more beggars at the barrier than usual, and I can't help but stare. Do they ever get any money? It certainly wouldn't be enough to live on, but that's more than I have right now.

Every fiber of my body aches as I climb our building's narrow stairs. Once we return to our apartment, the first thing I'm going to do is lie down. Sleeping in my room, with no cell-mates around, sounds almost like a luxury. Then, after about a day's worth of sleep, I'll come up with a plan. The boys can manage on their own for a few hours. After all, they were okay while I was in Lockup.

When we reach our apartment, I wave my ID tag over the sensor in the door and wait for it to open. Nothing happens. I try again, and this time, the sensor makes a strange beeping sound. I close my eyes as my insides prickle. This is exactly what I don't want to deal with right after getting out of Lockup.

"My door's broken," I say, fighting to keep my voice calm as I reach the front desk. "Or the lock is. I need it fixed."

"Tag," the landlady says, not looking up from her pile of crumpled papers.

Reluctantly, I hold out my arm, and she waves her scanner over it. I wince as the inside of my forearm grows hot. Why does she have to be so rude all the time? It's not like I broke the lock. This is the Slum. This can't be the first time something's broken in this building today.

"Lock frequency was reset two days ago," the woman tells me, sounding almost bored. "The apartment isn't yours anymore."

"What?!" I snap, unable to stop myself. How can the apartment not be mine? I've lived there for over a month!

"Breach of morality clause," the woman says, jerking her head toward her scanner. "Government housing, kid. AURA requires a clean record for two months to requalify."

I open my mouth, determined to tell the woman she's wrong. But no sound comes out. Since when are there criteria for living here? It's the Slum. The government is supposed to provide everyone in this dump with free housing. My history teacher always said the free housing is proof of Nomisman's kindness to even its poorest citizens. I guess they never looked at the fine print.

But now, I have a real problem. Thanks to that stupid baker, I now have no money and nowhere to live. A cold, hollow feeling blooms deep in my stomach, and my hands shake so violently that I can't keep them still. How can I keep my brothers safe if we don't have a home?

"Hey," Callias says, grabbing my arm and pulling me back. "Let's go."

"What?" I say, not really listening.

"C'mon," Theron says, taking my other hand and pulling me out the door. "We'll find somewhere else."

How are my brothers so calm? Didn't they hear what the woman said? I have an arrest record now. None of the buildings in the Slum will take us for the next two months, and that's assuming none of us get into more trouble in that time. What are we going to do? We can't live on the streets. We're not Slummers. We may have nothing, but I refuse to let that happen to Callias and Theron. I'll figure something out ... but I have no idea how.

Theron takes the lead, and I'm so consumed by my dark thoughts that I let him. We walk along the barrier, passing even more beggars, their hands held toward the invisible line between

Midtown and the Slum. For some reason, the sight pushes my fears from my mind. What are they expecting to happen? No Midtowner in their right mind would dare throw a single phys across the barrier. And it's not just because Midtowners are too focused on flaunting their minimal wealth; I doubt most of them even know what phys is. I surely didn't before getting to the Slum. And if by some miracle, a coin did make it over, what then?

My breath catches in my throat. I've seen Slummers fight over scraps and trash. What would they do if real money was up for grabs? I don't want to be anywhere near here if that happens.

Luckily, Theron turns down a side street, and soon, the barrier is far behind us. My eyes narrow as the alleyways grow dark in the fading twilight. Even here, people sleep on piles of junk or under sheets strung up into makeshift tents. I've always wondered why so many people are on the streets when the government provides free housing. Now I know. They're not down on their luck. They're criminals.

My insides tighten as I spot a man covered in dirt sleeping on the pavement. Is that how people will see me? I shake my head, desperate to rid myself of the thought. I'm not like these people. I never meant to break the law.

The street opens up, and it feels like we're right back where we started. I've avoided coming to the square since the Culling. It looks so different with no stage, crowds, or massive screens. Plenty of carts are parked around the open expanse, and even more people happily browse the selection.

"Hey, Theron, Callias." A man in his mid-thirties waves as we walk by, smiling broadly as he rearranges his misshapen candles. I can't help but stare. Why is this stranger talking to my brothers? I've never seen him before.

"Evenin', boys," a woman with thinning grey hair says, a long, wadded-up length of fabric in her skeletal arms. "Give us a hand?"

Theron and Callias slip through my fingers before I can blink.

They run to the woman and begin neatly folding the fabric. My mouth falls open. When did my Newtown-raised little brothers learn to fold anything? And how do they know all these people? There's no way they met them all when I was in Lockup. I was only gone for two days. And why would Theron and Callias talk to them? They're Slummers. My brothers should know better.

"Thanks, boys." The woman smiles, placing the folded cloth on her rickety cart. "You're little time-savers, you are. Who's this?"

The woman's amber eyes fall on me. I join Theron and Callias, crossing my arms over my ill-fitting clothes. I don't know why I'm so uncomfortable. Probably because this grown woman clearly knows my little brothers, and I don't know a thing about her.

"Ezariah. Who are you?" I say, trying not to sound too harsh. I don't think it works.

"Oh," the woman says, her eyes widening. "Theron and Callias talk about you all the time. I'm glad you're … back. I'm Velva."

I try to smile, but all it does is make my face hurt. Why would I be kind to this woman? She's a Slummer who clearly took advantage of my absence. What happened to Theron and Callias while I was away? It's like they lived another life while I was in Lockup.

"So, what brings you down 'ere? Didn't you say you were going back to the Fringe tonight?" Velva asks.

"Well…" Theron trails off. He looks up at me, his brown eyes wide. I want to say something, but I have no idea what Theron and Velva are talking about. What's the Fringe? Based on the name, it's a place I'd like to avoid at all costs. Why would Theron tell Velva we were going there?

"We … can't. Not anymore" is all Theron says.

"Oh," Velva says, her eyes softening as they fall on me. "Don't worry, Ezariah. It happens to the best of us. We've all been there."

I think I get it now. The Fringe must be where our old apartment used to be. But Velva lumping me in with the rest of the Slummers who are in Lockup on a regular basis doesn't make me feel better. According to her, it's not even a big deal. But it is. I'm the reason we're homeless.

The boys run off, and this time, I don't try to stop them. They flit from cart to cart, chatting happily with the vendors as they pack up their piles of junk. I sit at the base of one of the crooked buildings, burying my face in my knees as white-hot tears sting my tired eyes. Now and then, someone calls my name, but I don't look up.

I've been an idiot. Things were bad enough when we were just Renounced. But now, I've made everything even worse. I got arrested because I couldn't bother to keep track of our money. We have no home now because I have a criminal record. How can I keep us alive when I failed so miserably the first time?

More than anything, all I want is to go home. I'd rather live under the same roof as my monster of a father than spend one more night in this hellhole. At least there, the threat of starvation and homelessness wouldn't be hanging over me like a sword. But would he even take us back?

Shaking my head, I laugh into my knees. My father would never take us back. Elias Malkin is a proud man. Taking us back would mean admitting he made a mistake in Renouncing us. But it's not just that. No matter how much I want to deny it, Velva is right. I may not be a true Slummer, but my father wouldn't dare associate with anyone like me now.

"Rough day?"

I jump, my heart thudding against my ribs as I tumble sideways. Pain shoots through my elbow as it hits the uneven pavement. I push myself up, and I'm surprised to find someone sitting beside me. How long has she been here? It couldn't have been more than a few minutes.

"What're you doing here?" I ask, hastily wiping away my tears.

"I live here," Sera says flatly. "And I like to sit and watch when I have a chance. I usually don't though.

"Things probably aren't that bad, you know," she adds after a pause, clearly sensing how I'm feeling.

"If only you knew," I mutter, my eyes trained on my thin shoes. "You have no idea what's going on."

"Really?" Sera says, her tone indignant. "You know what? You're right. Clearly, I've never worried about how I'm going to eats or how to make it through the day."

"It's not the same," I snap before I can stop myself. She really doesn't get it. "It's not just me that I'm worried about."

That shuts her up. For some reason, her silence makes me feel better. She has no idea what it's like, worrying about two young boys all the time. If I were here on my own, maybe I could manage it. But I'm not alone, and the boys are so young. I've tried too hard to hide the horrors of this place from them. They aren't like Sera, who's clearly a born-and-raised Slummer. Things that feel like the end of the world to me are probably normal for her.

"You'd be surprised," she says, and there's a gentleness to her voice that wasn't there before. "What's going on?"

I don't want to tell her. Somehow, saying it all out loud without even a whisper of a plan feels worse. But I need to tell someone, for Theron and Callias's sake. I can't keep it all bottled up inside.

So, while Theron and Callias play in the square, I explain how I'm the reason we have no place to live. I expect her to laugh, to make fun of my foolishness and stupidity. But she doesn't. She just sits there, listening to me unload, her eyes occasionally darting toward the boys.

When I've talked myself out, we sit in silence for a while, and then Sera pushes herself up.

"Alright. C'mon."

"What?" I shake my head a little. "Where?"

"To my place. It's small, but we can make it work."

"Why?" I ask before I can stop myself. I'm not sure what I expected after our talk, but this isn't it. Why would Sera, a Slummer, let Theron, Callias, and I live with her? It's not like she owes me anything. In fact, I owe *her* for taking care of Theron and Callias while I was in Lockup.

But as Sera continues glancing at the boys every few seconds, I realize I'm wrong. She's not doing this for me. She's doing it for them.

"Look, if you don't want to, fine," Sera says. "Sorry for—"

"No!" I shout a little more forcefully than I meant to. This is the first good thing to happen since my Renouncement. "Thanks. I'm sorry. Staying with you would be great. It's just… Why are you helping us?"

Sera looks from me to the boys. I don't know her well, but I can tell from the way her eyes narrow that she's choosing her words carefully.

"Those two… They're special," she finally says. "I don't want anything to happen to them."

Sera walks across the square to one of the many alleys. The hairs on the back of my neck stand on end as Theron and Callias run past me to join her. Why is Sera taking us down there? Maybe agreeing to stay with her was a mistake.

Sera stops at the poorest excuse for a door I've ever seen. It's basically a flimsy piece of wood propped in a doorway. She doesn't even wave her ID tag over a scanner to open it. Tentatively, I follow her and Theron up the narrow, uneven stairs. The worn wood creaks with every step I take. I grab Callias's hand, partly to keep him close, but mostly to keep myself upright.

"Since when are there apartments on the square?" I pant as we continue to climb. Does Sera live at the very top? I hope not.

"Yeah," Sera calls over her shoulder. "I think they were the first. I've had this place for over a year. They're not as fancy as the newer ones at the Fringe, but they're not bad."

Sera continues up the stairs until she turns sharply into a

slanting wall. I hurry after her, a stitch blooming in my side, and walk right into the ceiling.

"What the—?"

"Oh, yeah, watch your head," Sera calls.

My forehead pulsing, I follow Sera and Theron. The hallway is tiny, barely wide enough for one person to walk through. I have to hunch over to stop my head from hitting the sloping ceiling. Even Sera, who's a good half foot shorter than me, stoops when she walks. What idiot built this place?

Finally, Sera stops at a door. I expect her to wave her tag over the handle, like I did at our old apartment. Instead, she rams her shoulder into the rough wood several times before it finally bursts open. I fight the urge to shake my head. It's like they built this whole building with mismatched pieces.

"There," she pants, stepping aside to let us in.

If I said her place is small, I'd be lying. It's microscopic. The single room is just big enough for her sleeping mat and a rickety chair in the corner. There's also a tiny window, about the size of a book, so filthy that I can't see through it. The room is so dark that I can barely see my hands.

"Where's the light?" I ask, reaching out for the wall. There has to be a switch somewhere.

Sera's hand emerges from the darkness and smacks my fingers away with such force that they sting.

"Ouch! What was that for?"

"Are you nuts?" Sera asks. "What's wrong with you?"

"What's *wrong* with me?" I can't believe she just said that. "What's wrong with *you*? It's just a light switch."

"Why the hell would you turn the lights on?" Sera says. Even though it's dark, I can almost hear her rolling her eyes.

"Um, so we can *see*?" What kind of question is that?

"I have candles," Sera says. Warm, orange light blooms from the chair in the corner, which I now see is covered with warped grey tapers.

"Sera never turns on the lights." Callias shrugs, sitting cross-legged by the chair.

"She says it's too expensive," Theron adds, plopping down on the sleeping mat. "Candles are cheaper."

Theron's words are matter-of-fact, like he's talking about the weather. But I can't help but shake my head. This isn't what I was expecting when Sera offered to let us stay. At the very least, I thought I'd get to turn on a light. But Sera says no. And according to my brothers, that's all the explanation they need.

"I need some air."

Out in the hall, I slide down the wall, the rough surface biting through my thin shirt. This can't be happening. Before I went into Lockup, we were okay. Sure, we were just surviving, but at least we were safe. But now, I'm so deep in the Slum that I can't see a way out.

I should just cut my losses and take the boys out of here. But where could we go? I have no money, and I doubt I'll find another kind Slummer to take us in.

"You okay?"

I look up. Sera is standing over me, her thin arms folded across her ratty sheet dress. There are several lines across her forehead, and her eyes are narrow. I shift uncomfortably. Does she need to look at me like that? I'm not some animal for her to study.

"It's just... I..."

"C'mon, dude. Spit it out," Sera says, sitting opposite me. "I don't have all night."

I take a breath. Does she need to be so aggressive? I'm not a Slummer like her. All of this, the lack of everything, is so new to me.

"The boys and I... I don't think we can stay." I've made up my mind. We're not Slummers, and we aren't going to live like we are. I'm going to find a way to get us out of here. Sera's tiny excuse for an apartment isn't getting us anywhere. "Thanks for the offer. And for taking care of Callias and Theron while I was... But I just don't think this will work for us."

"Why not?" Sera asks, her tone much softer than I expected.

"I..." Does she really need me to spell it out? I don't want to live on top of my brothers in a space that's no larger than a servant's closet. We deserve better than this. It's filthy, and it's on the square; Slummers are probably lurking around every corner. I can't think of a worse place to live.

"This ... isn't what we're used to."

"Wow," Sera says, shaking her head. "And here I thought you were different."

I'm so stunned that my mouth actually falls open. What right does she have to judge me? She thought I was different? Than what? A Slummer? Of course I am. I don't belong here, and neither do my brothers. Why can't she see that?

"You Renounced are all the same," she mutters. "You think you can live here like the other Hoarders in Newtown."

It's like Sera has kicked me in the gut. There's that word again: Hoarder. After hearing it for two days in Lockup, I figured it was some sort of insult. But all it means is that I'm from Newtown? I try my best not to laugh. These Slummers really are stupid. Newtowners don't hoard their wealth. Everything we had, we earned.

And how does Sera even know I'm Renounced? We've barely spent ten minutes together, and it's not exactly something I advertise. Am I really that easy to read?

"Look, if you wanna go, go," Sera says, getting to her feet. "I'm not gonna stop you. But for the sake of those two boys, come up with a real plan before you leave. That's the least they deserve."

I stay in the hall while Sera returns to her apartment. Her words rattle around in my brain, and I can't shake them. Even though I'd never tell her, Sera is right about one thing: I can't just take the boys and leave with no plan. If it were just me, I might be able to manage it, but I have Theron and Callias to think about. And until I come up with a way out of this hellhole, I need to keep them safe. But how can I protect them from the Slum now? We're trapped in the very heart of it.

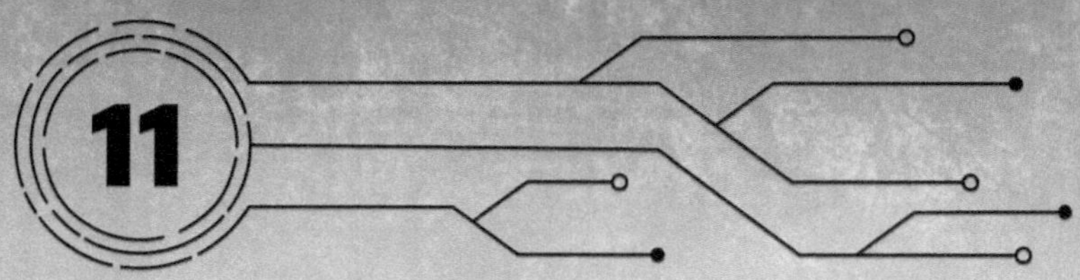

11

THE HARD WOODEN floor digs into my bones, making sleep nearly impossible. I shift for what feels like the hundredth time since lying down. The rolled-up sleeping mat we're using as a pillow is as uncomfortable as it is filthy. By far, the worst part is the smell.

My eyes open, but it makes no difference; Sera's apartment is so dark that I might as well be blindfolded. But I can still hear the heavy breathing around me. I try not to move. There's barely enough room for all of us to lie on the floor without touching. I don't want to wake Theron or Callias if I can help it.

So, I just lie here, staring into the dark silence. But no matter how hard I try, I can't shake the sinking feeling in my stomach. This is all wrong. I'm not supposed to be here, breathing in this thick, musty air. I try to swallow, but my tongue feels dry and swollen.

I sit bolt upright, my heart thundering against my ribs. Taking several deep breaths, I try to calm myself down. But I can't stop my arms from shaking. I rub my hands over my face, but they're rough as sandpaper.

I need a drink. I look around, but aside from the chair covered in melted candle wax, the apartment is empty. I want to scream so badly it feels like I'm going to burst. How can anyone live like this? I'll probably explode if I don't get out of here soon.

As quietly as I can, I rise, careful not to disturb Theron, Callias, or Sera. The worn floorboards creak, and I freeze, not daring to breathe. But the others are dead to the world. I shake my head. How can they sleep so peacefully in this dump?

I have to try several times to force the door. When it finally bursts open, I hurry into the hall and close it behind me. Well, "close" is too strong a word; I press on it until it gets stuck in the crooked doorframe.

My shoulder throbbing slightly, I stand in the slanting corridor, unsure where to go next. I really didn't think this through. I have no idea where anything is in this building. Sure, the hall is a little better than Sera's apartment. At least now I don't feel like I'm suffocating.

The narrow hallway is even creepier than it was last night. Every door I pass looks exactly the same. And even though I bend over, I still manage to hit my head several times. I furrow my brow as my face grows hot. Is there a single straight line in this place?

"Where's the bathroom?" I mutter. Does this place even have one?

A pungent odor burns my nostrils, making my insides lurch. Of course, my first impulse is to turn and run. Why would anyone in their right mind move toward such a repulsive smell? But I keep going, following the offensive scent to a cracked door at the other end of the hall. I clench my jaw, take one last breath, and push it open.

The bathroom is an utter disaster. A cracked mirror reflects the flickering light, casting eerie shadows on the discolored toilet. Foul smells fill the air, a nauseating mixture of mildew and human waste. If my mouth were open, I'd probably vomit right here on the floor. How am I supposed to use this disgusting place?

Tentatively, I approach the sink and turn the rusty tap. Thick brown water sputters out, pooling in the grimy basin. It almost looks like mud. My throat tightens as I take a step back. No. I'm not drinking that. Is it even water? But the sound of it running gnaws at my insides, and I know I have no choice.

"Gah!" I gasp as the thick, metallic liquid hits my lips. I swallow, the warm water sliding over my rough tongue. "Disgusting."

It's safe to say that I can't get out of here fast enough. But when I step into the hall, I freeze as I turn toward Sera's. I can't go back in there, and it's not just because it's so tiny that I can barely move without bumping into someone. Sera was right about one thing: if I want to get us out of here, I need a plan. And to do that, I need somewhere to think, to breathe.

But where can I possibly go? Outside? At this time of night, who knows what kind of Slummers are lurking in the square? A shiver runs down my spine at the thought. It's better if I stay inside. At least here, the floors are so creaky that I'd hear someone coming from a mile away.

So, I walk back to Sera's door. I slide down the wall just outside, and the horrid clothes I got from Lockup scratch my back. It takes all my will power to not rip them off right there. I bet they'd tear after one good pull.

"I need to get us out of this hellhole," I mutter, pressing my forehead into my knees. This is no way to live—not for me, or for Theron, and certainly not for Callias. They deserve better than a ratty broom closet in a crumbling building. But how can we get out? I wrack my brain, trying to think of some way out of the Slum.

Then it hits me: the Culling. It's our best chance to get out of here. But there won't be another lottery for months. Can we even make it that long? We barely lasted one month before everything fell apart.

A pit forms deep in my stomach as the realization hits me. I have no money. How can I win the Culling without it? I'd need to buy a ton of extra entries to ensure our ticket out of here. And forget the Culling—what am I supposed to do for food? Almost on cue, my stomach growls loudly.

I press the heels of my palms into my eyes. If the Enforcers hadn't incinerated my old clothes, I could've sold them to Bart.

No doubt he'd rip me off again, but at least I'd have some money. How can I possibly save up enough to win the Culling?

When I finally look up, my eyes fall on Sera's door. Maybe, if I ask her, she'll give me some money? She's already helping us, after all.

I barely stop myself from laughing. Why would she help me? She's a Slummer. I don't care how much she says she likes Theron and Callias; no Slummer will ever give money to a Hoarder like me. No, Sera won't help me. I need to figure this out on my own.

A sudden thud breaks the silence, making me jump. The door to Sera's apartment bursts open, and Theron steps out, his hair sticking up in all directions. He stares at me, his eyes narrow as I lie awkwardly on the floor. Quickly, I push myself back into a sitting position, fighting to keep my face neutral. What is he doing up this early?

"What's goin' on?" he asks, sitting beside me. "You've been out here for a while."

I guess I wasn't as quiet as I thought when I left. Should I tell him? It's not like he doesn't know what's going on. No matter how much I've tried to shield him, Theron has always been too smart for his own good. But this isn't his problem to solve. I got us in this mess, and I need to get us out of it.

"It's nothing," I lie. "Just … the bathroom's a bomb scene."

"Yeah." Theron chuckles, but there's no real humor in his voice. "I shoulda warned you. It's better if you hold your breath. But hey, it could be worse. At least we have a roof."

I nod, trying to agree with him, but the words catch in my throat. How is he okay with this? We're staying in a disgusting building that's on the verge of falling apart. The sooner I get us out of here, the better. I don't want Theron or Callias to think living like this is normal.

"C'mon," Theron says, standing up. "Let's go back inside."

We find Sera and Callias folding up the filthy sleeping mat.

"Thanks, Callias." Sera smiles. "You're such a good helper."

"Can we eat now?" Theron asks, and I hear his stomach growl. "I'm starving."

"Me too," Callias says.

My stomach sinks, but I try to put on a brave face. I thought I'd have at least an hour to figure out something for food. What am I going to do? We can't buy anything to eat.

"I'd join you," Sera says, pulling a small, worn bag from the folds of her sheet dress, "but I've got work in Midtown."

She hands Theron and Callias a few coins each, and my mouth drops. Theron's eyes widen as he clutches the large, square coins. They're so big that he can barely fit them in his tiny fist.

"This should be enough for some bread," Sera says.

"It's enough for the one with the nuts!" Callias exclaims, grinning from ear to ear.

I open my mouth, but it's hard to breathe. When I do, it's like a rock is sitting on my chest. Why did Sera give them money? Clearly, it's not like she has much of it. If she did, she'd spend it on decent clothes and not scream at me when I try to turn on a light.

The boys should just give the money back. We don't need charity from a Slummer. But my stomach growls again, and I bite my tongue. We need to eat, and my money bag is empty. I guess I can let Sera pay this one time.

"C'mon," she says, shoving her leather money bag back into the folds of her dress. "I need to get through the barrier before they close it."

We walk through the square, Theron and Callias on Sera's heels. Even though it's early, the streets are packed. My heart pounds in my ears as I trail behind them, fighting to keep my face calm. Why are so many people out? They're Slummers. It's not like they have anywhere to be.

"Mornin', Sera!" calls a stooped woman with a missing eye. She reaches into a worn bag on her back. My muscles tighten; I half expect her to pull out a weapon. Instead, she's holding what looks like a black-and-orange fruit.

"'Ere you go." she smiles, tossing the fruit to Callias. "Best I could find."

"Thanks!" Callias beams, clutching the squishy thing to his chest like a precious treasure.

"That orange looks good," Theron says, and I see his face fall slightly. "Better than the one I got yesterday."

The pounding in my chest slows, but only slightly, as Sera leads us down one of the wider alleys. How do my brothers know so many Slummers? And why would that woman give Callias an orange? Something's going on with the people here, and I don't like it. I really need to get us out of here, and soon.

A massive crowd is waiting when we reach the barrier. Even standing on my tiptoes, I can barely see the dark metal pillars over the sea of heads. I hate to admit it, but I'm impressed. All of these Slummers get to work in Midtown. But how? It's not like the Slummers have much to offer the Midtown factory owners. How do they even pick them?

"Do we need to stay?" I groan to Theron and Callias as the line shuffles forward a few inches. It's like we're deliberately moving at a snail's pace.

"Calm down." Theron shakes his head. "It's not gonna take too long."

"Yeah," Callias chimes in, digging into his orange with his nails. "We just wanna say bye."

It's hard to keep my frustration from my face. Why are Theron and Callias so attached to Sera? They've only known her for three days. And she's not even that nice. Aside from a few glances over her shoulder, she hasn't said anything to me today. The sooner I get us out of her cramped apartment, the happier I'll be.

"Fine," I concede. It's not like we have anywhere else to be.

Finally, after what feels like an hour, Sera steps up to the barrier checkpoint. Aside from the station where we got our ID tags, I've never seen a checkpoint up close. There's a hole in the pillar about as wide as a grown man's arm. Sera slides her arm into the hole, and several lines appear on her forehead as the inside of the hole glows green. She quickly pulls out her arm and steps across the barrier into Midtown.

"I'll see you when I'm done," Sera says from the other side of the barrier as Theron and Callias stand as close as they dare. Her gaze briefly meets mine, but I keep my mouth shut. Does she expect *me* to say something? I hardly know her.

"Bye!" Theron calls out as Sera joins the rest of the workers.

"See you later!" Callias yells, waving broadly while she vanishes in the crowd.

Enforcers escort the workers to the nearest factory, its tall smokestacks belching out black clouds. They disappear inside, and as the doors close, for the briefest of moments, I want to join them. But I shake my head. That's ridiculous. Why would I want to work in a dirty, smelly factory? Judging by Sera's apartment, they're not even paid well. What's the point?

The answer comes to me immediately: they get to leave the Slum for the day. For a few short hours they're free of this place.

"Let's go," I huff, turning my back to the barrier.

Theron and Callias race ahead, leading the way through the narrow alleys. I follow them, not really paying attention to where Theron is taking us. No matter how hard I try, I can't stop thinking about Sera. It's not that she has money, or a job, even though that does rub me the wrong way. Why does she, a born-and-raised Slummer, get to leave the Slum, while I'm stuck in this hellhole?

"C'mon." Callias takes my hand and pulls me down a cramped alley filled with piles of trash and people huddled at the bases of the buildings. "Theron says this way's quicker."

"Really?" I want to tell him no, but I have no idea where we are or where we're going. "How do you know?"

"We did some exploring while you were ... away," Theron

admits, avoiding my gaze. "We've been here a while, Ezariah. We should know our way around."

My jaw tightens as we continue walking. Doesn't Theron see how pointless knowing our way around is? If everything works out, we'll leave the Slum in a few months after the next Culling. Why learn to navigate the maze of alleys and streets when we won't be here for too long?

After a few minutes of us wandering, the alley opens onto a wider street. I sigh, letting go of Callias as bright sunlight warms my face. There's a crowd up ahead, a mixture of ragged Slummers and at least ten Enforcers. I stop dead in my tracks. Usually, I'd avoid any crowd that size. But I don't want to leave. Why would Enforcers stand with Slummers?

My curiosity piqued, I stand on my tiptoes. The crowd encircles two Slummers. They're at least ten years older than me, but just as thin as Theron. One takes a swing, and his knuckles collide with the other man's temple. Cheers erupt from the watchers as the other man staggers back, a dazed look on his face.

"What's happening?" Theron asks, jumping to try to catch a glimpse.

"It's a fight." I wince. I look to the Enforcers, expecting them to do something. Instead, they just stand there watching with the rest.

Another cry of pain from the fighters, and my stomach churns. Why aren't the Enforcers doing anything? Isn't it their job to protect people? They arrested me for getting beat with a club in the street. Why aren't they stopping this?

"Ezariah, let's go," Callias says, tugging on my sleeve.

"Wait..." For some reason, I can't bring myself to move. Why are these men fighting? Neither speaks, but I do overhear two others at the crowd's edge as I step closer.

"C'mon, Linden! You nearly got 'im!"

"Like hell he does! When Slate's finished, you'll think twice before you welch on me."

My eyes narrow as I stare at the two spectators. From the sound of it, the fight is between them. But why would anyone fight over something they're not involved in? Something strange is going on here, and I don't want to be anywhere near it.

I try to step back, but my foot hits something hard. I turn and find two men standing on either side of me. Their imposing shadows loom over me, and my mouth suddenly becomes very dry. They must be here to watch the fight. Do all Slummers find violence so amusing? I wouldn't be surprised.

The two men's eyes shift from the fight to me. My chest tightens, and my legs tremble violently. Why are they looking at me? I need to get my brothers out of here, now.

One of the men grabs my arm. "Ezariah."

I try to pull myself free, but his grip is like iron. "Wh-what?" How do they know my name? I look around wildly for Theron and Callias, but they're nowhere to be seen. My heart beats even faster. Where'd they run off to now?

"Come with us," the other man says, grabbing my other arm. "Let's take a walk."

The two men pull me from the crowd before I can catch my breath. My heart races as they drag me through the dark alleys. I desperately try to free my trembling arms, but it's useless. We pass several groups of people huddled around the buildings, and they don't even give us a second look.

When I was little, Uncle Galen would tell us stories about the Slum to try to scare us. He used to say that Slummers are savage creatures who thrive on the chaos of the Slum. They'll rob you without a second thought, he told us, and they kill for sport. Is that what these men plan to do with me?

Cold sweat drips down my spine. They can't possibly think I have any money. I probably look like a Slummer who slept on the side of the road. What do they want from me?

The men finally stop outside a drab derelict building. It's smaller than the others I've seen in the Slum, only three floors. They force me through the cracked door, which bangs loudly off the crumbling wall. Peeling paint hangs around us like scars, and the floorboards creak beneath our feet.

People linger around the edge of the space. I feel their eyes on me as the two men march me into the next room. Why are they all here? These two guys couldn't have grabbed us all, could they? The hairs on the back of my neck stand on end. What do these guys want from us?

The next room is dimly lit, with only a scratched-up table, a worn-out armchair, and a few wooden stools. There's even a boarded-up window. But unlike the previous room, there's no one else in here.

"Sit," one man huffs, pushing me toward the table. I catch myself just in time and shakily sit on a stool.

"Yarrow will be here soon," the other man says as they back out of the room.

My knuckles turn white as I grip the edge of the seat. I have no idea who Yarrow is, but I don't want to wait around to find out. My eyes fall on the boarded-up window. It's the only way out of here. But is there enough time to pry the wood off before Yarrow arrives? That could be any second. And what about Theron and Callias? These men could go after them next.

I'm on my feet and at the window in seconds.

"They're fine, Ezariah," I whisper, running my fingers over the worn boards. "You'll find them again, and they'll be fine, just like last time."

The sound of several feet approaching from the next room makes me freeze. I barely make it back to my stool before the door opens. The two men who grabbed me walk in, followed by a woman. She's tall, with short blonde hair and dark, sunken eyes. Like every other Slummer I've seen, she's thin as a rail. But as she sits in the old armchair, I see muscles bulging beneath her sallow skin. I take a shaky breath. She looks like she could snap me in half without breaking a sweat.

"Ezariah," she says, her slow voice dripping with authority, "you're a hard man to find."

"Who… You were looking for me?" I ask, my voice shaking despite my efforts to keep it steady.

"Of course I was," she says, raising an eyebrow. "Didn't Cassian…?"

At the mention of his name, it's like the world vanishes around me. I got so caught up in my release from Lockup and our encounters with Sera that I completely forgot about Cassian. I owe a debt to Cassian's boss, and he promised they'd find me. My insides shudder as I stare at the woman. How could I be so stupid? I must be sitting in the headquarters of Cassian's mob.

"It's a pleasure, Ezariah," the woman says, the ghost of a smile on her lips. "I'm Nyssa Yarrow."

Fear coils around my throat like a snake. I open my mouth to speak, but no sound comes out. Nyssa leans back in her armchair, her dark eyes narrowing as she cocks her head to the side. It's like she's studying me.

"You owe me a debt, Ezariah."

"I didn't mean… It was a…" I protest, but she cuts me off with a wave.

"You're responsible for Jackson's sentence getting extended," she says coolly. "Therefore, you'll assume his duties until his release."

I wait for Nyssa to explain further, but she only stares. Anger burns away some of my fear. How am I supposed to do Jackson's job when no one will tell me what it is? All I know about Jackson is that he's big and kind of stupid. What kind of job would Nyssa have someone like that do?

Can I refuse her? Of course, I know the answer immediately. This woman has Enforcers working for her. There's no telling what she might do to me, or to Theron or Callias if I get on her bad side. Realizing I have no choice, I clench my jaw and force the words out.

"Fine. I'll do it."

"Good," Nyssa says, her voice icy. "Be in the square at first light tomorrow. I'll send someone to show you the ropes."

She nods, and I hear the two thugs behind me step to the side. I stand so quickly that I knock over my stool. I pick it up with unsteady hands, fighting to keep myself calm. I need to get out of this run-down place before I lose it.

"Remember, Ezariah…" Nyssa's voice reaches me as I leave the room. "Our work here is crucial. I expect nothing less than perfection."

I manage to keep it together until I leave the building. I gasp for air like I'm trapped underwater. White-hot tears run down my cheeks, and my legs shake so violently that I can't stand. As I sit on the edge of the road, the last five minutes crash down on me like a wave. I'm working for the mob now—and there's nothing I can do about it.

Pulling myself together takes longer than I thought. When I finally do, I try to retrace the path Nyssa's thugs took here. I need to find my brothers.

Luckily, after following a group of Slummers to the square, I spot my brothers almost instantly. They're playing a game with some other kids, their laughter filling the air. I sigh as relief washes over me. They're fine.

"Hey, Ezariah!" Theron calls out, his eyes full of curiosity. "Where'd you go?"

I open my mouth to explain, but stop myself. I can't tell him about Nyssa, or my new "job." The truth would terrify him.

"Nowhere," I lie, forcing on a smile. "Just needed some air."

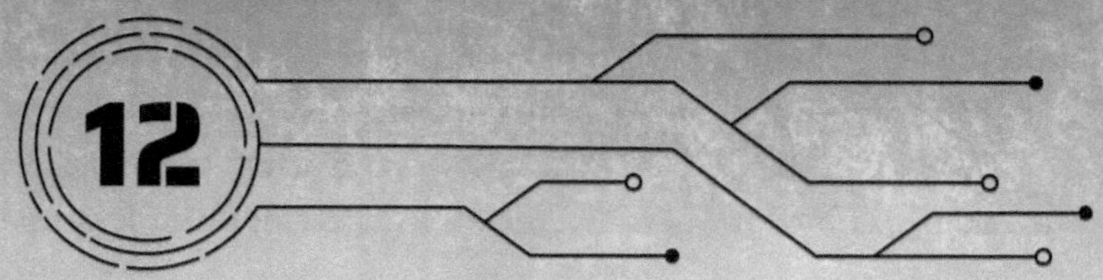

AS THE APARTMENT door closes behind Sera, I momentarily feel her eyes on me. I sigh, trying to slow my thundering pulse. I thought she'd never leave. She's been staring at me like it's her job ever since Callias told Sera I disappeared yesterday. Of course, she didn't say one word about it to me. I'm just glad she's gone.

Theron and Callias sit on the floor, rolling up the sleeping mat. I take a breath, wiping my sweaty palms on my rough pants. What am I supposed to tell them? My brothers aren't stupid. They'll notice when I leave to meet whoever Nyssa's sending to the square. I know I can't tell them the truth, but I need to tell them something.

"Hey, guys," I say slowly, trying to sound upbeat. "Guess what? I got a job."

"Neat." Callias shrugs before returning to shoving on his shoes.

Theron's eyes narrow as he looks up at me. I try to smile back, hoping he can't hear my heart hammering against my ribs. But I know Theron, and he doesn't believe me. Of course, I'm not lying—not really. I *do* have a job, even though I don't know what it is.

"What job?" Theron asks hesitantly.

"I ... uh..." I try to think of a plausible answer. "Around here. Delivering things."

"Delivering what?" he presses. "Who gave you a job?"

"Just stuff people need," I say evasively.

Theron cocks his head to the side, which sends my foot

tapping like crazy. He's still not buying it. I need to get out of here before he asks any more questions.

"Well, I gotta go. See you later."

Theron starts to say something, but I slip out the door before he can manage it.

Out in the square, Slummers push their carts around, getting ready for the day. One tries to sell me a cloth full of holes, claiming it's a blanket, but I barely hear her. My eyes rake over the crowd, my hands shaking slightly. Where's the guy from Nyssa's crew? It's not like they're hard to spot; they're all walking mountains.

A young girl pushes her way between the carts in front of me. She's small and wiry, with dirty blonde hair pulled back into a braid. I look right over her head, still searching for one of Nyssa's thugs. But after a few seconds I realize the girl has stopped right in front of me.

"Rowan," she says curtly, crossing her arms.

"Okay..." Why is this girl talking to me? I have enough to deal with without strange kids bothering me. She's probably looking for a handout; she's a Slummer, after all. I don't have time for this. I need to be ready for whoever Nyssa sends. I still have no idea what I'm supposed to do.

"Dude, let's go," she barks, snapping her fingers repeatedly in my face. "I swear, you're even dumber than Jackson."

"Wait ... what?"

Rowan turns on her heel and marches across the square. For a moment, I just stare. How does she know Jackson? Clearly, she doesn't like him. But she can't be part of Nyssa's crew. By the look of her, she's barely twelve.

I race after Rowan, a stitch growing in my side. I finally catch her as she ducks into one of the wider alleys branching off the square.

"... stuck me with a brainless slug," Rowan is muttering, shaking her head. "And after everything I've done for her... What's Nyssa thinking?"

I don't have time to be offended as Rowan speeds along, leaping around the heaps of trash lining the street. I practically run to keep up with her, trying to ignore the burning in my nose. Why would someone so young work for Nyssa? What horrible thing did she do to land her in this position?

"Umm, Rowan," I pant, trying to keep my voice casual. "Nyssa didn't … umm… What're we doing?"

"Just be quiet and watch," she says, shaking her head as she tosses me a ragged cloth bag. "Thanks to you, we're covering my route *and* Jackson's today."

Now I'm really confused. Rowan is barely taller than Theron, and just as skinny as Callias. Jackson, on the other hand, looked like he could knock over a building with his fists. Rowan may have an attitude, but surely she can't intimidate people like Jackson. How could they possibly do the same job for Nyssa?

We stop outside a shop a few blocks from the square. Rowan knocks, and I barely have time to breathe before the door creaks open.

"Hey, Row," a man whispers. "You're late."

"Sorry," Rowan huffs, taking the man's heavy cloth bag. "Got held up today."

Rowan throws the bag over her shoulder, and a faint white cloud bursts from the top. I bite my lip. Whatever's inside the bag is clearly illegal. I glance over my shoulder, expecting Enforcers to emerge from the shadows. But aside from a few people huddled soundlessly in the alley, the street is empty.

"Is he okay?" The man's eyes fall on me as he tosses Rowan a second, smaller bag that jingles slightly.

"Yeah," Rowan sighs, shaking her head. "He's just new."

She turns and walks quickly down the street, not bothering to see if I follow. I hurry after her, sweat pouring down my face while my lungs burn. How is she moving so fast? That bag must weigh fifty pounds. Whatever's inside, Rowan clearly doesn't want to be caught with it.

"Hurry up," she calls over her shoulder as she plops the bag in front of a new door.

Sweat stings my eyes as Rowan knocks. And suddenly, I realize this is not a new door—not to me, anyway. I've been here before. It's one of the better bakeries; they actually sell food a human can eat. Most days, the bakery we usually go to—the one where I got arrested—never has enough decent food. Theron and Callias always find something semi-decent here.

But why would Rowan bring a sack of drugs here? The hairs on the back of my neck stand on end. What does the baker do with it? Put it in the food? My stomach lurches, and I clamp my mouth shut.

"Oh, good," the baker says, taking the bag from Rowan. "I'm almost out of flour. I thought you forgot."

"C'mon, Dax," Rowan says, the corners of her mouth twitching. "You know Nyssa takes care of you."

The baker smiles, hands Rowan another small leather bag, then quickly closes the door. I stare from Rowan to the door, my mouth hanging open. Flour? It was just a bag of flour. Why would a baker pay Nyssa's crew just to deliver flour? Don't mobs do things like fight in the streets, rob people, or make them pay for protection?

Flour can't be too hard to come by. The Slum is full of bakeries, after all, even though most of them aren't that good. What kind of organization is Nyssa running?

"Here," Rowan says, tossing me both bags of money. "Keep track of those."

For the rest of the morning, I follow Rowan as she zips around the Slum. We pick up boxes of slightly rotten fruit, worn, discolored cloth, and even a case of glass bottles, and deliver them somewhere else. After each transaction, Rowan tosses me another bag of phys. The coins rattle loudly in the tattered bag hanging from my shoulder as I hurry to keep up. It's the most money I've seen since arriving in the Slum. But I still don't understand why people need Nyssa for these basic errands. One thing I've learned about the Slum is that money is scarce. Why would people pay Nyssa's crew just to do their chores?

"Rowan," I finally ask after we pick up some sweet-smelling herbs from a small shack tucked between two rotting buildings, "why are we doing this?"

Rowan rolls her eyes, rubbing her forehead with her palm. "You really are helpless, aren't you …?"

"Ezariah," I say, trying to keep my voice calm. I've been with her all morning; she should know my name by now. "I just wanna understand what we're doing."

"Fine, Eza… whatever," she sighs. "We're takin' the herbs to Floodway. They need them for medicine, I think."

"Floodway?" I've never heard of any place in the Slum by that name.

"It's a neighborhood," Rowan huffs.

"Then why doesn't the healer come get them?" I ask, furrowing my brow at the herbs.

"According to AURA they're a controlled substance," Rowan says slowly, like she's explaining something very simple to a child. "The healer can't grow them or transport them herself. Enforcers would throw her in Lockup in a second if they caught her."

So, we *are* doing something illegal. But that makes no sense. Why does AURA care who has flour or herbs or cloth? In Newtown, we had an endless supply of stuff like that. Just when I think the Slum can't get any stranger, somehow it does.

After we deliver the herbs to the healer, a short woman with huge, wide eyes, Rowan takes me back to Nyssa's. The front room is packed. I try not to breathe too deeply as people push past me. It takes Rowan and me a while before we reach the table by the back wall. A man sits behind it, squinting at me through heavy-lidded eyes.

"Good day?" the man asks. His voice sounds like a whistle.

"Good enough." Rowan shrugs. She shoves her hand into my satchel and throws our money bags onto the table. The man pours out the contents, and my breath catches in my throat as I stare at the pile of coins. With all that money, I could buy at least ten entries for the Culling! I'd be out of this hellhole in no time. But even as I stare, the man sweeps the coins into a small metal box and shuffles out of the room.

As we step out onto the winding street, Rowan says, "See you tomorrow, Ez... Eza..."

"Ezariah." I shake my head. Does she really still not know my name? Or is she just screwing with me? Probably the latter.

"Wow, that's a Hoarder name, dude," Rowan says. "And it's just hard to say."

"No, it's not!" Now she *is* making fun of my name. I can't believe this. "Ez-are-ee—"

"I'm just gonna call you Ezra." Rowan smiles as she backs down the street. "See you tomorrow, Ezra!"

"Why are you here?" The words fly out of my mouth before I can stop them. I've been wanting to ask her all day.

"What?"

"Why do you work for Nyssa?"

Rowan shrugs. "What else am I gonna do?" she calls, disappearing down a side street before I can say another word. "People need our help."

WORKING with Rowan is much the same over the next few days: we pick items up from one place and deliver them to another. After a while, we switch roles: I handle the exchanges, while Rowan holds the money. She says it's necessary, since she won't be there to "hold my hand" once I'm on my own. The thought makes my stomach do a backflip.

"Are you sure about this, Row?" Dax, the baker, asks. "Has Yarrow okayed this?"

He speaks to Rowan like I'm not even there. I focus on my thin shoes, trying to keep the frustration from my face. Why does it bother me? It's not like I care what some Slummer thinks. I just want to get out of working for Nyssa's crew in one piece.

"Yup." Rowan shrugs, taking Dax's money. "Ezra's gotta learn somehow."

A few days later, while we're making our daily drop-off with the man at the back table, Nyssa walks into the room. The room goes quiet as she weaves between the people waiting to turn in their hauls. Even though I don't look at her, I can feel her eyes on me. My skin crawls as I pass the money across the table. I haven't seen Nyssa since the night her goons grabbed me. Why's she here?

"How's he doing?" she asks Rowan, nodding in my direction.

"Okay," Rowan says, sounding surprised. "He hasn't made a mess of anything yet."

"Good." Nyssa's dark eyes fall on me. "Tomorrow, you'll work your route alone."

A mixture of relief and panic burns my insides like acid. For a moment, I thought someone must have complained to Nyssa about me. But no; Nyssa finally trusts me enough to let me do a route on my own. I don't know whether to be proud or mortified.

The thought of doing this without Rowan actually makes me a little sad. I'd never tell Rowan, but I'll miss having her around. She may not be much of a talker, but with her there, I always feel safe in the Slum. What's going to happen when she's not with me?

Thankfully, my route isn't as complicated as I thought. Every morning, I check on Dax, the baker, and Sorrel, the healer. I'm also assigned three side streets a few blocks from the square, where I'm supposed to wander around and offer Nyssa's services to anyone who might need them.

Mostly, I try to make as little of an impression as possible. Dax and Sorrel are one thing, but walking up to random Slummers who are lying in the streets begging for handouts makes my insides squirm. Sure, seeing them doesn't make me want to run in the opposite direction anymore, but that doesn't mean I want to talk to them. What would they ask me to do? Probably something foul.

I try not to think about it. I just have to hang on until Jackson is released. Then I can stop pretending the Slum is normal. There's nothing normal about a place where mobs walk the streets and everyone is starving or fighting to survive. The sooner I get out of Nyssa's mob, the faster I can focus on getting my brothers and me out of this hellhole. No matter how normal this place is starting to seem, it is not my home. I need to remember where I am.

The sun is setting behind the buildings as I deliver several bottles of a clear liquid to Sorrel. I hurry down my assigned streets, keeping my head down and making as little eye contact as possible. I feel like I haven't been back to Sera's apartment for days. I can't remember the last time I saw Theron and Callias for more than a few minutes. What do they do while Sera and I are gone all day? They must know I'd be with them if I could. As far as they know, I'm working to get us enough money to escape the Slum. Guilt claws at my insides, but I certainly can't tell them the truth.

Suddenly, two men burst out of a nearby shop. I freeze, my muscles tense as one tries to pull the other to the ground. This is precisely the type of thing I try to avoid on my rounds. I need to get out of here—now.

I turn to leave, but more people pour out of the shop, gathering around the fight, and I'm pushed in closer.

"You're short five phys!" cries one man with long, dark hair and a squished nose.

"You know I paid in full!" the other insists, leaning heavily on a worn walking stick.

The younger man throws a punch, and the onlookers gasp and laugh all at once. But I'm not laughing. The guy with the long hair is going to beat the old man for not paying. I know all too well what that's like.

"Stop!"

I run forward before I can think. The younger man raises his fist again, and I step between him and the old man. He freezes, his eyes narrowing as he glares at me. Every fiber of my being screams at me to run, but even though my arms and legs shake, I stay where I am. He may be a Slummer, but I can't ignore an old man getting beaten in the middle of the street for not being able to pay.

"Enforcers!" a voice hisses from the crowd.

I've never seen people disappear so quickly. They duck into shops and alleys as the unmistakable sound of heavy boots echoes around the battered buildings. The younger man with the long hair vanishes along with the rest. I take a few deep breaths before turning around. I want to make sure the old man is okay. But he's gone, just like the rest of the Slummers.

"Really?" I shake my head. At the very least, he could've thanked me.

I need to get out of here; I can't be late for my drop-off at Nyssa's. The last thing I need is to get on her bad side.

Just then, a woman quickly walks past me, and I feel her hand slip in and out of my pocket.

"Thank you."

"Hey!" I spin around, looking all over for her. But aside from the Enforcers, the street is empty. I shove my hand into my pocket, my face growing hot. What did she take?

My fingers brush against a few loose coins. My breath catches in my throat as I pull them out. These weren't there a second ago. All my collections for Nyssa are in leather bags in my satchel. That woman put these in my pocket and thanked me. But for what? Stopping a fight? Maybe.

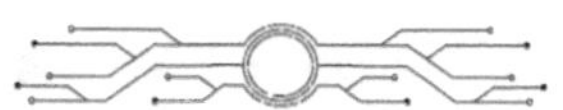

I STARE AT THE COINS—MY coins. It's the first money I've held since Lockup that's not destined for Nyssa. I return the coins to my pocket, my heart lighter than it's been in weeks. This is it. This is my way out of the Slum.

Finding fights in the Slum is easier than I thought it would be. I always stumble on one or two when I'm making my rounds. Oddly, stepping between two people brawling in the street feels a lot safer than transporting goods for Nyssa's clients. And every time I stop a fight, a few coins appear in my pocket. Most of the time, I don't see who put them there. But I don't care.

Before going to Nyssa's each night, I rush back to Sera's place. Luckily, it's always late afternoon, so no one's ever home. I hide the coins under the loose floorboard in the corner. In no time, my little money bag is fuller than ever. What I didn't expect is how hard saving it would be.

"C'mon, Ezariah," Theron says, nudging me in the side. "Just one extra blanket."

"We can't afford a blanket," I say, showing Theron the few coins I have. I take a handful with me whenever we go out. I don't like lying to him, but what choice do I have? We can't get out of the Slum if I don't keep better track of the money. I won't make that mistake again.

Most nights, Nyssa's place is packed. A lot of the crew hang out there after dropping off their hauls, playing cards, eating, and drinking. I try to get out of there as fast as possible. I don't care how normal working for Nyssa feels now. I'm not like the rest of her crew. I'm not a criminal.

"Hey, Ezra!" Rowan's yell stops me just as I open the front door. I turn and nearly step on her foot.

"What?" I try not to sound too annoyed. She really can appear out of nowhere.

"Touchy," Rowan says, raising an eyebrow. "Wanna stay and play a few hands?"

"No." I don't mean to say it so quickly. But really, what is

Rowan thinking? Why would I stay and play cards? I've worked too hard to throw my money away now. "I need to get home."

"Suit yourself." she shrugs. "Tell your brothers hi for me."

My chest tightens as Rowan closes the door. I've never mentioned my brothers to anyone in Nyssa's crew. But, of course, they all seem to know. Even Cassian knew back when I was in Lockup. Every time someone mentions them, I get uneasy. It's like they're reminding me that they're always watching.

I'm almost to the square when I spot a man struggling with a cart. The wheel is stuck in a pothole, and his ragged face shines with sweat as he tries to push it free. He looks up, and his pleading eyes lock on mine.

"Hey, kid! Can you give me a hand?"

Normally, I'd walk right past this man without a second thought. There are always plenty of people in the street to help with stuff like this. But tonight, of course, there's no one.

As I approach the cart, something rank hits my nose. My stomach lurches, and I clamp my mouth shut. No wonder no one is helping him. The cart is full of literal garbage.

It doesn't take long to free it. Several bags tumble out the back, and I suppress a shudder. I'd better get at least a few phys for this. I barely tolerate touching the trash in Sera's apartment.

I grab a particularly large bag, and pain erupts in my hand. Gasping, I immediately let it go. Blood oozes from a shallow cut in my palm. My face grows hot as I clench my jaw. Why didn't he tell me there was something sharp in the bags? And who carries around bags of broken glass? Slummers really are idiots.

"Thanks, kid." The man hands me a few coins, and I suppress a groan. Only four phys. I get at least double that for stopping fights, and even then, I don't get hurt. I should have left the man to his own devices after all.

"No problem," I mutter, trying to ignore my stinging hand as I pocket the coins.

Theron, Callias, and Sera are on the floor when I force open the apartment door. I keep my hand in my pocket and try to force my face into a calm expression. Theron and Callias smile, but Sera doesn't take her eyes off me as I slump between my brothers.

"How was your day?" Theron asks through a mouthful of very dry bread.

"It was okay," I say, trying to rip off a piece of rock hard break with my good hand. "Just a normal—"

"What's with your hand?" Sera asks, her eyes narrowing.

"Nothing," I say, pushing it deeper into my pocket. Why does she have to be so nosy all the time?

Sera moves quicker than I thought possible. She reaches out and yanks my hand from my pocket. I squeeze my hand into a fist, trying to cover the cut. But there's no concealing the dried blood coating my fingers.

"Ew," Callias says, his eyes widening.

"What happened?" Sera demands. "Did you get into a fight?"

"No." Of all the things Sera could have said, I didn't expect that. Why would I fight someone? I'm not a lawless Slummer. "I just helped an old guy with a cart."

"Really?" Sera's expression hardens as her eyes flicker between my bloody hand and face. "Must have been a slow delivery day."

I don't know if it's the way she emphasizes *delivery* or her rolling her eyes. Clearly, she doesn't believe my lie about being a delivery boy. Either way, I'm on my feet in seconds. Sera stands too, her eyes narrow and her brows knitted together.

"What's that supposed to mean?" I demand, my hands balling into fists.

"Oh, c'mon," she says, her eyes darting to Theron and Callias, who look like they've been slapped. "Do you really want to go there?"

She's right. I don't want to go there. What right does Sera have to judge me? I haven't said anything about her tiny apartment, ratty clothes, or lack of shoes. Why would she bring this up in front of Theron and Callias? I've worked so hard to protect them. Now Sera's going to ruin everything.

"I'm just doing what I need to do to survive, just like everyone else in this hellhole. Why can't you accept that?"

"Because of them!" she exclaims, throwing her hands in the air. "I don't want whatever you're doing to fall back on your brothers."

"You think I don't know that?" I would never put my brothers in danger. I'm doing all of this to save them. Why can't Sera see that? "You've lived in the Slum your whole life. But I'm trying to get us out of here, to give my brothers a better future. And I don't need a Slummer telling me how to do that!"

Sera's face hardens, and she storms out the door, slamming it behind her. I sit in the corner, my face hot and sweaty. I think Theron says something, but I can't hear him. This is the last straw. I don't care that Sera has looked after my brothers and given us a place to live. The first chance I get, we're leaving this tiny apartment.

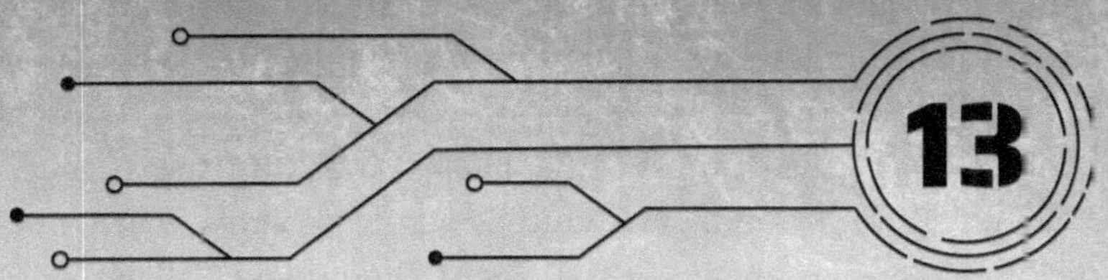

THE TENSION in the apartment hangs heavy, like a smog-filled sky blocking out the sun. Sera and I haven't spoken for days. Luckily, her job in Midtown means I only see her in the mornings and evenings. But even that feels like too much. When she's not talking with Theron and Callias, she just sits there, her dark hair hanging over her face.

It wouldn't bother me if we never spoke again. She still hasn't apologized for confronting me about my job. Why does she care if I'm lying? She's a Slummer. They lie all the time.

"Are you ever gonna say you're sorry?" Theron asks as he helps Callias with his shoes.

My throat tightens, and I have trouble swallowing. Why does he always take Sera's side? Doesn't he know how much I've sacrificed for him and Callias?

Of course he doesn't. He's just a little kid. He has no idea what I've done to keep us safe and earn the meager money we have. We're brothers. He should take my side no matter what.

"We're fine," I say, my voice shaking slightly.

"Oh, yeah," Sera says, not looking up as she rolls up the sleeping mat. "Why would anything be wrong?"

"Because you're glaring at each other," Theron says.

"No, we're not!" My hands ball into fists as I fight to keep my voice calm. Why does Theron keep pushing? Sera and I arguing has nothing to do with him.

"Ezariah, it's just..." Callias starts, grabbing my hand.

"Just drop it!"

Callias's eyes fill with tears as his fingers slip out of mine.

Immediately, Theron is there, wrapping his arms around Callias. The look he gives me is like a knife to the gut. I didn't mean to shout. I just don't want to talk about this anymore. Why can't they see that?

"Hey, you guys hungry?" Sera asks, breaking the silence. "Let's go get some food." Her voice is gentle, so she's clearly not speaking to me. As always, it's all about Theron and Callias.

"Really?" Theron says. He and Callias join Sera, and my chest tightens as she smiles at them. It's like I'm not even here.

Aside from the first few days we stayed with her, Sera never offers to buy food. Sometimes, she'll bring something home after work. I never touch the stuff. The food never looks right or even smells good. No doubt she buys it from Slummers who picked it up off the side of the road.

"Sure," she says, ruffling Callias's hair.

They leave the apartment, talking excitedly about what food they'll get. I stay where I am, my legs as still as stone. This isn't right. *I* should be taking my brothers to get food, not Sera. When did everything get so messed up? If Sera hadn't stuck her nose where it didn't belong, none of this would be happening.

This is the last straw. I pry up the loose floorboard beneath the rickety chair in the corner. In the weeks that I've worked for Nyssa, I've managed to earn two full bags of coins doing things on my own. Altogether, it's nearly one hundred phys. I have no idea how many credits that is exactly, but it's enough for Theron, Callias, and I to start over. I just have to survive living with Sera for a bit longer. That time cannot come fast enough.

I leave for my rounds before Sera or my brothers return. After I deliver the baker's daily flour, he has me take a sack of bread to Sorrel, the healer. It smells awful. Combined with the everyday odor of the Slum, I have a hard time not gagging. What can Sorrel want with moldy bread? Put it into medicine? My stomach lurches at the thought.

Once I finish my deliveries, I hurry down my assigned streets. Several shop owners stick their heads out as I pass, but I ignore them. I'm not finding more money for Nyssa—not today. If I'm lucky, I'll find a few fights to break up. There are always Slummers fighting about something.

As I turn a corner, something hard slams into me. I fall onto the cobblestones, pain exploding in my forehead and tailbone. Beside me, I hear the jingle of coins as one of the bags flies out of my satchel. I grit my teeth as I push myself up. What idiot doesn't watch where they're walking? I look up and see a pair of dirty, bare feet. My heart leaps into my throat. Sera.

It's like my insides turn to ice. I grab the coins as fast as I can. No doubt Sera saw them. Did she follow me? Why?

"What are you doing here?" I ask, getting to my feet.

"Callias, Theron, and I are getting food," she says slowly. She raises her eyebrows, and they almost disappear beneath her long, dark hair. "What are you doing?"

"Nothing," I say, shoving the coins back into my bag.

"Another delivery?" she asks, clearly not buying it. She doesn't take her dark eyes off me, and goosebumps appear all over my arms.

"Theron and Callias?" I repeat, peering around Sera's slight frame.

"Relax," she says, shaking her head. "They're not here."

The tension in my chest fades as I take a shaky breath. How would I explain all the coins to them? Callias would probably let it go. But Theron… If Theron found out, I don't think he'd ever trust me again.

"You should probably get a move on," Sera says as she steps around me. "Don't want to keep your boss waiting."

"What?!" I turn on the spot, my anger mounting. But Sera is gone. I take a few deep breaths, but it doesn't help. First, she questioned my job, and now she mentions my boss. How much does she know?

Over the next several hours, I make out well. There must be something in the air, because even by Slum standards, I stumble across more fights than usual. It's like Slummers are hardwired to be angry. I break up two fights and even help an old woman push her cart of clothing scraps to the square. It's been a good day—better than it started, at least. At any rate, my pocket is full of coins, and I don't see Sera or my brothers anywhere.

The Enforcers come out as the sun disappears behind the buildings. All the fights in the street scatter, and I know I'm done for the night. I can't help but feel disappointed, and it's not just because I'm out of chances to add coins to my pocket. I'll have to return to Sera's at some point. Maybe she and the boys are still out? Either way, I need to stash my earnings before dropping off Nyssa's money. The last thing I need is Sera asking more questions with Theron and Callias there.

As I round a corner, I see a group of Slummers a little ways down the street. They're young—maybe a few years younger than me. Their clothes look at least five sizes too big, and it's clear from the smell that they haven't bathed in a while. I slip my hands into my pockets as I walk past. There's something about the way they're looking at me. I've seen that look in the eyes of the animals Callias is always chasing after—a wild, crazed look.

"Hey. Whatcha got there?" One of them steps in front of me, blocking my path.

"Nothing," I say, fighting to keep my voice calm as my heart races. "Could you move?"

"C'mon, man," another says. He grabs my shoulder, and my muscles shudder. "You holdin' out on us?"

"Back off!" I snap, trying to shake his hand off me. But another appears, this time on my arm.

"Well, that's not very nice." The first boy steps right up to my face, his foul breath filling my nose. "I'd expect more from one of Nyssa Yarrow's guys."

My legs tremble so violently that it's a miracle I don't collapse on the spot. How do these Slummers know I work for Nyssa? Aside from Rowan, I doubt I could point out anyone from the crew in a crowd. But that's not what makes my heart race. Even though these Slummers know I work for Nyssa, they're still confronting me. Aren't they terrified of what Nyssa might do to them? I'm part of her crew, and Nyssa still scares the crap out of me.

But as I look into this kid's sunken, crazed eyes, I know he's not afraid. He's desperate.

"I … I don't know what you're talking about," I say, trying to keep my voice steady despite the adrenaline burning through me. "I'm just going home."

"Oh, we know exactly what we're talking about." He smirks, grabbing the strap of my satchel. "And you've got what we're looking for."

The boy's fist slams right into my jaw. I gasp, lights popping in my eyes as pain explodes through my face. Desperately, I try to pull my arms free, but they're pinned awkwardly behind me. I'm hit repeatedly in the side as hands that aren't mine force their way into my pockets.

"No!" This can't be happening. That money is mine! I earned it. What right do these Slummers have to take it?

Suddenly, my arms are free, I fall, and I taste blood. I try to push myself up, and a foot connects with my stomach. A mixture of blood and saliva flies from my lips as I fall back to the ground. My vision is blurry, but I still see the boys running off, their laughter echoing off the slanting buildings.

For a while, I just lie there. My head is pounding, and there's a ringing in my ears that won't stop. Somehow, my hands manage to find my pockets. They're empty. It's like someone's squeezing my insides. All of my money is gone. But that's not the worst of it. My satchel, which had the two bags of coins I'd collected for Nyssa, is gone too.

What am I going to do? If Nyssa finds out I lost all of her money…

No. I can't let her find out. Somehow, I need to get it back. So, even though all I want to do is lie still for about ten years, I push myself up.

"Ezra!" The familiar voice echoes down the street, and my heart skips a beat.

"Rowan," I croak, trying to put on a brave face as I struggle to stand. I can't let her know what happened. "What are you doing here?"

"Looking for you." Rowan's eyes narrow as she draws nearer. "You've usually made your drop-off by now. Why are you late?"

"I … um…"

"What happened to your face?"

The throbbing in my jaw intensifies as I try to smile. I can't tell her the truth; she'd run straight to Nyssa. I'd be dead before the sun rose.

Rowan reaches out and grabs my chin, and I gasp with pain. She drags me toward the nearest streetlight. I see her eyes widen in the flickering glow as she takes in the damage to my face. A shiver runs down my spine that has nothing to do with my injuries. I understand her look with chilling clarity: I'm trapped.

"We need to get to Nyssa's," she says, her voice uncharacteristically dark as she lets me go. "Now."

Rowan takes my hand and drags me through the narrow streets. Before I know it, I'm standing in the front room of Nyssa's place. The room, as always, is packed, but tonight it's dead silent. My arms tremble at my sides as I feel them stare. It's like they're holding their breath, waiting for something terrible to happen.

The back door creaks open, and Nyssa steps through. My throat tightens as her cool, unyielding eyes bore into me. It's like she's picking me apart. What is she going to do? Beat me, or something far worse?

"Explain," she says, her voice quiet but firm.

I try to swallow, but my tongue is like sandpaper. "Nyssa, I … I don't know what happened. Three guys jumped me on my way here. They took everything. I'm sorry. I was going to look for them when Rowan—"

"Enough." Nyssa silences me with a wave of her hand. "I must say, I'm disappointed, Ezariah. I expected better from you, given your ... situation."

Anger rises in my stomach as I look into Nyssa's dark eyes. No. I won't let her bring my brothers into this. I know I lost her money, and I am sorry about that. But she makes ten times the amount I just lost every day.

"Nyssa, I—"

"What is it we do here, Ezariah?" Nyssa cuts me off.

I wrack my brain, trying to remember what Rowan said about working for Nyssa. It was on our first day together, and Rowan had explained why Sorrel couldn't get the herbs herself.

"Deliver stuff that's illegal?" I say. I don't know how to make it not sound offensive.

"No." Nyssa shakes her head. She looks almost disappointed. But why? I'm not wrong. Every item I've delivered since working for Nyssa has been illegal.

"I thought you understood our goals here, Ezariah," Nyssa continues. "We protect the people of the Slum."

"From what?" The words escape my lips before I can stop them. I can't help it; it's the most ridiculous thing I've ever heard. Nyssa's crew doesn't protect anyone but themselves.

"Ezariah, we protect the people of the Slum from AURA." Nyssa takes another step, and I know I've crossed a line. But what is she saying about AURA? AURA saved Nomisman after the Great Fall. AURA creates order. All Nyssa's crew does is extort people for money.

"Who decides what's illegal? AURA. Who adjusts the exchange rate for phys to prevent us from accumulating wealth? AURA does." Nyssa is so close to me that I can see the flecks of gold in her eyes. I try to breathe, but it's like she's squeezing my lungs. "That's why everyone in my crew has a record. We've got nothing left to lose. AURA has trapped us here. But the people we help—their records are clean. We're giving them a chance for a better life. But doing so isn't cheap."

Nyssa's words crash around in my brain like waves. Have I been wrong about her all this time? I want to step away, to process what she's saying, but I can't.

"You need to repay the money you lost. Our benefactor used to send regular payments, but those stopped months ago. Without that money, we won't survive."

"I … I'm sorry. But I … I can't," I lie. My stash back at the apartment could easily cover what I've lost. But I'd rather Nyssa beat me than let her take that money. I don't care about stupid Slummers or Nyssa's dwindling resources. Theron and Callias are all I care about. That money is *their* chance at a better life.

Nyssa's eyes narrow, and I brace myself. Hopefully, whatever punishment she has in mind will be quick. My jaw is already bruised after I got the crap kicked out of me by some kids. What else could she do to me?

"Very well." Nyssa's voice is so calm that my eyes snap open. "If you can't pay, you'd better come with me."

Nyssa leads the way as Rowan takes my arm and steers me out onto the street. My heart pounds with every step as icy dread courses through my veins. No matter what I do, images of dark alleys full of menacing, faceless figures flood my mind. What's Nyssa going to do to me?

"Where are we going?" I ask, my voice shaking despite my efforts to keep it steady.

"Patience," Nyssa says, not even bothering to look back.

Rowan gives my arm a rough shove. I glance at her, hoping to find some comfort or understanding in her eyes. Instead, she stares directly ahead, her hollow face set. I want to scream. How is Rowan, a kid, acting like this is normal? How many people has she dragged into this alley for whatever twisted fate Nyssa has planned for me? I thought I knew Rowan, that she had my back. But I was wrong. She's a Slummer; all she cares about is herself.

Finally, we reach a large, dilapidated building. I think it may have been a warehouse at some point. Cheers and shouts emanate from inside, and goose bumps rise all over my arms as Nyssa opens the door. There are so many people inside that there's barely any space to move. They all face the middle of the room, which is illuminated by several spotlights.

My heart is beating so fast that I feel like I'm vibrating. Why would Nyssa bring me here? Clearly, teaching me a lesson in front of the rest of the crew isn't enough for her. She wants to do it in front of an audience.

"We have a winner!"

The cheers grow louder than ever. The sea of people parts, and I can finally see what they're looking at. It's a massive pit. Rusty metal sheets line the walls, which are easily ten feet tall. There are two people in the pit. One stands with her bloody fists in the air as she screams into the crowd. The other lies on the packed dirt, barely moving.

Every part of my body screams at me to run, to get out of here as fast as possible. My legs feel like they're made of lead as Rowan pushes me after Nyssa through the watchers. This isn't just some warehouse. It's a fighting ring.

"Wh-why are we here?" I stammer, my voice barely audible as Nyssa stops at the pit's edge.

"Eris Crane had a disagreement with some healer over a service she can't pay for. Eris contracted me to fight in her place to settle the debt," Nyssa says, her voice just as calm as ever. "But you're going to fight instead."

"Wh-what?" Nyssa can't be serious. I know Slummers fight to settle their debts; I've broken up enough of them in the streets. But those weren't anything compared to this. I don't know the first thing about fighting.

"If you win," Nyssa presses, "I'll forgive your debt."

"I can't… How am I supposed to fight?"

"You'd better learn quickly," Nyssa says before turning to Rowan. "It's time."

Rowan takes my arm and drags me along the edge of the pit before I can say another word. I look around wildly, my chest tightening as my breaths come in jagged, uneven bursts. There has to be some way out of here. But the crowd is packed so tightly that I can't even see the walls. I'm trapped.

When we reach the edge of the pit, I catch sight of my opponent. She's in her mid-twenties and at least a foot taller than me. Like every other Slummer, she's thin, but I can see her lean muscles twitching as she crosses her arms. Her eyes lock onto mine, and a knot forms in my stomach. This woman is clearly no stranger to fighting. She's going to tear me apart.

"Go on, then," Rowan sighs, nodding toward a ladder descending into the hole.

My legs tremble so badly that it's a miracle I don't fall off the worn metal rungs. The crowd roars, their bloodlust practically palpable in the air. My feet hit the hard, packed earth of the pit, and the crowd's jeers fade to a dim hum. Did they all suddenly get quiet, or is my heart pounding so loudly that it's all I hear?

Time seems to slow down. Somewhere, I think I hear a bell ring. Then, my opponent raises her fists. I try to do something—anything. To take a step, or lift my arms. But fear roots me to the spot as her knuckles hurtle toward my face.

There's a sickening crunch, and suddenly I'm on the ground. Stars explode in my eyes as the metallic taste of blood fills my mouth again. I try to get up, but my ears are ringing, and the world is spinning like a top. But even as my insides lurch, my opponent materializes in front of me, her arms outstretched. She grabs my foot and drags me across the dirt. My heart racing, I desperately dig my fingers into the rough ground. My leg screams with pain as she pulls even harder. I kick out frantically, and my foot connects with her side. Her grip on my leg vanishes, and I take my chance. I scramble away on all fours, my eyes scanning the metal walls of the pit. There has to be some way out of here. But the ladder I used to get down here is gone.

"*Gah!*" I scream as my shirt collar tightens around my neck. Suddenly, my feet leave the ground. I barely have time to register the fury in my opponent's eyes as her knee collides with my gut.

What little air I have explodes out of me. My limbs go limp, and her arms wrap around mine in a twisted hug. I watch her head reel back. Then, her forehead slams into my face. My vision goes hazy as her grip slackens. I crumple, the pain exploding through me, finally too much.

"Get up!" The voice is distant and echoing, like someone yelling from far away.

I try to push myself up, but my arms buckle, and I drop in a heap. I think I might hear the bell again as pain overrides my senses. But the pain is nothing compared to the dread coursing through me like fire. I didn't win. This was my chance to escape Nyssa's wrath, and I blew it. I didn't even land a single punch.

"Get him up!" Nyssa's voice cuts through the fog in my head.

Rough hands grab me, half carrying me out of the pit. I don't resist. How can I? My head is splitting, and it's hard enough just to keep my eyes open.

"That was … disappointing." Nyssa's hollow face swims in and out of focus. "You'll keep fighting until your debt is paid."

Even though I can barely keep my eyes open up, the words cut through my pain like a knife. This was Nyssa's plan all along. My insides shudder as the reality of my situation dawns on me. I was never going to win that fight, and Nyssa knew that.

What if I just disappeared—found some way back to my life before Nyssa? Before Lockup. Before my Renouncement.

But that will never happen. Nyssa's eyes are everywhere. I'll be fighting here for the rest of my life—however short that may be.

"Wait!"

A familiar voice cuts through the jeers of the spectators. I look up, and my neck feels like it's about to snap. I can't stop my mouth from falling open. Sera pushes her way through the crowd, her eyes wide and jaw set. For the shortest of moments, I think I see disbelief on Nyssa's face. But her normally calm expression returns as Sera reaches the crew.

"Here," Sera says. She slips her hand into the overlapping folds of her tattered sheet dress and retrieves three leather bags. Rowan walks up to Sera, but Sera doesn't give Rowan the bags. Instead, she tosses them to Nyssa.

"What's this?" Nyssa's eyes narrow as she opens one of the bags. Even though I'm slumped on the floor, I can still see the glint of the coins as they fall into Nyssa's slender fingers.

My mind is spinning, which doesn't help with the pounding in my skull. For the first time since getting out of Lockup, I'm actually happy to see Sera. But how did she even know where I was? And where did all of that money come from? If she had all of that, why is she still trying to pass off a tattered sheet as a dress?

"I'm confused," Nyssa says, returning the coins to the bag. "Do you owe me a debt?"

"Of course not. But *he* does." Sera's eyes momentarily lock onto mine. It's like the wind has been knocked out of me again. How does Sera even know I owe Nyssa a debt? "That should cover Ezariah's debt and then some. He's done with this. He's done with you."

Nyssa raises an eyebrow, her gaze flicking between me and the bag. It's like someone's squeezing my insides. Judging by the size of the bags, Sera's money will easily cover what I lost. But is it enough? Nyssa may want me to keep fighting, because in her cruel, twisted mind, I still need to learn a lesson.

"The payment is fair. Ezariah's free to go."

Nyssa's crew parts, and Sera rushes to my side. She takes my throbbing arm and drapes it over her shoulder. Once I'm on my feet, she leads me through the crowd and out onto the street. Even though every step feels like I'm breathing in glass, I feel lighter. Ever since I got mixed up with Nyssa's crew, I've wanted to be free of it. And thanks to Sera, I am. She saved me—even after the way I treated her.

It's like I'm trapped at the bottom of some massive pit. Sera has now saved me, Theron, and Callias. How can I ever repay her for that?

After we've walked down several streets, I can't help but ask the question that's been burning in my mind ever since she showed up: "Where'd the money come from?"

"From me. And from you," she sighs, shooting me a knowing look. "I used your stash."

My heart skips a beat, and for a moment, anger threatens to explode out of me. But as I look at her, I can only feel grateful. She knew what I was doing all along. She knew I was lying about my job and that I'd hidden money in her apartment, but she never tried to stop me. And still, after all of that, she came to rescue me. Maybe Sera's not as bad as I first thought.

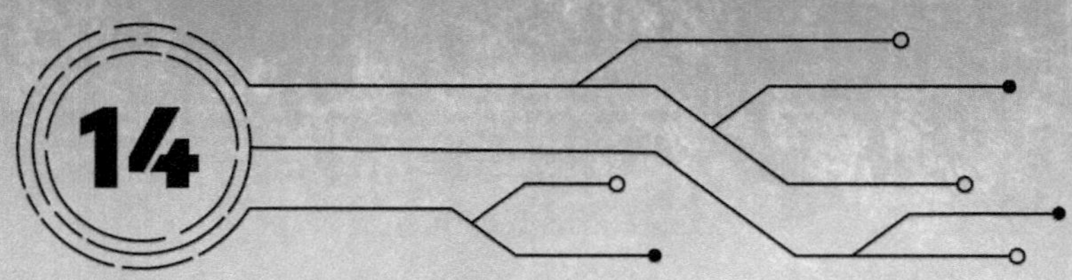

THE RICKETY FLOORS creak as I try to take a tentative step. It's like I'm walking on nails. I wince, pain exploding through me like a bomb. Gritting my teeth, I lean against the slanting walls. When Sera got me home last night, she said I'd feel better in the morning. And like an idiot, I believed her. Secretly, I'm glad she can't see me like this.

"C'mon," I groan, forcing myself to take another step. I don't care how much rest Sera said I needed. I need to find Theron and Callias.

So, I struggle my way down the uneven stairs. My legs shake, and I grip the worn railing so tightly that my knuckles turn white. But it's not enough to keep me upright. My legs buckle, and I slip down several stairs before I'm able to catch myself. Pain surges through me like fire. It's like a million tiny needles are being jabbed into me all at once. I close my eyes, trying to focus on something other than the pain. But what is there? I'm trapped in the Slum with no money. I joined a mob and was forced to fight in an underground fight club. Misery is all I have left.

By some miracle, I manage to make it outside. The dingy daylight stings my eyes as I half sit, half fall onto the stoop. I squint, and stabs of pain erupt in my cheek. Gingerly, I touch my face. My skin is tender and hot, and there's definitely a lump on my left cheek.

A mixture of high-pitched laughter and shouting reaches my ears. I sigh, and my pounding heart slows a little. I don't need to see them to know Theron and Callias are close by. Slowly, I open my eyes.

My brothers are running around the square, their footsteps echoing off the leaning buildings. But they're not alone. I recognize several of the children; they're always hanging around the square. My insides twist uncomfortably as I see the joy on my brothers' faces. How are they so happy? It's one thing to accept that this is our life, but it's another to actually enjoy it. How can they stand playing with those Slummer kids? I don't care how little they are, they're still dirty Slummers. Sooner or later, they'll turn on my brothers, just like Nyssa and Rowan did to me. How am I supposed to protect them from that?

The sound of heavy footsteps pulls me from my thoughts. I glance up, and I'm surprised to see Bart. I haven't seen him since I first met him in his shop. That day feels like a lifetime ago. More than anything, I wish I could go back there. At least then I'd have more than a bloody shirt and an aching body.

"Hey, kid," he says, sitting beside me on the stoop. "Looks like you've had a rough one."

"Thanks." My throbbing face burns as I avoid Bart's gaze. I haven't looked in a mirror lately, but I know I'm probably covered in bruises. But why does Bart even care? All he cares about is money. And clearly, I don't have any.

"Heard you got torn a new one at the Hollow," Bart says. "Tough break."

My breath catches in my throat as my heart skips a beat. I've never heard of the Hollow, but I don't have to guess what Bart's talking about. But how does he know about the fight? Was he there? And if he knows, it's only a matter of time before Theron and Callias find out.

"What… How?" I ask, fighting to keep my voice steady.

"Word gets around," Bart says, waving his large hand. "Especially when one of Nyssa's guys loses."

"I'm not one of Nyssa's guys." Nervously, I glance toward Theron and Callias. Clearly, Bart knows more than I thought.

"Relax." Bart pats me roughly on the shoulder. The pain is excruciating, and I barely manage to keep it together. "I doubt they heard us," he adds, jerking his head toward Callias and Theron.

But I can't relax. My fists tighten as anger rages inside me. The sooner I get us out of here, the better. But how am I supposed to win the Culling with no money? I'm grateful Sera saved me from Nyssa, but it literally took all the money I had. How can anyone live in this place? The Slum is nothing but violence and pain and hunger and fear.

"What am I supposed to do?" The words tumble from my mouth before I can stop them. "I lost everything. How can I keep my brothers safe?"

Bart's pudgy bloodshot eyes narrow as he looks at me. For a moment, I'm afraid he's going to leave. But he can't. I need him to tell me what to do.

"Look, I don' know, kid," he finally says. "This place is rough for little ones."

"Please?" The desperation in my voice makes my stomach churn. Has it really come to this? Am I really asking a Slummer for help? "Just tell me what to do."

Bart's eyes dart between me and my brothers. I hold my breath, and my heart pounds like a drum. I know Bart has a soft spot for my brothers. I don't know why, and frankly, I don't care. Bart doesn't need to help me; I need him to help Theron and Callias.

"Kid, no one here can tell you that. But you can start by telling those boys the truth."

My throat tightens as I watch Theron duck behind a trash can. Tell them the truth? How does Bart know I've been lying to them? And if I were to tell them the truth, where would I start? I've kept so much from them since we got to the Slum.

"Secrets don't stay that way for too long. Best they hear it from you."

Bart stands before I can respond. Deep down, I know he's

right. By some miracle, I've managed to keep secrets from my brothers since our Renouncement. But there's no way I can keep that up—not with my face covered in bruises.

"Theron, Callias!" I call out, my voice wavering. "Come here for a second."

The boys exchange confused looks before running over. As they get closer, I see their eyes widen. I'm sure in the harsh light of the day, I'm sure my injuries look worse than they did in the dark apartment.

"What happened?" Callias asks, his voice full of concern. "Sera made us leave while you were still asleep."

I swallow, but my tongue sticks to the roof of my mouth. Where do I even start? This isn't going to be easy.

"Guys, I ... I need to tell you something." I see Theron's eyes narrow, and sweat coats my palms. It's like he already knows what I'm trying to say. Callias sits beside me and rests his head on my aching shoulder. I don't know what's harder—keeping the pain from my face or not yelling at him to get off.

"Um…" Where do I even start? I've kept so much from them. "Remember when I was arrested? Well, some things happened while I was in Lockup."

Telling them everything takes longer than I thought. The whole time, I can practically see Theron's anger radiating off of him. So, I stare at my shoes. I tell them what happened in Lockup, and how I got Jackson's sentence extended. I explain how I've been working for Nyssa, and that I've been making money on the side. I manage to keep it together until I get to last night.

"Does Sera know all this?" Theron asks, his voice barely a whisper as I lapse into silence.

I nod my head. I'm glad she's not here for this. It's one thing to admit these things to Theron and Callias, but Sera knew all along that I was lying. Listing out every lie I've told to Sera somehow seems worse.

"So, what happened last night?" Callias asks, his tiny, dirty fingers gently tracing a bruise on my arm.

"I … um… I messed up. I lost Nyssa's money."

"Is that why you were in a fight?" Theron asks, his eyes narrowing to slits.

My words catch in my throat. How does he know about the fight? I hadn't told them that part yet.

"Yeah, it is," I say, my head dropping. "But don't worry. I'm not doing anything like that again. From now on, my only job is getting us out of here."

I know Theron is angry. But can't he see that I've done what I needed to do to keep us safe? Everything I've done was for him and Callias.

"Whatever, Ezariah," Theron shakes his head, and the look on his face is more painful than any injury. "Can we go now? Our friends are waiting."

"Sure," I say, forcing a smile as tears sting my eyes.

The boys rejoin their friends. I sit leaning against the stoop, my heart growing heavy as I watch them. That was worse than I could have imagined. Theron's not just upset; he hates me now, and I can't blame him. My brothers are in this mess because of me. Even if I manage to get us out of the Slum, I doubt Theron will ever trust me again. And I deserve it.

I need to get out of here. So, even though I'd rather lie on the filthy ground, I force myself to stand. Callias waves as I limp past, but Theron looks pointedly away from me. It's like another kick to the gut, but ten times more painful. Will he ever look at me again?

Pain creeps through my bruised and battered muscles with each step, but I grit my teeth and keep going. Somehow, the farther I get from the square, the less pain I feel. Is the pain actually fading, or am I just getting used to it? Sadly, it's probably the latter.

Several blocks from the square, I see a man pushing a rickety cart, filled with what I can only call trash. No; *trash* is too strong a word. There's nothing of value in the cart, just some cobble-stones and jagged pieces of wood. Why would any Slummer want junk like that?

"Hey," the man calls gruffly. "You lookin'? Got some quality stuff 'ere."

"No." I shake my head. Slummers really will do anything for a few phys. Who in their right mind would buy this crap?

"Lemme guess: low credits?" The man parks the cart right in front of me, blocking my path. "I can help."

Of course, I want to tell him to move along. But he grabs my arm, and I wince. I stagger back, unable to keep the pain from my face. Why would this Slummer grab me? Anyone with eyes can see that I have nothing.

"Relax, kid." The man steps back, raising his hands. "I don't want any trouble."

"Then what *do* you want?" I ask, although I'm not sure I want to know the answer.

"Look, I'm jus' a collector." He shrugs. "And I pay fair. If you're interested..."

The man pulls a small leather bag from his ragged jacket. Anger burns through me like fire. Who does this guy think he is? I'm not a Slummer collecting junk off the street. I don't need his charity.

But as I turn to leave, I can't look away from the bag of coins. I can't turn him down, no matter how much I want to. I'm bloody and bruised, and thanks to Nyssa, I'm completely broke. I'm going to have to start making money at some point. I guess I'm starting now.

"Fine."

For hours, I drag the cart along the winding streets. It doesn't take long before my arms feel like they're splintering. The man stops every few yards and roughly tosses more heavy stones and planks of rotting wood into the cart. We don't speak as the cart slowly fills, but I don't mind. I don't even care why we're collecting junk anymore. There's a stitch in my side and my shirt is soaked in sweat. All I want is to finish this and get paid.

The cart is practically overflowing when we reach the square. I'm so tired, it's a struggle to just keep my eyes open. My mouth is dry, and a dull pounding started in my head several blocks ago. The old man, however, looks perfectly fine. In fact, he looks ecstatic. He hands over my coins without a word, and I pour the contents into my palm. Five phys. My hand shakes as I stare at the small, square coins. That's it? After all that work, these little coins are all I have to show for it? I dragged this man's stupid cart around the whole Slum. I deserve ten times this!

"Hey!" I call out, but the man and his cart have disappeared into the crowd.

Frustration rages inside me, but I grit my teeth as I stow the coins in my pocket. This really was a waste of a day.

Most of the vendors in the square are packing up their things as I pass. They shove their wares in my face—bruised fruit, a pack of mismatched nails, a warped metal pan. I ignore them. Why would anyone buy this stuff? It looks like they found it on the side of the road.

"New blankets!" An old woman waves what looks like an old sheet in my face. The edges are frayed, and it has a huge stain down the middle. As I stare at the filthy thing, I can't help but want it. I haven't had a proper blanket since my Renouncement, and Sera's cramped apartment keeps getting colder. Sooner or later, we'll need to buy one.

My fingers have nearly grasped the coins in my pocket when I stop myself. I shake my head, taking several steps back. What am I thinking? I can't waste what little money I have on a piece of garbage like this! I need to save every credit I can for the Culling. It's our only chance to get out of this hellhole. I've been through too much to forget that now.

My muscles ache as I climb the stairs to Sera's apartment. The tiny room is empty when I force the door open. I can't help but sigh as I step inside. Almost automatically, my eyes fall on the loose floorboards beneath the rickety chair. My hand closes around the phys in my pocket. Of course, my first impulse is to hide them before Theron and Callias see them. But no—I promised I'd tell them the truth.

"No more lies," I whisper, stowing the coins back in my pocket.

It doesn't take long for Theron and Callias to arrive, practically bouncing off the walls. Callias's face lights up when he sees me, and he jumps into my arms. I smile at Theron, but he stays back, his face set. Anger boils up inside me, but somehow, I manage to keep my face calm. Theron has every right to still be mad. I did lie to him, after all.

Awkwardly, I fish the coins out of my pocket.

"Hey!" Callias's face light's up as he stares them.

"Where'd you get those?" Theron asks, his tone lighter than it's been since my confession.

I crouch down, my heart pounding against my ribs. I need to be honest with them. "I helped an old guy with his cart today, and he paid me these coins."

"Can I get some new pants?" Callias pipes up. He points to the gaping hole in his pants, so large that I can see his whole leg.

"We'll see." It feels like all the air has been sucked out of me. How long have Callias's pants been like this? And how did I not notice?

I hand the coins to Theron. "Can you keep these safe for us?"

Theron's eyes widen a touch, but he takes the coins. He runs to the window with Callias, where they examine the coins in the faint light. I'm pretty sure I see Theron's face soften a little, and the tightness in my chest lessens. Good. At least I've done one thing right today.

The door bangs open again, and Sera steps inside. Her eyes lock on the coins in Theron's hand, and her face goes blank. She looks at me, and there's no mistaking the anger in her face. "Where'd that come from?" Her voice crackles through the air like lightning.

"I helped a guy with his cart." I shake my head. Is it too much to ask for one day without her judging me?

Sera crosses her arms over her chest. "Did you 'help someone,' or did you go back to Nyssa?"

"Are you crazy?" I snap. "Why would I go back there? She's the reason I got the crap kicked out of me!"

Sera scoffs. "Whatever. It's your life, Ezariah. Throw it away, for all I care."

"Shut up, you filthy Slummer!" My insides feel like they're on fire. What right does Sera have to tell me what to do? Sure, she saved me last night, but that doesn't mean she can order me around. She's a Slummer; she doesn't know any better. But I do.

"Stop fighting!"

Callias's cry stops me in my tracks. The fire in me dies as I see the look on his face. It feels like all the air has been sucked from my lungs. What am I doing? Sera saved me. She saved Theron and Callias. I'll never be able to repay her for that—and I just insulted her. What's wrong with me? Why do I keep doing this?

"Let's talk outside," Sera says, her voice trembling slightly.

Shame settles on my shoulders like a ton of bricks as I follow her out the door.

Sera leads the way down the hall and narrow stairs without saying a word. Finally, she stops at a door on the second floor. She forces the door open, and I follow her inside. The room is barely larger than a closet, with nothing but dust dancing in shafts of light that pierce through the boarded-up windows.

"Why are we here, Sera?" My voice echoes slightly off the bare walls.

Sera turns to face me. I see her take a deep breath, like she's fighting to keep herself in check. "Because out there—" She gestures toward the stairs we descended. "—isn't just about us." Her eyes bore into me, her arms crossed tightly over her chest. "Where'd the money come from, Ezariah?"

"I told you, I got it from helping some guy," I say, fighting to keep my voice calm. Why doesn't she believe me?

"Seriously?" Sera shakes her head. "I thought you'd have learned after what happened last night."

"Learned what?"

"That what you're doing isn't working!"

"You don't understand," I snap. "You're a Slummer."

Sera's eyebrows nearly disappear into her hair. "What does being a Slummer have to do with anything?"

"You don't get it," I press on, my voice rising. "This place is all you've known. But my brothers and I don't belong here. We're from Newtown."

"Not anymore, Ezariah. You're in the Slum now." Sera's voice is quiet but firm. "You need to accept that."

"No." I shake my head. She really doesn't get it. My life has been a living hell ever since we got to the Slum. Why would I ever accept living here? "All I have to do is make it to the next Culling."

Sera shakes her head, and I see her expression soften. For some reason, her look makes my anger flare up. "You really think you can buy your way out of here?" she asks.

"I *know* I can." Why is she doubting me? I know I can get my brothers and me out of here. If she doesn't think I can, my brothers and I will be better off somewhere else. "I just need to buy enough entries to—"

"Ezariah," she cuts in gently, "you'll never win the Culling."

"Why not?" I throw my hands in the air.

"Because you need a clean record to even enter the Culling."

Sera's words fall on me like physical blows. I lean against the rough wall, trying to steady myself as I struggle to process what she said. I can't enter the Culling? No. She has to be wrong. But as I look into her eyes, I know she's not lying. It's like the bottom has dropped out of my stomach. Everything I've done—lying to my brothers, breaking up fights—I've done it to win the Culling.

The realization crashes over me like a wave. My plan—my only plan—shatters into a million irretrievable pieces.

"What?" I say dumbly.

"You were arrested," she continues softly. "Your record isn't clean anymore."

"But I need to get out of here." I open my mouth, but it's like there's no air in the room. My vision darkens until all I can see is Sera's face. "I can't stay here… I can't…"

Her hand grips my shoulder, and it's then that I realize I'm shaking. The pressure of her fingers slows my thundering heart, but only a little. My eyes grow hot, and I turn away from Sera. This can't be happening.

"I know you want to protect Theron and Callias," she says quietly as I slide down the wall, "but this isn't the way."

"I won't make it here," I confess in a whisper so faint that it's almost lost in the stillness.

Sera's hand moves from my shoulder to clasp mine, her touch warm and strangely comforting. "You've made it this far."

I shake my head, white-hot tears stinging my cheeks. "I'm not like you."

Sera's grip on my hand tightens. I look up and see her soft blue eyes—eyes that have seen more of the Slum's cruelty than I'll ever know. "Don't give up, Ezariah."

"C'mon, Sera," I say, shaking my head. "I'll never make it here like you."

Her lips press into a thin line. "You can. I know you can. Because I…" She hesitates and takes a deep breath before continuing, "Ezariah, my family Renounced me over a year ago."

Of all the things she could have said, I never would have imagined this. I stare at Sera, from her black, filthy feet to her ragged clothes. All this time, I'd pegged her as a Slummer, someone born into chaos and despair. But I couldn't have been more wrong. Sera's Renounced. All this time, she's been just like me, Theron, and Callias.

"I'm sorry," I mutter. There's so much more I want to say, but

I can't find the words. What could I say? I've been horrible to Sera these last few weeks. All I've done since moving into her apartment is lie and argue with her—not to mention calling her names. No wonder she hates me.

Sera nods, her face regaining some of its usual sternness. "Whatever. It's fine. But you need to get your shit together You can't keep acting like you're not a Slummer. Face it: you are now. There's no getting out of here."

"But if I can just—"

"Ezariah, how many Renounced have you seen since you got here?" she asks, cutting me off.

I open my mouth, but quickly close it. Other Renounced? As far as I know, Theron, Callias, and I are the only Renounced in the Slum. Well, I guess there's Sera too. But I haven't seen any others, and well-dressed people being dropped off in the square by Enforcers would be a hard thing to miss.

"Why does it matter?" I shrug.

"There've been seven," she says firmly. "Where do you think they are now?"

"I don't know," I say, my stomach twisting uncomfortably.

"They're dead, Ezariah. The Slum wasn't what they were used to either. They tried to keep going, just like you are, acting like nothing was different. Sooner or later, they ran out of money, and they starved. Or acted like idiots and got on someone's bad side.

"But I didn't. I stopped pretending I was still in Newtown the moment I got here. This is the Slum, so I lived like I'm a Slummer. I've done things I never thought I would ever do in my life. But I'm still here."

I look towards the stairs, and a pit forms in my stomach as Sera's words wash over me. I will not let what happened to those other Renounced happen to Theron and Callias. I won't let them suffer just because I refuse to accept reality. No matter what it takes, I'll find some way to get them out of here—even if I'm doomed to stay.

"Sera," I start, my voice barely above a whisper, "I don't know what to do."

"I'll help you," she says slowly, her eyes narrowing. "But you have to do everything I say, even if you hate it. Can you do that?"

Slowly, I close my eyes and take a breath. Even though I know what to say, it still takes me a moment to form the words.

"I guess I have no choice."

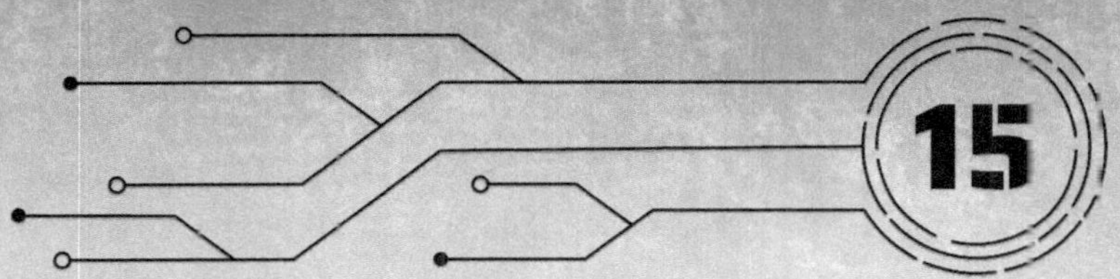

THE HARSH SCRAPE of wood assaults my ears. My eyes snap open, and I see Sera looming over me. She's already dressed, her silhouette fuzzy against the weak dawn light seeping through the grimy window.

"Up, now," she says, her voice firm.

My face drops like a rock onto the filthy sleeping mat. This is ridiculous. Why on earth is Sera waking us up this early? The sun isn't even up yet. I'm still sore from getting the crap kicked out of me at the Hollow. Doesn't Sera know I need to rest?

"C'mon. We gotta go before the good stuff's picked over."

That gets my attention. Good stuff? Even though I'd rather do anything else, I open my eyes and sit up. What is she talking about?

Theron and Callias are already up, and even through the gloom, I see the excitement in their eyes. I can't help but shake my head. How are they okay with this? Back in Newtown, waking before the sun was unheard of—except for servants, that is. But my brothers are acting like it's perfectly normal.

The chill air stings my skin as we step out into the square. Theron and Callias trail behind Sera, chattering about what we might find. I don't say anything, mostly because I have no idea where we're going. The narrow streets are empty, save for the occasional Slummer shuffling along. Their faces are downcast, and they all have dark circles under their eyes. I can't help but stare. What were they doing all night?

"Keep up," Sera calls back, her pace as fast as ever. I hurry to catch up with her, Theron, and Callias. Why does she always have to walk like she's in some crazy foot race?

Theron grins when I reach him. "What do you think we'll find?"

"Um…" I have no idea what to say. Clearly, Theron knows where we're going. But how? He and Callias only stayed with Sera for two days while I was in Lockup. I never thought to ask what they did while I was away. Now I wish I had.

We emerge onto a wider street. The grey dawn light casts long shadows across the cracked pavement. The silence is eerie, no chattering voices or clattering carts, just our footsteps echoing between the buildings. I shudder, but it has nothing to do with the cold.

"C'mon," Sera calls over her shoulder.

The smell hits me first, a pungent mix of rotting food and something sour that burns my nose. Up ahead is a vast fence topped with barbed wire, surrounding piles at least thirty feet high. As Sera pushes through a gap in the fence, a gust of wind sends a plastic bag dancing over my feet. The hairs on my arms stand on end as I look more closely at the piles. Sera's brought us to a literal dump.

"Look for anything edible," Sera says as she starts sifting through the base of the nearest pile.

Edible? I stand as still as a statue, gazing at the mountains of waste towering over us. The sight alone is enough to turn my stomach—rancid scraps of food intermingled with unidentifiable sludge. Every fiber of my being screams at me to run. Why would Sera bring us here? There can't be anything of value in all this garbage.

I step forward, ready to tell Sera no, but something stops me. Our conversation last night forces its way to the front of my mind. *"You need to do everything I say, even if you hate it."* I stop dead in my tracks. My eyes shift from Sera, waist deep in garbage, to my brothers. They're already scrambling up the side of a mound, their laughter bouncing around the piles of decay. I guess acting like a Slummer starts now.

Gritting my teeth, I step forward. My hands shake as they plunge into the cold, wet muck. My throat tightens and my stomach jolts as my fingers brush against something slimy. I close my eyes, trying not to think about what I'm doing. Hopefully, Sera won't make us stay here too long.

"Look!" Theron's excited cry makes me look up. He's sliding down a nearby pile, his hand held over his head. "This isn't too bad!"

He's holding up what I think may have been a pear, its wrinkly skin covered with brown spots. I clamp my mouth shut and try to keep the disgust from my face. "Theron, that's—"

Sera's hand appears on my shoulder, stopping me mid-sentence. "It's okay."

I turn to Sera, my blood boiling. How can she say that rotten thing is okay? But as my eyes meet hers, I know it's pointless. There's no way I'm going to change her mind.

"We'll cut away the bad parts." She smiles.

Theron beams, showing Callias his find. I force a smile as they return to the piles, both unfazed by the reality of what they're doing. Don't they realize they're digging through literal garbage? How can they be okay with this? If I'd had it my way, I'd have run out of here screaming.

"I can't believe you're making us do this," I mutter under my breath.

"Believe it," Sera replies, and her tone is so calm that we could be talking about the weather.

It's a struggle to hold the scream in my chest. I know I said I'd listen to Sera, but I had no idea that meant this. We're supposed to be working to get Theron and Callias a better life. I don't care what Slummers do; digging through the trash for food isn't the life I want for my brothers.

"Sera," I start, my voice shaking with restraint, "this isn't food. It's trash."

"To you, maybe," she says. "But in the Slum, food is food, Ezariah. It doesn't matter where it comes from if it keeps you alive."

"But there's a line," I argue, gesturing to the mountains of filth surrounding us. "We can't just eat *anything*!"

She turns to me, brushing a grimy strand of hair from her face. "You need to be more open-minded. We take what we can get here. It's not pretty, but we survive."

Survive? She can't be serious. This feels more like an act of desperation. I know I said I'd stop acting like a Newtowner, and I meant it. But this can't be the only way.

It doesn't take long for Theron and Callias to return, holding up a banana peel and an apple core like trophies. They look so pleased with themselves. I try to act impressed, ignoring my writhing insides.

"Nice job, boys." Sera smiles, taking the rotten fruit from Theron and Callias and handing it to me.

My skin shudders as I take the squishy food. Reluctantly, I nod and force myself to smile. Arguing with Sera won't do me any good now. Whatever I say, Theron and Callias will side with Sera. I guess I'm stuck rummaging through garbage.

"Keep looking," Sera says. "See if you can find anything we can sell."

Theron and Callias dive back into the piles, laughing excitedly. It's like they're playing a game. How long until they realize they're not? My eyes drift to the apple core and banana peel in my hand. I hope they never do.

"I gotta go," Sera says quickly, rushing past me. "When you're done here, head to the rations bank," she calls over her shoulder.

"The rations bank?" A mixture of anger and confusion swirls inside me. Why would Sera have us dig through trash if there's a rations bank, whatever that is? I want to ask what she's talking about, but Sera has already slipped through the fence and vanished.

I slump onto the least filthy spot I can find. It doesn't smell as bad here, or maybe I'm just getting used to it. Theron and Callias don't even notice. They're so focused on their search that I doubt anything could pull them from it. I watch them, their hands smudged with grime, their faces alight with excitement.

"Look!" Callias exclaims, holding up a scrap of cloth. It's filthy, but Theron's eyes light up.

"That looks great!" Theron says, his eyes wide. "I bet we can sell it in the square!"

I force myself up, even though my aching muscles protest. I want to tell Theron it's pointless—that no one in their right mind would buy those rags—but I bite my tongue. What's the point? This is the happiest I've seen my brothers in weeks. I can't take that from them.

"That's not a bad idea," I say, mustering what enthusiasm I can. "But we should get going."

"But Sera said—"

"I know," I say quickly, fighting to keep my temper in check. Just because Sera said it, that doesn't mean it's the law. "But you have enough now. And Sera said we need to go to the rations bank."

Saliva floods my mouth at the thought of real food—something that hasn't been picked out of the trash. I steer Theron and Callias through the gap in the debris refinery fence, grateful to finally be leaving the place. My brothers prattle on about their finds, wondering how much they'll get for their morning's work.

After about thirty seconds I realize that I have no idea where I'm going. I freeze, scanning the tangle of identical streets. Where are we supposed to go? It's not like Sera bothered to tell me where the rations bank is; that would actually be helpful.

"Which way?" I mutter, more out of frustration than anything else.

"It's this way." Theron shakes his head as he takes my hand and pulls me down a street lined with makeshift tents.

"How do you know?" I can't keep the skepticism from my voice.

"It's not exactly easy to miss," Theron says, letting go of my hand and running ahead.

I exchange a look with Callias, who just shrugs and smiles and hurries after Theron. I bite my lip as I run to catch up with my brothers. I wish we had a better plan than this. Why does Theron always have to run off without explaining what he's actually doing? He's just as bad as Sera.

A stitch blooms in my side as I race after them. Theron sprints through the labyrinth of alleys, darting in new directions seemingly at random. My legs burn as I fight to keep up with them, but I don't stop. I can't lose them here; I have no idea where we are.

We spill out onto a wider street, and the sudden bright light stings my eyes. I skid to a halt, narrowly avoiding Callias, who's stopped in the middle of the road. I double over, trying to catch my breath as my muscles ache.

Slowly, I lift my head. The streets are full of people, swarming around like ants. Why did Theron stop here? It can't be because of the people. I look to my brothers, but they're not looking at me. They're staring at something behind me.

I turn, and then I see it. A massive concrete building looms over us. Unlike the rest of the Slum, which always looks like a good wind could knock it over, this place looks like it could survive a nuclear blast. DEPARTMENT OF RESOURCES is carved into the stone above the massive doors, where a line of people stand waiting.

Even though I want to move, I can't help but stare. The idea of people handing out food here feels alien, even wrong. How have I not seen this place before?

"Told you it was easy to find," Theron says smugly, grinning as he nudges me in the side.

We join the line, flanked on either side by Enforcers. It takes Callias and Theron about five seconds before they ask to look around. I clench my jaw, trying not to look too annoyed. Why can't they just stay in one place? Besides, what's there to see here? It looks like any other part of the Slum. But their relentless shuffling and questions have me on the verge of exploding.

"Fine," I finally say. Maybe now I'll get a few moments of peace. "Just stay where I can see you."

Their faces light up, and they disappear into the crowd before I can blink.

It doesn't take too long before I'm inside the rations bank. The interior is just as stark as its exterior, all grey concrete and buzzing fluorescent lights. I reach the front and slide my forearm into the scanner. A beep sounds, and I try to ignore the burning under my skin. A slot in the wall opens, spitting out a couple of silver packets and a plastic jug.

"This is it?" I take the items, but I can't stop my head from shaking. Tentatively, I open one of the packs and find it full of a pale yellow powder. How is this supposed to feed Theron, Callias, and me? We need real food, not whatever this crap is. "I need more than this."

"*AURA regulates rations allocation based on individual records and economic impact,*" the computer says in a cool female voice.

"Economic impact?" My free hand balls into a fist. "There are three of us, and we're starving!"

"*AURA regulates rations allocation based on individual records and economic impact,*" the computer repeats.

I'm filled with a burning desire to kick the machine. It's like arguing with a brick wall. No, worse—at least a wall doesn't pretend to listen. Even though I know it makes no difference, I shoot one final glare at the machine before stepping out of the line with my meager packs and water jug.

Outside the rations bank, I spot Theron and Callias almost instantly. Theron's eyes are wide, and he's waving his fist over his head. I try to force my face into a smile, even though all I want to do is throw something.

"Look!" Theron beams, holding out his hand to show me the square coins in his palm.

My eyes widen. "Where'd those come from?"

"I sold what we found at the refinery!"

My stomach churns as I look at the coins. Three phys? That's nothing—barely enough for a stale loaf of bread. I feel my face growing hot. After a few hours of listening to Sera, what do I have to show for it? A few phys clutched in Theron's dirt-streaked hand, some nutrition packs that might as well contain chalk, and a jug of water that's probably not even clean. I know I promised Sera I'd do as she does, but this isn't surviving; it's barely existing.

"That's great, Theron," I manage, though my voice lacks any real enthusiasm. "We should get back to the square."

Theron's smile falters. "But—"

"No buts," I snap, my temper finally getting the best of me. Why does Theron have to question me all the time? I'm doing all of this so they have a chance to get out of the Slum.

Reluctantly, Theron leads the way back to the square. I'm grateful that he doesn't run off this time. As soon as we reach the cobblestone expanse, Theron and Callias join a group of kids as they run and shout between the carts and stalls. I slump against the base of a building, the coolness of the stone seeping through my worn shirt. From here, I watch my brothers play, their laughter cutting through the heavy air. It's like they're in their own world—a place where the filth and danger of the Slum don't mean anything. A small part of me wishes I could join them. Even just one minute of escape would be enough. But there's no escaping the grey and filth that is now my reality.

The sound of Callias's laughter sends a dull thud through my insides. How long can innocence like his survive in a place like this? The Slum has already killed all the hope and happiness I once had. How long will it take before that carefree spark in their eyes disappears forever? The thought twists around my heart like a vise.

I shake my head as I wrap my arms around my knees. No matter what I have to do, I won't let Theron and Callias's laughter die. They're stuck in this hellhole because of me; the least I can do is protect their joy. But how, when the Slum seems determined to snuff it out?

The sky turns from pale blue to a mix of oranges and pinks, but the colors feel like they belong to another world. I'm not sure how much time has passed when I see Sera walk into the square. I fight the impulse to run and hide. I don't want another lecture. Can't she leave me alone for five minutes? But of course, she doesn't.

"How'd it go?" she asks, closing her eyes as she leans against the wall.

Anger burns through me like fire as I shove my rations into Sera's lap. I kick a stray pebble, watching it skitter across the cobblestones. "It was a joke. The rations bank barely gave us enough to last a day. Theron sold some garbage from the refinery, but the coins won't go far."

Sera frowns, and I know she's going to say something stupid about making do or staying strong. But that's easy for her to say; she's used to this. I'm not. How can anyone get used to living this way?

"How do they do it, Sera? How do they live like this day after day?"

Sera pulls her knees up to her chest and wraps her arms around them. "It's not about living, Ezariah," she says, her voice as rough as the pavement beneath us. "It's about surviving."

"Surviving? Is that what you call this?" My hand sweeps over the square—the broken buildings, the listless faces of people passing by, and the emaciated children who known nothing but these decrepit streets.

"It's all we've got," Sera replies as she watches Theron chase Callias around a cart selling bruised fruit. "The strongest make it because they have to. They find ways to scrape by. They barely make it, sure, but they do survive."

"I don't want to just survive! There has to be more than this." My voice breaks as I look at my brothers again. They deserve so much more than this hand-to-mouth existence.

Sera's gaze hardens as she turns to me. "You think I don't know that? You think I haven't dreamed of something better than this place every day since I was Renounced? I have, Ezariah. But I'm also realistic."

"Easy for you to say. You get to leave this hellhole." The words explode out of me before I can stop them. The injustice of it all is just too much. All I want is to leave this place. But thanks to my arrest, I'm stuck here. But Sera, a girl who wears a ratty sheet and no shoes, gets to leave every day.

"Yeah, I get to leave," Sera snaps back, her patience clearly wearing thin. "But it's not like I'm off to some paradise, Ezariah. The foreman works us to the bone, and I barely get seven credits a week if I'm lucky. That's not even enough for food! If you want something different..." She pauses, her eyes narrowing on me. "You could get a job."

"What?" The idea slams into me like a ton of bricks. Get a job? Ever since arriving in the Slum, the thought has never once crossed my mind. My sole focus has been on getting Theron, Callias, and me out of here. A job—a real job—seems so permanent, so final—like I'm surrendering to being stuck here.

"I … I don't… How am I supposed to get a job?"

A mixture of shame and embarrassment washes over me, making me feel dirtier than ever. How had I not considered it? It seems so stupid not to. Here I am, trying to get money to get Theron and Callias out of here, and I hadn't thought of the most basic way of earning it.

Sera's expression softens a little, but not by much. "You can go to the Department of Labor," she suggests. "They'll find something for you, based on what you can do."

The Department of Labor. Unlike the rations bank, this is something I've heard of. We even have one in Newtown. After we graduate, we go to the Department of Labor to get our first work assignment. Nearly all Newtowners are assigned some government position, like Uncle Galen.

"Do we have to go today?" I can't stop the bitterness from seeping into my voice. I know I need a job, but after the day I've had, all I want is to not move for about eighteen days. I scoff at the thought, bitterness creeping into my voice. "No way I'm going there now."

"Tomorrow." Sera sighs, shaking her head as she pushes herself away from the wall. "You've done enough for today."

Sera jerks her head toward Theron and Callias. Slowly, I push myself off the ground, my muscles protesting. What is Sera doing? She said we could wait until tomorrow to go to the Department of Labor. When I catch up with Sera, she, Theron, and Callias are standing near one of the carts as a man ladles something steaming into rough wooden bowls. Theron passes the coins he earned to Sera, who exchanges them for a bowl of the murky broth. My eyes narrow as I look at the thick, brownish liquid. Does Sera even know what's in it? It's not like there are a lot of options for finding fresh food here.

"What's in that?" I ask, even though I'm not entirely sure I want to know.

"Don't think about it," she says without looking at me, swirling the soup around the bowl.

The smell drifts into my nose, and saliva instantly floods my mouth. It's savory and rich—a stark contrast to the dry bread and old fruit we've been eating lately. The thought of eating something warm makes the hairs on my arms stand on end. Sera carries the bowl with such care, you'd think it was filled with gold.

We settle on the front steps of a nearby building, the worn stone cool beneath me. Theron and Callias are all smiles as they take turns sipping from the bowl. The sight tugs at something inside me, evoking a warmth I thought I'd never feel again.

"Here." Sera nudges me with her elbow before passing me the bowl.

I hesitate only a moment before bringing it to my lips. The broth is hot and full of flavors I can't quite place—meat, maybe, or some kind of vegetable. Normally, I'd question any food I couldn't name. But my hunger wins out, and I savor every drop.

"Good, right?" Theron asks, his eyes wide and expectant.

"Yeah." I hate to admit it, but Theron's right. The soup is good.

The warmth spreads through me, pushing away the evening chill. Theron and Callias chatter between mouthfuls, excitedly wondering what they might find at the refinery tomorrow. Sera watches them, her eyes softer than I've seen in days. Their laughter is infectious, and I can't help but laugh too. It's a strange, almost foreign feeling.

"Look at Ezariah." Callias giggles. "It's like he doesn't know how to laugh!"

Sera snorts, covering her mouth in a failed attempt to stifle her own laughter. "Don't! You'll scare it away."

Now that makes me laugh. I double over, tears streaming down my face as I let the joy sweep me away.

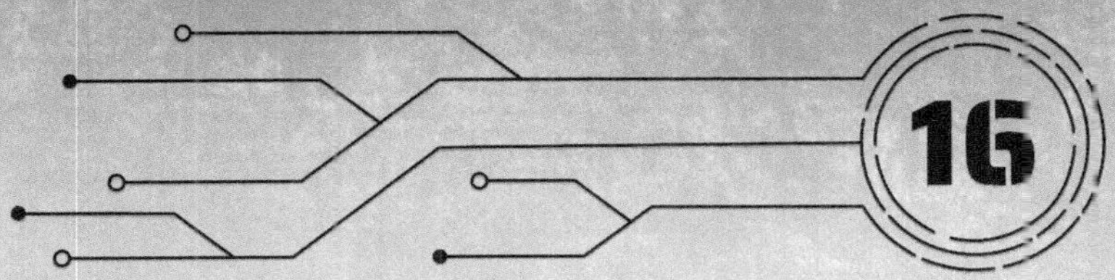

THE HUMAN POWER Generation plant looms before me, a grey monstrosity of steel and stone. I stare at its skeletal structure, my fists clenched. Even though it's been a few hours since I left Sera at the Department of Labor, the sting of the system's "options" are still burned into my eyes. Toxic waste handler, day laborer, human power generator—that's all AURA thinks I'm suited for.

Of course, Sera had her own spin on it. "A job's a job," she said. I wanted to throw something. This isn't like her job in Midtown. At least there, she's not reduced to nothing more than a cog in a machine.

Reluctantly, I join the line of Slummers as they're funneled into the plant. I can't help but jump as a rhythmic high-pitched ringing hits my ears. The smell doesn't help—a mixture of sweat, stale air, and something slightly fouler. Bodies push against me the closer we go, their faces etched with deep lines. No one talks; we just move. I can't help but stare. Do they look that way from years of work in the Slum, or is this just how all Slummers look?

An Enforcer silently thrusts a sledgehammer into my hands. It's so heavy that I nearly drop it on my foot. I tighten my grip on the rough handle, the splintered wood digging into my palms. I open my mouth to say something to the Enforcer, but I'm pushed forward before I get a chance.

Finally, I stop at what must be my workstation. The number forty-seven is roughly scrawled on the concrete floor. The workstation is empty, except for a large metal plate connected to an intricate system of wires and cables that disappear into the ceiling above. My eyes move from the plate to the hammer in my hands. What am I supposed to do? Hit it?

"This has to be a joke," I say, my voice so low that I doubt anyone can hear me.

A shrill whistle cuts through the din, making me shudder. An Enforcer's voice, harsh and devoid of empathy, orders us to begin. I grip the sledgehammer, my hands already slick with sweat. Raising it is a struggle; it feels heavier than anything I've ever lifted in my life. With all the force I can muster, I bring it down onto the metal plate. There's an echoing clang, and the circuits connecting the plate to the wall momentarily glow. They fade quickly, like the dying embers of a fire.

The other workers around me swing their hammers like machines, automatic, unthinking. I try to find that rhythm, but my arms shake with each strike, the impact jolting through me. My strikes become heavier as a stitch grows in my side. In no time at all I've easily fallen behind the others.

I stop, leaning on the sledgehammer like a crutch. Sweat pours down my face, stinging my eyes. I gasp, my bones shaking as the pounding continues around me. How are they keeping this up? It's only been five minutes, and I'm about ready to pass out. I shake my head. AURA was wrong; this job isn't for me at all.

"Hey, you!" The harsh voice cracks through the air like a whip. I push myself up as an Enforcer marches into my workstation, his baton at the ready. "No stopping," he barks, pointing at my hammer with his baton. "Get going!"

"I ... I just..." My words trail off under his glare. I turn back to my workstation, fighting to keep the anger from my face. What's wrong with this guy? Isn't it his job to protect me? Besides, it's my first day; he should cut me a little slack.

Pain erupts through my shoulder as a crackle of electricity fills the air. My muscles contract, squeezing so tightly that it's like they've turned to stone. I stumble forward, and narrowly avoid hitting my head on the handle of my hammer.

"I said, get back to work," the Enforcer commands, this time pointing his baton at my face.

Clenching my jaw, I push myself up on my good arm. My shoulder throbs; I can already feel a welt forming beneath my shirt where the Enforcer's baton touched me. I want to scream, to fight back, but I don't. What good will it do? So, I raise the hammer again. My strikes are weak and clumsy, but I force myself to push through the pain. After a while, the Enforcer backs away, and I hear him yelling at someone a few stations away.

Anger boils up inside me like lava. I want to take my sledge-hammer and smash his stupid baton. Doesn't he know how hard this is? I doubt it. To him, we're all just Slummers, expendable and replaceable. So, I keep swinging, tears blurring my vision, determined not to give him another reason to punish me.

When the whistle finally blows to signal the end of the day, I'm nothing but raw muscle and bone, held together by sheer force of will. Even so, I doubt I'll survive the walk home. I'm grateful as I return the sledgehammer to a rack near the front. My hands look like I shoved them into a grinder, covered in blisters that sting, thanks to my sweaty palms.

The line to leave the plant is sluggish, but for the first time, I don't mind. My feet drag across the grimy floor, heavy as lead. I blindly follow the Slummer in front of me, not even paying attention to where he's going. It's only when I reach the doors that I finally snap back to my senses.

I place my forearm in the scanner, and it beeps. My tag grows hot in my forearm, leaving behind an uncomfortable warmth that lingers too long. I stare at the flickering screen, unable to stop my foot from tapping. How long is this going to take?

"Three credits," the computer says in a cool female voice.

I stare at the flashing three on the screen. That's it? This can't be right.

"Are you kidding me?" My voice is louder than I intended,

and I can feel people staring at me. But I don't care. "That's all I get?"

The machine remains silent for a beat before responding in its monotonous drone. *"Quotas and pay are set by AURA. Please contact the Department of Labor if you have concerns regarding your work placement."*

My hand balls into a fist, my nails digging into my stinging palms. Fury rushes through me like lightning, and I have a sudden impulse to drive my foot into the screen. But my anger fades as quickly as it came. What's the point? The computer just does whatever AURA tells it to do—and if I've learned anything in my time here, it's that what AURA decides is final.

So, I step aside, allowing the next Slummer to collect their pay. One by one, they scan their tags, and each time it beeps, my frustration grows. A few of them pat me on the back as they pass by. "First day's always the hardest," one says with a worn-out smile. "You'll get used to it," murmurs another.

I know their words are meant to comfort me, but they only make me angrier. How are they all okay with this? They're acting like being treated like this is normal.

Making my way back to the square takes a lot longer than I thought it would. My muscles scream with each step I take, and it's like I'm dragging a sack of rocks behind me. The smell of sweat and metal clings to me; it's like I'm still at workstation 47. Even my blistered hands seem to hurt more with every step. More than anything, I just want a shower. Back in Newtown, they had soaps for everything—smooth, fragrant soaps that would heal my battered, raw, blistered skin. I can't remember the last time I cleaned myself properly.

People swarm the square, quickly flitting between the carts. I find Theron and Callias almost instantly. They're weaving through the carts like two tiny birds, their hands shoved deep into their pockets.

I lean against the nearest building as Theron passes what looks like an old, crumpled-up wire to one of the cart owners.

Somewhere deep inside of me, I think I feel a glimmer of pride. I'd have never guessed the three of us would have found ways to honestly earn some money when we first arrived in the Slum. But as I take in the grime on their hollow faces and the holes in their clothes, the pride fades.

Theron and Callias shouldn't have to scavenge. The whole reason I took the job as a human power generator is to make enough money for them to be safe. But how safe can they be, running around the Slum without me or Sera to protect them? With both of us working now, surely there's a better way.

"Guys!" I call, waving my arm to stop Theron from entering a shop. "Time to go!"

I can tell by the look on Theron's face that he'd rather keep selling. But he must sense my irritation, because after a few seconds, he joins me at the door to Sera's building. I'm actually grateful when Callias forces open the door to the apartment.

Theron and Callias sprawl on the sleeping mat, a tangle of limbs and laughter. They're telling stories, each more ridiculous than the last. It's a game to them, and I don't have it in me to tell them to be quiet. All I want to do is sleep.

"Make room," I mutter, easing myself down beside them with a wince. The mat is as uncomfortable as ever, but today, it's enough that a sigh escapes my lips.

"You okay?" Theron asks, propping himself up on his elbow.

"Yep," I lie. The thought of telling them about my job tonight is too much. "When's Sera getting back?"

"Soon." Callias nuzzles into me, and my muscles relax slightly at his touch. "Is everything okay?"

"Yeah," I lie again, closing my eyes. "Just wake me when she gets here."

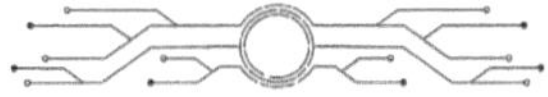

WHEN I OPEN MY EYES, Sera's apartment is so dark that it's almost suffocating. I sit up, and my muscles feel like they're splintering beneath my skin. It's the middle of the night; I can tell by the deep silence that has settled over everything. Theron and Callias are dead to the world, their breathing steady and soft. How long was I asleep?

I turn, expecting to see Sera asleep beside Theron, but she's not here. My eyes narrow in the darkness. Where could she be at this hour? My pulse quickens as I push myself up, careful not to wake my brothers. As quietly as I can, I force the door open.

"Sera?" My voice is barely a whisper as I step out into the slanting hall. I'm greeted with nothing but silence.

I slip back onto the mat, careful not to disturb Theron and Callias. In the short time I was out in the hall, the space between them has vanished, their chests rising and falling in the darkness. I slip between them, and almost instantly, my eyes begin to droop. A strange feeling pulls at my gut—a mixture of concern and something else I can't quite place. Sera's never been out this late before. Where could she be?

THE SOFT MURMUR of voices pulls me from sleep. My eyes drag open, and I see Sera's silhouette hunched over a flickering candle. Theron and Callias sit beside her like it's any other morning. I rub my face, pretending to wipe away the sleep as I try to keep calm. But on the inside, I'm screaming. Where did Sera go last night, and why is she acting like she never left? When I was working for Nyssa, Sera constantly tried to make me tell the truth. But now, she's the one who's lying. I want to confront her about it, but now is not the time; I can't ask her in front of Theron and Callias. They practically worship her, and as far as they know, things are finally good between Sera and me.

Weak rays of sunlight seep through the grimy window. Theron and Callias are all chatter and laughter as they get ready to head off to the refinery to do some scavenging. They're excited about what they might find; apparently, someone told them fresh food scraps are delivered on Thursdays. I don't know whether I'm more excited or disgusted.

Once they're gone, the silence in the apartment presses down on me. It's time for answers. I wait for the sound of their footsteps to fade before I turn to Sera.

"Sera, where were you last night?"

The moment the words leave my lips, I know I've messed up. Sera's back stiffens, and she doesn't turn to face me. In fact, she doesn't even acknowledge that I've spoken. She simply collects her few belongings, and the silence is deafening.

"Sera," I repeat, trying to keep my voice casual, "where were you?"

Sera pushes past me and is out the door in seconds. I race after her, my head nearly smacking the sloping ceiling. I don't understand what her problem is; I just want to know where she went last night. After all, she was the one who told me off for keeping secrets.

"Sera!" I call after her, but she just hurries down the stairs.

The square is already packed with people when I reach the cobblestones. Sera weaves through the carts and stalls, but I'm right on her heels. I don't lose sight of her as she darts down the nearest side street. Why won't she tell me where she was? It's not like she could have done anything bad, right?

"Why won't you talk to me?" I hiss once I finally grab Sera as she joins the line at the Fringe. People crowd around us, all waiting to cross into Midtown.

Sera's thin arm easily slides out of my fingers. For a brief moment, her blue eyes lock on mine. But they're gone in an instant as the line shuffles forward. "It's none of your business," she says, her voice as cold as the morning air.

It feels like she's kicked me in the gut. None of my business? How can she say that? Sera took in me and my brothers when we had nowhere else to go. I trusted her to look after Theron and Callias. We've been living together for months now. I thought

Sera was the one person in this hellhole I could trust. Clearly, I was wrong.

"I thought we were being honest with each other now," I say, trying to stay with her as the line pushes forward.

"We are," she says, sticking her arm into the barrier pillar. She crosses into Midtown, leaving me stuck in the Slum. "And I've told you everything you need to know."

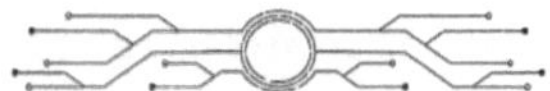

EVERY NIGHT for the next week, I fight against the pull of sleep, my eyes heavy with exhaustion from the relentless pounding at the plant. The sledgehammer might as well be an extension of my arms now, a part of me I can't shake off even in the cramped space of Sera's apartment. But no matter how much my body screams for rest, I push it aside. I need to know what Sera is up to.

Each night, as Theron and Callias slip into dreams, I lie on the hard floor, feigning sleep, while keeping one eye on Sera's still form. It's a waiting game. The candle burns down to a stub, flickering out and leaving us in darkness that seems to thicken with each passing hour.

Then it happens, like clockwork: Sera rises. I hear the rustle of her makeshift dress as she eases herself up. She thinks we're all asleep, that her secret is safe. But not anymore—not from me.

I wait until the darkness of the hall swallows her before I follow. My muscles groan in protest, but I ignore them. I keep my distance, always careful not to make a sound. I don't know why I bother; the building is so creaky, I doubt she'd even hear my footsteps. But it's not our building that's the problem.

Out in the dark streets, I tread softly over the uneven cobblestones, keeping to the shadows as much as possible. But Sera is like smoke slipping through my fingers, disappearing around corners or vanishing into doorways whenever I think I'm close.

The maze of streets and alleys consumes her every single time, and that's when I lose her.

But what I don't understand is why she's being so secretive. Is she in trouble, or part of something dangerous? No. She can't be. She was furious when she found out I was part of Nyssa's crew. But if it's not that, what could it be?

One night turns into two, then three, and each night ends the same way: I return to Sera's apartment empty-handed, with dawn breaking over the horizon. And each morning, she's back before me, acting as if she never left. I thought I had Sera figured out—the tough exterior, the kind heart—but really, I don't know her at all.

After a week of sleepless nights, I'm about ready to burst. I'm so exhausted, I'm falling behind at work. Today, I got shocked twice by an Enforcer. And I have absolutely nothing to show for it. But for some reason, I can't bring myself to stop following her.

Sera rounds another corner, and I hustle to catch up, but as I turn into the alley, she's gone—again. A gust of wind sweeps past, carrying away any trace of her. I lean against the grimy wall, and I can't help but close my eyes. Sadly, this is the most relaxed I've felt all week.

I straighten up, rubbing my burning eyes with my fists. "That's it," I whisper, shaking my head, "I'm done." There's a part of me that feels like giving up entirely, but I shove it down. All I need is a decent night's sleep, but I doubt I'll get that at Sera's place.

As I wander back through the streets, I can't help but replay my every failed attempt to follow Sera. I have to be missing something. But what?

"Ezra! What are you doing out here?"

I spin around, my heart hammering against my ribs. Rowan is leaning against a doorway, her arms crossed. Her presence is like a splash of cold water, and suddenly I'm alert again.

"Just out walking," I say, though it sounds like a lame excuse, even to me.

Rowan smirks, as if she knows there's more to it than that. "Sure you are. You're out late."

"Couldn't sleep," I mutter, shoving my hands into my pockets and looking away from Rowan's piercing gaze. I haven't seen her since my fight at the Hollow—right before Sera saved me from being Nyssa's punching bag. Even though I never want to set foot in Nyssa's place again, I do miss having Rowan to talk to.

Should I tell Rowan? Apart from Sera, Rowan knows more about the Slum than anyone I know. She has to know something about Sera.

I open my mouth to ask her, but something stops me. What good would it do? I don't even know what Sera's up to, after all. And dragging Rowan into this feels like pulling her into quicksand, messy and dangerous. But maybe…

"So, you know Sera?" I ask, trying to sound casual.

Rowan raises an eyebrow. "The girl who saved your butt at the Hollow? No, not really. Why?"

"No reason." I shrug, hating how defensive I sound. "Just curious."

She shrugs back, as if the question is of little consequence to her—which it probably is. "She seems to keep to herself. After she bailed you out, Nyssa asked about her. But no one in the crew knew anything," she says with a nonchalance that makes me envious.

"Have you seen her lately?" I press on, sweat coating my palms. "Early in the morning? Late at night?"

Rowan shakes her head. "Haven't seen her." She pushes off the wall and glances down the alleyway, where a figure looms in the shadows—probably another crew member waiting on her. "Gotta go. We're doing a pickup in Floodway. Catch you later, Ezra."

I trudge back to the square, my feet growing heavier with every step. Sleep—real, deep sleep—has eluded me for too long. Maybe tonight I'll catch more than a fleeting glimpse of it. The square is quieter at this hour, the hustle of day replaced by a rare stillness. My eyelids are heavy, and it's a struggle to simply keep them open.

As I climb the steep steps to Sera's apartment, my muscles protest with every heave. My hand grazes the cold, uneven railing, and my breath comes out in ragged pulls. When I reach the top floor, I see a sliver of light from where I know Sera's door is. I stifle a groan. What are Theron and Callias doing up this late? I'd hoped they would be asleep when I got back. How can I explain where I've been, or why Sera isn't here. What will I say?

Tentatively, I push the door open. But there's no sign of Theron or Callias. Instead, Sera is here—along with three women I've never seen before. Their dresses cling to them like second skins, tattered and cut in ways that reveal more than they hide. Their faces are masked with even more makeup than the old Newtown ladies who desperately try to conceal their age. One of them is sprawled out on the sleeping mat, a bruise blooming across her cheekbone like a dark stain on a canvas. Her eyes are shut tight, pain etched into the creases of her forehead.

"What the hell?" I blurt out before I can stop myself.

Sera doesn't even look at me. Her focus is entirely on the woman on the mat, her brows furrowed with concern. "What happened, Jewel?" she asks, her voice gentle but firm.

The woman's lips part, releasing a whisper of sound that never quite forms words. Jewel tries again, a string of sounds tumbling out, disjointed and desperate. It's like she's speaking through a mouthful of broken glass. I step closer, my heart pounding franticly. What could leave someone so utterly shattered? And what is she doing in Sera's apartment?

"Where was Jewel tonight?" Sera asks, her eyes narrowing at the other two women, like they have on me countless times

"She was with a regular," one of them murmurs in a tremulous voice. "He's never been rough before."

The other nods in agreement, her arms crossed over her

chest. "She must've been jumped after she left him," she adds, her eyes dark with worry.

Sera squats down and slides her fingers into the folds of Jewel's dress. My eyes narrow as I see her jaw tighten. She's looking for something, but what?

"Her money's gone," Sera says, straightening up.

My heart hammers against my rib cage as the truth slams into me. These women are prostitutes, and Jewel... I feel a surge of anger so intense that it nearly chokes me. Sera brought them here—to the only refuge Theron, Callias, and I have. This place is supposed to be safe, away from the filth and darkness of the Slum.

Is this what she does at night? My hands clench into fists. The idea that she's mixed up in … in *this*, and right under our noses, makes my skin crawl. How could she? Doesn't she realize how dangerous this is? Doesn't she care about us at all?

The door bursts open with a force that it makes me jump. Theron and Callias stand there, eyes wide, faces reflecting the dim candlelight like startled deer. My heart leaps into my throat.

"Can we come back yet?" Theron asks.

"No!" I lunge forward, arms outstretched, desperate to shield them from the scene before us. They don't need to see this, to know this kind of ugliness exists.

Sera's head snaps toward the noise, and her gaze locks onto Theron and Callias. For a moment, nobody moves; the air in the room is thick with tension. Then Sera's expression hardens.

"Lina," she says, looking to one of the women, "take the boys downstairs. Now."

Lina, the slighter of the women, nods quickly. She scoops up Theron's hand while the other woman takes Callias's. They don't resist, but their confusion pierces me more sharply than any blade.

I stand there, frozen, as Lina and the other woman usher my brothers down the hall with hurried whispers. My little brothers glance back at me, their eyes searching for an explanation I'm not ready to give. The door bounces shut behind them, leaving me, Sera, and Jewel's pained whimpers in the cramped room.

I can't stand the silence. The way Sera tends to Jewel screams of untold stories. There's something she's not telling me about her, and I've had enough. I can't have any more secrets.

"How do you know her?" The words come out harsher than I intend, a demand rather than a question. "And don't lie to me. I know you've been sneaking out at night. I need answers. Sera. Right now."

Sera doesn't flinch at my tone, continuing to dab at Jewel's face with the edge of her sheet dress. "After I was Renounced, I got robbed." Her voice is steady, but there's a flicker of something in her eyes. "Jewel found me in the street. She took care of me."

Her words hang in the air between us, and I feel the heat of my anger dissipate like steam into a cool night. I can't bring myself to look at her. I'd been so quick to judge Sera, to assume the worst about her actions, without truly understanding. The way Sera looks out for Jewel isn't much different from how she watches over Theron and Callias. She's extending a hand in the dark, just as she did for us.

A question claws its way up my throat, and it tastes bitter on my tongue. "And are you… Do you…?"

Sera's expression softens, and I know she understands. "No. I'm one of the lucky ones." Her face is full of pity—I can tell it's not for herself, but for those like Jewel. The realization that she's never had to sink that low to survive carves a hollow space in my chest, filling it with both relief and an overwhelming sense of sorrow.

I take a deep breath, the weight of my own judgment pressing on my shoulders. What does it matter what Sera does at night? She's been nothing but good to Theron, Callias, and me. After everything I've done, she still trusts me, and I trust her— and for me, that's enough.

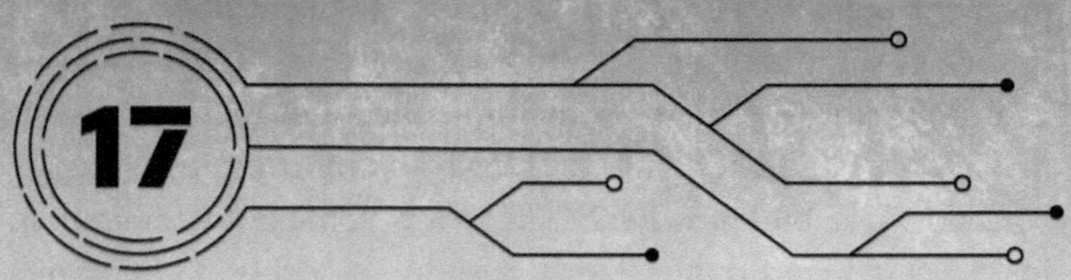

17

THE COLD WINTER air bites at my skin, worming its way through the threadbare fabric of my shirt. I used to love winter, when the world would be blanketed in a layer of pristine white. The first frost was always a time of excitement for me. But now, all I feel is dread and an aching cold that nothing can take away.

Theron skips ahead of me and Callias, kicking at the icy puddles with worn shoes that are more holes than soles at this point. "Ezariah," he calls over his shoulder, his breath a shimmering cloud of mist. "Let's go in there!"

I follow his finger to a shop huddled between two dilapidated buildings, its windows fogged by the warmth within. Callias clings to my side, shivering in his baggy shirt. The idea of heat makes goose bumps rise all over my arms. We've been wandering around all morning. This place looks as good as any.

Inside, the air is thick with the smell of leather and glue, a stark contrast to the biting cold outside. The shop is mostly empty, save for a few shelves lined with shoes that have seen better days. A space heater hums in the corner, casting a warm glow on Theron's face as he sidles up to it.

The owner stands behind the counter, his eyes narrowing as we approach the glowing coils. I know we don't look like customers—because we aren't—and it's only a matter of time before he kicks us out. But as the warm air hits my skin, all my worries seem to fade away.

Theron glances at me and then back at the owner. "Sir," he says, his voice about three octaves higher than normal, "could you help me? My shoes are full of holes, and I can't feel my toes anymore."

The man's face softens a fraction as Theron lifts his foot to show his tattered shoe. "Alright," he concedes with a sigh. "Let's see what we have in your size."

The shop slowly fills with people seeking refuge from the cold, or perhaps they're genuinely interested in purchasing something. I pull Callias into the back of the shop. I can't help but be impressed with Theron. Maybe if he milks it, we'll get at least ten minutes of warmth before the owner realizes we can't afford new shoes.

Suddenly, a chill that has nothing to do with winter sweeps over me as the door bangs open and an Enforcer steps inside. To say everyone steps back is an understatement; we all retreat into whatever shadows we can find. I pull Callias close, my eyes trained on the worn wooden floor. I know I've done nothing wrong, but Enforcers don't need a reason to be cruel.

The Enforcer makes one lap through the shop. He grabs me, along with a few others, and quickly runs his hands over our clothes before moving on. I bite my lip, waiting for him to say I've done something illegal and take me away. After what feels like an eternity, but probably lasts only a minute or two, he leaves. A collective sigh ripples through the room.

Gratefully, I shove my freezing hands into my pockets, and my fingers brush against something unexpected: neatly folded paper. Curious but cautious, I pull it out just enough to see the elegant script gracing the front. My mouth falls open. It's my mother's handwriting.

It's like someone has dumped cement into my brain. How did a letter from my mother end up in my pocket? That Enforcer must have put it there when he searched me! But why? I haven't heard from her since my Renouncement, and why would I? She's the perfect Newtown wife: doing everything my father says without question. She barely lifted a finger when he Renounced us. So, why would she write me now?

I slip the unopened letter back into my pocket before Callias can see it. This isn't the time or place. My brothers have suffered enough when it comes to our former parents.

That night, it takes Theron and Callias forever to fall asleep. I watch them from the corner, their chests rising and falling in sync. They look so peaceful, so unburdened. How I wish I were them! But I remain silent, my mother's letter, still unopened, growing heavier in my pocket.

As the night deepens and Theron's soft snoring fills the space between silence and solace, I know it's time.

I rise, careful not to disturb the boys, and step over to where Sera lies wrapped in her purple sheet. "Sera," I whisper, nudging her shoulder gently.

Her eyes pop open, alert and questioning. "What's wrong?" she murmurs.

"Nothing," I say quickly. "I just… Can we talk? Outside?"

She nods and follows me into the hallway, wrapping her sheet quickly around her. I hand Sera the letter without a word. The thought of reading those words myself makes my blood boil. So, Sera unfolds it under the bulb flickering from the ceiling, her eyes flicking over my mother's elegant handwriting.

"I don't believe it," she whispers.

"What?" What could my mother possibly have to say to me?

"It's an invitation for you, Theron, Callias … and me," she says slowly. "To your family's winter gala tomorrow."

"What?!" I don't know whether to be upset or angry. I expected her to apologize, or at least offer her sons some support after not bothering to stand up for us when our father Renounced us. But to invite us to my family's winter gala? It's one of the biggest social events in Newtown. "She can't be serious?"

Sera doesn't miss a beat. "Ezariah, think about it. This could give you … closure."

"Closure?" The word tastes bitter in my mouth. "My father tossed me out for attending my grandmother's funeral, and then he threw Theron and Callias out for not wanting me to go. How can I find closure after that?"

She steps closer, her eyes soft but firm. "It's not for you. Theron and Callias deserve to see your mother again, don't they? And it's a gala. There will be tons of food, warmth."

An image of Theron and Callias laughing with full bellies makes my chest relax. It's been so long since they've had a decent meal—one that didn't come from scavenging or the rations bank.

"And you," Sera continues, her hand resting lightly on my arm. "You'll get to face your father. Not as the boy he Renounced, but as the man who's survived, despite everything he threw at you."

Her words echo in the hollow space where my anger lives. Could I really go back there? Could I stand to see the man who used to be my father?

But as much as I hate to admit it, Sera's right. I let out a deep breath, hoping I won't regret this. "Okay," I finally say. "We'll go."

EVEN THOUGH THE thought of seeing my father again makes my stomach churn, I know there's no backing out after Sera gives Theron my mother's invitation. Sera insists on buying decent soap, and I can't argue with her. We use every coin we have; even Theron and Callias pitch in their meager savings, though it means they can't buy new shirts for the event. But what can we do?

The bathroom is as grim as ever. The four of us take turns scrubbing under the weak, brown trickle from the faucet. It's cold and unpleasant, and I try not to think about it too much. But Sera's right: the soap makes a world of difference. With the grime and filth washed away, the dark patches under Theron's eyes and Callias's hollow face are even more pronounced.

When we're as clean as we can manage, Sera starts to work on our clothes. The shirt I got from Lockup hangs off me like a tent, but she knots it at the back, so it clings to my frame in a more flattering way. Theron and Callias giggle as she does the same for them, but all I can see are their ribs pressing through their skin.

Sera rewraps her sheet dress, and now it looks more like a gown, with her old scarf accentuating her waist. Even her feet look cleaner than I've ever seen them. She's still barefoot, but at least her skin isn't the same grimy color as the ground.

We're a far cry from gala material, or even presentable by Newtown standards, but it's the best we can do.

"We don't look too bad," I acknowledge with a small nod.

Sera meets my eyes with a hint of pride in hers. "We'll fit right in," she says with far more confidence than I feel.

We stand huddled together in the square, our breath misting in the frigid air. A sleek, black car pulls up to collect us, just as my mother's invitation said it would. Out of the corner of my eye, I see several Slummers stop in their tracks. I don't blame them. Aside from the occasional Enforcer vehicle, cars aren't a very common thing in the Slum; no one can afford them. In fact, I can't remember the last time I saw one.

The driver steps out, tall and stiff in his uniform, his face completely devoid of surprise or judgment. He pulls out a hand-held scanner and motions for us to line up. One by one, he checks our ID tags—Theron's first, then Callias's, then Sera's, and finally mine. Our tags glow green under the scanner's light.

"Master Malkin has granted you clearance to Newtown until midnight," the driver says stiffly, opening the rear door.

We pile into the car, its shining interior a stark contrast to our rough, stained clothes. As we pull away from the square, the Slum's decrepit buildings and filth vanish into the distance. The road becomes smoother, and even the air looks cleaner. We soon pass through the barrier to Midtown, and before I can even think, the sleek, imposing structures of Newtown rise in the distance. Somehow, it all looks too bright, too clean. It's so different from the world I've been living in. My old life in Newtown feels like another world, like the memories are not even mine.

"Why would he invite us back?" I mutter under my breath, but Sera hears me.

She leans close, her voice barely a whisper. "I guess we'll find out."

I want to believe her, but I know my father. He Renounced his kids without a single thought to preserve his own reputation. No matter what Sera says, he doesn't want to reconcile with me. So, why would my father, a strict upholder of Nomisman's values, invite four Slummers into his home for an upscale event?

The car glides through Newtown, and I can't help but notice how Theron's eyes widen with each passing light, each towering building more grandiose than the last. Callias presses his face against the window, his tiny hand smudging on the glass as he points out familiar sights.

"We're really back!" Theron whispers, his voice a mixture of disbelief and awe.

I manage a smile for them, hiding the unease churning in my gut. "Yeah. Should be fun, right?"

Callias turns to me, his wide eyes shining. "Are we there yet?"

I nod, forcing myself to smile while my stomach does a backflip. I know they're excited, but personally, midnight can't get here fast enough. Ever since my Renouncement, all I've thought about is leaving the Slum. But I'd rather sleep in the gutter with the filth than beg my father to take us back. The sooner we leave, the better.

As the car rolls up the graveled drive, I stare out the window. The glittering white marble facade of what used to be my home now looks out of place to my eyes. It's easily bigger than four whole blocks in the Slum. My fingers twitch as the car slows to a stop. I take a deep breath, trying to contain the whirlwind inside me. But how can I?

"C'mon," Sera says, nudging me in the side. "It's just one night."

I nod and close my eyes one last time before exiting the car. The gravel crunches under my feet, sounding both familiar and strange. Theron and Callias spill out after me, their faces alight with excitement that I can't muster.

We climb the sweeping steps—the same steps where my father Renounced my brothers—and cross the threshold. It's like I've traveled forward and backward in time all at once. Miles of shimmering fabric cover the foyer walls, while priceless stone vases at least six feet tall line the main hall. My feet move automatically as a servant appears out of nowhere to guide us down the hall, the faint sound of music growing with every step. I turn a corner and see the doors to the ballroom wide open. I take a deep breath, resisting the urge to turn and leave. I've already come this far.

The ballroom is a sea of people dressed in velvet and silk, their jewels sparkling like stars in the night. They all move as one, swaying to the choreographed dance I never bothered to learn. Just one of their outfits must easily cost more than I've held since my Renouncement. But of course, none of them see that. They simply laugh and chatter on, oblivious to the harsh world lurking just outside their walls. Was I this shallow too?

The tables, piled high with food, seem obscene now, even as my mouth waters. Platters of roasted meats, exotic fruits, and pastries glisten under the crystal chandeliers, their sweet aromas making my head throb slightly. It's a feast fit for those at the top, not those who scavenge for crumbs.

Theron tugs at my sleeve, pointing at a mountain of sweets that would have him bouncing off the walls for days. "It looks *so* good," he says, his eyes as wide as the plates. "Let's go, before they take all the good stuff!"

Callias and Theron run off before I can even open my mouth.

The sight of their backs retreating twists something deep inside me. I genuinely want them to enjoy a decent meal for once; that's the whole reason I agreed to come here. Hopefully, they'll eat their fill. Who knows when we'll get another meal like this?

Sera and I walk through the crowd, and I feel every eye on me. Newtowners are many things—ambitious, arrogant, spiteful—but one thing they aren't is subtle. Their eyes slide over our worn clothes, lingering on my rough hands or Sera's bare feet.

A woman's gaze meets mine, and I instantly see the fear in her eyes. It's like we're a contagious disease. My chest tightens, and I feel a heat in my cheeks that has nothing to do with the warmth of the room. Sera was wrong. As unwanted reminders of the world these people despise, us coming here was a mistake.

"Sera," I whisper, leaning close so only she can hear. "We should just go. We don't belong here."

Sera stops dead in her tracks. She turns to face me, her hand squeezing mine tightly as her soft blue eyes bore into mine. A shudder runs through my arm, only partly due to the throbbing in my fingers. "Ezariah," she says, her voice steady and sure, "we're here now. Stop worrying about what these people think."

Before I can even form the words to argue, Sera is weaving her way through the crowd, pulling me along after her. Her grip is firm, and I know from the glint in her eyes that I'm trapped. The crowd practically parts for her as she positions us right in the middle of the dance floor.

I'm about to tell her that I don't dance—at least, not these kinds of dances—when the music sweeps over us. It's a gentle melody, soft and graceful. Sera's hands find mine, guiding them into the right position. I follow her lead, clumsily at first, but she's surprisingly patient with me.

The room spins as we turn in time with the beat, and something strange happens: my worries begin to slip away. The whispers and stares of the crowd fade until there's only Sera, her long, brown hair swaying behind her, leading me through steps I never bothered to learn.

As we move around the dance floor, I see Sera's face soften, the ghost of a smile flickering on her cracked lips. "I used to love dancing," she murmurs, closing her eyes as the music swells.

"You used to dance?"

"Don't sound so shocked. My dad taught me. Before…"

I can hear the longing in her voice as she trails off. Aside from that one night, Sera never mentions her life before her Renouncement—the life that was taken from her. Now, here she is with me, in a place neither of us belongs. But for the first time in I don't know how long, it doesn't matter; we're just two Renounced souls finding solace in each other's company amidst a world that's tossed us aside. The music wraps around us like a cocoon, shielding us from the whispers and glares. Sera's hand is warm in mine, her steps sure and graceful. I let go, allowing the rhythm to carry me, to fill the void where my anxiety used to be. We spin, and for a moment, it's like we're alone in the world.

But then I see them. My father stands rigid at the edge of the dance floor, his eyes scanning the crowd like he's searching for a flaw in his perfect, glittering world. My mother is at his side, her face a perfect mask of quiet grace, though her eyes hold a sadness that I don't recognize. My feet stumble to a halt, and the music might as well have stopped. My heart hammers against my ribs, a caged bird desperate for escape.

"You should go talk to them," Sera says softly, clearly following my gaze. "It'd be rude not to."

I hesitate, and somehow, the weight of their betrayal is heavier than before. But she's right. Taking a deep breath, I muster every ounce of the poise I was taught in my former life and approach my parents, Sera right by my side.

"Mr. and Mrs. Malkin," Sera says, inclining her head to both my mother and father. "Thank you for inviting us."

Silence follows Sera's words. My parents look through us as though we're not even here. My father's eyes narrow as his mouth recedes into a thin line. Beside him, my mother's gaze flits to the floor, a shadow of sorrow crossing her features.

I clench my jaw, my anger rising like lava. What is their problem? *They* invited us here, and now they're ignoring us? I know they're supposed to ignore me, since my father Renounced me. But Sera? They don't even know her.

"Can we speak privately?" I ask, my voice steady despite the storm brewing inside me.

Of course, my father doesn't respond. Instead, he takes my mother's hand and walks to the nearest exit. Sera and I hurry after him, my anger seething just below the surface.

My mother closes the heavy door behind us, muffling the music. As I stand beside Sera, the tension in the small sitting room is thick enough to choke on.

"I have no desire to see Ezariah, Theron, or Callias," my father says, his voice as cool as ever. "If it were up to me, you'd still be in Lowtown, where you belong. However, I have my wife's well-being to consider."

It feels like I've been slapped in the face. Why would my father invite us here if he didn't want to see us? To tell me to my face how much he despises me? I know he doesn't like me, but this is cruel, even for him. And for what? To satisfy some warped sense of family duty, or to appease my mother's heartache? Either way, it's a sick joke, and we're the punchline.

"So, why are we here?" Sera's voice cuts through the tension, clear and unwavering. "I assume you're having Ezariah followed. How else could you slip him your invitation?"

My father's face turns stony, and I'm surprised that Sera doesn't crumble beneath his gaze. "You," he says slowly, "are entitled to nothing here. By AURA's grace, I allowed four Slummers, four Renounced, into my home. Where is your gratitude?"

My hands ball into fists at my sides. I've had enough of this. My father is free to treat me like garbage; he always has. But Sera? She took us in when *he* cast us out. My father should be thanking *her*.

"Ezariah."

My mother's voice is no more than a whisper, but the sound

is enough to temper my anger. I look at her and see her eyes brimming with tears. That sucks the fight right out of me. My throat tightens, and I can't tear my eyes away from hers. There are so many things I want to ask her. Why didn't she fight for us? Why does she let my father walk all over her? But there's one answer I want above all others.

"Why'd you send that invitation?" I say, my voice cracking.

I expect my mother to answer. Instead, she looks to my father.

"It was a moment of weakness," he says curtly, not looking at me. "One that won't be repeated."

A moment of weakness? That's how my father describes a mother's love? Heat courses through my veins, and I can feel the blood pounding in my ears. I'm sick of him speaking for her, like she's just another one of his possessions, not a person with thoughts and feelings. My eyes lock onto hers, searching for some sign of defiance, some glimmer of the woman who used to read me bedtime stories and smooth back my hair when I was sick.

"Mom," I say, and the word feels foreign on my tongue, "why'd you invite us here?"

My mother's eyes are pools of sorrow. Again, she looks to my father, but this time, he's not looking at her.

"Ezariah," my father says, finally turning his gaze to me, "I'll compensate you for the return of Theron and Callias."

It feels like I've been hit over the head with a mallet. I'm sure I must've misheard him. But as the words bounce around my mind, I feel Sera stiffen beside me. My stomach churns as my eyes dart between my father and mother. Is this why he brought us here—to *buy* back my brothers?

"No," I spit out, the word tasting like poison. "You can't have them."

Sera's whisper joins mine, but there's no mistaking the fire in her voice. "You think you can just throw money at everything? They're not yours to claim anymore."

My father's cold eyes fall on Sera, and I can almost see the disdain radiating off him. "Look at you," he says, eyes raking over her appearance with contempt. "A whore dragged out from the gutter. What kind of future can you offer Theron and Callias?"

Her eyes glitter. "You pig!"

"Hey!" Anger drives me forward, and I step between Sera and my father. "She helped us, which is more than you did—you Renounced your youngest sons for loving me!"

"You're no better, Ezariah," he says with a shake of his head. "Less than a month in the Slum, and you already had a record. You're incapable of caring for anyone."

My chest tightens with every word my father says. Blood pounds in my ears, and my legs tremble beneath me. "They deserve better than this," I say, my voice cracking as it rises. "My brothers are kind and caring and good. You don't deserve them! They're worth more than any credits you could ever offer!"

My mother steps forward, her hands clasped in front of her like she's praying. "Ezariah, please," she says, her voice breaking with emotion. "We know your situation. Your father has agreed to give you five thousand credits for—"

"I don't care!" The words explode out of me like fire. Tears well up in my mother's eyes, but I couldn't care less. I mean what I said. "You can't fix what you did. He Renounced us—and you did nothing to stop him. You're just as bad as he is."

I turn to Sera, and in her eyes, I see my own determination staring back at me. Her fingers slip into mine, and I'm surprised to feel myself shaking. I've been right all along. Coming here was a mistake.

"We're leaving," I say, disgust dripping from every word. "We have two boys that need us. It's their bedtime soon."

We storm out of the room, the echo of my parents' last words fading behind us. Out in the ballroom, the guests continue to dance and mingle, completely unaware of what just transpired in the next room. We find Theron and Callias at one of the buffet tables, grinning ear to ear as they stuff their pockets with sweets and treats.

"Grab whatever you can," I whisper, snatching several pastries and shoving them in my own pockets.

Theron looks at me, and I see the confusion in his eyes, but he follows my instructions. Callias, of course, is totally focused on making sure his sweets don't crumble as he wraps them carefully in a napkin.

As Sera leads the way toward the massive front doors, I keep my face turned from my brothers. It's hard, but I try to keep my voice as normal as possible. But I know I have to. What happened in that room... They don't need to know what our parents just tried to do. My father offered to *buy* them from us, but not because he misses them or regrets Renouncing us.

"Take us home, please," I say to the driver after we pile into the car.

As we zip back through Newtown, my anger slowly fades. Of course, Sera is focused on Theron and Callias, making sure they're happy and unaware of my inferno raging inside me. There's a determination in her eyes, a fierce protectiveness that reminds me of someone else: Gram. Gram always defended me whenever I did anything my father disapproved of. And that's been Sera all along. She took us in when we had nowhere else to go. She saved me from Nyssa, and stood up to my father. How have I not seen it before?

Something stirs deep inside me as I watch Sera stroke Theron's dark curls. It's an odd feeling—one I don't think I've ever felt before. It's warm, full of longing and hope, and oddly, peace. I settle back in my seat as the feeling fills me up. It's nothing any amount of money or food could provide. It's better.

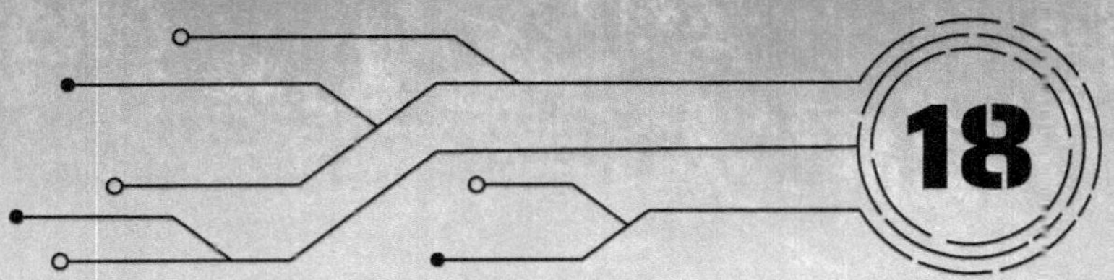

18

SNOWFLAKES DRIFT FROM THE SKY, blanketing the cobblestones of the square in a soft white powder. I sit on a stoop, knees drawn up to my chest, my breath bursting from my lips in glittering puffs. Theron and Callias run around the carts and stalls, their laughter easily the loudest of the bunch. There are other children too, chasing each other around, greying snowballs held in their tiny hands.

As they run, the hollow spaces beneath their clothes catch my eye more than their snow-dusted hair or wide grins. Some of the other kids must be older than Theron. But even with his thinning frame, Theron is easily the biggest. It's a sobering thought— these kids, shadows of what they should be, darting around with more joy than their little bodies should be able to hold. Theron hurls a snowball with more strength than I expect from his thin arms, and Callias's laughter fills the freezing air. They are completely unaware of how much they've changed.

It's been weeks since the winter gala—since my father tried to buy back his youngest sons like they're nothing more than property. Every time I think about it, it's like rubbing salt into a wound. But I've stayed strong. I haven't told Theron or Callias about what happened that night, even though both of them have asked. I don't even think Callias would understand—but Theron would. He takes things so personally, he'd let his anger toward our father consume him. I can't let that happen. Besides, I have enough hate for the three of us.

Gram has been on my mind a lot since that night. Of course, after my Renouncement, I was so focused on just surviving that I didn't have room for anything else. But after seeing my parents again, and the life I've been trying so desperately to reclaim, it's like I'm seeing the world with fresh eyes. Why would I want to go back to a place where people Renounce those closest to them, only to offer to buy them back? But seeing Theron and Callias playing in the square, free and full of joy ... I know I made the right choice. It's what Gram would have wanted. I'm not just looking out for myself.

Tonight, the apartment is so cold that I can see my breath curling in the air every time I exhale. We're all huddled together under a blanket Sera finally conceded to buy, though it's thin and riddled with holes. It's a poor shield against the chill that seeps into our bones, but it's better than nothing.

I lie here, trying to find warmth in the press of our bodies. Theron's thin form is against my chest, his deep breathing punctuated by coughs he can't shake. Callias is no better, constantly kicking off the blanket between raspy breaths. Each time he does, I reach over to pull it back up to his chin. I don't mind, really; it's not like I can sleep between the cold and all the coughing anyway.

The cold has a way of seeping into my bones, making me shiver, despite the warmth of my brothers' bodies against mine. Sera lies across from us, her silhouette barely visible in the darkness. Then, as I've seen her do countless times, she stirs. She slips out from the blanket without making a sound. She's out the door in seconds, her bare feet barely making a sound on the creaking floorboards.

My eyes narrow as the door bounces quietly in the warped doorframe. Really? Of all the nights she could have picked, she chooses this one? It doesn't make sense. I know I've given up on discovering Sera's nighttime activities; what she does is her business. But this... This is different. Sera's smart—almost too smart. Why is she going out into a blizzard in the dead of night with nothing but her sheet dress and bare feet?

Without thinking, I untangle myself from Theron and Callias

and pull on my thin shoes. Through the grimy window, I can see the snow falling as thick as ever. A shiver runs down my spine. I wish I had a coat, but Theron and Callias need the blanket more. I slip out the door, leaving it slightly ajar so I won't wake Theron and Callias.

The cold stings my face, and every breath is like breathing in shards of ice. It's not exactly hard to find where Sera went. Aside from a single line of bare footprints, the streets are a pristine blanket of snow. My insides quiver as the snow seeps through my shirt and shoes. How is Sera managing this? I can barely stand it, and I have shoes.

I push the thought away, focusing on Sera's trail as I weave between buildings and through alleys. The walls trap the wind, and the howling is so loud, I'm surprised that anyone can sleep through it. I cross my arms tightly over my chest, hoping it might provide some relief from the cold. It doesn't.

But the cold seeping into my bones isn't my only problem. Sera's prints disappear as I step onto one of the main roads. Here, the snow has been trampled by countless feet throughout the day, forming a solid sheet of ice. I look around, desperate for some sign of Sera. Why would she come this way? Then, I spot a single fresh footprint on the other side of the road, pointing toward the Fringe.

"What the hell?" I whisper, shoving my hands deeper into my pockets. The Fringe? Why would Sera go there, especially at this hour? It's not like she works the night shift in Midtown, and I've never seen her join those desperate enough to beg the Midtowners on the other side of the barrier. So, what is she up to?

I trudge through the snow toward the Fringe, my teeth chattering uncontrollably. The barrier looms ahead, its metal pillars standing like silent sentinels in the night, the invisible current between them all that stands between the Slum and Midtown. The only sound is the muffled crunch of snow beneath my soaked shoes and the low hum from the nearest pillar.

Sera's standing beside the pillars, her back to me. I press myself against the side of a ratty building, my heart pounding so fast that I'm surprised she can't hear it. What is she doing here? This isn't a crossing point. Besides, she's only cleared to cross during her work hours. So, why is she here?

Sera glances around cautiously before she pulls off her scarf —the black knit one she wears like a belt. She wraps it carefully around her forearm, covering her ID tag with several layers of the filthy fabric. She secures the scarf with a knot, once again looking over her shoulders. The action is deliberate, calculated. Clearly, she's done this before. After she brought Jewel to her apartment, I just assumed she spent her nights checking on the other people she cares about. But I never expected this. Why would she cover her tag? To trick the system? But the scanners read our tags even through fabric. I thought Sera was all about survival; taking unnecessary risks isn't like her at all.

My breath catches as Sera steps up to the barrier. She pauses for a heartbeat, then walks through as if the barrier isn't even there. My heart lurches. Any second now, she'll crumple to the ground, the electric current stunning her like it does to anyone who dares to cross without authorization. Enforcers will be here within a minute, and they'll take her away for who knows how long. How could Sera be this stupid?

But nothing happens. Sera just keeps walking into Midtown like it's the most natural thing in the world.

"What the—?" I mutter under my breath. My feet move before my brain can catch up, carrying me closer to the barrier. I stop short of crossing over, sliding on the snow-slick ground. Even though Sera crossed with ease, there's no way I can follow her. But how did she even do it?

"Sera!" I call out, not even bothering to keep my voice low.

She whirls around, her eyes wide with shock—and something else. Fear? Anger? It's hard to tell in the dim light.

"Ezariah? What are you doing here?!" Her voice is a hiss, carried away almost instantly by the wind.

I shake my head, trying to rid myself of the disbelief. "What am I doing? What are *you* doing? How'd you cross the barrier?"

Sera glances back at Midtown, then at me, biting her lip. "You need to go home," she says firmly. "Now."

"No." The word comes out stronger than I mean them to. My hands are shaking, but it's more from adrenaline than the cold. "I want answers, Sera. You owe me that much."

I see her face soften, but it hardens almost instantly. "Please," she says, "you shouldn't be involved in this."

"I'm already involved," I counter stubbornly. "I saw you cover your tag with your scarf and just… You walked through like it's nothing." My voice rises with every word, my frustration and worry boiling over. "Tell me what's going on."

Sera's eyes flick back and forth, like she's weighing her options. I can see the gears turning in her head, the same way they do when she's calculating how much food we can afford with our meager coins. But I don't budge. I need to know what she's up to, what kind of danger she might be getting herself into.

"I never told you why I was Renounced," she finally says, her voice barely above a whisper.

My arms drop limply to my sides. All this time, I've never thought to ask. We all have our stories, our scars from being tossed out like trash. But it's always felt too personal, too raw to dig into Sera's past. Now though, as I watch her struggle with the truth, I realize just how little I actually know about her.

"My mother," Sera starts, then stops as if the words are lodged in her throat. "She was … is … the head of our family. She was strict and controlling to a level you can't imagine." Her hands clench and unclench at her sides.

"Um, my father…"

"It's not the same," she says, cutting me off. "Your father's a piece of work, for sure—but he's nothing compared to my mom. She welded a tracking bracelet onto my wrist," Sera continues, her eyes darting to her bare wrist as if she can still feel the thing.

"It was like an ID tag, but for a child. She wanted to keep tabs on me all the time."

A chill that has nothing to do with the cold creeps over my arms. I've never heard of anything like that before. My father may be cruel and self-obsessed, but I could never imagine him welding a tracker to me. To be tracked every moment of your life... That's a level of control that makes even AURA seem benign.

"I hated it," Sera admits, and there's a fierceness in her voice that I've never heard before. "Newtown was worse than a cage for me. It was a prison. That's when I figured out that my scarf— *this* scarf..." She touches it gently. "... blocked the tracker's signal."

"And you used it to sneak into Midtown," I conclude, the pieces falling together almost perfectly.

"Yes." Sera nods slowly, and some of the hardness in her face melts away. "I wanted to be free. I'd go out to random bars in Midtown, and for a few hours, I wasn't trapped."

"What happened then?" I ask, my voice barely carrying above the howling wind. I've stepped as close to the barrier as I can, and even though there's only about a foot between Sera and me, it feels like she's miles away.

Sera's gaze drops to the snow, her shoulders hunching as if the weight of the memory is too much to bear. "I was careless," she says, her voice tinged with regret. "One night, the scarf slipped off my wrist while I was out. The Enforcers came. I don't know if it was a random check or because my mom knew where I was. Either way, they caught me before I even knew what was happening."

In my mind, I can almost imagine Sera, a younger, less starved version of the girl standing before me. I can see the Enforcers dragging her away, just like they did to me at Gram's funeral. My stomach twists at the thought.

"They took me home," she continues, and there's a bitterness in her words that cuts through the cold air. "My mother was waiting. She was so mad." Sera's soft blue eyes meet mine again, and they're like ice, hard and unforgiving. "She Renounced me on the spot. Didn't even let me explain or say goodbye."

The finality in her voice stings. Renouncement isn't just a punishment; it's a severing of all ties, a complete rejection by those who are supposed to love you unconditionally. My chest tightens with anger—not just at her mother, but at all of Newtown and its twisted values that can turn parents against their own children so easily.

"I'm sorry" is all I can manage to say—a pathetic response to the depth of the betrayal she must have felt.

Somehow, the cold seeping through my bones lessens as I stare at Sera. I realize I've always seen her as some kind of machine—perfect, constantly pushing forward under any circumstance. But she's not. In fact, she's more like me. Her mother Renounced her for simply wanting her freedom. I can't imagine what it must have been like to grow up like that. At least I had Gram to protect me from my father.

But Sera's story doesn't explain why she's out here now, crossing the barrier in the middle of a snowstorm.

"Sera," I start, my voice gentler now, "that's … that's rough. I'm so sorry. But… Why are you sneaking into Midtown now?"

For a moment, she hesitates, and I can almost see the wheels turning in her head again. Then, without a word, she unwraps the scarf from her arm and tosses it to me. It lands in the snow at my feet with a soft thud.

"Trust me," she says simply.

I pick up the scarf. It's heavy—heavier than I expected it to be. My hands tremble slightly as I wrap it around my forearm, covering the scar from my tag with layer after layer of knitted material. Excitement flutters in my chest, and it feels like there's no air in my lungs. I don't know why I'm so nervous; Sera just successfully crossed the barrier minutes ago, and nothing happened to her.

I take a deep breath, bracing myself for what might happen.

With one last look at Sera, close my eyes, and step forward. A low hum fills my ears as I pass the pillar, my every muscle tensed for the electric shocks. But they don't come. Slowly, I open my eyes. I'm now standing beside Sera on the Midtown side of the barrier.

"C'mon," Sera says, taking back her scarf.

It feels like I'm vibrating we navigate Midtown's streets, each step away from the Slum feeling like a breath of fresh air. The buildings here aren't like the ones I've grown used to; they're tall and clean, and there's no feeling of being trapped inside a crumbling maze.

I can't stop my hands from. Ever since my Renouncement, this is what I've wanted: to escape the suffocating Slum and join a world where there's a chance for something better. And here it is, right in front of me. If I could just stay here, everything would be perfect. With Sera's scarf, my life in the Slum could be a thing of the past.

My eyes lock on Sera; now a few paces ahead of me. Sera can leave the Slum whenever she wants. Unlike everyone else there, she's not trapped. So, why would she stay?

"Sera, where are we going?" I ask, unable to keep it in any longer. "You're not taking me to a bar, are you?"

Sera laughs, a genuine sound that surprises me with its lightness. "I haven't done that since I was Renounced," she says, shaking her head.

Her words stir something inside me—admiration, maybe, or a kind of kinship I hadn't realized was there. Either way, she still hasn't explained what we're doing in Midtown. In our ragged clothes, we stick out like a sore thumb. If anyone sees us, we're dead.

"So, what are we doing here?" I ask. "Why cross the barrier at all?"

We turn down a darker street, and Sera doesn't say a word. She glances at me, and I can tell she's contemplating sharing something. Clearly, there's still more to her story. But why is she holding back? She knows all the grim details of my own past. Does she think I'll judge her?

"When Jewel found me after I was mugged, I had nothing," she begins slowly, not meeting my eyes. "No money, no food. I had to survive however I could. So, I used my scarf to get into Midtown ... and I robbed a house."

"You *what*?!" I stop dead in my tracks. Of all the things she could have said, I wasn't expecting this. Sera, a thief?

"I did what I had to do," Sera says, her voice remaining calm. "I mean, I barely earn any credits at the factory. Everyone in the Slum does shady things to get by. You did."

Sera's words hang in the frosty air, and it's like I've been punched in the stomach. The Sera I thought I knew—she wouldn't do something like that. But the Sera I thought I knew wasn't her at all.

I look at her—really look at her—and see the shadows beneath her eyes, the lines of strain around her mouth. She is survival in its rawest form, and who am I to judge? I worked for Nyssa, broke up fights for money, and fought in a fight club. I'm no saint.

"Sera," I start, my voice rough with emotion, "I ... I'm sorry. I know what it's like to be desperate."

She turns to me, her soft blue eyes searching mine. There's a vulnerability there that I've never seen before. "It's okay,' she says quietly. "You didn't know. But now, you know everything. I have no more secrets with you."

Sera's fingers lace through mine, and my insides give an unexpected flutter. She pulls me through the clean snowplowed streets. Soon, we turn into what must be a neighborhood. Unlike the chaotic clutter of the Slum, here there's space to breathe between the homes, each one standing proudly with its own patch of cleared ground. Sera stops in front of a modest two-story house, its windows dark and uninviting. Five of these houses could easily fit in the home I grew up in, but compared to her apartment, it might as well be a palace. Her thin frame easily slips through the front gate. She turns back to me, her silhouette framed by the metal bars.

"Don't come if you don't want to," she says, her voice barely above a whisper.

I know I should be afraid—we could get caught at any second—but all I feel is a strange sense of excitement. I take a shaky breath and glance back at the empty street behind me. Does Sera really want me to come with her?

Before my mind has even formed an answer, I step forward and easily pass between the metal bars.

I follow Sera as she runs around the house and opens the back door, which is unlocked. I don't have time to question how she knew it would be unlocked as she slips inside. The halls are shrouded in darkness, and the silence is almost suffocating. I feel my pulse in my throat, each heartbeat like a drum in the quiet.

"Stay close," Sera whispers, her hand finding mine again.

We move in silence, the moonlight filtering through the tall windows. The place is filled with shadows that could easily be mistaken for furniture—or people. Every creak of a floorboard makes me want to run. But Sera's grip on my hand keeps my fears at bay.

In the living room, Sera heads straight for a bookshelf lined with various knickknacks. She picks up a small ceramic figurine —a dog covered in small gemstones—and slips it into the overlapping folds of her sheet dress. I pick up another trinket. My first thought is that they're gaudy—a clear sign of a Midtowner attempting to show off their growing wealth. In Newtown, such displays are seen as a clear sign of desperation.

We continue through the house, taking only what we can easily hide on our person. I slip a pair of cuff links from a dresser into my pocket, as well as an old watch that no longer ticks. There are so many items that I doubt the owners will even notice they're gone when they come home.

With each trinket I pocket, my heart thunders a little faster. But it's not because I'm taking things that don't belong to me, even though that may have something to do with it. Tonight, I feel more alive than I have in months. The thrill of potentially being caught is almost intoxicating. Is this how Sera feels every time she crosses into Midtown?

We don't stay more than five minutes. Before I know it, Sera's pulling me from the house, the cold air biting my skin as we run back to the barrier. She crosses first, her scarf wrapped around her tag. Then she throws it across the barrier, but as I reach out to grab it, the fabric slips between my numb fingers. I quickly snatch the scarf from the snowy ground. I start wrapping it around my tag, but stop. The grimy black fabric looks different in the moonlight, almost cleaner. Has Sera ever bothered to wash it? I narrow my eyes, looking more closely at the fabric. Woven into the material are strands of glittering golden thread no thicker than a strand of hair.

My mouth falls open as I look from the scarf to Sera. It's easily worth ten times what we just stole. In the moonlight, the golden strands glisten like stars. They must be what's blocking the signals from our tags. But how is that possible?

My heart races as I step back into the Slum. I slip the scarf from my forearm and return it to Sera.

I see her eyes narrow as they fall on the strands of glittering thread now shining in the night. "Damn." Sera turns slowly on the spot, her eyes trained on the ground. I'm about to ask what she's looking for when she throws the scarf into a nearby pothole. The fabric sinks into the grimy freezing water before Sera retrieves it, wringing it out. She returns the damp scarf to her waist, and it looks just as black and filthy as it used to.

We make our way back through the twisted alleys, neither one of us saying a word. Sera stops as we reach the square, and I follow her lead, stopping just outside the expanse of cobblestones. She turns to me, and in the flickering light from a nearby streetlamp, I see her face clearly for the first time since we left Midtown. There's a softness there I haven't noticed before—or maybe I just haven't been looking?

"Thank you," she says, her voice barely above a whisper. "For following me."

I nod, unable to find my own words. But as I search her eyes, I know she's not just thanking me for a successful theft. There's more to it than that. Because I followed her, Sera has showed me who she is—who she really is. She let me in, and that's something I don't think she's ever done before.

"I should be thanking you," I say, my voice cracking slightly. "You've been there for Theron, for Callias … for me. You … you saved me."

"And I'd do it again." Sera steps closer, and I can feel her breath on my freezing skin. "Even though you're a pain most of the time."

My hand finds her cheek, and to my surprise, she leans into my touch. Our lips meet, tentative at first, but more hungrily a heartbeat later. The feel of her lips on mine fills me up, driving away even the bitter cold. Nothing else matters. Not my Renouncement. Not the Slum. Not everything I've endured. Right now, it's just us, and that's enough.

We pull apart, and Sera's words float to me through the haze of my own happiness. She's talking about waiting a few hours to go to Bart's to sell what we stole, but I can barely hear her. My head is swimming with a joy that I haven't felt in so long. It feels foreign, almost wrong. Yet it fills every crevice of my being.

I open the door to her apartment as quietly as I can. We slip inside, careful not to make a sound. The morning chill seeps into my bones as I stand over Theron and Callias, still cloaked beneath the thin blanket. I reach down, nudging Theron's shoulder.

"Hey, wake up," I whisper, trying not to startle him. There's no response. A smile tugs at my lips; they're pretending to be asleep.

"Come on, time to wake up," I say a bit louder, my annoyance creeping in as I shake Callias gently.

From the doorway, Sera's laughter breaks through the silence. "Give them a minute," she says. "It's still early."

Ignoring her, I reach under the blanket for Callias, my voice firm. "Get up, Cal." But there's no squirming, no sleepy protest. I nudge Theron, but he too is still. "C'mon, Theron, wake up," I urge, my fingers dancing across his back. But he still doesn't move.

Something isn't right. I pull my hand from beneath the blanket, and Theron's arm flops to the ground, ghostly and blue. My insides freeze as I stare at his little fingers.

"Theron?" My voice cracks as I rip back the blanket. Why is their skin so pale? They're curled up around each other, their lips a deep, dark blue.

"No, no, no…" I mutter, grabbing Theron's shoulders, which feel like ice in my hands. "Theron! Callias! Wake up!"

I drop to the floor, pulling my brothers into my lap. They're sleeping. Surely, they're both just sleeping. But Theron is like a doll, his limbs flopping this way and that as my arms tremble. I hear Sera's voice, but it's oddly muffled and distant. All I can do is hold my brothers close. I collapse, falling to my side as white-hot tears stream down my cheeks and onto the still-peaceful faces of Theron and Callias.

PART THREE

THE SPRING

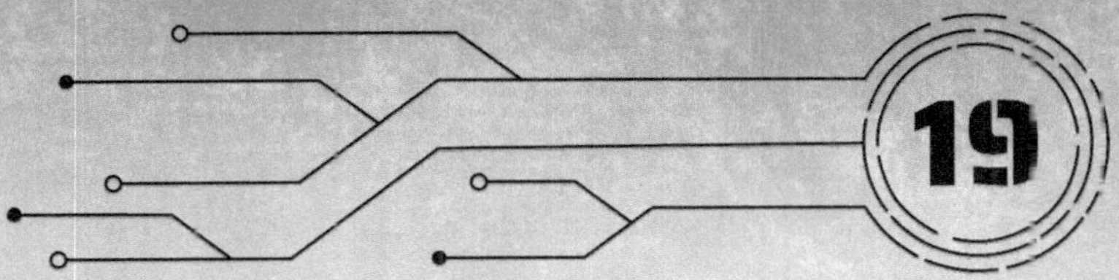

PALE SUNLIGHT FILTERS through the grimy window, casting a faint glow over the apartment. The cold seeps from the floor into my bones, but I barely notice. All that matters is Theron and Callias, still held tightly in my arms. Their faces are so calm, so peaceful. It's like they're sleeping, lost in a world of dreams.

But this is no dream. It's a nightmare.

How long has it been since I found them? Minutes? Years? A lifetime? Whatever it is, it doesn't matter. Nothing matters anymore.

Tears slide down my face, stinging against the chill of the room. "I'm sorry," I whisper into the silence, my voice breaking with each word. "Wake up. Please. Don't leave me here…"

But my brothers can no longer hear me. I pull them closer, waiting, praying for them to respond. Pressed against my chest, their bodies feel oddly small, as if everything that made them slipped away like shadows in the night. My brothers don't stir, and their stillness is more painful than anything I've known.

Somehow, Sera's cramped apartment feels even smaller, claustrophobic. Every inch of the rough wooden walls creaks with memories—Theron's mischievous grin, Callias's bright-eyed wonder. Things I'll never see again. This is my fault; I see that now. I shake with sobs that threaten to rip me in two. If I hadn't been so obsessed with following Sera, if I'd just stayed home, maybe this wouldn't have…

My chest tightens, and every breath feels like I'm breathing in glass. I failed them. I couldn't protect them from the Slum, from the hunger, from the cold. Everything they've endured, up to the very end, was all because of me. And now, without Theron and Callias, I have nothing left.

The door creaks open, the sound grating against the silence. I hear my name—Sera's voice. It's like an echo, distant and strange, a sound from another life. I can't bring myself to answer.

Sera's face appears beside me, but it's fuzzy and out of focus. I squeeze my eyes shut. I can't hear her now. Not now.

"Ezariah." Her voice cracks as my name leaves her lips. My eyes open as I feel her hand on my shoulder, but it's like a touch from another world—one where things aren't broken beyond repair.

"We ... we can't leave them here," she says, her eyes puffy and bloodshot. "We need to move them."

Move Theron and Callias? Somewhere, deep inside me, a tiny spark of anger burns through my undying grief. Why would we take Theron and Callias from here? This tiny apartment... It's their home. It's where they belong. Why would Sera try to take that from them?

"No," I choke out, the word strangled and. My arms tighten around Theron and Callias, as if I can somehow keep them with me if I just hold on long enough.

"Ezariah, we have to."

My arms shake around my brothers. Sera doesn't get it. She's used to having nothing. But me—I've always had Theron and Callias. How am I supposed to let go of the only thing I have left —the thing that kept me fighting? How do you say goodbye when it feels like your soul is being crushed?

"I can't," I whisper, unable to meet Sera's eyes. "I just ... can't."

"Ezariah, you have to let them go."

I can't. I won't. After everything we've been through, I can't let Theron and Callias go now.

Sera's hand reappears on my shoulder. Her touch is gentle,

no doubt meant to comfort me. I shrug it off. Can't she see that I don't want her here? If I talk to her, I'd have to open my eyes, and that's something I can't face. Not now.

"We're running out of time," she says, her voice cracking. "The dead… They have no place in the Slum. No matter how much we want to keep them here."

Every part of me wants to explode. Clearly, Sera didn't care about Theron and Callias as much as I thought. She didn't love them. If she did, she wouldn't say this to me. I don't care about the stupid Slum or how things are done here. All I care about is my brothers.

My gaze drifts to Theron and Callias, their hollow cheeks, the skin that clings to their bones like wet paper. They look so small, so fragile. It's as if the Slum drained away every ounce of their spirit, their joy. The sight of them drives all the fight out of me. There's no sign of my brothers in the bodies held in my arms. All I see is hunger snuffed out by the cold.

As gently as I can, I return Theron and Callias to the sleeping mat. I push myself up, and surprisingly, I'm able to stand. I look into Sera's tear-filled eyes, but the sight stirs nothing inside me. I'm empty—as hollow as the bodies I placed on the floor.

"Fine," I mutter.

Sera picks up the thin, tattered blanket from beside the sleeping mat. My throat tightens as she shakes it out, laying it on what little floor we have left. Sera only let us buy it just last week, when the snow started to fall thick and fast. Theron had been so excited. Finally, after months without a blanket, we'd finally had one to keep us warm. If only he'd known how wrong he was.

Sera moves toward Theron and Callias, but stops. She looks at me, and her eyes are full of tears. In another life, her expression might have stirred something in me. But not today.

She's looking for something—a word, a nod, a look. She wants me to tell her it's okay to start. The thought sends a shudder down my spine.

Sera's fingers find mine, and she pulls me forward. It feels like I'm underwater. Everything is distorted—the sounds muffled, the world blurry. Together, we lift Theron's frail body from the sleeping mat and place him on the blanket before moving to Callias. I stare at the wall, determined not to look down. Between the two of us, they're lighter than air. We fold the frayed edges neatly around them, and it's like I'm tucking in their icy bodies for another night. It's a relief when their faces finally disappear beneath the fabric.

"We'll take care of them," she whispers, taking my hand. Her grip is firm, but it's not enough to stop my hands from shaking.

I stand there, numb, as Sera tells me it's time to lift my brothers. Her voice is urgent, but it's like she's speaking from the end of a long tunnel. I can't find the words to respond, to tell her that I'm not ready—that I'll never be ready. So, I stay silent.

Sera squats beside the neat little bundle we made. She looks at me with eyes that say everything words can't. *"We need to do this,"* they tell me. *"Whether you're ready or not."*

I doubt I'll ever be ready. I stoop down, my heart feeling like it's made of lead, and together, we lift Theron and Callias. Even in my state, I'm surprised by how light they feel. They weigh almost nothing in my arms, their bodies limp as we carry them from the apartment. The door groans as we pass through it, leaving behind the small room that's been our sanctuary.

The square is empty when we step. A fresh dusting of snow covers the cobblestones, masking the footprints Sera and I made last night. There are no stalls set up, no Slummers trying to pawn off what they dug out of the refinery. The silence is deafening, leaving me with only the pounding in my chest. The cold stings my face as the snow crunches beneath our feet. I can feel Sera's eyes on me, but I can't bring myself to look at her. Instead, I focus on a hole in the blanket. I see Callias's tangled mop of hair through the rip, and the pain is worse than anything I've ever felt.

I want to stop, but Sera keeps going. Where is she taking us?

The words claw up my throat, but I can't make my lips form the question. Honestly, I don't know if I want to hear the answer.

A creaking noise breaks the silence as a cart pulled by two Slummers trundles into the square. Sera stops, and I do the same, sliding on the icy ground. The cart is rickety and worn down, like everything else around here, but it's very large. A hole-riddled tarp is draped over the back, flapping in the freezing breeze.

Even in my state, I know it's odd to see scavengers out. I doubt there's anything useful to be found at the refinery; no doubt the snow ruined any salvageable food. Even now, the snow is still falling, blanketing everything in a hush. Yet here they are, dragging their rickety cart through the streets. But why come to the square? Of all the places in the Slum, it's always the most picked over.

The cart stops a few feet ahead of us, its wheels groaning against the packed ice.

"It's time." Sera's voice cuts through the cold air like a knife.

Time? Time for what? My mind races as fury bubbles up inside me like lava as I see Sera's eyes fall on the cart. She can't be serious. I thought we were taking Theron and Callias somewhere safe. But no. Sera wants me to throw my brothers into this … this garbage heap on wheels.

The Slummers don't notice my growing rage—or if they do, they don't care. And why would they? One of them reaches for the tarp with gnarled hands and pulls it back.

My breath catches in my throat as I stare at the wrapped bundles filling the cart. Bodies. This cart isn't carrying trash at all; it's full of people, piled up without a second thought. This is where Sera intends to put Theron and Callias—just two more bodies to add to the heap.

My stomach lurches, and I feel like I'm going to be sick. The cold has seeped into my bones, but this… This sight burns hotter than any fire inside me.

"No!" The word explodes out of me, raw and ragged. "We can't… I'm not putting them in there."

Sera's eyes narrow as she adjusts her grip on my brothers. "Ezariah, this is how it's done here."

"No," I repeat, white-hot tears burning my frozen face. I cannot accept that this is the only fate for my brothers. Even Gram, with her ornate mausoleum and poorly attended funeral, had a better send-off than this. No one deserves to be thrown into a cart and forgotten for the rest of time.

"There has to be another way," I plead, my voice barely above a whisper.

Her eyes meet mine, and I see the pain in them—but Sera's pain is nothing compared to mine. "There isn't," she says softly. "I wish there was, but in the Slum … we take care of our own until the end."

It's not enough. Nothing will ever be enough to make this right. But as I look at Sera, seeing the resolve in her face, I know there's no changing her mind. This is how it must be done. So, even though it feels like I'm ripping my heart in two, I nod.

Together, we approach the cart, and with hands that don't feel like my own, Sera and I lift Theron and Callias into it. We place them gently on the pile—the pile of people who were loved, who mattered to someone. But now, they're nothing more than nameless, faceless bundles, bound for whatever final resting place the Slum provides.

The cart creaks away the moment Theron and Callias leave my hands. But as it rumbles over the cobblestones, a gust of frosty wind catches the edge of our tattered blanket. It slips, revealing Theron and Callias's pale faces. If I didn't know any better, I'd have said they were sleeping. But I do know better, and the sight of their faces cuts deeper than any wound.

I lurch forward, chasing after the cart as if my life depends on it. My feet slip on the icy cobblestones, but still, I don't stop. I can't.

The cart jolts to a halt, but I'm too close to do the same. I crash into the worn wood, but the pain feels subdued, like a memory of pain. Awkwardly, I pull myself up. I think the Slummers pulling the cart say something, but I don't care. Gently, I run my shaking hands over Theron's and Callias's overgrown hair. My lips touch Theron's cold forehead. Callias's sallow skin is just as icy, the memory of his laughter echoing through me. Slowly, I pull the blanket back over their faces, shielding them from the world they never should have known. But as I step back, my fingers cling to the fabric, every fiber of my being screaming against letting go.

"Goodbye."

The cart groans as it rolls forward, carrying Theron and Callias away from me forever. My knees buckle, and the cobblestones are cold and hard against my legs. But there's no pain—no anger, even. As I watch the cart disappear, all I feel is a vast emptiness consuming my insides. Tears carve icy trails down my cheeks, but even they bring no relief. Why would they? I've lost everything that ever mattered.

I'm not entirely sure when Sera appears at my side. But she's there, her hand on my back, her whisper barely able to break through the numbness. "C'mon, let's go home," she says, pulling gently on my arm.

Home? The word feels strange to my ears. I have no home—not without Theron and Callias's laughter echoing off the rough wooden walls. Besides, that tiny room isn't a home anymore. It's a tomb—a place where my brothers slowly starved right under my nose.

"You need to get out of the cold," Sera says, her voice edged with worry.

Slowly, I stand, my legs trembling from the combined and something much worse. The square spins around me, a whirl of grey and white as the snow continues to fall. Sera reaches for me again, but I step back. Her face falls, and I think she says something else. But I can't hear her—not now. I'm the reason my brothers are gone. Sure, the lack of food and biting cold didn't help, but in the end it was all me. I don't deserve her pity.

Without another word, I turn from Sera—from everything that once was. She calls after me, but I don't stop. There's nothing left for me here—not in the apartment where my brothers died, not in the square where my brothers played. So, I walk on, letting grief lead me wherever it may—anywhere but here.

My feet drag over the cobblestones, the snow muffling my heavy steps. I'm a ghost haunting these streets, hollow and invisible. Emptiness consumes me, and the world is nothing more than shades of grey. Slummers hurry past me, their laughter and voices a distant hum, their shapes just a passing blur. I don't know where I'm going, nor do I care. Time loses all meaning as the image of the cart taking my brothers away plays over and over again in my mind. All I know is the void inside me, the place where my brothers' smiles once lived.

A sudden cacophony of laughter and music pierces my sorrow, like a hook through my gut. I blink, and it takes a few seconds for my vision to clear. But slowly, I take in the cracked walls and worn front door. I'm outside Nyssa's place. Sounds of revelry—laughter, clinking glasses, and the odd hum of music— seep from the boarded-up windows.

A flare of rage ignites in my chest, filling the deep void inside me. How can they celebrate? How can their world keep spinning while mine is shattered? Don't they know what I've lost? What the world has lost? Their laughter is a slap to my face, mocking the silence that can never be filled without Theron and Callias. My hands ball into fists, and pain radiates through my palms as my nails dig into my skin.

The door creaks open, and light spills out onto the street. Rowan steps out, her face flushed, her blonde braid swaying loosely around her. She spots me immediately, her brow furrowing in confusion.

"Ezra? What are you doing here?" she asks, stepping closer.

Normally, I'd feel a twinge of annoyance at her refusal to use my real name. But today, for some reason, I don't mind. Ezariah has suffered enough, but Ezra doesn't know any of his pain.

But I can't answer her; there are no words powerful enough to describe what I'm feeling. I turn to leave, to return to the shadows of the Slum, where grief and sadness thrive.

Rowan moves faster than I thought possible. Her hand grips my arm with surprising strength, her fingers digging into my flesh through my thin, soaking shirt. I stare at the fabric. When did I get wet?

"Come on," she says firmly, pulling me toward the door

I resist, but only halfheartedly. There's no point fighting—not anymore. Rowan drags me inside the house, where I feel out of place amongst the warmth and light.

The front room is packed with people crowded around tables, playing cards, laughing too loudly. The air is thick with smoke and a stale smell that that I cannot shake. Rowan shoves me down onto an old couch, its springs creaking in protest. She squats down in front of me, her eyes narrowing as she stares into my face.

Her voice cuts through the noise. "Why are you here, Ezra?"

I can't bring myself to say it. Saying it would make it real, and I'm not ready for that. Not yet—maybe not ever. I stare at my shoes, which are soaked and covered in grime. How long was I walking out there?

"Ezra?" Rowan shakes my knee with all the subtlety of a hammer. I squeeze my lips, determined to hold myself together. "Ezra, talk to me."

A shadow looms over us, and I look up. Nyssa is standing behind Rowan, her face wearing that same unreadable expression she always wears. Somewhere deep inside me, I feel a pang. I haven't seen Nyssa since that night at the Hollow. I honestly never thought I'd see her again.

"Rowan," Nyssa says, her voice firm, "that's enough. Leave us."

Rowan does as Nyssa says, and my insides relax slightly. The girl casts me a worried glance before melting into the crowd.

I expect Nyssa to follow Rowan, so it's a surprise when she sits beside me, the couch dipping under our combined weight. Luckily, she doesn't say anything. She just sits there, staring at her crew as they continue with their merriment. Then she lifts a bottle and hands it to me.

I look at the bottle—the way the dim light dances through the amber liquid—and back at Nyssa.

"I heard about your brothers" is all she says.

The words hit me like a physical blow. Unable to speak, I bring the bottle shakily to my lips. The liquid burns as it slides down my throat, but it's nothing compared to the pain threatening to consume me.

"For what it's worth, I'm sorry, Ezariah," Nyssa says. "Those little ones deserved better."

I take another swig. The warmth from the drink spreads through me, burning away some of my grief. Nyssa's right: my brothers did deserve better. They deserved more than to be taken away in a cart full of bodies. They deserved to live in a world where it isn't a struggle not to starve and where parents don't throw away their kids. They deserved a brother who could take care of them better than I did.

Everything blurs around me as I continue to drink. The noises fade to dull hums, and the edges of my vision grow fuzzy. I don't even notice as Nyssa's crew packs up their cards, their laughter and chatter receding into the background like a fading dream.

"Rowan," Nyssa says, her voice oddly distant, "take Ezariah home."

Home? The word echoes in my spinning head. I don't have a home—not anymore. A home is where a family lives. Sera's place stopped being my home the moment I let my brothers die.

"C'mon, Ezra," Rowan says, her arm sliding beneath my armpit. "Let's go."

"No," I choke, my voice ragged as panic constricts my chest. I can't go back there. I won't.

Nyssa's eyes meet mine, and there's something like understanding in their dark depths. I take another sip from the bottle, and the liquid burns away some of my fear. She knows why I can't go back there. She knows what I've done, after all.

"Fine," Nyssa says, her gaze shifting to Rowan. "Bring him along."

Relief washes over me as I take another drink. At least for now, I'm safe from Sera's apartment. The thought is enough to keep me from falling apart.

The world spins, and I'm floating in its wake. Rowan's grip on me is the only anchor keeping me from slipping into the abyss. I can't tell if my feet are dragging along, or even if they're moving at all. We leave Nyssa's place and start walking the dark, cold alleys. How long has it been since I got here? My head lolls on my shoulders as Rowan half drags me through the snowy streets. My feet slide on the slick ground, and a giggle escapes my lips. It sounds odd to my ears. Rowan says something, but it sounds like she's underwater. I giggle again.

The sounds reach me first—the roar of a crowd, punctuated by harsh shouts and the unmistakable smack of flesh against flesh. My stomach churns as we draw closer, and it hits me with a jolt that sparks through my stupor: Nyssa is taking us to the Hollow.

We slip inside, the warmth from the packed bodies a stark contrast to the biting cold outside. The chaotic noise pounds against my skull, and my temples throb painfully. I blink, trying to focus as Rowan leads me through the crowd. Through the tangle of legs and torsos jostling for a view, I catch a glimpse of the pit. Two figures circle each other, their breath forming misty clouds in the harsh light. One fighter lunges, but his opponent is faster. Her fist connects with her opponent's jaw with a sickening crunch, and he falls to the ground in a cloud of dust.

The violence grips me, pulling the world into sharper focus. Each thud, each grunt of pain, is a jolt to my senses. I stare at the victor as she raises her fists, the cheer of the crowd filling my ears. It's raw, brutal—life stripped down to its bones.

"Next fighter!" a voice cuts through the cheers. "Nyssa Yarrow!"

My head lulls up, and my blurry eyes slowly lock on Nyssa. She's standing by the ladder to the pit, removing her tattered outer shirt. The crowd chants her name, and the sound ignites something in my addled mind. Excitement? Fear? Desire? Whatever it is, it's better than what I've been feeling. Anything is better than that.

Before I know it, I'm staggering forward, the world tilting on its axis. I grab Nyssa's wrist, and her eyes narrow dangerously.

"Lemme fight," I say, my words slurring together. "I wanna do it."

"Ezra, you're drunk," Rowan says, stepping between me and Nyssa. "Back off."

Rowan's right: I am definitely drunk. But that makes it really easy to tune her out. Nyssa's gaze meets mine, and there's a long moment where the only thing I can hear is the ragged sound of my own breathing. What's she going to do? I can never tell what's going on in Nyssa's head.

"Alright," Nyssa says slowly, her voice cutting through the din.

Cheers fill my ears as I stumble down the ladder into the pit, each step an effort to stay upright. My head is swimming, and the noise around me becomes a distorted symphony. However, I do hear the name "Ezra! Ezra!" bouncing off the walls, chanted by voices I don't recognize.

I squint, trying to focus on the figure across from me. He's well built for a Slummer, with shoulders like boulders and arms as thick as my head. I raise my hands, trying to mirror his stance, but I can't stop my legs from wobbling. Then somewhere, I hear a bell ring. My opponent lunges, his arm darting forward like a snake. I blink as his fist draws nearer. What am I supposed to do? Dodge? Strike back?

His fist connects with my stomach. I gasp, doubling over as all the air is forced from my lungs. The crowd's cheering fades, replaced by a sustained, high-pitched ringing. Pain explodes in my shoulder, and I stagger backward. I swing my arm wildly, but it's like moving through molasses. My opponent easily side-steps me, and in one fluid motion, he swings his leg into my ribs. My legs wobble beneath me as I try to regain my balance, my vision turning fuzzy.

My opponent kicks out again, this time hitting my stomach. I feel my feet slide out from beneath me, and I fall. I slam into the hard packed earth, but oddly, the pain just feels like a dull throbbing. I look up just in time to see the man's fist hurtling toward my temple. My head snaps to the side, stars exploding across my vision. Next thing I know, I'm lying in the dirt as something trickles down my face. The world tilts dangerously as I lie there, pain radiating through my skull.

Hands grab me under the arms and drag me out of the ring as the crowd's enthusiasm fades to a distant buzz. Rowan's face swims before me, while the ground feels like a boat rocked by the waves. My stomach lurches, and I retch, the mixture of alcohol and stomach acid burning my throat and nose. My entire body convulses as I vomit again, and this time tears burn my eyes. Someone pats me on the back—Rowan, I think—and I look up. Nyssa towers over me, her silhouette blurry but unmistakable.

"Had enough?" Her voice is almost gentle, like she's speaking to a small child.

I shake my head, and my stomach threatens to empty itself for a third time. My skull is throbbing, and my muscles ache, but as I lie here, an odd sense of calm washes over me. For the briefest of moments in the ring, I was just Ezra, getting beaten to a pulp. I wasn't Ezariah, whose brothers died because of his incompetence. For a few fleeting minutes, under the floodlights and shouts of the crowd, I was free—free from the pain now welling up inside me. And I liked it.

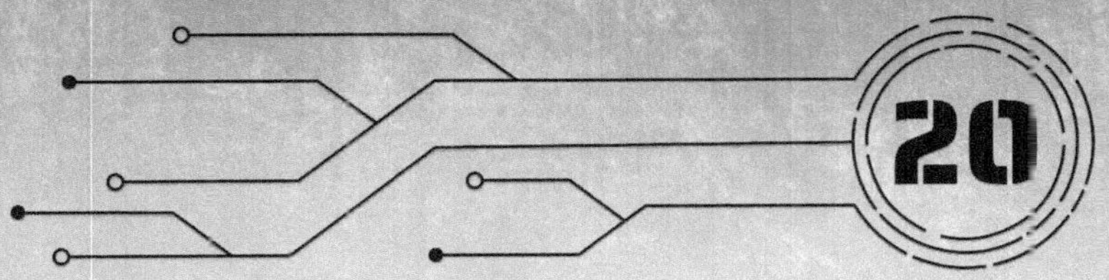

20

I SPRINT ACROSS THE FIELD, the tall grass tickling my legs. The sun is high, its rays warming my face. Theron and Callias laugh as they zip back and forth, their shouts mingling with the rustling leaves. I smile as I chase after them, careful not to close the gap between us. Not yet, anyway.

"Come on, Ezariah! Bet you can't catch us!" Theron shouts, his eyes gleaming as he darts behind a massive bush covered in pink blossoms.

Callias joins in, "Yeah, Ezariah! Too slow!"

I let out a dramatic yell that's more like a growl. Their squeals fill the air as they each dart in a different direction. It's a real struggle to keep my face serious. After all, I'm supposed to be the "bad guy," and according to Callias, bad guys aren't happy.

"Alright, you asked for it!" I call out, breaking into a run. "Here I come!"

I fly over the grass, my heart pounding in my ears. Theron screams and zips through the undergrowth until he's easily out of my reach. But I'm not going for Theron; he's always been faster than me. Callias, with his short legs and wild grin, is a much easier target.

"You can't get away!" I shout.

Callias's cry is a mixture of a shriek and a giggle. He pumps his little arms, but it's no good. I'm gaining on him, and he'll be mine in seconds. Just as he looks over his shoulder, I reach out and grab him by the waist. He yelps in surprise, then erupts into fits of laughter, squirming as I swing him around.

"Gotcha!" Callias wriggles like a fish in my arms, laughing as I spin him around. "I win!"

Theron runs circles around us, smiling as sweat shines on his brow. "My turn! My turn!"

Grinning, I set Callias down and hoist up Theron by his—

MY EYES SNAP OPEN. For a moment, I'm frozen, unable to move. The pounding in my ears drowns out everything else as I try to catch my breath. It was so real this time. I look down and I can almost feel Theron in my arms. It's like he was just here. But I know better. My brothers are gone, and they're never coming back.

A groan escapes my lips as my head throbs painfully. I cover my face with my arms, trying not to look at the cracked ceiling. Why did I have to wake up?

With some effort, I push myself up, wincing as pain shoots through my ribs. The room tilts dangerously, and I clamp my mouth shut, willing the world to stop spinning. Why hasn't it gotten better? It's been a month since I started crashing at Nyssa's—one month of getting myself beaten raw every night in the Hollow. But no matter what I do, I can't escape them. No matter how hard I try, Theron and Callias are there whenever I close my eyes.

I run a hand through my greasy tangle of hair and reach for one of the many bottles scattered across the floor. After all this time, the liquid does nothing more than warm me up. It's not enough to numb the pain, physical or otherwise, but it does take the edge off, even if just for a little while.

The door bangs open, bouncing off the cracked wall. Light floods the room, chasing away the darkness. I squint, raising an arm to shield myself from the harsh reality. A small figure marches to the window and grabs the worn blinds. I try to roll away, but I'm too slow. The morning sun stabs my eyes, and I bury my face in the crook of my arm.

"God, Rowan," I groan. "Take it easy."

"This isn't your personal crash pad, you know." Rowan's voice cuts through my haze. "If you don't like it, you can always go home."

I roll over, turning my back to her and pressing my face into the lumpy couch. It smells like sweat, dust, and old booze, but at least it's dark. Why would Rowan think I'd go back there? No matter how she barks at me, my answer hasn't changed. If I never set foot in that tiny, cramped apartment, with its worn wooden walls haunted by the laughter I'll never hear again, I'd be okay with that.

"I'm fine right here."

"Clearly," she says dryly. I hear her footsteps creak over the floorboards, and I brace myself for whatever she has in store. "C'mon, Ezra. Get up." Rowan grabs my ankle and pulls. For such a little girl, she's surprisingly strong—or maybe I just don't put up a fight. Either way, I slide off the couch, my graveyard of empty bottles scattering in every direction.

"Ow," I mutter, rubbing my throbbing hip.

"Oh, boo-hoo," Rowan says flatly. "Like you said, you're fine. And if you leave now, you can actually make it to work today."

"I'll get there when I get there." I grab a bottle off the floor. I'm not sure how long it's been sitting there, but there are still a few gulps of clear liquid lolling in the bottom. It's better than nothing.

"Uh-huh. That would require you being conscious before noon," Rowan huffs. "Well, if you're just gonna lie here, you could clean yourself up. You reek worse than the refinery."

I take another drink. Why does Rowan care if I go to work or not? It's not like I have any use for it now. I only took the job to make money to keep Theron and Callias...

Wham. It's like I've been hit in the chest. Tears sting my eyes, and my breathing becomes shallow and shaky. I close my eyes and bring the bottle to my lips until there's nothing left. The alcohol burns through me, and my heartbeat slows a little.

"I ran into Sera on my way here," Rowan says as she picks up several of my empty bottles. "She asked about you again."

My arms tense, and my blood turns cold. Anger swirls inside me, threatening to explode. I find another mostly empty bottle, and it tempers the storm a little. Why can't Sera just leave me alone? Almost every day, Rowan says something about Sera wanting to see me. Can't she take a hint? I don't want to see her. I can't.

"Drop it, okay?" I say sharply.

"You can't avoid her forever—"

"Watch me."

Rowan's lips part, a retort at the ready, but then the back door creaks open, and the words die in her throat. Nyssa steps into the room, her eyes flitting from Rowan to me, squatting on the dirty floor, surrounded by my mess of bottles. I sigh. Nyssa is the only person who can get Rowan to stop when she's on a roll.

"Ezariah," she says slowly, "make yourself useful and take this to Bart."

Nyssa holds out what must have been a piece of paper in a former life. With a grunt, I push myself up and take the note. It's so wrinkled and worn that it feels more like cloth. Several notes have been scribbled and crossed out all over it. I hate delivery duty. I don't even work for Nyssa anymore, but she still gives me a random task every couple of days. But if I do it, she won't complain about me staying at her house.

I stumble through the streets, a bottle swinging loosely in my grip. I squint against the sun, which feels somehow brighter than usual, my head pounding with every step. The Slummers I pass don't even try to hide their stares, all giving me a wide berth. I can't help but laugh. Slummers avoiding me? What a joke.

I'm not sure when I notice the pain shooting through my leg. Maybe it was always there? I look down. There's a semi-healed cut just below my knee. The edges are jagged and red, but it's already starting to scab over. When did that happen? At the Hollow? It wouldn't be the first time I left the ring with a bad scrape. It's hard to say, since I don't actually remember going there last night. I close my eyes, trying to conjure up something —anything. But all I can conjure up are some distant shouts and the faint taste of blood.

I take another swig from the bottle, trying to wash away the uncertainty gnawing at me. The liquid does nothing to ease the sting of the cut or to clear the fog in my mind. But at least it's something to do while I walk.

The square is busier than it's been in weeks, but the usual carts and makeshift stalls are nowhere to be seen. The remnants of snow have vanished, piled against the surrounding buildings. In the center of the cobblestone expanse, I see a half-built stage taking shape, workers fitting the pieces together like a puzzle.

My eyes narrow as several workers rush past me, followed closely by two Enforcers. Why would the Enforcers build anything in the square? This is the Slum; nothing new is ever built here. And where are the Slummers who are trying to eke out a living? I try to make sense of it, but my mind is a swirling jumble. It's hard enough to keep myself upright.

A little ways away, an Enforcer stands on a crate, slapping a poster on the grimy, slanting wall. I stagger closer, squinting to make out the large, bold lettering:

BY DECREE OF THE GOVERNMENT OF NOMISMAN:

PER THE LAWS OF ECONOMIC STABILITY ESTABLISHED BY AURA, RESIDENTS OF LOWTOWN MUST PRESENT THEMSELVES IN THE TOWN SQUARE ON THE 15TH OF JANUARY AT NOON FOR THE CULLING. THE WINNER WILL RECEIVE NEW RESIDENCY STATUS, INCLUDING FOR IMMEDIATE FAMILY MEMBERS, PERMITTING RELO-CATION TO SELECT PARTS OF MIDTOWN.

ATTENDANCE IS MANDATORY.

IN AURA WE TRUST.

In AURA we trust. Each word feels like a punch to the gut, worse than any I get in the Hollow. The Culling. A lifetime ago, I stood in this square, full of hope that I had no idea was pointless. Everything I did was supposed to lead me here, to the next Culling. This was supposed to be Theron and Callias's way out of this cesspool. I take another long gulp from my bottle, but it's no good. No amount of alcohol can quiet the pain coursing through me like fire.

The creak of the floorboards inside Bart's shop is almost comforting. It's like stepping into another world—a world where everything has its place, even if that place is on top of something else. The air is heavy with dust and something else I can't place. The shelves are crammed with items that have no business being together: chipped mugs next to rusted tools, even a stack of yellowed books leaning against old boots.

My eyes linger on the books. Ever since arriving here, I've never seen a single book in the Slum. I'm not even sure if most Slummers can read. Theron would've exploded if he'd seen these. He never missed a chance to duck in here, his fingers running over everything within reach, no matter what it was. And Callias... He'd always find the strangest things. Once, he even found an old chess set. Half the pieces were missing, but it was so strange to find something like that in here.

My throat tightens, so I take another drink. It doesn't help.

"Ezariah?" Bart's voice reaches me from a long way away. He's standing behind the counter, wiping his hands on a rag that's seen better days. "Been a while, kid."

"Yeah." I nod, digging Nyssa's note out of my pocket.

Bart takes it, his bloodshot eyes flicking to mine before he unfolds the crumpled paper. He starts to say something else—probably trying to make small talk—but I can't handle it. Not when my head is splitting open and my heart feels like it's been dragged through razors.

"I gotta go," I mutter, my fingers tightening around my bottle. I turn to leave, but the door swings open before I can take a step. My muscles turn to stone as she steps between the shelves. Sera's eyes land on me, and there's a moment—just for a heartbeat—where her face softens. Is it relief?

Whatever it is, it doesn't last. Her gaze sharpens, taking in my baggy, stained clothes as I sway on the spot.

"Ezariah," she says, her voice carrying that tone that always sets my teeth on edge. "You look like shit."

No. I don't want to hear this now. Not from her.

She steps closer, her blue eyes narrowing like I'm her newest problem in need of solving. "Where have you been?"

My heart pounds so loudly that I'm surprised Sera can't hear it. Why does everyone keep asking me questions? Can't she see I want nothing to do with her or my old life? I'm fine with the way things are. Why can't she, and Rowan, and every other person in this godawful Slum accept that?

"I'm fine," I lie, taking another drink.

Of course, she doesn't buy it for a second. "Ezariah—"

I push past Sera before she can finish. I burst through the door, the world tilting as I stumble through the crowded streets. My breath comes in ragged gasps, the bottle's neck gripped tightly in my hand. Blurred faces flicker past me. I don't see them, don't hear their protests as I barrel into them.

Why did I have to run into Sera today? After my dream, and then learning of the upcoming Culling, seeing her in person was too much. So, I run, desperate to put as much distance between me and the ghosts of my past as I can.

Somehow, I find my way to the Hollow. The dim lights and the roar of the crowd envelop me, and I breathe a sigh of relief at the familiarity. The crowd is a hazy blur, but many turn their heads toward me. They know me—or at least, they know the version of me that haunts the pit every night.

"Ezra!" someone shouts, and the sound of the name does more to calm my nerves than any drink. Ezra, not Ezariah. Not the brother who failed to protect Theron and Callias. Just Ezra, the mediocre fighter. Here, no one cares what I do outside of these walls. All that matters is the fight.

Even though the world sways dangerously, I find Nyssa easily enough. She's standing at the edge of the pit, Rowan and a few others at her side. I push through the sea of bodies and reach Nyssa as the crowd erupts. Down in the pit, I see the loser crumpling in a cloud of dust.

"That settles Quinn's debt," Nyssa says, nodding to the man standing in the ring as one of her bookies makes a note in his ledger. "You want in tonight?" she adds, her voice easily cutting through the din.

Rowan steps forward, her eyes wide. "He can't," she pleads. "Nyssa, not tonight."

A bitter laugh flies from my lips. I can't help it. Rowan should know better by now. Like it or not, I'm going to fight. It's not like I have anything left to lose. I nod and take a long drink from my bottle. Rowan quickly yanks it away, but it doesn't matter. It's empty now anyway.

I stagger forward, my feet taking the path they know all too well. The edges of my vision blur as Rowan's voice fades away, drowned out by the thunder of blood in my ears. I slip down the ladder, only hitting half the rungs. But as my feet slam onto the hard-packed earth, even the cheers of the crowd fade away.

My opponent is already here, a thin woman with muscles like chiseled stone. I can't help but stare as she raises her arms. We used to have statues like her back in Newtown. Gram even bought a few to display in the garden.

Without warning, dull pain blooms across my face. I stagger back, my ears ringing as the faint roar of the crowd hits me. I try to blink, but one of my eyes won't open. But why? What happened?

Through the haze, my opponent appears in front of me. She swings her fists, and I raise my arms. I think I block one punch, maybe two. But it's all a blur. She swings around, and her foot connects with my arm.

A sickening crack splits through the noise of the crowd, and pain sears through my arm. The fog in my head clears, and I stumble back as she lunges for me. I hit the ground before I can even think, and immediately taste blood. Somewhere, I think I hear the crowd cheering. I lie back, and let the pain take me, driving away everything else. No more past. No more regrets. Just pain.

Laughter spills out of me, along with a mixture of saliva and blood. Rough hands haul me to the ladder and hoist me out of the pit. The world wobbles dangerously, but I can make out Rowan's scowl, her lips moving fast. Luckily, the ringing in my ears means I can only make out some of what she's saying.

"… one of the stupidest … ever done…" Her voice fades in and out, like a bad signal. "Why do you keep doing this to yourself?"

I chuckle, the sound raw and grating even to my ears. I try to push myself up, but the pain in my arm stops me. "I'm ready for another round," I say, my words blending together.

"Shut up, Ezra," Rowan hisses.

Nyssa's face swims into view. I sigh, tuning Rowan out completely. Rowan doesn't get it, but Nyssa does. She knows how much I need this. I try to stand, but Nyssa grabs my shoulder, pinning me down. "No more," she says, her voice a cold slap to my face.

"But—"

"No."

I know the crowd is cheering, but Nyssa's voice is all I hear. I stare at her, and there's something in her eyes I haven't seen before: pity.

"You're done fighting for me, Ezariah."

Fear courses through me like fire, burning away my pain. She can't be serious. I thought Nyssa understood why I needed to be here. The fighting—the pain—is the only escape I have.

"Please…" My voice cracks as tears burn my eyes. "Please don't take this from me. It's all I have left."

Nyssa's gaze doesn't waver as she pushes herself up, but I think I see it soften a little. I can't lose this. Not now. Not when everyone else has abandoned me.

"You're done here."

My steps are shaky as I move through the moonlit alleys. Shadows cling to the walls, and I'm nothing more than a ghost haunting the streets. The nightly chill stings my skin, but it's nothing compared to the pain. Not even the bottle I swiped from the Hollow does much to numb the that agony.

After a while, my legs feel like they're about to split open. I lean against a building that looks like it's on the verge of collapse. Even the window has seen better days, the glass thick and warped. In the glass, a Slummer looks back at me— hollowed cheeks, skin stretched tight over protruding bones, and a wild tangle of hair frame a face I used to recognize.

"Look at you," I whisper, my words slurring together. "You're just like the rest of them."

With nowhere else to go, this broken, forgotten building seems as good as any place. At least its walls will offer meager shelter from the biting wind. I stagger inside and collapse into a corner, pulling my knees close to my chest. The last swig of alcohol burns my throat before the bottle slips from my fingers and shatters. I close my eyes, fighting to keep the pain at bay as sleep slowly takes me over.

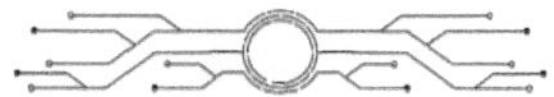

A BLARING sound rips through the darkness, and my eyes snap open. My head is pounding, and my arm throbs with a dull, persistent ache. I blink several times, and the half-demolished room around me comes into focus. How did I even get here?

I stagger to my feet, using the crumbling wall for support. As

I step out onto the street, the harsh daylight burns my eyes. The street is deserted, an eerie silence hanging over the slum like a shroud. My stomach churns, and I press a hand against the rough brick to steady myself.

Suddenly, a cool, female voice cuts through the silence, echoing off the slanting buildings. *"Residents of Lowtown, please report to the square. Per the Laws of Economic Stability, all Lowtown residents will present themselves for the Culling. Attendance is mandatory."*

"Crap." I squeeze my eyes shut. Vaguely, I remember seeing a sign about the Culling yesterday. Did I go to the square. Of course, I'd rather dig through the refinery than attend the Culling. What's the point? Thanks to my record, I can't even enter. But like the voice said, attendance isn't a choice.

My feet feel like cinder blocks as I make my way to the square. The check-in line is easy enough to find, completely taking up one of the larger streets. When it's my turn, the Enforcer barely glances at me before scanning my tag. It blinks red as the inside of my forearm grows hot, and I step through without another word.

I join the edge of the crowd as the previous winner, a middle-aged woman whose dress doesn't quite fit her, steps up to the podium on the newly built stage. I lean against a cold brick wall, my gaze wandering over the sea of faces—faces filled with hope, desperation, and everything in between. The sight claws at my insides as my head throbs. It must be nice to have hope.

The crowd grows silent as everyone's ID tags blink in their forearms. I turn to the massive screens flanking the stage. First, they show images of the crowd. Then, the picture zooms in on the only ID tag glowing green. A young man steps forward, two kids clutching his hands. There's a collective gasp, and applause breaks out around me.

The sight of those kids, their hollow faces alight with a future that's suddenly bright and free, cuts me deep. A searing pain burns from the pit of my stomach, lodging itself in my throat. It should be Theron and Callias standing up there, basking in the crowd's cheers, about to escape this hell. But they can't now—and it's all my fault.

I stumble back, a raw, animalistic noise clawing its way out of me. I push through the crowd, their cries nothing more than a hum as I yank open the first door I can find. I slam the door behind me, muffling the cheers, and sink to the floor, clutching my stomach. I gasp, but it's like there's no air in the room. My face grows hot, and my fists shake at my sides. I want it to go away—the pain, the guilt.

I grab a small figurine from a nearby shelf and hurl it against the wall. It shatters, and for a second, everything fades. But the pain returns, rebounding against my splintering heart. I grab more things from the shelves—an old vase, a tattered shirt, an odd misshapen ball. With each throw, I feel relief, but my fury keeps building, like a fire that will swallow me whole. My chest heaves with ragged breaths as I reach for something, anything.

"What the hell you doin'?!"

The voice crashes through my chaos like lightning. I whirl around, my arm throbbing with pain. Bart is standing in the doorway, his eyes wide with anger, and the room snaps into focus. Crap—I'm in Bart's shop!

"Get out!" His face is red, his eyes narrowed into slits. "You're wrecking my shop!"

"Leave me alone," I hiss, sounding like some cornered animal. I've had enough. Why don't people listen when I tell them to leave me alone? I swing my fist—the one that's been throbbing all morning—and it collides with a shelf. Pain erupts up my arm, a white-hot agony that's still nothing compared to the turmoil inside me. Bottles crash to the floor, their contents spilling like blood.

The door bangs open again, and this time, it's Sera who rushes in. Her eyes find mine, filled with a worry that I can't stand to see.

"No," I snarl, my voice breaking. "Get out!" I grab the nearest thing I can find—an old, worn-out boot—and hurl it at her. It misses by a mile and bounces off the wall.

Sera doesn't retreat, or even flinch. Instead, she moves closer until she's standing right in front of me. She takes my hand—the one attached to the arm screaming in agony. A shudder runs down my spine that has nothing to do with pain. The last time Sera touched me, we were in the square as the cart took Theron and Callias away.

Tears well up in my eyes, and my knees buckle. Sera's arm slips under mine, and together, we sink to the floor as the grief I've fought so hard to keep at bay finally consumes me. I want to run, to hide someplace where my pain can't reach me. But Sera's arms tighten around me, anchoring me to reality.

"I tried to save them," I choke out, finally saying the words that have haunted my dreams every night for weeks. "I tried so hard."

Sera pulls me close, her hand cradling the back of my head. "I know," she whispers softly against my hair. "I know you did. I'm so sorry, Ezariah."

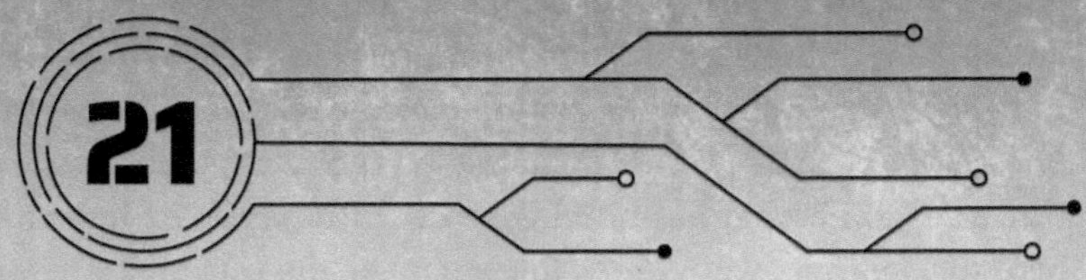

"YOU TRASHED MY SHOP!"

Bart's gravelly voice cuts through the air. I press my face into Sera's shoulder as the tears sting my skin. Her arms tighten around me, and my fingers twist into the worn fabric of her sheet dress. I can't let her go—I won't. Right now, her arms are the only thing holding me together.

"What's wrong with you?!"

Slowly, I lift my head. There's a fire in Bart's bloodshot eyes that I've only ever seen in one other person: my father. There's so much hate radiating off Bart that I'm surprised he's not floating.

"I ... I don't know," I stammer, and that's the truth. The anger that surged through me during the Culling feels like a distant memory, like it happened to someone else.

"Figures," Bart huffs, shaking his head. "Gonna take months to rebuild my stock."

Sera stands, leaving me on the floor. She moves around the aisles, gathering the broken fragments now littering the ground. Each piece she picks up is like she's hitting me in the stomach. After everything I did—abandoning her after losing Theron and Callias—she's still here, cleaning up my mess. She's still looking after me, just like she did when we first met. My stomach twists uncomfortably. I'm never going to stop owing her.

"The kid's losin' it," Bart says from several shelves away. "If he keeps this up, he's not gonna make it."

"He's been through hell." Sera's voice is a whisper, but I can still hear every word. "He's lost ... everything. Give him a chance."

I wait for Bart to respond, but all I hear is a muffled huff. I sigh. I guess that's the best I can hope for.

It doesn't take Sera and Bart long to clean up my mess. When they're done, I force myself to stand, despite every muscle in my body screaming in protest. My head is throbbing with a mixture of exhaustion and pain. My mouth is oddly dry, and my hands won't stop shaking. More than anything, I just want to lie down. But I can't. There's something I have to do first.

Gingerly, I walk up to the counter. Bart is sorting through my wreckage, no doubt trying to salvage whatever he can. It would be easier to look at my shoes, but I force myself to look right at Bart.

"I'm sorry." My voice sounds small and distant, even to my ears.

"Whatever." Bart shrugs. He doesn't look at me, but he doesn't have to. His voice tells me everything I need to know; he's only forgiving me because Sera asked him to.

Sera's hand slips into mine, and it's like some of the weight rises from my chest—but only a little.

"C'mon," she says gently. "Let's go."

We step out into the square, which is practically deserted now that the Culling has ended. Sera leads me across, and for a moment, I feel relief. For the first time in a long time, I'm not making the decisions. But as we near the building on the other side of the square, my insides turn to ice. My muscles tighten, and I can't bring myself to take a step. No. I can't go back here. Not the place where Theron and Callias slept and played, not the place where they drew their last breaths. Their laughter echoes through me, and my chest tightens as fresh tears threaten to spill onto my cheeks.

Sera's grip on me tightens, as if she knows exactly what's going through my head. "You're okay," she whispers, pulling us toward the building, the door still hanging off its hinges. "We'll do it together."

"Together"—that's a word I thought I'd never say again. But

as Sera leads me up the stairs, I know she's wrong about one thing: even with her at my side, I'm far from okay.

Sera's hand doesn't leave mine as she rams her shoulder into her door. It bursts open, banging against the wall. Her fingers slip out of mine, and immediately, my throat tightens. I know it's selfish, but I want her here for what I know is coming. But I know better. She let go for a reason: she wants me to do this alone.

Stepping into Sera's apartment is like stepping into a dream. The small, dingy space was barely big enough for the four of us to fit on the floor. But now, without Theron and Callias, it seems too big to fill. Sera lights the candles, and a faint glow fills the room where my brothers ate their meals. Here, inside these old wooden walls, they were supposed to be safe.

I sigh, and all the fight seeps out of me. My legs give way, and I fall to the floor. My body shakes uncontrollably as tears course down my cheeks. Somewhere—in my arm, maybe—I think I feel pain. But it's nothing compared to the agony ripping through me.

"I killed them." The words are like acid in my mouth, eating me from the inside out. "I killed my brothers."

"No." Sera's hand finds my shoulder, her grip firm, yet somehow tender. "Don't say that. You didn't kill them, Ezariah."

"How can you say that?" I snap, anger momentarily driving away my grief. I know she's trying to comfort me, but why is she lying? "I was supposed to protect them, and I failed. They're dead because of me."

Sera sits beside me, her face surprisingly calm. "You didn't kill your brothers," she says bluntly. "Hunger did. The cold did. The Slum did. It destroys anything good and innocent. But you're letting your grief swallow you. Somehow, you need to find a way to move on."

"Move *on*?" I echo, my voice rising in disbelief. The words are like a slap to the face. "So, I should just forget them? Is that what you're saying?"

"Of course not," she says, her voice regaining its usual bite. "I'd never ask you to forget your brothers. But you can't live like this."

I'm shaking now, but not from sadness or grief. There's so much rage swirling inside me that it consumes everything else. "You don't get it!" I yell, shoving her hand off my shoulder. "No one understands what it's like—what I'm going through!"

"I do."

"No, you don't! You didn't love them. If you did, you'd be a wreck, just like me."

Sera's gaze hardens, and even in my state, I know I've crossed a line. "I miss them every day," she says, her voice breaking. "But I can't let myself fall apart."

I shake my head. How? How can she just move on from this? How can she wake up knowing Theron and Callias aren't here? My brothers... They were everything. And now they're gone— really gone—and I feel like I'm being torn apart.

I knew Sera couldn't understand. She's too strong, too much of a survivor to let something as simple as death stop her. But me? I can't just stop caring about them.

"It's ... it's not the same," I say, my words barely audible. "The only family I had left is gone. Now I have no one."

Sera's fingers find mine again, and this time, I don't push her away. I close my eyes, bracing myself for what will surely be another gut-wrenching statement. I know Sera thinks she's helping, but sometimes there are things people can't bear to hear.

"So, what does that make me?"

Sera's words hang in the air, and a chill settles over me that has nothing to do with the cool chill. Sera ... family? To be honest, the thought has never occurred to me. But now that she's said it, it feels almost obvious. After my father Renounced us, Sera was the one who took us in. She took care of us, even when I treated her like a dirty Slummer.

Sera's right. She *is* my family—not by blood, but by something stronger. She chose me, just like I chose her.

"I'm sorry," I corke, feeling the words stick in my throat. "I didn't mean…"

Sera nods, her eyes full of understanding. "You have to make a choice, Ezariah. Right now. Do you want to live?"

Almost instinctively, I nod. But it's weak, hollow. Honestly, I'm not entirely sure if I believe it. Do I want to live? The thought of living feels almost insurmountable. How can I, after everything I've lost?

"I won't forget them," I repeat, pulling my knees close to my chest.

"Good," Sera says, and I feel her body move closer to mine. "Remember Theron's laughter when he found a shortcut to the Fringe. Think of Callias, always finding some dog to love on. They were perfect—and that's how you should remember them."

I close my eyes, and I can see Theron and Callias running through the square. They're smirking, playing some game with the other kids who always seem to find one another. A smile tugs at my lips, and it feels so out of place, it almost hurts. I can't remember the last time I smiled.

The happiness fades faster than it came, and the ache I've grown to know comes back in full force. My chest tightens, and it's like all the air has left the room. How can I smile, be happy? I lost the right to feel that when I lost my brothers. Wouldn't it be easier to just stop—to give in to the current I've been fighting against and let it take me?

"Wouldn't it be easier?" I ask, my voice a mere whisper. "To just … let go?"

Sera's grip becomes so tight that it's like a jolt to my senses. "No," she says, her voice more forceful than before. "Theron and Callias wouldn't want that. They'd want you to keep going. And so do I."

"I don't know if I can." It feels pathetic to say it. Ever since Theron and Callias died, just waking up in the morning feels insurmountable. The thought of moving on—of living a life—is impossible.

"You can." Sera's rough, callused hands find my face. "You're stronger than you think. You've survived this long. You just have to choose to keep going."

And with that, all the fight fades out of me. Sera's words swim around my mind as my head falls, resting on her slender shoulder. Keeping my eyes open is like fighting a losing battle. Gently, Sera guides me to the sleeping mat, and it's like a weight lifting off my chest. I think she tells me to try to sleep, but her words blend into the background, nothing more than a light hum.

Sera's hands are gentle as she inspects the cut on my leg then wraps my arm in a sling made of scrap fabric. I think it may be broken. In some distant part of my mind, I think I feel pain. But I've felt so much today that I have no more feelings to spare. It's almost a relief, the absence of pain. I drift off, surrounded by a warmth that feels vaguely like forgiveness.

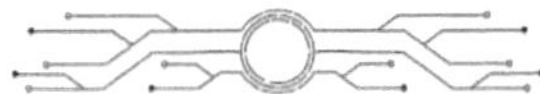

SERA SHAKES ME AWAKE, and it's like she's ripping my muscles in two. My head throbs dangerously, and I wince with every heartbeat. The faint light from the grimy window feels extremely bright against my stinging eyes. I roll over, pressing my face into the old sleeping mat. I'm not sure how long Sera let me sleep, but it wasn't enough.

"Why?" I croak, my tongue as dry as sandpaper.

"C'mon." Sera's voice sounds louder than usual, like she's speaking into a microphone. "It's time to get up."

Get up? I can't remember the last time I was up before noon. Was Sera always this bossy?

"What time is it?"

"Early." Sera's hands slide under my arm and pushes me into

a sitting position. There's still a sling on my arm—the one I hurt at the Hollow. Gingerly, I try to flex my fingers. They move, but it's slow, like dragging them through cement. I don't dare try to move the rest of my arm.

"You should go to the square this morning." Sera ties her scarf around her waist. "Before it gets too busy."

"Really?" I groan, unable to stop myself from rolling my eyes. Didn't Sera just tell Bart that I've been through hell? I guess her sympathy is only good for one night.

"It's something to do." She shrugs.

"That's not an answer." My brain feels like a pile of mush. Keeping myself upright is hard enough; now I have to decipher Sera's weird behavior too. This day has only just started, but it already sucks.

Sera grunts as she rams her shoulder into the door. "I guess you'll have to see." She whips out the door, vanishing before I can even open my mouth. Slowly, I shake my head and push myself to my feet. Sometimes, I really don't get her. First, she's telling me to keep fighting, to not give up. But now, she wants me to go to the square, so that I what—don't get bored?

The square is quiet when I arrive. Thankfully, the stage, screens, and speakers from the Culling are all gone. Save for a few people skulking around the edges like shadows, it's nearly empty. I stop in the middle of the square, biting my lip. When it's packed with people, there's always something to do. But now, in the early hours, all I can do is watch.

It's then that the low creak hits my ears. I turn and see the massive cart emerging from a side street. The hairs on my arms stand on end as the two Slummers pull it along, its tattered tarp flapping.

I want to run, to scream, to find something to dull the pain. That's the cart—the one that's haunted my nightmares ever since I placed Theron and Callias inside it. Even now, I can feel their tiny, weightless bodies in my arms, the infinite sadness crushing my soul.

As I stand frozen, people move towards the cart, their steps slow. One by one, they place bundles beneath the tarp. Each wrapped shape is someone's brother, sister, parent, child ... all taken by the cruelty of the Slum. As they step away from the cart, their wails are all I hear. My hands clench into fists at my sides. Sera must've known the cart would be in the square. She wanted me to see this. But why? After all the grief and suffering I've endured, why make me witness more?

"Why?" I demand the moment Sera returns to the apartment. "Why did you make me watch...?"

As usual, Sera's face remains impassive as she closes the door. For some reason, it rubs me the wrong way. I take a deep breath, fighting to keep my anger in check.

"I didn't make you watch anything," she says calmly. "I told you to go to the square. What you did there was entirely your choice."

"But you knew," I insist, my voice growing louder with frustration. "You knew what would be there!"

"I did," she admits, pulling her money bag out from the folds of her dress. "Don't worry, it'll get easier."

"*Easier?*" My mouth falls open, and my arm throbs painfully. "I'm never doing that again."

"Whatever you say, Ezariah," Sera says, now producing a loaf of bread.

I don't know what takes over me. Stupidity? Recklessness? Maybe a burning desire to prove Sera wrong. Whatever it is, it consumes my every thought. She can't be right—not about everything.

The square is exactly the same the next morning. I tell myself I'm there to pass the time, to prove that something like this cannot get easier. The death cart creaks down the road, and again, dread fills me like lava. In some small part of my mind, I feel a strange sense of accomplishment. Sera isn't right after all.

I try to focus on whatever I can—the cracked cobblestones, the sky as it slowly shifts from indigo to blue, my shoes. But no matter how hard I try, my eyes always find the cart. I see a woman, her slight frame shaking with sobs, holding a small bundle in her arms. My jaw tightens, and my legs shake. It's like I'm staring back in time. The child in her arms can't be much smaller than Callias. But somehow, the wrapped bundle looks tiny as she places it into the cart like a child's toy.

I don't notice that I'm moving until I'm right beside the woman. She looks at me, her eyes swollen and red, and takes a shaky breath. Her head lolls to the side, and she falls. By some miracle, I catch her with my good arm. Together, we sink to the ground, her body shaking with sobs that feel so familiar, it's almost eerie. I know I'm supposed to do something. Tentatively, I pat her shoulder. It's awkward; lately, *I'm* the one in need of comfort. It feels strange, helping someone else, but not entirely wrong.

Ever since arriving in the Slum, I've felt like I know nothing. But this—this woman's grief—I know all too well. Nothing I say will matter. When you lose a child, nothing can dull that pain.

"I know," I say as the woman grabs a fistful of my shirt. "I know."

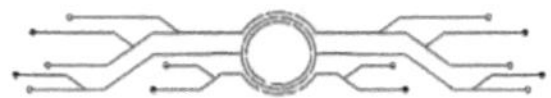

DAY AFTER DAY, I find myself drawn back to the square each morning. But as the days pass, I find myself looking at the cart less and less. In fact, after a while, I hardly notice it. Instead, I watch the people as they emerge from the shadows, carrying the wrapped bodies of their loved ones. Each time, my heart jumps into my throat, the pain on their faces all too familiar.

Of course, it's the smallest bundles that haunt me the most. There are so many of them—so many little lives claimed by the Slum. Yes, the thought of Theron and Callias still stings, and I doubt that pain will ever go away. But now, it feels muted, like a half-healed wound.

It's those people—those who've lost little ones—who draw

me in. I find myself approaching them, people I don't even know, and offering what little comfort I can. Typically, I don't say much; nothing I do can erase their pain. I know that better than anyone. But I'm here to help them up when they're ready.

After about a week of daily visits to the cart, I find myself wondering what has happened to the people I've seen. Where did they go after experiencing the worst thing possible? Not everyone has someone like Nyssa to let them spiral for weeks. Surely, someone should check on them.

So, in the afternoons, I make my rounds. After the cart passes, there's always someone who needs help finding their way home. It's a struggle at first; they don't want to talk, and I don't exactly know my way around here that well. But eventually, I'm able to find my way.

I go to see Sola a few times a week. She's the first woman I met at the cart—the one who lost her five-year-old son. She lives a few blocks from the square. Her home is nothing fancy, just one large room. There's a rickety table in the corner by a wood-burning stove, and a brown mattress under the cracked window. Sola barely spoke when I first started popping in, but after a while, she slowly started to open up. She can't afford to wallow in her grief—not when she has three other mouths to feed.

I find myself staying at Sola's longer and longer, trying to help out wherever I can. Of course, I'm no good at washing things, or at any other household chore, but Sola still finds things for me to do. Once my arm's out of its sling I help her carry supplies from the rations bank, but mostly, I watch her other kids. Luca is happy as long as he's kept busy, while Tace will spend hours constructing whatever new thing has filled her mind. Halyn, the oldest, keeps to herself, her brows knitted like she's trying to solve all of Nomisman's problems.

Even though I try not to think about it, they remind me of Theron and Callias. But oddly, that thought doesn't hurt me the way it used to. In fact, when I'm having a bad day, it's Luca's laugh or Tace's insistence that she need to finish building her house that makes me smile.

But Sola and her family aren't the only ones in need of help. There's Wren, whose husband died after an accident at the chemical plant. Most days, she just needs someone to talk to. But there's also Talon, whose sister caught an infection no healer could shake, and Cypress, who lost his son. It just keeps going, on and on and on. I wish I could do more than just check in and offer a helping hand. But what can I do? I'm no healer or miracle worker; I'm just a Renounced kid who's been through the wringer and come out the other side. What can I give these people that could make any real difference?

My first impulse is to ask Sera, but for some reason, whenever I think to bring it up, something stops me. Maybe it's my own insecurity, or maybe it's the very real possibility that Sera might not agree with me. Sure, she took me, Theron, and Callias in. But Sera survives the Slum by always being three steps ahead, always making sure she's safe, whatever it takes. To her, helping every random grieving person I come across will probably sound like an idiotic idea.

"Sera," I say one night as we sit together in her apartment, "I've been thinking … about all those people at the death cart."

"And?" She stares at me so intently that it's like she's trying to see right through me.

"I want to help them—to do something more than visit and make small talk." I get the words out quickly before I lose my nerve. Sera's eyes narrow as she takes a bite from a burned loaf she found at the refinery. But as the seconds stretch on, I know I've made a mistake. Asking Sera was a long shot to begin with. I'll have to come up with a plan on my own.

"Okay," she says softly.

I'm so shocked that my mouth falls open. She's going to do it; Sera's actually going to help me.

"We just have to be smart about it," she says, the corners of her mouth twitching. "Make sure we do things right."

"Of course." I smile, and it feels like I'm being warmed from the inside.

The flame flickers as Sera gently extinguishes the candle. The room fades into darkness, and the world outside the thin walls disappears as well. I roll out the thin sleeping mat, and we lie down beside each other. I shift closer to her, closing the gap that once seemed as wide as the Slum itself.

I don't remember when exactly the chasm that Theron and Callias's deaths created between us began to close. It wasn't a single moment, but a series of them—shared meals on a stoop in the square; feeling her eyes on me, but not being quick enough to see; our hands lingering a little too long as we roll up the sleeping mat. Gradually, as the nights pass, we've moved closer to each other.

I feel her steady breathing beside me, the slight warmth radiating from her body into mine. There's a comforting ease between us that wasn't there before, something born of shared pain. So, we lie there in silence, but it's not empty; it's full of words and feelings I've never dared speak aloud. If I did, then they'd be out there for everyone to hear. What if she doesn't feel the same way?

"Thank you," I whisper so quietly that not even the creaking walls can hear.

"For what?" Her voice is soft, barely audible above the sound of our breathing.

"Everything. For making me go to the death cart," I say, finally voicing what I've wanted to say for weeks. "I ... I didn't understand why you made me go. But now I do."

Sera rolls toward me in the dark. I hold my breath, waiting for her to say something. Whenever I've asked her why she sent me to watch the death cart—to watch the grieving—she'd never gives me a straight answer. But I don't think it's that simple anymore. There wasn't just one reason.

"It wasn't about the death, was it?" I continue, now sure I'm on the right track. "It was about life—finding life after death. It was about living."

In the dark, I can almost feel her smile. "Took you long enough to figure it out," Sera whispers back. "I knew you'd get there in the end."

I close my eyes, feeling the warmth of her body seep into mine. Sera's right: the Slum is always going to try to tear us down. But it can't, as long as we have something to fight for.

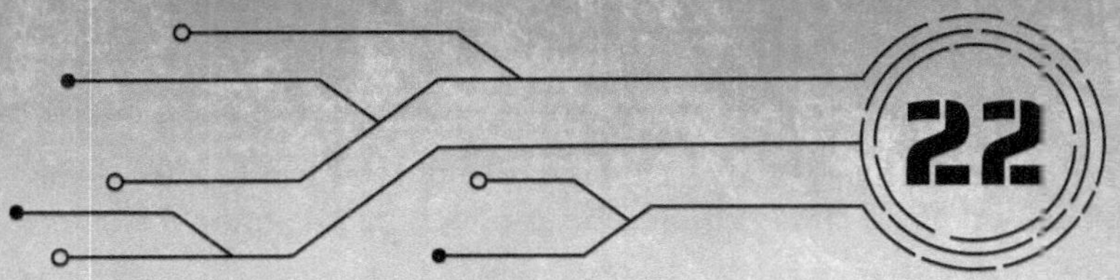

WHEN I WAKE UP, the first thing I notice is the silence. No soft, shallow breathing, no sign of warmth in the darkness. I roll onto my side and find Sera's place on the sleeping mat empty. I reach out, my fingers brushing the spot, then I push myself up, rubbing the sleep from my eyes. She's been gone for a while. But I don't have to think very hard to figure out where she is.

Yesterday, after I did a really bad job of patching a hole in Wren's wall, I kept Luca and Tace busy while Sola and Halyn washed some of their neighbors' clothes for a few extra coins. When I got home, my stomach was aching, and the thought of any food made saliva flood my mouth. But when Sera got back from her shift at the factory, her money bag was empty, and all she had was a few strips of dried meat for us to share.

Sera has snuck into Midtown; no doubt she's already there. The thought stings more than I expect it to. It's not that she left without telling me—well, maybe a little. It's the fact that our current situation is mostly, if not entirely, my fault. In the months since Theron and Callias died, I haven't gone to work once. Granted, I was a drunken mess for the first several weeks, and in no condition to swing a heavy sledgehammer at the power plant. But even after Sera pulled me back from the edge, I still never thought to go back. I had the death cart; I had Sola, Cypress, and all the others to check on. Going back to work just never occurred to me.

Slowly, I pull on my shoes. I think they were grey when I got them at the Department of Corrections, but now, they're so dirty that they might as well be black. The soles have worn down to nothing, and there are several holes in the left one. But they're better than walking around barefoot, like Sera does. I don't know how she stands it.

If she's really in Midtown, she'll have to cross back into the Slum before sunrise to avoid attention. There are only a few places on the Fringe where she can do that. I guess I'll check those—not that Sera needs my help. I just want to make sure she's okay. I decide I might as well check some of her other haunts. It's a long shot, but most of them are on the way anyway.

The night air is warmer than it's been in weeks, and for the first time in a long time, I'm not longing for the coat I can't afford. The market's not too far from the square, but it might as well be another world. Unlike the rest of the Slum's dark streets, at night, the market feels almost alive. People wearing clothes that are almost see-through stand in and around the doorways, calling out sweetly as men, women, and Enforcers pass by.

Even though I've been here a handful of times with Sera, I still feel out of place. But it's not because the buildings here are smaller than the ones in the square, and in far worse condition. Many have holes in the walls, and as far as I can tell, none of the windows have glass. Surprisingly, I'm even okay with the activities I know are happening inside the buildings. If there's one thing I've learned in the last few months, it's not to judge what people do to survive the Slum. No, it's the Enforcers that make me feel uncomfortable. They look so out of place in their dark uniforms, chatting happily outside the buildings before being pulled inside. Somehow, it all feels wrong—like the Enforcers are just like us. But they're not.

Jewel is easy enough to spot. She's outside one of the larger buildings, leaning against a shattered doorframe. The flickering light from inside casts weird shadows over her face, not helped by her thick layer of makeup. When was the last time she washed it off? Probably never. Makeup is a luxury most Slummers could only dream of.

"Evenin', Ezra," Jewel says as I walk up the slanting steps. Ever since I began fighting at the Hollow, more and more people have started calling me Ezra—even Sola's kids. It doesn't bother me the way it did when Rowan first called me that. Actually, I don't mind at all. "Fancy seein' you out this late, dear."

"I know." I smile, stepping aside as one of Jewel's girls leads two Enforcers inside. "Have you seen Sera?"

"Haven't seen her since she brought us spare rations yesterday." Jewel frowns, slipping some coins her girl handed her into a leather bag. "Why? She's not in trouble, is she?"

"No." I shake my head, trying not to laugh. Of all the people in the Slum, Sera is the last person I'd expect to be in any kind of trouble. "I'm just trying to find her."

"I'll have my girls keep an eye out," Jewel says. 'But I wouldn't worry, Ezra. That girl always turns up."

With the market growing more crowded by the minute, I happily duck down the first alley I reach. I can't help but smile as the jeering, laughter, and other sounds fade behind me. How many times since I met her has Sera just popped up out of nowhere? And it's not like sneaking into Midtown is a new thing for her; she's been doing it ever since her Renouncement. Jewel's right: I really shouldn't be worried.

As I pass the crumbling remains of a wall, a figure stumbles through the rubble, a piece of twisted metal in their hand. I start, my heart racing, and step back into the shadows, not daring to breathe. But the figure doesn't follow me. Instead, they continue down the rubble, trip, and land in a heap on the ground.

"Damn!"

My muscles relax as the voice reaches my ears. This man isn't a stranger at all. I step out of the shadows and hurry to his side. He's a few years older than me, but he doesn't look it. A dark layer of scruff covers his face, and scars highlight his thin arms.

"Ezra?" He brushes the dirt off his clothes while still clinging to the twisted piece of metal like a trophy.

"What are you doing, Talon?" I ask, offering him my hand. "Why aren't you home with your grandpa?"

"He's asleep." Talon shrugs. "I'll be back before he wakes up."

I can't help but smile a little. Talon's grandfather is easily the oldest person I've seen in the Slum. I'd guess he's in his eighties, but who knows, he could be even older than Gram. I first met Talon's grandfather after I found Talon putting his sister in the death cart. I've been to their apartment a few times. Whenever I'm there, Talon's grandfather won't get out of bed. Talon says it started after his sister died.

"So, what's that for?" I ask, eyeing the rough, twisted piece of metal.

"A new knife," Talon says, lifting it up for me to see. "What do you think?"

"Um…" The piece of metal looks like Talon ripped it out of a crumbling wall. Why wouldn't he just go buy a knife? I'm sure Bart has some; he's always saying he has everything in his little shop.

"I know, it's not much," Talon says, hopefully misreading my pause as concern. "But Skye said he could only make me a little one. And he made me pay in advance! It's not my problem that the Enforcers have stopped ignoring his business."

"Yeah." I nod, trying to make my face look sympathetic. Clearly, I'm missing something. Why do the Enforcers care about some guy named Skye making Talon a knife? Last I checked, having a knife isn't a crime.

Talon disappears into the darkness before I can ask him. I shake my head, turning in the opposite direction. I thought I'd finally figured this place out, but I should know better. The only constant in the Slum is that nothing stays the same for too long.

Honestly, the last time I visited the Fringe is a blur. That was the night I first caught Sera crossing the barrier—the night when Theron and Callias… Well, it's safe to say that I've avoided the place since then. But even though I don't remember a lot from that night, I do know that the Fringe was basically deserted. So, when I turn the corner, I stop dead in my tracks.

It's like the whole Slum is pressed right up against the edge of the barrier. The makeshift tents and shelters that normally fill the smaller alleys have spilled out into the main road. Some people sit huddled around small fires, thin blankets or rags draped over their shoulders. Others don't even have that.

I walk slowly between the rows of tents, fighting to keep the disbelief from my face. What happened to drive all these people here? Did a building collapse? Or maybe there was a fire? But no, that can't be it. The Slum isn't exactly large; it only takes twenty minutes to walk across it when there are no crowds. I'd have seen the smoke if something bad happened, and someone would have said something.

The roar of engines rips through the silence, and I spin around so quickly that I almost fall. Armored cars—at least six of them—barrel out of the nearest side street. I know I should run, but I can't get my feet to move. All I do is stare as Enforcers spill out, their crackling batons filling the darkness with an eerie blue glow.

"By order of AURA," one shouts, his voice blaring through the car speakers, *"all residents must sleep in an official residence. Violators will be apprehended."*

Chaos erupts. Shouts fill the air as people scatter in every direction. Somewhere, a child's scream cuts through the madness. Something clicks in my brain, and I stumble back as the Enforcers start grabbing people—men, women, kids. My fists tighten as I watch an Enforcer carry away a screaming girl—she looks no older than ten. They can't do this. Why, after being okay with it for months, is AURA suddenly making sleeping outside illegal? For some of the Slummers, it's the only choice they have. I have to do something.

As I step forward with nothing more than a whisper of an idea, a hand grips my arm firmly. I'm pulled back, and fingers slide over my mouth before I can cry out. I stumble, desperately reaching out for the rough alley wall. I can't let this happen. There's no way I'm letting the Enforcers take me. This time, I know I've done nothing wrong.

"Shut up, you idiot," a familiar voice hisses in my ear, "or you'll get us both caught!"

"Sera!" A mixture of shock and relief surges through me as I spin around.

"We need to stay out of sight," she breathes, her eyes scanning the chaos at the Fringe before she turns her gaze back to me. "What are you doing here?"

"Looking for you," I say, shaking off her hold. "What's going on? Why are they doing this now?"

"I don't know." She shakes her head, and even in the darkness, I see the worry in her eyes. "I walked the entire barrier— twice. Enforcers are everywhere. And the people…"

"Did you make it to Midtown?"

"No," Sera huffs. "I couldn't risk it. These aren't just random patrols, Ezariah. They're actively looking for people to arrest. Like AURA gave them some quota or something."

I run a hand through my hair, trying to make sense of it all. This new rule… It's not just cruel; it's crazy. AURA has to know how many people are in the Slum. Isn't that why we all have to sign in at every Culling, even those of us who aren't allowed an entry? Why would AURA make sleeping outside a designated residence illegal when it has to know there's not enough space for everyone? I know AURA's job is to maintain order in Nomisman's cities, but how is this order?

"C'mon," Sera says, taking my hand. I expect her to stick to the shadows, skirting along the edge of the Fringe. So, when she turns around and starts walking back into the Slum, I can't help but stop.

"Where are you going?"

"Back home," she says, also stopping. "Before something worse happens."

"But what about Midtown?" I ask. "We need the money."

"Are you crazy?!" Sera hisses. "Didn't you see what just happened? Enforcers are arresting people just for sleeping outside, Ezariah! What will they do if they catch me trying to cross the barrier?"

"We'll be careful," I argue, my mind racing. "We'll watch each other's backs."

"'We'?"

My stomach flutters as Sera looks at me. I brace myself, waiting for her to say something. Sure, I had no intention of crossing into Midtown tonight. But standing here, with the barrier so close, I remember the last time I was here. The thrill of crossing, of taking what we needed to survive, of Sera's lips on mine makes the hairs on my arms stand on end. I know that finding Theron and Callias eclipsed everything else that night. Maybe tonight, I can change that?

"Fine," she says slowly. "We'll try it."

"Yes." My lips spread into a wide smile.

Sera's grip on my hand is tight as she leads the way through the smallest alleys, always sticking to the shadows. Every rustle and shout sends shivers down my spine—but it's not fear. For so long, all I felt was sadness. Then, that was slowly replaced by a drive to help those like me. But this feeling—it's like electricity coursing through me. I can't remember the last time I felt excitement like this.

"There." Sera points to a narrow space between two crumbling buildings. The heaping piles of debris create a small opening that's shielded from the main road. Before my Renouncement, I doubt I could have made it through the narrow gap. But now, I easily crawl through with room to spare, my stomach barely grazing the dusty stones.

We emerge right next to a barrier pillar. Sera removes her scarf from her waist, wrapping it quickly over her ID tag. My head moves slowly, the low hum of the pillar mixing with the pounding in my ears. But there's no blaring siren, no thud of an

Enforcer's boots. Sera steps safely across the barrier, unwraps her scarf, and throws it back to me.

I'm across the barrier in seconds. Sera leads the way through Midtown's wide streets, the cool night air filling me up. I close my eyes, my heart hammering against my ribs. Even though the Slum is right behind me, I feel lighter than I've felt in weeks. And the farther I get from the narrow streets that have become my home, the more my skin feels like it's vibrating.

But it's not just the thrill of leaving the Slum that's taken over me. Sure, the rush of doing something drastic is intoxicating, but there's something more. Is it the fact that for the first time in I don't know how long, the air in my nose doesn't burn? Or is it the feeling of Sera's hand in mine?

When Sera finally stops, we're standing outside one of the gaudiest houses I've ever seen. It looks like someone visited a house in Newtown and then threw every idea they ever had at it. There are so many windows that the whole thing is basically made of glass. Large bushes trimmed into the shapes of strange animals adorn the slowly greening lawn. But the worst offender sits at the end of the front drive. Two of Sera's apartments could easily fit within the giant fountain. Large golden fish sit around the rim, jets of water spraying from their mouths.

I can't help but roll my eyes. Clearly, this isn't the home of some random Midtowner. Whoever lives here wants everyone to know how much money they have. They're trying desperately to look like Newtowners; I wouldn't be surprised if they're hoping to buy their way across. Sadly, even if they ever get enough money to make it, the Newtowners won't have anything to do with them. The one thing they hate almost as much as the Renounced are social climbers.

The back door, an awful collage of stained glass, is easy enough to spot. I half expect it to be locked, but when I turn the knob, it swings open easily. "That was lucky," I mutter, unable to stop myself from smiling.

Sera glances back at me, the corners of her mouth twitching.

"It's not luck. All the thieves are either rotting in the Department of Corrections or trapped in the Slum—like we should be. Why would Midtowners bother locking their doors?"

I don't know how, but the inside of the house is even worse than the outside. The intricate designs carved into the walls clash with the overstuffed furniture. Chandeliers dripping with crystals hang in every room, reflecting moon light onto paintings that are at least three feet taller than me. The whole thing feels like a slap in the face, which is probably what the owner wants.

"This place is…" I start, trying not to snort.

"Perfect." Even though Sera's voice is just a whisper, I can still hear her excitement.

We move from room to room, grabbing whatever objects won't be missed. After only going through three rooms, I've got a silver letter opener, a small diamond pinky ring, and three silk scarves covered in gold thread—and that's just the stuff that fits in my pocket. I don't even feel bad about taking any of it. Whoever lives here clearly just bought this stuff because they were told it's expensive. Why else would someone have eighteen different handkerchiefs embroidered with glittering stones?

Up on the second floor, I slip into what must be an office. Here, dark wood panels line the walls, and the floor is made of a smooth, polished stone. A massive black desk sits in the middle of the room, surrounded by bookshelves that reach to the ceiling. Like the rest of the house, each shelf is stuffed with books, trinkets, and little mechanical devices that look like they're at least a hundred years old—that is, except for the shelf directly behind the desk.

The polished metal rectangle could easily fit in my hand. A credit drive. I stare at the little device, unsure of whether to be shocked or impressed. Credit drives are typically for Newtowners, especially the wealthier families. They can store more credits than anyone can spend in three lifetimes. When Gram was still alive, she always had two or three credit drives locked away in the study.

Suddenly, my mouth feels very dry as I take a step closer to the drive. I was right about whoever lives here. Whoever they are, they're clearly attempting to move up into Newtown. How many credits are stored on the drive? Easily enough to keep Sera and me fed for the rest of our lives. Slowly, almost absentmindedly, my hand reaches out.

"Proximity alert" a robotic female voice announces. Strobe lights pulse around me, making my eyes water. There's a grinding sound, and two camera drones deploy from the ceiling, their blades whirring as they swivel toward me.

Adrenaline surges through me like acid. I bolt from the room, my heart pounding so hard that it feels like it might explode. Behind me, I hear the drones closing in. Instinctively, I duck my head, my face growing hot. Why did I try to touch the stupid credit drive?

Sera barrels around a corner, her eyes wide with panic. "What happened?!" she demands.

"Drones," I gasp, my sides burning as I point over my shoulder. "We need to go—now!"

Sera doesn't need me to tell her twice. I race past her, the whir of the cameras' blades growing louder with every step. But I don't slow down as I barrel down the stairs. We need to get out of here; we can't get caught because of my stupid mistake. Luckily, the drones aren't that good at making sharp turns. We're able to put a few yards between us as we skid around a corner, and as we run outside, Sera slams the back door before they can catch up.

Pain burns through my sides as we sprint through Midtown, the cool air slicing my lungs. We don't stop until we're back at the barrier. Sera quickly wraps her scarf around her ID tag and steps back into the Slum. She tosses me the scarf before crawling back through the gap in the debris shielding this part of the barrier. I follow suit, the low hum of the pillar filling my ears. I take several deep breaths, trying to slow my heart, which feels like it's about to break my ribs. But oddly, it's the sight of the slanting buildings and blackened cobblestones that calms me.

Sera collapses on a nearby stoop, her face shining with sweat. I sit beside her, the cool stone leaching the heat from my back.

"That ... was too close," I manage to wheeze.

Sera nods, her breathing just as ragged. "You can say that again."

I shake my head, replaying the whole thing again in my mind. "Have you ever seen security like that?"

Sera's eyes lock on mine, and it makes my throat tighten. There's something in her eyes I don't think I've ever seen before: fear. "Only in Newtown," she admits.

This doesn't make any sense. Why would a Midtowner have advanced Newtown security when they don't even bother to lock their doors? And why would Newtown let them use it? If there's one thing Newtowners don't do, it's share their technology with Midtowners. That would violate the Laws of Economic Stability.

"Freeze!"

An Enforcer emerges from the shadows, her baton filling the darkness with a faint blue light. I stand, trying to keep my face calm while my hands shake violently. Did this Enforcer see us cross over? She can't have; all the rubble from the building should have blocked us from view. So, why is she here?

"This isn't a designated residence. Come with me."

My feet move before I can think. I grab Sera's hand, turn on the spot, and run in the opposite direction of the Enforcer. Behind me, the thud of the Enforcer's boots against the cobblestones explode like gunfire.

"Stop!" The Enforcer's shout cracks through the night like a whip.

But we don't stop. We can't. It's not just that we look like we're sleeping on the streets. My pockets and Sera's dress are full of stolen items. If the Enforcer catches us ... I don't even want to imagine what will happen.

We skid around a corner, and I see Nyssa's house, light seeping through the cracks in the boarded-up windows. I don't hesitate—in fact, I don't even think. I pull Sera inside before slamming the door behind us.

"Ezra?"

"Dude, slow down!"

But I don't stop. I keep moving, pulling Sera until we're at the very back of the main room. Normally, the bagmen would be here, counting up the daily haul. But tonight, the tables are covered with playing cards and several bottles of alcohol. I walk right past Rowan, her mouth hanging open, and try to open the door to the back room. It bursts open before I even reach the handle. I back up, nearly treading on Sera as Nyssa steps into the room.

"What's this?" Nyssa's voice is quiet, like it always is, but the hairs on my arm stand on end. Her eyes fall on me, and it feels like she's staring right through me. I open my mouth, not really sure what I'm going to say. Whatever it is, it will be a lie. I can't let Nyssa know we snuck into Midtown. But what else can I tell her?

Boom. The pounding stops my words in my throat. I look around Nyssa and see the dust flying off the rough boards of the front door.

"Open up!" the voice of the Enforcer booms through the door. "This is your only warning!"

I don't dare breathe as Nyssa's eyes quickly flick between Sera and me. Will she turn us in, after everything we've been through? Nyssa always takes care of her own, but I haven't been part of her crew for a long time. Even when I crashed here, she only took care of me out of pity.

Slowly, Nyssa turns to Rowan. "Take them to the basement. Now," she says before turning back to Sera and me. "Not a sound from either of you."

Rowan nods, her expression serious as she gestures for us to duck behind one of the couches. I do as I'm told, although I don't know why. I lived here for almost a month, and I never once saw a basement. Granted, I wasn't exactly fully aware the whole time I was here, but how could I miss a whole basement?

I have to eat my words when Rowan pulls back an old, faded rug, revealing a trapdoor. I tighten my grip on Sera's hand as I descend the rickety stairs. The air is thicker down here, the foul, sour smell burning my nose. My eyes struggle to adjust as the door closes over us. Through the gloom, I can just make out what looks like stacks of boxes and crates. Even though my heart is racing, I can't help but stare at the boxes. Why would Nyssa store anything down here?

Sera and I crouch between the crates, staring up at the ceiling. Nyssa's voice, as calm as ever, drifts through the floorboards.

"How can I help you, Enforcer Rina?"

"I'm looking for two nonconformists," the Enforcer barks. "I saw them come in here. Step aside so I can search the premises."

"Of course," Nyssa says, although this time, I hear a slight edge to her voice. "By all means. But when you're done, please inform your superiors that, unfortunately, my crew may not be able to make its delivery to the barracks. Such a shame that in tough times, our Enforcers may go hungry."

Suddenly, I'm aware of how loudly I'm breathing. Above, the room is so quiet that you could hear a pin drop. I always knew Nyssa had the Enforcers in her pocket, but since when does the crew do their grunt work? I guess it makes sense. Why would the Enforcers risk doing something illegal when that's all Nyssa's crew does? But is her influence enough to make them leave?

"My apologies, Ms. Yarrow." Even through the floor, I can hear Enforcer Rina fighting to keep the anger from her voice.

Sera's hand finds mine in the dark, and relief floods through me like ice. We stand, and I can't help but sigh as the front door closes with a soft click. Above us, the trapdoor opens, flooding the basement with light. With the threat of arrest fading, I lean against one of the crates. Unlike most everything in the Slum, these crates aren't all battered and bruised. In fact, they look almost new.

I walk around the nearest box—and my jaw drops. There's a symbol on the side of the box—a symbol I know all too well. It's a fox sitting in front of a gilded tower, with the words Lumen In Umbra at its feet. The exact same thing was printed on every piece of paper Gram wrote on, as well as on the door of her mausoleum.

Nyssa descends the stairs. Sera steps forward, but I stay where I am, unable to take my eyes off the crate. How is this even possible—Gram's crest, here in the Slum?

"Thank you," Sera says, pulling me out of my thoughts.

Nyssa opens her mouth to say something, but the words explode out of me before I can stop them. "Why do you have boxes with my Gram's crest?"

Nyssa doesn't even flinch. Instead, she crosses her arms and considers me with those dark eyes. For some reason, it rubs me the wrong way. Why should she care if I'm asking questions? It's *my* Gram's crest, after all.

"Ezariah, Lady Malkin was more than just your grandmother," she begins, and my pulse quickens with every word. "She was my benefactor."

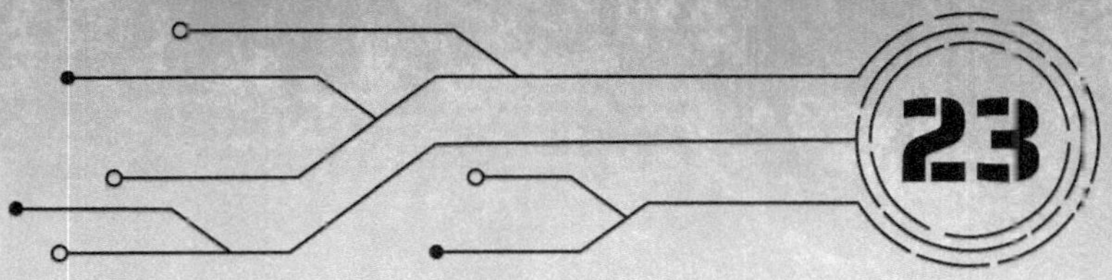

I LEAN against the grimy stone wall, my hands pressed deep into my pockets. For the most part, the square is deserted, just a few early risers hurrying through the morning breeze. The sign above Bart's door creaks slightly. If it fell off, I wouldn't be shocked at all. Sera is inside, finally pawning off what we stole from Midtown three days ago. She said I should come in, that Bart isn't holding a grudge after I trashed his shop. I shot down that idea. Bart doesn't strike me as the forgiving type.

Besides, I have enough on my mind at the moment. What happened in Nyssa's basement keeps playing on a loop in my head. Even though I saw the crest with my own eyes, I still can't believe it. Gram wasn't just some rich lady with odd hobbies and a soft spot for her rebellious grandson. She actually gave money to Nyssa to help the people in the Slum. After all this time, my father was actually right: Gram was really a nonconformist.

In the past, that thought would have shocked me—maybe even scared me. But now, all I can think about is how amazing she was. But how'd she do it? How did my Gram, a little old lady, get stuff to Nyssa? Somehow, now that I know more about her, Gram feels more like a stranger. But more than anything, I wish she'd told me. I'd have thought she was crazy, but everyone else in Newtown already thought that.

The door creaks open, and Sera steps out. She hands me a small bag, and my eyes narrow as I take it. I notice how light it is almost instantly. I pull it open and dump the assorted small and medium coins into my palm. They're all different thicknesses, like someone made them in a rush in the dark.

"That's not a lot," I sigh, returning the coins to the bag. "You sure he didn't rip you off?"

"Of course he ripped me off," she mutters. "But it's better than nothing."

"C'mon, Sera." I try not to sound too annoyed. "That stuff was worth at least—"

The heavy grinding of wooden wheels cuts me off. I look up —the death cart is rumbling into the square. My chest tightens as people emerge from the nearby buildings, their wrapped burdens in their shaking arms. Even after seeing it practically every day for the past few months, it's still like a knife to my heart. One by one, they place their loved ones into the cart as it rolls past before collapsing to the ground, their sobs filling the air.

I don't really remember moving. The next thing I know, I'm crouching beside a woman, her tiny bundle shaking in her thin arms. Gently, I grab the woman's shoulder, an act I've done more times than I can count. But this time, it feels different, almost hollow. There has to be more I can do.

Gram would do more. There may be things I never knew about my grandmother, but I do know one thing: she wouldn't just sit here while this woman goes through the worst day of her life and only offer her kind words. Gram would've scooped her up and filled her hands with all the coins she could carry. The thought brings a shy smile to my lips.

"I'm sorry." I pull a few coins from my bag and press them into the woman's palm. It's not as much as Gram would give, but it's enough for ... something. A meal? A night to grieve without worry? Whatever it is, it's better than nothing.

The clatter of the death cart fades as Sera and I walk through the narrow streets. She doesn't say anything, but I can tell there's something on her mind. She keeps looking at me every few steps, lines etched on her forehead. I know that look; she's trying to solve a problem. And it doesn't take a genius to know what that problem is.

"Spit it out," I say, trying and failing to not sound annoyed.

"Why'd you do that?" she asks, and unlike me, she's able to keep her annoyance in check. "Give the phys away? We barely have enough as it is, Ezariah. And now you're just handing it out?"

A mixture of a laugh and snort flies past my lips before I can stop it. Sera shoots me a look, and I bite my lip, trying to compose myself. I know; it's not funny. We are running really low on money. A few days ago, the thought of giving it away would never have crossed my mind. But that was before I saw Gram's crest in Nyssa's basement.

"It's what Gram would've done," I say, turning to Sera. "If people need our help, shouldn't we help them if we can?"

Sera rolls her eyes. "Ezariah, I know your grandmother gave money to Nyssa. But she *had* money to give. We don't. And the money we have … we nearly got arrested getting it. Why risk our lives if you're just gonna give it away?"

I stop and turn to Sera, my mouth hanging open. I know how her brain works; I've lived with her long enough. For her, everything is about survival—staying one, five, ten steps ahead. That's how she's made it in the Slum for so long. But at some point, we need to do more than just survive. Isn't that what Sera told me when I was spiraling out of control?

"That woman needed the money more than us. We'll make do. We always do."

Sera huffs and marches off, her bare feet slapping against the cobblestones. I hurry after her and slip my hand into hers. Surprisingly, she doesn't shake it off. But even as we walk, she still refuses to look at me.

I don't want to say it, but this is kind of her fault. She's the one who wanted me to find a purpose after Theron and Callias died. She can't be angry now that I've found one.

But I know better than to pick a fight right now. So, I drop the subject. Luckily, we turn onto one of the larger streets, which is packed with people heading toward the massive building at the end of it. Even from the other end of the road, I can hear the ring of sledgehammers on metal. The sound makes my stomach twist into a knot.

"Do I… Are we sure I should go back today?" I ask, my voice shaking slightly. I haven't set foot in the Human Power Generation plant since Theron and Callias died. I haven't missed swinging the heavy hammer around, or the Enforcers watching me like a hawk. Working there was a nightmare. But with our money running dangerously low, Sera and I have decided it's time for me to go back. Okay, maybe it was more Sera telling me to go back, but I didn't disagree.

"We need the money," Sera says, her grip tightening on my hand. "And it's not like we're gonna get to Midtown anytime soon. Last night, there were Enforcers at nearly every pillar. We couldn't have crossed, even if we'd tried."

I want to keep arguing, but I stop myself. It sounds more like an excuse than an explanation. I know we're scraping by as it is; Sera doesn't need to constantly remind me of that. But I doubt that Enforcers are everywhere along the barrier. Sure, last night, there were a ton of them. But how long can that last? Sooner or later, the Enforcers will calm down, AURA will slacken the crazy rules it's put in place, and everything in the Slum will go back to normal.

"You'll be fine," Sera says with more confidence than I feel. "We do need the money—especially if you insist on giving it away."

I manage a weak smile. I know she's trying to lighten the mood, and in her own way, admit that she's not totally against my act of kindness. For now, I'll take it as a win. Maybe she's right. Maybe it will be fine. All I have to do is make it through my first shift. How hard can that be?

The familiar din of the plant swallows me as I step inside. I scan my tag, and the computer makes a low beep as a warm pain fills my arm. It fades quickly. If I'm being honest, I don't really notice it anymore. I pick up a sledgehammer—which feels even heavier than I remember—and follow the sea of workers into the plant.

The heat hits me like a wave. Was it always this hot? No, it can't have been. But one thing I do know for sure is that there weren't this many people here last time.

"Hey, Ezra!" A familiar voice cuts through the chaos. I turn and see Talon and Cypress pushing through the sweat coated workers. They both have smiles on their faces. I can't imagine why.

"What are you doing here?" I ask, my eyes darting between their hammers.

"What do you mean?" Cypress asks, resting his hammer over his shoulder. "We work here."

"Since when?" I can't help but sound shocked. I don't remember ever seeing them here.

"I've been here for years," Talon says. "Cypress too. We thought you'd quit."

"Oh. Umm…" I had no idea either of them worked here. But clearly, they knew I did. There's a sinking feeling in my stomach that has nothing to do with being back here. I've visited them several times a week for months now. How did I not know where they worked?

Somehow, workstation 47 seems even smaller than I remember. In fact, it's so small that I barely have enough room to swing the hammer. The metal plate embedded in the floor is dented in several places, and the number on the floor is so faded that I can barely read it. But the lines separating me from my neighbors are so vibrant, they almost look new. Has it really been that long since I've been here? I thought nothing ever changed in the Slum. I guess I was wrong.

Sweat drips down my face after the first few swings. Every time the hammer hits the plate, it's like my bones are exploding. I try to keep up with the pace, the steady rhythmic clang assaulting my ears, but I can't. No matter how hard I try, I only manage one good strike for every four. I hate to admit it, but the past few months have taken their toll. After all the injuries from the Hollow, barely eating, and the month of near-constant intoxication, my body is a wreck. But that's not even the worst of it; the room is so hot from all the bodies that I'm on the verge of vomiting.

A heavy hand appears on my shoulder, as if out of thin air. I turn, and my throat tightens as the sledgehammer slips a little in my hand. The Enforcer is at least a foot taller than me, his dark uniform practically pristine. Even though I should be scared, I can't help but be impressed. My clothes are soaked, and they're thinner than tissue paper. How is this guy not boiling?

"You're behind," he growls, his voice barely audible over the ring of the hammers.

It takes all of my willpower not to say, *"Well, duh. Of course I'm behind. I haven't been here for months."*

Pain sears my side before I even open my mouth. My muscles tense, and it's like I've turned to stone while the crackle of electricity fills the air. It doesn't take too long for the pain to subside. I stagger back, dropping my hammer as I gasping like I'm just breaking the surface.

"Not good enough," the Enforcer says, waving his baton.

I clench my teeth, swallowing the retorts I want to hurl at him. How is tasing me going to make me work any faster? I lift the hammer, but now, it's like moving through mud; everything's so slow and heavy. I feel the Enforcer watching, waiting for me to mess up again. The pain doesn't help my already poor aim, and I end up hitting the concrete floor beside my panel.

The shock erupts again across my back, and this time, my knees give out. I hear someone shout—I think it may be me—but the sound is oddly distant. Stars pop in my eyes as I try to push myself up with the hammer, my arms and legs trembling. However, in some small, distant part of my mind, I feel vindicated. I was right: working here is a nightmare.

To say I'm grateful when the whistle blows would be a massive understatement. I practically crawl to join the giant line of workers inching toward the payment terminal. I drag my hammer behind me; picking it up seems like a task for ten men right now. I'm so tired that I don't even notice Talon elbowing me in the side when I reach the drop-off rack.

"You okay?" he asks, his eyes wide.

I want to say no, but I can barely manage to keep my eyes open. So, I nod my head, which feels like a brick. Cypress appears on my other side, his leathery hand squeezing my shoulder. I think he says something encouraging, but I'm not entirely sure. All I can think about is how much my shoulder's throbbing under his thick fingers.

When I finally reach the scanner, I shove my arm inside and stare at the scratched, staticky screen. As soon as it's done, I get to go home. I don't think I've ever been so excited to go to Sera's place in my life. Finally, a number appears on the screen.

"One-and-a-half credits?" I'm so shocked that I don't even take my arm out of the scanner. This can't be right. I made more than this on my first day.

"*Pay deduction due to unsatisfactory attendance. Quotas and pay are set by AURA. Please contact the Department of Labor if you have concerns regarding your work placement,*" the computer says in its flat female voice.

"I've been here all day!" My voice cracks with exhaustion and irritation.

"*Please contact the Department of Labor if you have concerns regarding your work placement,*" it repeats.

I want to scream, to throw something. How is this right? Sure, I missed some days. Okay, I missed a lot of days. But one-and-a-half credits is barely enough for a stale loaf of bread these days. This job was supposed to help with Sera's and my dwindling money situation. I'd have been better off begging at the Fringe.

"Ezra, let it go," Talon says, pulling my arm out of the scanner. "It's not worth it."

Cypress scans his tag, but he keeps his dark eyes locked on

me. "He's right. In AURA we trust—but talkin' to AURA's like talking to a wall."

"But it's not fair!"

"Life isn't fair," Cypress says simply, stepping away from the terminal.

Talon's eyes drift to something behind me. I turn and see an Enforcer moving slowly down the line, her baton already drawn. I clench my jaw, fighting to keep my anger in check. It's like she's waiting for us to cause trouble.

"Let's get outta here," Talon says.

Talon and Cypress half lead, half drag me out of the plant before I can say anything. With every block between me and that electric-humming nightmare, I breathe a little easier. However, the streets practically press in on me. People sit on stoops, on the narrow sidewalks, or even in the middle of the street. The chatter really doesn't help with the pounding in my head.

"Has it always been this packed?" I ask, pressing my newly blistered palms into my temples.

Talon shakes his head, glancing around as if noticing for the first time. "No, this is new. Maybe in the last few months."

"AURA upped the energy quota for the city," Cypress huffs. "A higher quota means more workers. The Hoarders are squeezin' us dry."

I'm so taken aback that I nearly stumble over a loose cobblestone. I haven't heard anyone say Hoarder since Rowan started calling me Ezra; according to her, Ezariah is a Hoarder name. Even though it wasn't that long ago, it feels like a lifetime. I don't even recognize the person I was back then.

"But why? H-hoarders can afford—"

"It's not about affording, Ezra," Cypress cuts me off. "It's about control." His gaze hardens as he surveys our surroundings. "AURA doesn't give a damn about us. Just numbers and efficiency. As prices rise, people fall."

I'm slumped in the corner when Sera finally enters the apartment. Somehow, the room feels smaller than ever—like someone moved the walls in a few inches while we were out. No matter what I do, I can't get Cypress's words out of my head. They buzz around like a fly I can't seem to swat.

Sera doesn't say much as she lights a candle and places it on the rickety chair. She hands me a crusty roll, her fingers lingering over mine before she sits beside me. It's not much of a meal, but I'm grateful for it, especially after the day I've had.

We eat in silence at first. After a while, she leans against me, and I gasp. I can't help it. Sera doesn't say a word as she lifts up my thinning shirt. There's a massive welt on my side, the skin stretched tight like a balloon.

"Rough day?" Sera asks, her fingers brushing the welt.

I wince, and the hairs on my arms stand on end. But this time, I don't think it's from the pain.

"Cypress said it's about control," I finally conclude after recounting my day at the plant. "He says AURA doesn't care about us, just … numbers and efficiency."

"You just figured that out?" Sera says, raising her eyebrows. "I thought it was obvious."

"Well, it wasn't to me," I say, unable to keep the bite out of my voice.

I want to shuffle away and put some space between Sera and me, but in her tiny apartment, there's literally nowhere to go. Why, after all this time in the Slum, are there still things I don't understand about this place? Somehow, I feel trapped and lost all at the same time. It's like being stuck in the world's worst puzzle.

"I just wish there were something we could do."

"Not this again, Ezariah," Sera says. "I know you want to help people, and I love that. But like Cypress said, the system that keeps Nomisman going, it's … it's stacked against us. You can't help anyone if we starve to death."

Sera and I don't speak as the candle burns down to a nub. It doesn't take long before her slow, heavy breathing fills the darkness. But no matter how much my muscles ache, I can't close my eyes. Cypress and Sera can't both be right. I don't care what they say. After everything I've been through, I refuse to give up on hope—mostly because hope is all I have left. One way or another, I'll show Sera just how wrong she is.

The street's just as busy when I leave Sera's apartment the next morning. And even though my stomach is rumbling, I don't stop to get anything to eat. But I do pull out my money bag. I'm not sure what I'm looking for exactly, but I try not to think too hard. Rational thinking flew out the window when I left the apartment without waking Sera.

So, I follow my gut. There's an old man with one leg sitting in a broken doorway. I slip a coin into his hand and walk off before he even lifts his head. Then there's two little kids running toward the refinery, their bones clearly visible beneath their grimy skin. I give them each a coin, and their eyes grow wide as dinner plates before they run off. I can't help but smile as I keep moving toward the plant. Sera might be right about a lot of things, but she was wrong about this. Giving to these people does make a difference, no matter how small.

My day at the plant is much less fulfilling. Sweat stings my eyes, and my muscles ache with every strike. The welts on my back and side are still tender, and the fresh blisters on my hands are on the verge of bursting. But I can't stop—not with Enforcers prowling the aisles. So, I keep my head down, focusing on each strike as the heat wraps around me like a suffocating blanket. Surprisingly, I manage to keep pace this time. Nothing like the threat of a beating to keep workers motivated. The thought makes my stomach churn.

"Get up!"

Even though I know he's not talking to me, the Enforcer's shout still makes me wince. I know I shouldn't look, just keep my head down and mind my own business. But I can't help it. I turn, making sure my strikes don't fall behind. A few workstations over, an man is leaning on his hammer. He's old—older than most people in the Slum—with deep lines covering his face.

"Pick it up!" the Enforcer shouts, his baton inches from the man's back. The old man tries to lift his hammer, but even I can see his arms shaking.

"No!"

I'm not sure what's more surprising: the fact that I'm the one who spoke, or that my hammer slips out of my grip. I run from my station, and all around me, the constant clang of the hammers falters. In a second, I'm standing between the old man and the Enforcer. Through the slit in his helmet, I see his eyes widen. No doubt my sudden appearance took him by surprise. I know it surprised me.

"Impeding disciplinary action is punishable," he growls, pointing his baton at my face. "Step aside and get back to work."

"No." The word flies out of my mouth before I can stop it. I take a breath, my legs shaking violently, but I stand my ground. I don't care what Sera or Cypress says. I refuse to accept that this is the way things are in the Slum, and that there's no way to change it. I won't let an Enforcer beat an old man right in front of me.

So much for keeping my head down.

The baton hits my stomach, and it's like the air disappears from my lungs. I fall, gasping, tears streaming from my eyes. I look up, and that's when I see the Enforcer's boot. I curl up, trying to shield my head as the Enforcer kicks me again and again. I cough, and the metallic taste of blood fills my mouth. I'm not sure if it's the ringing in my ears or if everyone's too stunned to make a sound, but the world goes oddly quiet.

The Enforcer finally stops when my arms go limp. Somewhere, way off in the distance, I hear him order the workers back to work. But I stay where I am, curled up on the cold concrete floor. Every breath feels like my ribs are exploding into a million pieces. However, even all that pain can't extinguish the tiny flicker of pride inside me. I may be hurt, but at least the old man is okay.

When the whistle finally blows, I know I have to get up. It's a struggle. Every move sends the world spinning, making my stomach lurch. I stop, crouched on my hands and knees, trying to will the world to right itself. At this rate, I'd be better off staying right here; at least I'd be on time for work tomorrow.

Then, several pairs of dirty, thin shoes appear in my wobbly vision. Hands slide beneath my arms and hoist me to my feet. I close my eyes and clamp my mouth shut. After all of this, I can't vomit now.

"You're crazy, man," Talon's voice says. "Why'd you have to do that?"

"I … couldn't just … watch." Every word I say is a monumental effort.

"When are you gonna stop gettin' yourself in trouble?" Cypress's voice says on my other side. I can't tell if he sounds more annoyed or concerned. Probably a little of both.

Talon and Cypress practically carry me out of the plant. I tried to walk after they got me to my feet, but even those few steps felt like I was stepping on glass. So, they lead me through the crowded streets in silence. But I can still feel them looking at each other over my shoulders. I know they think I'm an idiot, but I don't care. Even with all the pain, I'd do it again in a heartbeat.

"What happened?"

My eyes snap open at the sound of Sera's voice. She's standing in the doorway of her apartment, her eyes moving so fast that it makes me dizzy. I try to smile, but I think it comes off as more of a grimace. That wipes the concern from her face.

"Your boy here decided to play the hero," Talon says dryly, helping me inside. He and Cypress lower me cautiously onto the sleeping mat, like they're afraid I might break. I sigh when they finally let me go, the pain subsiding slightly. I see them exchange a look with Sera, but they leave without saying anything.

For a moment, Sera just stares at me, her face oddly blank. I brace myself. This isn't going to be a fun lecture.

"Why do you keep doing this?" Sera huffs as she kneels

beside me. I know she's trying to be gentle, but as her fingers prod my bruises, it's like she's jabbing a million needles into my skin. I wince, but it's not just from the pain.

"Because it was the right thing to do."

Sera can't hide the disapproval on her face as she shakes her head. She doesn't understand. How can she, when her whole world is solely focused on her own survival? But as I lie here, I feel a strange warmth spreading through me. Sure, it's pain, but there's something else too: pride. Today, even though I took a beating, I stood up for someone when they couldn't stand up for themselves.

"Ezariah, just…" Sera trails off, and I can tell from the look on her face that she's struggling to find the right words. But how hard is it to reprimand me? She does it all the time.

"… just give it a little more thought next time," she continues, brushing my hair out of my face. "How are we supposed to do what your Gram wanted if you keep getting beat up at work? You can't save anyone if you can't walk."

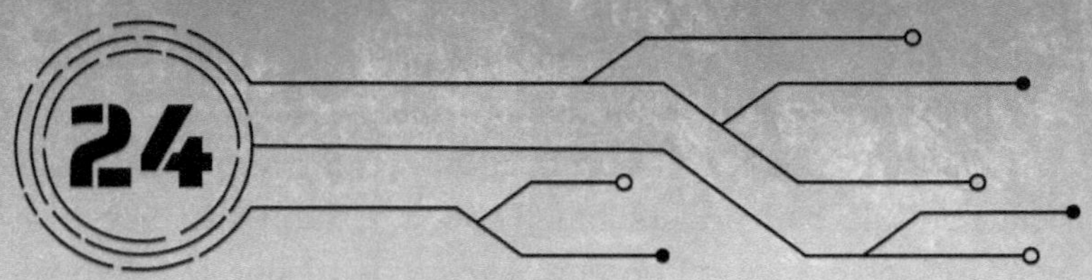

THE FRINGE IS SO PACKED that I barely have room to move. My eyes rake over the crowd, their hands held toward the barrier to Midtown. It's late afternoon, and the Midtown side of the barrier is buzzing with people. I see them look at us, not even trying to hide their disgust. To them, we're nothing more than animals, safely caged in the Slum. Every once in a while, some Midtowner might toss a coin across the barrier, but it's too rare to count on. Besides, why would a Midtowner give away the money they're meant to hoard? They can't get to Newtown if they take pity on us Slummers.

Fortunately, I don't care about the Midtowners. They're just a distraction. While several people scurry forward to fight over a tossed coin, I sit in one of the newly vacated spaces. It's hard to keep my head down, but Sera made me promise that I wouldn't draw attention to myself. And I hate to admit it, but she has a point.

But I don't need to look up to know who's sitting beside me. I saw her when I first got to the Fringe. Her legs are too thin, and her eyes look overly large above her hollow cheeks. This girl can't be older than five.

My hands tremble as I slip my hand into my pocket. Of the coins Sera gave me, I only have a few left. If I had it my way, I'd give it all to this girl, her vast eyes almost identical to Callias's. I want to do more for her, but I can't and that thought almost rips me in two. I guess it's a good thing Sera is in charge of the money.

I've gotten really good at being unnoticeable. I pull a coin from my pocket and wait for another Midtowner to throw one. The girl looks up, roused by the noise and excitement, and I slip the coin beneath the frayed hem of her dress. When she looks down, my hand is already back in my lap.

I'm about to get up, to find the next person I can help, when the sharp thud of boots makes my insides freeze. Enforcers. Panic surges through the air like an electric current, making the hairs on the back of my neck stand on end. Slowly, subtly, I return to the cobblestones.

"Move!" The unmistakable crackle of an Enforcer's baton fills the air, followed by a man's scream. I look up. A man is being supported between two Enforcers while a third brandishes his baton. "Refusing to obey an Enforcer? Last I checked, that's three nights in Lockup."

I want to act, to do something to protect these people. They've done nothing wrong. Sitting on the street in broad daylight isn't illegal. But I know there's nothing I can do. So, I stay put, staring at my shoes as my overgrown hair falls over my face.

At least five others are arrested by the time the Enforcers leave the Fringe. I slip away, my face a calm mask while my hands shake. I can't even think straight. I know firsthand how cruel Enforcers can be. And lately, it's like they've been told to turn it up a notch. But this, arresting the poorest the Slum has to offer for no reason… This is low, even for Enforcers.

Unlike the Fringe, the market is practically deserted. A few workers stand in doorways, their faces long with dark circles beneath their eyes. I sit on an abandoned stoop, struggling to control the anger raging inside me. But sitting only makes it worse.

It doesn't take long for Sera to emerge from a building across the street. Her eyes lock onto mine, and for a moment, the storm inside me fades, replaced by a soft, warm feeling that makes my fingers tingle. More than anything, I want the feeling to last forever—but of course, I know it can't. In the Slum, happiness is a luxury I can't afford.

"How'd it go?" she asks, nudging me in the side as she sits beside me.

My hands clench into fists as my face turns hot. "Not great," I say, trying to keep my voice level. "The Enforcers came out today. They arrested several people for … I don't even know what."

"Jewel said it's the same here," she sighs, nodding toward the building she came out of. "Enforcers stirring up more trouble than business. By the way, she says thank you."

Now that's enough to make my raging pulse slow. I lean against Sera, a rare smile threatening to spread across my lips. I can't help but feel proud of her. She's been hesitant about my desire to help people. She's always had a hard time letting people in; I know that firsthand. But lately, she's come around to seeing things my way, at least a little. We've found our rhythm: she checks on the people we've grown close to, like Jewel, Talon, and Sola, while I focus on the people we'll probably never meet.

"Ezariah, just … remember to be careful," she says, her eyes narrowing the way they always do when her mind is racing ten steps ahead. "I wouldn't put it past the Enforcers to arrest you if they caught you handing out money."

I open my mouth to retort, but close it quickly. There's no winning this fight—not when Sera's actually right. I've barely got her on board with this plan as it is.

"I know," I huff, trying not to sound too defeated. "No unnecessary risks."

If I had it my way, I'd give all the money we could to those who need it. Sera and I can survive without it. Of course, Sera shot down that idea before I even finished saying it. But even with the few coins we've stashed away, going to the rations bank has become a weekly occurrence. Today, the walk there feels even longer than usual. The dull ache filling my stomach doesn't help. Even though I've been in the Slum for months now, I'll never get used to that feeling.

The crowd in front of the bank is massive, and it only grows, practically swallowing us whole. Sera presses into me, her head in almost constant motion. I take her hand, but she doesn't even look at me. My insides prickle as I bite my lip. I know crowds aren't her favorite thing, but does she need to constantly be on guard?

Time stretches on, and the line doesn't move an inch. In fact, it only grows. More people press in around Sera and me until we're practically standing on top of each other. I cross my arms, trying to make myself as small as possible while my foot practically vibrates. I crane my neck, but all I can see is a sea of faces.

"What's taking so long?" I shake my head. This really is ridiculous.

"Something's not right," Sera mutters under her breath.

She can say that again. After getting our rations, I was supposed to watch Halyn, Luca, and Tace while Sola went shopping. But at this rate, I doubt we'll be home before the sun goes down.

I'm not sure when the murmuring starts. It moves through the crowd like a wave. People shuffle around, bumping into each other as the noise grows louder. Then I hear something—the sound of breaking glass, followed by the thud of several hard things colliding.

"What do you mean, 'closed'?"

Even with the rising commotion, I hear every word as though the speaker is right beside me. Closed? No. The rations bank can't be closed! It's never closed. My insides turn to ice as my chest tightens. All I have is two phys—not even enough for a scrap scavenged from the refinery these days.

Sera's grip on my hand is so tight that I wince. I turn to her, trying to pull my hand free, but she only holds on tighter. I open my mouth, ready to tell her to let go, and that's when I see her face—eyes wide, mouth slightly open, skin pale. The shock in her eyes knocks the wind from my lungs. I know that look, although I've not seen it often. She's afraid.

"We need to go," Sera says, her voice shaking slightly. "Now."

Before I can take a step, the low rumble of engines fills the air. My stomach drops as I whip around. I don't have to stand on my tiptoes to see the glint of the armored cars barreling into the street. The vehicles don't even stop before their back doors fly open. Enforcers spill out onto the cobblestones, batons in hand, while several hold clear shields at least a foot taller than me.

"*Disperse,*" an amplified voice blares over the crowd. "*You are disturbing AURA's peace.*"

"Open the bank!" a voice yells from the crowd.

"AURA promised us food!" another shouts.

The crowd surges forward, sweeping me and Sera along with it. My muscles tense as my eyes dart in every direction. This can't be happening—not again. First the Fringe and the market, and now here? Why would AURA close the rations bank? It makes no sense; AURA is meant to maintain order. But this… This is chaos.

"Move." Sera's voice is so quiet that I can barely hear it over the raging crowd. She pulls me behind her, weaving through the throng with surprising speed. I stumble after her, fighting the urge to slip from her grip. We're almost at the edge of the street when I hear it: glass shattering against metal. I've never heard a bomb go off, but this has to be ten times louder. Shouts and screams blend with the telltale crackle of the Enforcer's batons. Thuds fill the air as the crowd swells like a wave crashing on the shore.

"Keep your head down and run!" Sera shouts, glancing over her shoulder.

I sprint after her, my pulse pounding in my ears as Sera slips into the nearest alley. The screams and shouts echo off the dilapidated buildings, but I don't look back.

After a few more turns, Sera runs into a shell of a building.

It's empty except for a few blackened sleeping mats and an old dented can filled with ash.

"Why?" I pant, trying to catch my breath. "Why would AURA do this? They're starving people—people who just want a little food!" I squeeze my fist so tight that my knuckles turn white and my muscles are so tense I feel like I'm going to break in two.

"Ezariah, I know you're mad," Sera says, grabbing my shoulder. "I am too. But getting angry isn't going to help anyone."

"No." I pull away, and her hand slides off me. She doesn't get it. She never has. What we're doing… It's more than just helping people. We're giving them something more than money; we're giving them hope. "We need to do more."

"We're doing all we can," Sera says. Her voice is calm, but I can hear the tension she's fighting to keep out of it.

"No, we're not. If we just had more money… If we went back to Midtown, just once—"

"Are you crazy?!" Sera's expression hardens, reducing her blue eyes to slits. "With the Enforcers out for blood like this? It's suicide."

"But—"

"Ezariah." Her voice cracks through the air like a whip. "You need to stop. You're gonna drive yourself crazy trying to keep this up."

When the commotion finally fades, we make our way back to the square. The sun dips low, and the buildings cast shadows across the cracked cobblestones. While Sera goes off to do who knows what, I go back to the apartment. Sera doesn't say a word as she leaves, and neither do I. I'm not going to be the first one to break the silence. I don't care how logical her thinking is or how impractical my actions are. I can't give up. Not when the alternative is accepting that things in the Slum will never change.

Several hours pass before Sera finally returns. She leans against the warped doorframe, her arms crossed tightly over her chest. I stare at her, not even bothering to get up. At the very least, I deserve an apology.

"Follow me."

I didn't expect that. She turns and walks down the hall before I can get up. I hurry down the stairs and finally catch her as she steps out into the square. Sera stays a few steps ahead of me, the fresh night air cool on my face. She turns down alleys and streets at the last possible moment, and after a few turns, I have no idea where she's taking us. I doubt we're going anywhere good. She's probably taking me to some horrible, downtrodden place that I haven't seen yet to give me a talking to. But after the day I've had, a lecture is the last thing I want.

We turn a corner, and I see the massive warehouse, its old, thick windows full of soft orange light. The Hollow. I'm so taken aback that I stop right in the middle of the road. Why would Sera bring us here, to a place where people fight for sport? But as I stand here, I notice something. Actually, it's the absence of something—no angry shouts or cries of pain. Instead, I hear music, lively and warm.

Sera glances back, and I'm even more surprised to see her smiling. She opens the door and holds out her hand. A shudder courses through me, and I take a shaky breath before joining her.

The inside of the Hollow is unrecognizable. Wide wooden boards cover the pit, which supports a rickety stage for the band. Their music fills the cavernous space, seeping into every corner. A couple of the instruments have seen better days, but the sound still makes my bones vibrate. It's so inviting and full of life. Laughter echoes off the walls as people dance across the floor, and I can't help but smile. This is not the place where I tried to drown my grief with pain.

"Why are we here?" I ask, my voice barely audible above the music.

Sera looks at me, her eyes softer than they've been in a long time. "You're so busy helping everyone else. But who's looking after you? You deserve a little fun, Ezariah."

Sera doesn't wait for me to respond. She grabs my hands and pulls me toward the dance floor. It takes me about three seconds before I stumble over my feet. My face grows hot, and suddenly, I feel like everyone is watching me. This music is nothing like what I grew up with in Newtown. Everything there was so poised, almost regal. But this… Sera's bare feet move so fast that they're practically a blur.

I'm not sure if it's customary for the woman to lead in the Slum, but Sera's a natural. She pulls me along, her eyes closed as she leans her head back. Slowly, the world outside fades. I stop caring about missing steps as Sera's laughter fills me up, making my insides warm. I step closer, leaving only a breath between us. I'd never admit this to her, but Sera is right. I do need a little fun.

Then a chill runs down my spine that has nothing to do with Sera. It's like someone's watching me. I turn, and the bottom drops out of my stomach. A massive figure is pushing his way across the dance floor, his arms as thick as my head. I freeze, unable to move my legs, as Jackson stops right in front of me.

"Look at you, Ezariah," Jackson says, nodding to the music. "You look nothin' like a Hoarder now."

I don't know what's more shocking—the fact that Jackson knows my name, or that he's even here at all. The last time I saw him, Enforcers were dragging him away in the Department of Corrections. At the time, I thought he deserved his extended sentence. But now, after months in the Slum, all that has changed. No matter what I told myself at the time, his extended sentence was my fault. My stomach twists around itself, and I can't bring myself to look up at the man towering over me.

"Do you need something?" Sera asks, her grip on my hand tightening.

What is Sera thinking? We both know why Jackson's here. He blames me for screwing him over, and he wants revenge. In the past, I would have run for the hills. But not now. He wants to settle the score—and I'll let him. I've gotten the crap kicked out of me more times than I can count in this building. What's one more beating? At least this time, it's one I actually deserve.

"Nyssa's here," he says simply, his head still nodding to the beat. "She wants to talk."

It's like our time in the Department of Corrections never happened. I don't know if I'm more shocked or relieved. But if Jackson is over it, I'm not going to argue with him—especially since he could snap me in half with one hand.

I give Sera's hand a reassuring squeeze before leaving the dance floor. I know she probably wants to come with me, but Jackson was clear; Nyssa wants to talk to me. But why? I haven't spoken to her since the night I found Gram's crest in Nyssa's basement. If anything, I'm the one who should want to talk to Nyssa. I have so many things to ask her.

Nyssa's at a table near the back. Here, away from the dancers and music, the Hollow seems smaller somehow. Her cool eyes meet mine, and my hands shake slightly. It's a struggle to keep my nerves from showing. Why does Nyssa still make me feel so uncomfortable?

"Ezariah," she says, her voice as flat and controlled as ever.

"Nyssa." I join her, my voice surprisingly steady as sweat coats my palms. "Jackson said you wanted to see me."

"I do. To discuss your current … activities."

I try to swallow, but my tongue is like sandpaper. My activities? How does Nyssa even know what Sera and I have been doing? I've been so careful, making sure no one sees my face as I slip them a coin. But why does Nyssa care? It's not like I'm stepping on her turf. I'm not charging people; I'm just giving them a few coins.

"I must say, I'm impressed, Ezariah," Nyssa says, the corners of her mouth twitching. "Your … your grandmother would be proud."

After everything I've experienced, it takes a lot to shock me these days. So when I open my mouth to respond, I'm surprised that no words come out. I always thought I was someone Nyssa tolerated at best. I mean, I've screwed up enough times for that to be true. But she's been watching me all this time. But it's not her approval that makes my heart twinge.

"How ... how'd you know my Gram?"

Nyssa leans back, her usually stern face softening a little. "I only met her once. Most of the time, she paid drones from Midtown to bring us messages and supplies—money, mostly. She's the one who showed me how AURA keeps us here, by making things so hard that escape becomes impossible."

The memory surfaces from some deep, distant part of my mind. I'm standing in front of Gram's mausoleum in the meadow, three Midtown workers standing off to the side. At the time, I wondered why drones were at Gram's funeral. They seemed so out of place, almost like intruders. But they weren't. They, like Nyssa, were part of Gram's quiet fight against AURA.

I thought I knew Gram—my quirky, opinionated grandmother who always defended my kindness. But I didn't—not really. Gram had a whole other life outside the shining walls of Newtown, and that's the woman I want to know.

"No offense, but your grandmother was a kook," Nyssa says, pulling me back to the music. "A few years ago, she paid off some Enforcers to bring her down here. I thought she'd run screamin'. Instead, she practically drank me under the table. That was the only time I met her in person."

Hearing Nyssa talk is like seeing something from another time. Of course Gram wouldn't run when faced with the true face of the Slum. She joined right in. I can't help but smile. That's my Gram, after all.

"Here." Nyssa sets a rough metal cup full of clear liquid in front of me. "To Lady Malkin. She may be gone, but her soldiers fight on."

Nyssa raises her drink—first to the ceiling, and then to me. My eyes dart between Nyssa and the cup in my hand. Me, one of Gram's soldiers? But I'm nothing like Nyssa. I don't have a crew willing to put themselves on the line to protect the people of the

Slum from AURA's control. I'm just me—a kid who's suffered too much and can't stand to see others feel the same pain—a pain I tried to drown with alcohol.

Slowly, I set my drink down, not touching a drop. "No, thank you."

"You've come a long way, Ezariah." Nyssa smiles, taking back my cup. The expression looks odd, but not entirely out of place. "You're not like most Renounced. The Slum… It breaks your kind. But not you. You've suffered, but now, you're one of us. This is where you belong."

Nyssa's words echo around in my mind as I leave her. I return to the music, my insides growing warmer as the volume increases. I find Sera right where I left her. She dances through the crowd, her eyes closed as her tattered purple sheet swirls around her. There's a grace to her movements that the other dancers lack. I can't help but smile. Her dad taught her well.

I position myself in her path. She spins right into me, and I stagger back, trying to keep myself upright. Her eyes snap open, and for a moment, her face hardens. Then, as her soft blue eyes find mine, I feel her muscles relax.

"Thought you'd left me." She smiles.

"Never." The word slips out before I can stop it.

My hand finds hers, and our fingers intertwine. Sera pulls me along, and I gladly follow her lead. I pull her closer, and I feel the warmth of her breath on my chest. Without thinking, I lean in and press my lips to hers. Sera's hand slips from mine, and I almost expect her to pull away. Instead, she wraps her arms around my neck, kissing me back. I'm not sure if we've stopped dancing, because the world feels like it's spinning. My heart thuds against my ribs, and more than anything, I don't want the moment to end.

Nyssa's right. Right now, in this moment, is exactly where I belong. The music pulses through me, and it's like I'm floating. Nothing else matters. It's just me and Sera.

Suddenly, the doors to the Hollow burst open. The music screeches to a halt, replaced by the heavy stomp of boots.

"Enforcers!"

The scream rips through the air like gunfire. People push past us, knocking Sera into me as they scramble to get away. All the warmth inside me vanishes, replaced by an icy dread. These people aren't running for the exit; they're running from the Enforcers toward the opposite side of the Hollow, where there are no doors or windows.

"Come on!" Sera yells over the noise, her grip on my hand tightening.

As Sera pulls me through the crowd, I see Nyssa standing on a table. "Rowan! Get these people out of here! Nelda, get the others! Jackson, with me!"

Nyssa jumps off her table and disappears into the crowd. My feet move instinctively. I step forward, but not toward the door. I know what Nyssa's doing: she's buying Rowan time to get as many people out of here as possible. My eyes dart from a woman, screaming as a baton strikes her in the back, to a man, pulled to the ground by his hair.

Nyssa's words push through the chaos, filling my mind until there's nothing left. *"Gram may be gone, but her soldiers fight on."*

Nyssa's right: I am one of Gram's soldiers. And it's my job to protect these people, just like she did.

"We need to help!" I say, pulling against Sera's grip, but she doesn't let go.

"There's nothing we can do!" Sera's voice is desperate. "We have to go!"

"No!" Sera pulls me towards the exit, but my feet feel like lead. This isn't right; we promised to help people. How can we do that if we run?

"Ezariah, please!" Sera shouts, and I hear the panic in her voice.

Even though all I want to do is fight, I can't ignore the terror in Sera's eyes. Somehow, it drowns out the chaos, and I know what I have to do. Sera's right. I can't protect everyone in here—but I can protect her.

The doors of the Hollow are hanging off their hinges, and an armored car fills most of the doorway. Luckily, the Enforcers have more important things to worry about. Even with all the screaming, Nyssa's shouts still rise over the din. It's hard to keep my eyes fixed ahead. I double my grip on Sera as we force our way through the small opening between the Enforcer's car and the doorframe.

We run, our feet pounding over the cobblestones. The music and warmth of the Hollow, all the happiness I felt mere moments ago, slips through my fingers like water. Tonight was supposed to be about letting go, taking just one night for myself. But the Enforcers won't even let us have that. Today, I was almost arrested three different times. I thought I'd seen the worst the Slum has to offer. But I was wrong. Things are getting much worse.

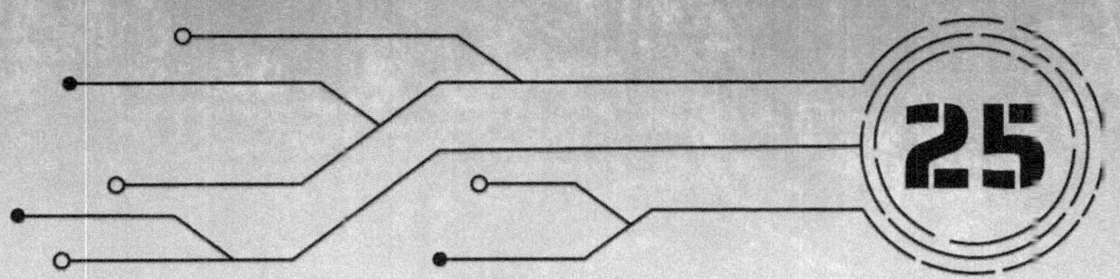

MY EYES ARE heavy as I follow Sera through the streets. It's kind of amazing, the difference twenty-four hours can make. Yesterday, every possible path was packed with so many people that I couldn't take two steps without running into someone. But now, I'd be lucky to find two people. The tension in the air is as thick as the grime clinging to the slanting buildings.

Neither Sera nor I say a word. Every time I try to speak, last night flashes through my mind like a whirlwind. Dancing with Sera. Talking with Nyssa about Gram. Sera's lips pressed against mine. Enforcers throwing people to the ground. Somehow, it still doesn't feel real; it's more like a twisted nightmare. If that's the case, I'd really like to wake up now.

We turn down a street a few blocks from the square. New posters hang every few feet, all covered in the same bold writing, the seal of Nomisman stamped in the corner. I stop, letting go of Sera's hand as I approach the nearest one.

BY DECREE OF THE GOVERNMENT OF NOMISMAN:

IN ORDER TO MAINTAIN THE LAWS OF ECONOMIC STABILITY ESTABLISHED BY AURA, THE FOLLOWING REGULATIONS SHALL BE PUT INTO IMMEDIATE EFFECT TO ENSURE THE SAFETY AND STABILITY OF ALL LOWTOWN RESIDENTS:
-ALL RESIDENTS MUST RETURN TO THEIR DESIGNATED DWELLING BY SUNDOWN.

-LOITERING AND SOLICITATION FOR ALMS ARE STRICTLY PROHIBITED.
-ALL RESIDENTS WILL CONSENT TO RANDOM SEARCH AND INSPECTION.

COMPLIANCE IS MANDATORY.
IN AURA WE TRUST.

With every line, it feels like someone is burying me beneath slabs of concrete. This… It can't be real, can it? Life in the Slum is hard enough with AURA controlling the price of everything, squeezing every last coin out of our pockets. I don't care what the notices say. Thanks to Nyssa, I know the truth: AURA and the Enforcers don't care about protecting us. All that matters to them is keeping us Slummers under control. This isn't an act of protection; it's a declaration of war.

"This can't be happening," Sera breathes.

My hands ball into fists, my nails digging into my palms. "This is why they came to the Hollow." It's so obvious. They probably enacted the new laws yesterday without telling anyone. Then, they waited until the gathering at the Hollow was in full swing. They arrested so many people for things they didn't even know were illegal yet. The thought makes me want to throw something.

"You gotta keep your head down," Sera says. "The last thing we need right now is for the Enforcers to catch us."

Oddly, staying out of trouble is easier than I thought. But it's not because I want to. Ever since the orders went up, Enforcers are everywhere. They're always marching through the streets, their batons in hand. They stop people at random, shoving them against the walls as they pat them down. Sera should really stop worrying. With all of these Enforcers so busy upholding the new laws, I couldn't get into trouble even if I tried.

This morning is no different as I walk toward the plant. Somehow, even the larger roads feel small with the Enforcers patrolling on either side. Normally, I'd cut through a few of the narrower alleys to get to the plant. But the Enforcers have taken to stalking there, looking for easy pickings. So, I stick to the main roads.

But as careful as I'm trying to be, that doesn't stop the Enforcers. I turn a corner and almost walk right into one. I see her eyes narrow through the slit in her visor, and I force my face into a neutral expression. It's surprisingly easy to look innocent, especially when I've done nothing wrong today.

"Tag," she demands.

Without hesitating, I hold out my arm. She holds a scanner over my tag, which beeps once as the inside of my forearm burns. Then her hands are on me, pushing me against a wall as she pats down my shirt, my pants. I take a deep breath, fighting to keep myself calm. She finds nothing, of course. Aside from my clothes, I have no real possessions. I don't even have any coins on me; I gave my last phys to an old man after he received a more brutal search.

"Move along," she says gruffly, stepping aside.

I nod, stepping around her without a word. As I walk away, I can't stop the corners of my mouth from twitching. It's a small victory, but right now, I'll take what I can get.

The clang of sledgehammers hits me before I even cross the threshold. It's louder than ever, with even more people standing in line to sign in. Enforcers stand on either side of the crowd, their helmets in constant motion. I shake my head as I shuffle forward. It's like they're expecting us to riot at any moment.

I reach the terminal and shove my forearm into the scanner. It beeps twice, and a message flashes across the screen.

"Work quota increased by twenty percent," the flat female voice drones. *"Shift duration extended by two hours. Noncompliance will result in immediate penalization."*

Whatever fight I have vanishes like smoke. It's the third time they've raised the quota in the past week. I sigh and take my sledgehammer. The Enforcers are worrying about nothing; we're more likely to collapse from exhaustion than fight back. I can't help but shake my head. That's probably exactly what the Enforcers want. We can't fight back if they work us to death.

Workstation 47 looks just like I left it yesterday. I grip my hammer, the rough handle biting the new callouses on my palms. My muscles tense as I step up to my generation plate. Behind me, I can feel an Enforcer watching me. They showed up a few weeks ago—one at every workstation. I thought they were cruel before, but now they're on a whole new level. Yesterday, I stopped to adjust my grip. No, it wasn't even a full stop; it was a pause, not even a full second. But that didn't stop the Enforcer from pressing his baton into my back. I can't see the welt, but Sera said it doesn't look too bad. With how much it still stings, I'd disagree.

The whistle blows, and I try to get into the rhythm. The ringing is deafening, but after a while, it's like I'm underwater, oddly muffled and distorted. Strike after strike, I bring my hammer down on the plate, and the wires extending from it glow. Sweat pours down my face, stinging my eyes. But I don't dare wipe it away; I grit my teeth and swing again and again. Today, I'm not going to give the Enforcers any reason to punish me.

Others aren't as lucky. I see them falter—a missed strike here, a slower swing there. The Enforcers don't waste a second, and soon, the pained cries of workers mingle with the rhythmic clang of the hammers. The sound ignites something in me. I bring my hammer down on my generation plate with all the strength I have. I imagine it hitting an Enforcer, knocking them back from their helpless prey. I smile and swing my hammer again.

The end of the day brings no relief. My back is aching, my muscles feel like I've run them through a shredder, and my head is pounding in time with the hammers. I try to focus on the positive as I shuffle into line with Talon and Cypress, dragging my hammer behind me. At least I didn't get tased today. I want to laugh, but I don't even have the energy for that. This is my life now; a good day is not getting beaten repeatedly.

I slide my forearm into the scanner at the front terminal. The jolt of warmth from my ID tag feels oddly soothing against my throbbing muscles. The screen flickers, and then words flash across the display.

"Daily quota: met," the computer says, followed by a single number.

Three credits. I sigh and pull my arm back. It's barely enough for a decent meal. Hopefully, Sera earns more from her shift at the fabric warehouse. Maybe if she had a really good shift, we'll have enough to visit the Fringe before sundown. With all the new rules, I haven't been down there in a few days.

"Look at you, Ezra." Talon claps me on the back, a weak smile on his face. "Finally getting the hang of it."

I nod, forcing a half-hearted smile as we walk toward the doors. I know Talon's just trying to be nice; he's that way all the time. But I don't know what's stranger: the fact that I am getting better at this job, or the tiny glimmer of pride I feel at actually meeting the quota.

"Daily quota: not met."

I spin around so quickly that I almost trip. A shudder runs through the warehouse, and it's like all the air has been knocked from my lungs. Cypress is standing at the scanner, his face draining of color as he silently mouths the words still ringing in my ears.

"It … it's three strikes," Cypress stammers, his voice cracking as his dark eyes grow wide. "It's only three strikes."

It happens so fast. The Enforcers converge on Cypress, one pinning his arms behind his back while another pulls the hammer from Cypress's side.

"No! Please! My record's clean!" Cypress's plea echoes off the vast walls as the Enforcers drag him away.

The crowd is silent, like everyone is holding their breath, waiting. I step forward, my hands shaking, struggling to blink, to think, to do something more than stare. This can't be happening. All Cypress did was miss the quota. I've done that countless times, and I've never been arrested for it.

"Don't, Ezra," Talon hisses, grabbing my arm. "You'll just end up with him, or worse."

His words don't do anything to temper my anger. I watch as Cypress disappears into the crowd. I know I can't help him, but that doesn't stop the fire now raging inside me as more workers step up to the terminal like nothing happened. Cypress missed the quota by just three strikes, and now, I don't know when I'll see him again.

Somehow, things go from bad to worse. All of the bakeries and shops raise their prices, which means Sera and I have no chance of eating anything decent. We can't even afford a rotten apple or a bowl of mystery soup from the carts in the square. So, we slip into the refinery just as the sky turns from indigo to pink.

I'll be the first to admit that I've changed a lot since my Renouncement. I'm no longer terrified of every person I see, I've got a job, and I will eat basically anything if it fills my stomach. But the one thing I still can't get over is the refinery. The smell hits me like a punch to the face, burning my nose and making my eyes water. And there's something about eating food I've literally dug out of a pile of trash. At least in the square, it smells a little better.

"Find anything?" Sera asks.

"Just this." We've been searching for an hour, and all I've found is the discards from some Midtowner's dinner. It's mostly picked over, just the remains of a chicken carcass. If I had it my way, I'd leave it here. Surely we can find something better. But with the rations bank closing all the time now and the rise in prices, I guess I'll have to suck it up.

"Here." I toss the remains of the chicken to Sera.

"Watch it," Sera snaps, barely managing to grab it.

That really was the easiest throw in the world. If she'd dropped it, that's on her. I bite my tongue. We're both on edge;

two days with no food will do that to you. Even though she'd never tell me, I know Sera's freaking out. She's survived the Slum by knowing the system and bending it to her advantage. But all of these new laws have her hands tied. And with the foreman at the factory where she works extending their shifts too, Sera hasn't gotten much sleep lately. If I were her, I guess I'd bite my head off too.

It doesn't take long for more Slummers to arrive at the refinery. Sera and I lock eyes, and I know what she's thinking without her even saying it. It won't be long before this place is packed with starving people fighting over what few scraps remain. Worse, a crowd like this will no doubt draw the attention of Enforcers. So, Sera and I leave with our chicken carcass and what I think may have been a potato—it's hard to tell.

My feet drag over the cobblestones as Sera goes to the market to check on Jewel. I head to Floodway, where Cypress lives with his wife and daughter. Well, lived. My chest tightens as I knock on the door. I don't know why I'm nervous; it's not like Cypress's arrest was my fault. But when the Enforcers took him away, what did I do? Nothing, that's what.

The door creaks open, and a woman peeks out. Her face is red and puffy, and there's a vacant look in her eyes. "Ezra," Cypress's wife says, her voice oddly distant.

"I'm just … checking in." What can I say to her? In the past few months, she's been through hell. First her son died, and then Cypress got arrested for no reason. If I were her, I'd be falling apart. "Anything you need?"

She shakes her head, a weary smile on her lips. "We're fine. We've been through worse."

I nod, although I don't know what could be worse than this. I leave Cypress's wife, promising to return in a few days, and make my way to Sola's. With everything that's happened in the Slum, I haven't been to see them in over a week. I can't wait to just lie on the floor, playing with Luca while Tace builds some contraption. The thought makes me smile a little.

But when Sola opens the door, the smile vanishes from my lips. Her face is pale, and there are dark circles under her eyes. It's like I've swallowed an ice cube. Something's wrong.

"What is it?" I ask, stepping inside.

"Ezra, don't be mad," she whispers, grabbing my arm.

If she intended to calm me down, that was the wrong thing to say. Immediately, my heart starts to race, and I feel like I can't breathe. I look around. Tace is sitting on the floor, building what looks like a house out of old roofing material.

"Where's Halyn? Luca?"

"They're at the Department of Labor."

"No!" The word flies from my lips before I can stop it. But I don't care. There is no way I'm going to let this happen. Halyn and Luca—they're too young to start working, especially at the jobs given out at the Department of Labor. For a moment, I see Theron and Callias swinging hammers at the plant. Rage boils inside me, and I clench my fists so tight that my hands shake.

"Ezra," Sola says, pulling me into her arms before I can take a step. "We're barely scraping by. Halyn and Tace wanted to help. It's their choice."

I try to pull away from Sola, but she only hugs me tighter. The gesture feels odd, almost foreign. I can't remember the last time someone other than Sera touched me like that. Even though I don't want to, I understand. These days, putting food on the table is a daily battle. I don't know how Sola has managed this long with three little mouths to feed. Slowly, a warmth seeps into my bones, my muscles relax, and I let out a breath I didn't know I was holding.

My mind's a blur as I leave Sola's. I can't get the image of Halyn and Luca in a place like the plant out of my head. It's not right. They should be playing, enjoying what little freedom they have, not slaving away for a few measly credits. I remember what Bart said to me the first time we met. He told me the Slum is no place for little ones. At the time, I thought he was talking about the potential dangers here. But now, I don't think he was. How can kids stay kids in a place like this?

As I turn a corner, I stop. Sera's emerging from the crowd, her sheet dress billowing around her. I'm equally shocked and relieved. I didn't expect her back so soon.

"Hey," I say, jogging over to her. "I thought you were at Jewel's?"

"I was barely there," she says, shaking her head. "Enforcers are scumbags."

"I … know…" There has to be something I'm missing. I'm always the first one to say how horrible the Enforcers are; I have the welts to prove it.

"Jewel is at the end of her rope," Sera huffs. "She and her girls rely on their clients for everything. You know, most of the time, they pay with rations. But ever since AURA started cracking down, they've stopped coming."

A sour taste fills my mouth. AURA doles out rations based on economic impact. Since Jewel's work isn't exactly official, she and her girls only qualifies for the bare minimum. The same is true for everyone working the market. It's so unfair, especially when the bulk of the market shoppers are Enforcers.

"How're Sola and the kids?"

When I tell her about Halyn and Luca going to the Department of Labor, I expect her to be just as outraged as I am. So, I'm shocked when instead of sharing my horror, she looks almost relieved. It almost makes me angrier than them having to get jobs in the first place.

"Don't you see how wrong this is?"

"Ezariah, they have jobs. They're helping Sola put food on the table. What's wrong with that?"

"They're just kids!" How can she not see how wrong this is? Has Sera been in the slum for so long that she's forgotten what the real world is like? "This is all my fault."

"How can this possibly be your fault?" Sera demands, stopping dead in her tracks.

"Because I couldn't help them."

I've been thinking about it since I left Sola's. If AURA hadn't added these stupid laws, none of this would be happening. Sera and I would still be sneaking into Midtown, and we would have plenty of money to help those we care about. Jewel wouldn't have to go begging the Enforcers for scraps. Halyn and Luca could still be kids.

"Don't do that," Sera says, her eyes narrowing the way they always do when she's on edge. "You've helped them more than you know."

"But if I could just give—"

"No." Sera cuts me off and takes my hand. "Short of starving yourself, there's nothing more you can do. And I promise you, that's the last thing Sola wants."

I want to scream that it's not enough, that we have to do more. But I know that look in Sera's eyes. It's the same look she wore after bailing me out of Nyssa's crew. Even if I was right, which deep down I know I'm not, there's no way I'm winning this one. So, I swallow my words.

We walk into the square, but it's practically unrecognizable. Enforcers stand around the perimeter while Slummers run around with an urgency that makes me shudder. They're erecting a stage in the center of the square, its skeleton already casting a long shadow over the cobblestones. Huge speakers flank the stage, while behind it, massive screens hang precariously from cranes, shielding the buildings.

"What's going on?" My voice comes out harsher than normal.

Sera doesn't say anything. Instead, she takes my hand and drags me to the nearest building. Like every other wall in the Slum these days, it's covered with posters. I noticed the new ones this morning when we left for the refinery, but didn't bother to read them. Every poster has the same list of decrees and regulations from AURA. Why would I waste my time?

"It's for the Culling."

I laugh, but it sounds more like a snort. The Culling. I'd completely forgotten about the Culling—the one chance Theron and Callias had to escape this place. It was their only way out. But me—thanks to my record, I'm stuck here. On my priority list, the Culling ranks just below digging through the refinery.

I turn away, but Sera's grip tightens. "Wait," she insists. Her eyes narrow as they scan the large, bold writing. I can't imagine why. We both already know what the notice says.

"They changed the rules," Sera says slowly, like she can't quite believe what she's saying.

New rules? The way Sera says it makes me stop dead in my tracks. I don't want to care, but a small part of me can't help it. I return to the poster, the seal of Nomisman proudly displayed on the bottom corner.

BY DECREE OF THE GOVERNMENT OF NOMISMAN:

PER THE LAWS OF ECONOMIC STABILITY ESTABLISHED BY AURA, RESIDENTS OF LOWTOWN MUST PRESENT THEMSELVES IN THE TOWN SQUARE ON THE 15TH OF APRIL AT NOON FOR THE CULLING.
TO COMBAT RISING POPULATION IN THIS RESIDENCY ZONE, MULTIPLE WINNERS WILL BE SELECTED. THE WINNERS WILL RECEIVE NEW RESIDENCY STATUS FOR THEMSELVES, AS WELL AS FOR IMMEDIATE FAMILY MEMBERS, PERMITTING RELOCATION TO SELECT PARTS OF MIDTOWN.

ATTENDANCE IS MANDATORY.
IN AURA WE TRUST.

I read the poster through four times, sure I missed something. But there it is, plastered all around the square. There will be more than one winner. My stomach practically does a backflip at the thought. This is what I've needed. Not for me, of course; I'm still ineligible. But with multiple winners, so many people now have a real chance to escape the Slum. This one day will do more good for the people here than I could do in a year.

We hurry across the square, carefully avoiding the Enforcers and workers buzzing around like flies. I feel like I'm walking on clouds. Finally, after weeks of living in what feels like a war zone, this is our reprieve. I want to laugh, cry, and smile all at the same time, but I hold it in. However, when the door to Sera's apartment creaks shut, I can't keep it in any longer.

"Can you believe it?" I ask, smiling so broadly it hurts. "They're allowing multiple winners! Sola and her kids—they have a real shot at getting out, at having a real life."

Sera bites her lip, her eyes narrowing again. "It … sounds good on paper," she says slowly. "But Ezariah, this is still the Slum. It's not exactly known for giving people second chances."

"Oh, c'mon!" I roll my eyes. Why can't she just be happy? It's like she's always waiting for the other shoe to drop. "They've announced it. This Culling could change everything for someone like Talon or Sola … or even you."

I take her hand, and it feels like someone is sitting on my chest. I may be trapped in the Slum forever. But Sera—she's too smart to have a record. This Culling is a real chance for her to escape all this hardship for good.

"Me?" Sera pulls away, looking almost insulted. "Why would I go?"

I'm taken aback by the question. Isn't it obvious? "To be free?"

She lets out a laugh that doesn't quite reach her eyes. "Ezariah, here in the Slum, I'm freer than I've ever been."

Sera sits on the sleeping mat, her words hanging in the air. I stare as she caresses her wrist—the one where her mother's tracking bracelet used to be. I feel like an idiot. For Sera, the Culling isn't the escape it is for everyone else. Before the crackdown, she left the Slum whenever she wanted, thanks to her scarf. She didn't have to come back—she's clever enough to blend in anywhere—but she did. The Slum may be a prison, but for her, it's one without chains.

I join Sera on the sleeping mat. My hand finds hers, and our fingers intertwine. I open my mouth, but no words come out. What am I supposed to say to someone who has more strength than I could ever have?

She leans in, pressing her forehead onto mine. "Don't worry. I'm staying right here," she whispers. "Besides, who's gonna keep you out of trouble if I leave?"

I can't help but laugh. As much as I hate to admit it, Sera has a point. She's pulled me out of danger more times than I can count in the past few weeks. Without her, I doubt I'd last three days before doing something stupid.

"Then I guess I'm stuck with you," I say, my thumb tracing small circles on the back of her hand.

We lapse into silence, just lying together, watching the single candle Sera lit slowly warp and melt. No matter what happens at the Culling tomorrow, at least we have this. We have our tiny, cramped apartment. We have each other.

And honestly, that's all I really need.

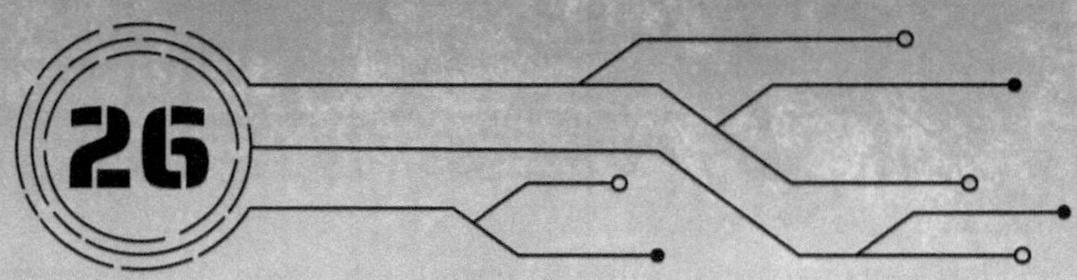

IF WE HAD it our way, we'd stay in Sera's apartment all day. I have no real desire to attend the Culling. After all, I can't win. And Sera's even less interested, if that's possible. She takes a long time getting dressed, which is impressive, since all she wears is a sheet. But I know she'll go in the end. We both will. It's not like we have a choice; attendance is mandatory.

The sun has barely peeked over the slanting buildings as we step outside. Despite Sera's apartment being literally feet from the square, we take the nearest alley away from it. Last night, the Enforcers blocked off all but one of the main entrances to the square, and it doesn't take a genius to know why. It's a lot easier to keep tabs on a population when there's only one entrance.

The main street is already packed when we get there. People stand shoulder to shoulder, practically stepping on each other as the line moves forward like a glacier. The last time I stood in this line—well, the last time I fully remember, anyway—I was so excited. I thought that after only a month in the Slum, Theron, Callias, and I were going to get out. I can't help but laugh now. It's hard to believe how much things have changed.

When we finally reach the check-in table, I present my arm first. The Enforcer manning the table scans my tag, the inside of my forearm burns for a second, and the screen on his scanner flashes red, followed by a sharp beep.

"Ineligible," he drones, waving me forward. "Next!"

I step forward while Sera signs in. I watch, almost bored, as Sera's tag glows green. She moves on before the Enforcer can even ask if she wants to buy more entries. I can't help but smile as she takes my hand and pulls me down the street. Even if Sera wanted to leave the Slum, she's too smart to buy more entries.

It's amazing what a difference twenty-four hours can make. The massive stage in the middle of the square is now complete, draped in white cloth and covered with chairs. An upbeat track blares from the speakers, while the massive screens behind the stage blast images of previous winners living their supposed Midtown dream lives, cut with shots of the growing crowd.

We find a spot near the edge of the throng, leaning against an old brick building that looks like it's being held together by sheer force of will. More and more people funnel into the square, and the growing excitement makes my insides hum. I've never felt anything like this since arriving in the Slum. I stand on my tiptoes, searching for any faces I recognize, but the bodies are already packed so tightly that I can't tell one from the next. It doesn't matter though. They're all here, somewhere.

"Well, at least it's exciting," I say, looking down at Sera.

"Yeah," she says slowly. Her eyes are narrow, the way they always are when she's thinking. She looks around the square, but I have no idea what she's looking for. Half the time, she's not even looking at the crowd. Instead, her eyes shift over the tops of the buildings or back to the main street.

After what feels like an hour, several Midtowners, all dressed in the loudest outfits I've ever seen, mount the stage. After they've taken their seats, a man dressed in a plain blue shirt and pants takes the last chair. He's oddly familiar, but I can't place his face. The music cuts off abruptly as one of the Midtowners swaggers up to the podium. His blue-and-green suit is covered with so many tiny stones that he looks like he's been dipped in dew. He clears his throat, and silence falls over the square.

"Welcome, ladies and gentlemen of Lowtown," he begins, his voice echoing around the square. "The Culling is about to begin!"

The crowd's cheers are so loud, it's almost deafening. People push forward, as though being closer to the stage will help their odds. Even though I know I can't win, that doesn't stop my heart from beating a little faster. I take Sera's hand. She glances at me, her expression unreadable, before turning back to the crowd.

"Per the Laws of Economic Stability, established by AURA after the Great Fall," the man begins, his voice so upbeat it makes me jump, "the government of Nomisman declared that the residents of Lowtown will present themselves four times a year for the Culling."

He pauses for effect. A few people clap, but most just stare at the stage. It's not hard to guess what they're thinking. No one cares about the history of the Culling. This guy just needs to get on with it.

"The winner will be granted relocation clearance to Midtown, as well as for their immediate family. And today is no ordinary Culling," he continues with a flourish that makes my stomach turn. "Today, by the grace of AURA, we will have not one, but multiple winners! In AURA we trust!"

"In AURA we trust!" the crowd echoes back before erupting into cheers. I can't help but clap along with them. The announcer may be over the top, but he's right about one thing. Today is a special day, and we should celebrate it.

I glance at Sera, but she's not looking at me. Her brows form one severe line as she continues to scan the crowd. I shake my head. I can't help it. I know she doesn't trust the Culling, but everyone else seems to. I think for the first time Sera might actually be wrong.

The man in the plain blue shirt stands and walks to the podium. The Midtowner hands him a tablet, and I feel like I'm emerging from underwater. The memory is fuzzy, but I do know this man. After he won the last Culling, he brought two young boys on stage with him. After that, I think I threw a lot of stuff.

"In AURA we trust."

The previous winner presses something on the tablet, and pain blooms in my forearm. All around me, the crowd gasps as every ID tag flashes red. I stare at mine, the pulsing light oddly soothing. Mine will never turn green. In the past, that thought would have terrified me. But not anymore.

The screens behind the stage show quick shots of the crowd as the rhythmic red pulsing increases. The shots come faster, and I hold my breath. I can't help it. I'm actually excited.

Then the picture on the screen zooms into the crowd. It shows a man with a heavily lined face, his eyes wide with disbelief as he stares at his green ID tag. The crowd claps and whistles as the old man hobbles forward. It takes him a while to reach the stage, and when he does, he struggles with the stairs. I smile, clapping with the rest when he finally reaches the podium. He may not be Sola, but this man has definitely earned his chance at an easier life.

This happens again and again. Each time the camera zooms in on a new winner, the crowd cheers louder than before as they join the old man on the stage. A woman with dark hair and skeletal arms. A short man with a squished face who's missing a hand.

The screens flash, and a fresh wave of excitement surges through me as my tag pulses again. How many people are they going to pick? The notices never said. Five? Ten? No matter how many they pick, it won't be enough.

The screen zooms in on the next winner. The crowd cheers again, and I look up. A small part of me hopes it's Sola or Talon, even though I know the odds are stacked against them. But I recognize the winner, and my mouth falls open.

Jackson's face is plastered across the screens, and for a second, I can't quite believe it. I watch him lumber through the crowd like a walking mountain, wide-eyed, a slight frown on his brow. His expression is identical to mine. Murmurs swirl around the crowd as Jackson mounts the stage. He looks like he just got hit in the face.

But this can't be happening. Jackson's got a record, just like me. He shouldn't be able to win. That's the rule. So, why is he up there?

"What's going on?" I shake my head, turning to Sera.

Sera's eyes are glued to the stage, her arms crossed tight against her chest. "Something's not right," she murmurs, her eyebrows furrowed.

Another winner is announced, and I recognize this face too. He's been at Nyssa's, dropping off his collections, just like I used to. He's got a rap sheet too; everyone in Nyssa's crew does. The crowd claps as expected, but there's an edge to their cheers that wasn't there before.

Then there's a girl in a dress so thin that it's practically see-through. She stands frozen for a moment before shuffling forward. I know her too. I've seen her standing with Jewel enough times at the market.

This time, there's no hint of excitement from the crowd as they press closer. Enforcers mount the stage, drawing their batons as they form a human wall between the crowd and the winners. I feel Sera tense beside me, and I take her hand in mine.

"This isn't right." Sera shakes her head slightly, eyes still fixed on the stage.

"Stay back!" the Enforcers shout, their amplified voices making my bones shake.

"Why are these people winning?" A voice rises over the square, asking the question we're all thinking. "They've got records!"

All the excitement from earlier is gone. Something's off—and it's bigger than AURA picking the wrong winners. As the crowd reaches the stage, the Midtown officials rise from their chairs. They hurry to the edge of the stage, then disappear, looking just as stunned as I feel. A sour taste fills my mouth. That's it? They're not even going to explain what's happening?

The Enforcers step right up to the edge of the stage. One of them, a bulky figure at least two heads taller than me, raises his baton high, as if to signal silence. That's a mistake. The crowd roars even louder, and a few attempt to mount the stage. I tighten my grip on Sera's hand, her pulse racing against my fingers.

Crack! Screams fill the air as all through the square, people fall. My ears ring, and I'm frozen, a statue unable to move. I've heard that sound before, back in school, when they'd show us old films from the Great Fall. Gunfire.

"Run!" Sera's grip on my hand turns to iron. She pulls me along, pushing headfirst through the crowd as more shots ring out. Somehow, instinct kicks in, a desperate, primal thing that overrides everything else. I focus on Sera, determined not to let her out of my sight.

Then my foot catches on something. Sera's hand slips from mine, and I fall, pain exploding in my leg. Suddenly, the world comes crashing in around me. All I hear is the sound of gunfire mixed with the screams of the crowd. I try to push myself up, but the pain in my leg is too much. It gives out, and I fall back to the ground.

"Get up!" Sera yells, taking my hand. "C'mon!"

She hoists me up, draping my arm over her shoulder. Together we stagger toward the square's entrance—the only one that's not blocked off. My leg burns with each step, but the terror coursing through me eclipses the pain. More people collapse, clutching bleeding wounds, while others trample over them in their desperation.

I crane my neck. Where are the Enforcers? They're supposed to protect us, to maintain AURA's peace. But there's no sign of their dark uniforms anywhere in the square.

Sera's breaths are ragged as we push through the panicked mass of bodies. The entrance to the square is a bottleneck—too many people frantically trying to squeeze through a tight space. Sera leads me to the side, and we force our way through a small gap between a building and the temporary barricade. My back scrapes against the rough brick, but I ignore it as we burst out onto the street. Before I can even look back, Sera takes my arm and pulls me from the gunshots and screams still piercing the air. Adrenaline surges through me like fire as my pounding heartbeat thuds against my skull. Sera's grip on my arm is the only constant as we duck and weave through the maze of alleys. But no matter how far we go, the crack of gunfire and the screams seem like they're right behind us.

After running for several blocks, Sera pulls me inside a random building. It has no door, and the glass from the windows lies shattered on the floor. My breaths come in ragged gasps as she slowly lowers me to the floor. She crouches beside me on the concrete, her eyes full of concern. She quickly rolls up my pant leg, revealing a long gash oozing blood. The sight sends a shiver down my spine, and the world wobbles dangerously.

"What's happening?" I demand, my voice shaking. "Why are they shooting people? They're supposed to protect us!"

Sera's eyes meet mine, her expression steely. "Right now, it doesn't matter."

"Doesn't matter?!" I shout, my voice cracking. "They're shooting at us!"

"We need to get somewhere safe first," Sera says, tearing a strip from the bottom of her sheet-dress. She wraps it tightly around my leg, and I hiss as my blood instantly soaks through the thin fabric.

"C'mon. Get up," she says, helping me to my feet. "We're going to the barrier."

"The barrier?" I wince as I gingerly put weight on my leg. Why would Sera want to go to the barrier now? With all the shooting, we shouldn't be out in the open. We need to find some-where to wait this out.

"Yes," Sera says firmly. "Whatever's happening here isn't over. But it's not happening in Midtown. We'll be safe there."

I lean heavily on her as we navigate our way out of the build-ing. My mind is racing with so many questions that I don't know where to start. But Sera's right: questions are pointless if we don't make it through this. Survive first; answers later.

Pain stabs my leg with every step, but I push it down. We

stick to the shadows, the narrow back alleys, only stepping onto the main roads when absolutely necessary. But even though we're blocks from the square, the crackle of gunfire and screams stabs me like a knife. Every now and then, a Slummer barrels past us, their face twisted in fear. They don't spare us so much as a glance. Right now, everyone's only concern is themselves.

We're almost at the barrier when I see it—a rough chain-linked fence stretched between the pillars. My heart sinks as I take it in, reaching all the way up to the top of the pillars. Sera stops, her breath shaky and uneven. The Enforcers have turned the barrier into a real fence. Even with Sera's scarf, there's no way we can climb over it.

Sera's hand tightens on mine. "We can't get through," she says, her voice breaking slightly. "They've blocked it off."

I lean against the wall, wincing as I adjust my weight off my injured leg. "What do we do now?"

"Um…" She peers around, her eyes narrowed, no doubt searching for some solution.

Boom! A wall of light slams into me, followed by a blast that punches the air from my lungs. I fly back, screaming as dust fills the air. Ringing fills my ears, and I have trouble opening my eyes. I try to push myself up, but my arms are as stiff as stone.

"Sera!" I know I'm shouting, but I can't hear my own voice. I crawl like an animal, the world tilting dangerously. My stomach lurches, and I clamp my mouth shut, bile burning my nose.

Another explosion, closer this time. The light sears my eyes as the bang rattles my skull. I crumple, my face slamming into the hard ground. All thought vanishes from my mind. I can't think; I can barely breathe.

Then hands—Sera's hands—stretch out of the gloom. The sight of her lying there, her eyes half open, covered in dust, jolts something in my brain. Even though it's agony, I push myself up. I crawl on all fours until I'm beside her. I take her hand, and with all the strength I can muster, I pull both of us to our feet. We stumble together, a strange, broken creature. Sera's head lolls on her shoulder, her mouth hanging open. A storefront looms ahead, its door blasted off its hinges. I guide us inside and prop the door in place just as another flash fills the street.

I slide down the wall, Sera collapsing beside me. It takes a while for the ringing in my ears to fade. The pounding in my head slows, and the world stops spinning around me like a top. Sera takes a little longer to recover. I try to keep her upright, and after a while, her eyes slowly open.

"You okay?"

"No." She shakes her head, and a pained look shoots across her face. "Where are we?"

"Some shop." I shrug. "I can't believe the Enforcers started this—just because the crowd got upset."

"Oh, c'mon," she says thickly. "That's not why they did it."

I stare at her, my mouth hanging open. Was she not at the same Culling as me? The Enforcers opened fire on the crowd when they got angry about ineligible people winning. What other proof does Sera need?

"Think about it," Sera says, pushing herself up. "They blocked off the square. They've never done that before. And they had Enforcers stationed on the roofs … with guns."

"So what?"

"Ezariah, this was their plan all along."

I stare at her, unable to process her words. I know Enforcers are awful, but why would they just start shooting at us? There has to be a reason.

"The posters said this Culling would be different because of the overpopulation in the Slum," Sera says, sounding more like herself now. "This is how AURA's solving the overpopulation— by reducing it."

I feel like I'm going to puke. I shake my head, trying to come up with some other explanation. But Sera's right: these aren't events driven by emotion or reason. This is the work of a machine—one that only cares about maintaining order. The Enforcers targeted the whole crowd, not just the people causing trouble. They sealed off the exits, meaning we had nowhere to go. And for those who made it out, they fenced off the barrier, so those desperate enough to face electrocution have no chance of escape.

"What are we supposed to do?"

"I don't know," Sera says, her head falling. "But this can't last forever. Sooner or later, they have to stop. Unless AURA plans to kill us all." She tries to stand, but her legs give out almost instantly.

"We need to wait," I say, unable to mask the urgency in my voice. "Until you're feeling better."

"Fine." Sera nods, her eyes darting to the door every few seconds. "But we can't stay long. Ezariah, if they find us…"

"We'll leave soon," I say quickly, and I mean it. I don't want to think what might happen if the Enforcers find us. So, I focus on what Sera said. This can't last forever. Sooner or later, the Enforcers will stop, and this nightmare will be over. But how long will that take?

Suddenly, canisters fly through the broken windows. They bounce off the walls and floor, filling the shop with dense white clouds. The gas claws at my eyes and burns my nose. I choke, my body convulsing as I try to draw breath.

"Go!" Sera's hoarse voice cuts through the haze. She grabs my arm, pulling me up. We stumble towards the back of the shop. I fumble at the door, but it's locked. I look wildly around. There has to be something I can use to pry it open. But Sera doesn't waste any time, slamming her shoulder against the door. It gives way, and we spill into the alley.

Fresh air hits me like a wave, but it's not enough to clear my head. Tears stream down my cheeks as I try to blink away the burn. Around us, other figures emerge from nearby buildings— more people driven out by the gas.

"Let's … move!" someone coughs.

I don't know these people, but right now, I don't care. I pull Sera with me, joining the group as we run down the alley. More canisters fall around us, filling the narrow street with smoke. It sears my lungs as I run, fighting to keep ahead of it. My injured leg trembles with every step, but I can't worry about that now. All that matters is moving forward—moving as far away from this wretched smoke as I can.

"We can't go this way."

"Sera, we need to keep going!" I pant, my lungs burning with every breath. I look at her, expecting to see some kind of injury. But aside from looking a little beat up, she looks fine. In fact, she looks almost alert.

Sera stops so abruptly that I almost fall over. She stands in the middle of the street, blocking me and the rest of the group from going forward. If I could, I'd pick her up and throw her over my shoulder. What is she thinking? The gas is going to catch up to us if we just stand here!

"We need to stop," she insists, her voice raspy.

"Girl, you're crazy!" an older woman says, her grey hair hanging limply over her face.

"No, Ezariah, look!" She shakes her head and gestures down the street we were about to follow. "Look where we are."

I do as she says—and my heart drops. I know this street. We're not near the barrier anymore. The white plumes of gas weren't meant to hurt us; it was meant to drive us back into the Slum like animals. A chill runs down my spine as the realization dawns on me.

"They're herding us back to the square," Sera says, as if reading my mind, her voice urgent. "Come this way."

Sera takes a few steps toward the nearest building. I follow, eager to get out of the open. But as she glances over her shoulder, she stops again. Most of the Slummers haven't moved. It's like they're rooted to the spot. Frustration temporarily masks my fear. What's wrong with them?

"You need to come with us," Sera insists, retracing her steps. "We need to get off the street."

"Not when they're firing gas into the buildings!" one man yells at her, his eyes wide.

"I promise, we're safer here," Sera says, and I hear the anger in her voice. "They want us to go that way."

"You're gonna get us killed!" another woman shouts, her voice raw.

I turn to Sera. Her jaw is set as her eyes dart between the Slummers, who continue to stand in the middle of the street. She's trying to save them—to save all of us—but their panic has driven all reason from their brains. If they keep going, the gas will drive them to the square. And if that happens, there's nothing standing between them and an Enforcer's bullet.

"Listen," I say, my throat tightening. "She's right! If you keep going that way, you're as good as—"

The sound of boots on concrete stops my words in my throat. Enforcers emerge from the alley—the same alley we were about to run down. They stop, their dark armor glinting as they raise their guns, pointing them right at us.

My breath catches in my throat, and I stumble back until I hit the wall. Sera's hand finds mine, her fingers shaking like crazy. I look down at her, expecting to see her mind whirring. Instead, her eyes are wide, and I know the truth: we have nowhere to go.

With nothing left to do, I close my eyes.

That's when the Enforcers open fire.

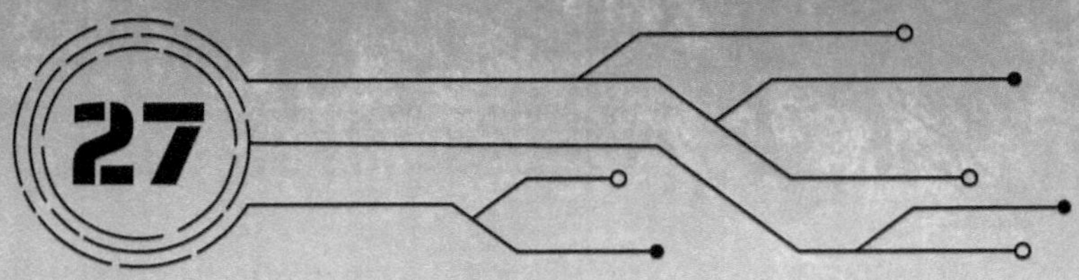

27

"NO!"

Hands slam into my side, and I stumble. Sera's scream pierces the air, a sound so raw and desperate that it cuts right through me. My eyes snap open, and I spin toward her, heart hammering against my ribs. She crumples to the ground, her hands clutching her stomach, dark red seeping through her sheet dress. An Enforcer looms over us, his gun still raised as the others race after the scattering Slummers.

Something inside me snaps. I lunge forward, and my fist connects with the underside of his jaw—the only part not covered by his helmet. The gun falls from his hand as he staggers back. I swing again, but this time, his baton strikes my side. Pain explodes through my ribs with a zap of electricity. But I barely register it; pain means nothing to me now. All that matters is making this Enforcer pay.

He may be trained to keep us Slummers in line, but now I've spent enough time in the pit at the Hollow to hold my own. And there, we fight dirty. He swings his baton at me again, but I'm ready this time. I hurl a handful of mud right in his face. It slips through the slit in his helmet, and he cries out in pain. I swing my leg around, and it hits him right in the side. He falls, hissing, and pulls his helmet off.

I react before I can even think. I grab the gun from the ground and swing it with all my might against his temple. The thud of metal on bone echoes through the alley. His head drops like a stone, and he doesn't stir.

"Sera!" My voice is hoarse as I fall to my knees, throwing the gun away.

She's pale—too pale—but she's conscious, eyes wide with shock and fear. "I'm okay," she says through gritted teeth as I help her to her feet.

"You're not," I retort, unable to stop my voice from shaking.

We limp down the alley, Sera's arm draped over my shoulder. We only make it a few feet before I know we can't go on. Sera grimaces with every step, and even though I'm holding most of her weight, she's shaking like a leaf. But I know Sera. She won't give up until we're safe or her body finally gives out.

I need to find us somewhere to hide. If I don't...

No. I can't think about that. Not now, not ever.

Blood pulses in my ears as I half carry, half drag Sera into the first building I can find, my injured leg screaming. She's lighter than she should be—or maybe the sight of her like this has made me stronger. The air inside is musty, and dust drifts through shafts of light from the boarded-up windows like stars.

"Here," I whisper, easing Sera down onto the hard floor. She winces, her lips pressed so tightly together that it's like she's determined to never open her mouth again.

"Don't move," I say, more to myself than to her. My hands shake as I limp around the room, dragging out broken chairs and a warped table and stacking them in front of the door. It's not much, but it will at least keep the door shut. And right now, that's the least of my worries.

In the few minutes it took me to barricade the door, Sera is looking worse—a lot worse. Her breathing is shallow and ragged, and her skin is ghastly, like someone who hasn't seen the sun for months. But that's nothing compared to the red stain growing on her stomach. Gingerly, I lift the layers of her sheet dress, and blood oozes from the wound in her stomach.

"It's ... fine," I lie, fighting to keep the panic from my face. Sera doesn't need me freaking out. But how can I keep it together when all I want to do is scream? "You're gonna be fine."

I tear my gaze from the wound and spot an old tarp crumpled in a corner. It reeks, and is covered in about five hundred stains, but it's all we have. I press it against Sera's stomach. Hopefully, it's enough to stop the bleeding. Her eyes flutter open, and it's enough to break me in two. All the fight, all the determination to survive is gone. Now, all I see is a girl who's suffered too much pain.

"Just hang on," I urge her, more a plea than a command.

But it's not her hanging on that's the problem. I look down at my hands, coated in Sera's blood. Every breath she takes feels like a tick of the clock, counting down until…

No. I shake my head and wipe my hands on the tarp. Thinking like that isn't going to get us out of here.

"Ezariah," Sera says, her voice airy and weak. "I … I don't—"

"Shh," I say, smoothing back her dark hair, her skin cold against mine. "Try not to talk."

Gunshots punctuate the silence as flashes rattle the boarded-up windows, sending tremors through the floor. Outside, AURA's culling of the Slum carries on, but somehow, it feels distant—like it's happening to someone else. Right now, all that matters is the girl lying beside me. But even as I stare at her, I feel the warmth fading from her hands, the color from her cheeks. If she dies, I'll have no one. After Theron and Callias died, Sera brought me back to life. How am I supposed to live in a world without her?

"I'm going to find help," I say, making up my mind. It's a long shot, but if I get to Floodway, maybe I can convince a healer to help—if anyone is even there. We just have to make it through the shooting, but if I double back to the barrier, I might make it.

"No." Sera's voice is barely audible over the chaos outside. "Stay with me."

Her gaze digs into my heart. She knows as well as I do that going out there is a death wish. But I don't care how dangerous it is. Doesn't she see that? I'd walk through a battlefield to save her. She's saved me more times than I can count.

"Sera," I say, dropping to my knees and taking her cold hand, "I can't just sit here while you—"

"Just sit," she insists again, cutting me off with a feeble squeeze of my fingers.

I obey, although every fiber of my being screams to move, to do something to stop this. "Sera, please," I whisper, my voice breaking.

"Ezariah," she says, her voice barely a whisper. "Tell me a story."

Even under the best of circumstances, I'm a horrible storyteller. Every time Theron or Callias asked me to tell one, I refused. But as I look into Sera's pale face, I know I can't say no. I nod and gently ease her head into my lap, brushing a strand of hair from her face. Her eyes flutter, but she manages a faint smile.

"Okay," I begin, my voice low and shaky, "there was this one time when Theron and Callias..."

Sera nods, the corners of her mouth twitching. Her breaths are shallow and fast, syncing with my heartbeat.

"... they were little. I think Callias was three. Our uncle, Galen, he had this dog—it barked all the time and drooled all over everything. My dad got so mad when it ruined his new suit." A wry smile tugs at the corner of my mouth at the thought. "Anyway, Theron thought he could outrun it."

Sera's hand squeezes mine ever so slightly. I take a shaky breath, trying to focus on what happened next.

"So, Theron and Callias were in the garden, and the dog came barreling out from behind the hedge. Both of them screamed like I'd taken their favorite toy, and they ran for the nearest tree." I can almost picture their tiny legs scurrying up the trunk. "The dog was just playing, but you couldn't tell them that. They climbed up that tree faster than squirrels. Then the dog got bored after a while and left them alone. Of course, then it became *my* problem. They realized they couldn't get down.

"I was so annoyed," I admit, staring at the dusty ceiling "I had to climb up there and get them down while they were both wailing."

I glance down at Sera. Her eyelids are heavy, but she's fighting to keep them open.

"But the whole thing was kinda funny," I say, swallowing hard against the lump in my throat. "Theron hanging onto that branch for dear life, while Callias hid under his shirt."

Her lips twitch in an attempt at a smile, and I can't help but smile back, even if mine is weak.

"I yelled at them the whole way down. We could have gotten in so much trouble if our father found out. But once we hit the ground..." My voice trails off, the ghost of a chuckle escaping my lips. "Theron... He just stared at me with those big eyes and said..."

"Said what?" Sera breathes, her voice so faint that it's almost carried away by the still air.

"He said, 'Ez, you're our hero!'" My voice cracks as the last word leaves me. It's like retelling something from another life, where being a hero means climbing into a tree to get my brothers. It almost doesn't feel real. I blink several times, forcing back my tears. I can't break—not now. Sera needs me to be strong. Her breathing is slower now, and her eyes have finally closed. Silence falls around us, only broken by the occasional gunshot or blast. But I stay right where I am, Sera's chest rising and falling against my trembling hands.

Time slips away as silence presses in around us. Sera's hand grows colder in mine, her breaths more labored. She hasn't spoken in a while, but maybe that's a good thing. She needs to conserve her strength.

"Just rest," I whisper, smoothing her hair as her body shakes.

"Ezariah..." Her voice is a ghost of itself, each syllable fractured with pain.

"Please, don't talk. Just rest," I urge.

But she's stubborn—always has been. "You ... gave me..."

Her words break off as I feel her shudder. Tears glisten at the corners of her eyes, and her eyelids flutter like butterfly wings.

"Sera, please," I plead, my voice barely above a murmur. I don't want to hear it. I know the words she's struggling to say.

"… a reason to live…" she continues, her breath hitching with every word. "Not just … survive."

I shake my head fiercely. "I should be the one thanking you. You're the one who saved *me*."

"We saved … each other," she gasps. "You need … to live … Ezariah. Don't let this … destroy your heart."

"I won't," I choke, even though my heart feels like it's being crushed into a million pieces.

Her eyes flutter open again—those soft blue eyes that have seen too much. "I'll tell … Theron and Callias … you love them."

I don't let go of Sera's hand, afraid of what might happen if I do. The room fades around me, the chaos outside nothing more than a dull echo. Her skin grows colder with each shallow breath, and I feel her pulse slowing beneath my fingers.

"Sera," I whisper, my voice breaking as much as my hands. "You can't… Please, don't go!"

But she doesn't respond, her chest barely rising now. Her grip on my hand loosens, her fingers growing limp in mine. I lean closer, desperate for any sign that she's still with me. I hear Sera's soft exhale and wait for her to breathe again. But all that follows is silence.

Gently, I stroke her face, expecting her to respond. But as the seconds tick by, I know I must accept the truth. Sera's gone.

Somewhere, I think it starts to rain. The soft patter fills the silence, like fingers drumming on a table. But even as the cold seeps through my clothes, I don't move. Sera's hand is still in mine, her skin cooling with each minute that slips by. I stare at her face. It's so calm, so peaceful. I wish I could have some of that peace. For myself, all I know is pain.

But this is an agony I know well. I've been here before— standing on the edge of a cliff, ready to drown my grief with alcohol and pain. Losing Theron and Callias nearly broke me. But now, I don't even have Sera to pull me back. It would be so easy to just let go—to give in to the sorrow until I'm nothing but an empty shell. Anything would be better than what I'm feeling now.

But then, Sera's words push their way through my sadness, echoing around my mind like a mantra. *"You need ... to live."*

Live? How am I supposed to do that when I have nothing to live for? No matter how much she taught me, I'm not Sera. I don't have her strength, her will to keep pushing forward when all hope is lost. She was a survivor. Even when facing her own death, she wanted more for me. How can I ever be like that?

But that isn't all Sera was. After everything she endured, all she wanted was to live her life free of the chains others tried to place around her. She didn't just survive; she lived—really lived. And that's all she wanted for me: to live. To move past tragedy. To not let it consume me.

I close my eyes, squeezing them tight until everything goes black. No. I won't let myself slip into that place. Not again. Sera's gone because she pushed me out of the way. If I give up now, she died for nothing—and she can't have died for nothing. She wanted me to live. And even if it kills me every day, that's exactly what I'm going to do.

Daybreak creeps in, the rain's patter dwindling to silence. I sit, numb and hollow, watching as light creeps across Sera's pale face. It's odd, seeing her so still. All the joy she fought so hard for seems like a distant dream. She looks so different now—no laughter, no fiery determination in her eyes. The hollows of her cheeks are deeper, and several fine lines cover her face. Her arms are as thin as sticks, and she doesn't look like she'd weigh one hundred pounds soaking wet. It's like looking at a stranger.

As gently as my shaking fingers allow, I remove Sera's scarf —the one thing from her past she couldn't part with. The fabric feels heavy in my hands, like it's more than just cloth and fine wire threads. It's like I'm holding a piece of her—the piece she kept hidden from everyone, except from me. I was the only person in the Slum who knew who Sera really was. And now, no one else will.

My eyes fall on Sera's bare feet. She never needed shoes, even when the ground was covered in snow and ice. Carefully, I set the scarf aside and slip off my shoes. They're frayed at the edges with holes in the bottoms—the same shoes I got when I left Lockup. I hated them when I got them. But now, I don't really think I need them anymore.

I take Sera's hands and place them over the wound in her stomach. No one should have to see that. Then, I take the tarp and cover everything but her face. In another world, Sera could be sleeping, dreaming of her next nighttime adventure in Midtown.

I lean forward and press my lips to her forehead. It's cold, void of all the warmth and joy she used to possess. I pull back, white-hot tears burning my eyes as I drape the tarp over her face.

"I love you."

My voice is barely a whisper, but the words are truer than any others. I love Sera. I *loved* Sera. And I'll never love anyone the way I loved her.

Sera's scarf feels oddly heavy as I wrap it around my neck. With nothing more to do and nothing left to say, I stand up, the pain in my leg little more than a throb, and limp to the door I move the broken chair and table out of the way, my hands surprisingly steady. Then, after taking one final look over my shoulder, I step outside, leaving Sera behind.

The air smells fresh after the rain—a stark contrast to the thick, pungent stuff that usually fills the Slum. After yesterday's chaos, the streets are a ghost town, the slick cobblestones cold against my bare feet. Bodies lay scattered like discarded playthings, with men, women, children strewn across alleys and doorways. The early morning sun casts long shadows over their still forms, but it can't warm the ice flooding through me.

A lump forms in my throat as I move through this place that used to be jam-packed with life. Every corner reveals another tragedy—a mother clutching her silent child, an old man crumpled against a wall. Their faces are frozen in time, some in fear, others in surprise. But all of them are gone. How many did the Enforcers kill before they finally stopped? Talon? Sola and her kids? Nyssa? Each one of their faces flashes through my mind. I need to find them, need to know that they're still here. If I've lost them too… No, I can't think like that. I've lost too much already.

With a sigh, I turn my feet toward the square. It's the last place I want to go. The deaths in the streets are one thing, but I know that whatever's waiting in the square is another beast entirely. That's were AURA wanted us, after all.

My heart jumps into my throat as I step into the square. Armed Enforcers patrol the area, prodding the bodies on the ground with their batons. People wearing hazmat suits walk around in pairs, throwing bodies carelessly into the backs of trucks. My throat tightens as I clench my fists. It's like the people lying on the ground aren't even people at all. How can anyone be so heartless?

But I don't stop until my eyes reach the stage. Newtowners, their clothes adorned in glittering gemstones and metallic threads. A few consult tablets, but overall, they just look bored or repulsed.

I turn on my heel, my shoulders shaking with suppressed fury. I can't stand this—the bodies of the poor discarded like rubbish, lives reduced to nothing, while those who have more than enough simply watch. I need to get out of here. Maybe I'll find Sola back at her house. If she made it through the night, that's where she and the kids would be.

"Check over there. Ensure everyone's accounted for!"

I stop dead in my tracks. I know that voice. It's haunted my dreams ever since I was seven, when he first caught me playing with a servant. Slowly, I turn back to the stage—and there he is.

Elias Malkin stands in the middle of the stage, the golden

embroidery of his black suit glinting like stars. He's barking orders at the Enforcers, a large tablet in his hand. My chest tightens as I watch him, bile burning my throat. How? How is my father a part of this? Sure, I always thought he was a horrible human being. After all, he Renounced his own kids just to save his reputation. But this—coordinating AURA's massacre of the Slum—is a low I didn't think possible for him.

I should leave, just turn my back on the stage and disappear before he sees me. It's not like he cares. But something roots me to the spot. Even though his voice still sends a chill down my spine, it doesn't evoke the dread it once did. I've suffered too much to be scared of one man.

My feet carry me closer to the stage, almost against my will. The disgust on my father's face as he looks over the square stings; it's a look I know all too well. But I don't walk away. I wait, holding my breath as his eyes sweep over me. I don't know what I'm expecting—a flicker of recognition, maybe. What I'm not expecting is for him to look away, turning up his nose as he barks orders at another Enforcer.

"Hey!" The shout leaves my lips before I can stop it. But I don't care. I want him to look at me, to see me.

"Run along, Slummer," my father says, waving me off.

I'm so stunned that I can't even move. How does he not recognize me?! My face grows hot as my hands ball into fists. I guess I really didn't mean anything to him. After all, it takes a special kind of monster to forget their own son's face.

"Excuse me!" another voice calls out, making me turn around.

I feel like I've been hit by a truck. My mother, Aelia Malkin, walks through the square, her glittering dress barely skimming the blood-soaked cobblestones. My mouth falls open. This doesn't make any sense. Why would my mother, the perfect Newtown wife who tried to buy her youngest kids back, be here?

Before I can even find the words to ask, my mother shoves

something under my nose. "Have you seen this boy?" she demands, her eyes wide with panic. "Please, tell me you've seen him."

I stare at the person in the photo, barely able to breathe. It's me—or at least, who I used to be before I got here. The boy in the photo is well groomed, young, and well-fed—someone who had the whole world at his fingertips.

The picture in my mother's hand blurs as my eyes widen in disbelief. How can she not recognize me? I'm standing right in front of her! But it's like she's looking at a complete stranger.

"Answer the lady, vermin! Or I'll call an Enforcer." my father snaps, stepping down from the stage to join my mother. "I knew I shouldn't have let you come. Finding that boy is a waste of time," my father adds, his eyes narrowing at my mother.

Aelia's hands tremble as she holds out the photo, practically shoving it into my face. "Please," she implores, tears cutting through her makeup. "If you know anything…"

I feel something stir inside me—pity, maybe, or shock. The Slum has stripped me bare. My skin is dry and cracked, my cheeks are hollow, and I now have dark circles beneath my eyes that never go away. My once perfectly groomed hair practically reaches my chin, and I am covered in more scars than I can count. I am a Slummer through and through; no trace of the Newtown boy remains.

My heart pounds as I step back. The Malkins, so polished and perfect, so concerned with their own standing with AURA that they'd Renounce their kids to save their own necks. They don't deserve to be here, standing on the bloodied stones of the square. They don't deserve to know if their son is alive or dead.

"I've never seen him," I say quietly, my voice surprisingly steady.

Without another word, I turn my back on them—the two people who were supposed to love me no matter what—and walk through the chaos they've helped create. My bare feet slip slightly on the slick cobblestones as I weave between bodies and debris. The rain has washed away some of the blood, but not enough to wipe the stones clean. Will they ever be clean after something like this?

The farther I get from the square, from the people who used to be my parents, the more something inside me settles into place. It's not peace—I think I've endured too much pain to ever feel true peace. Ezariah Malkin is dead. If I'm being honest, he died with Theron and Callias, and whatever was left went with Sera. Now, there's only Ezra.

I shuffle through the streets, my bare feet numb against the damp ground. I look at the buildings leaning on each other like old friends, and the narrow streets, an intricate network that connects everyone here. I used to think the Slum was a prison, a filthy, disgusting place that needed to be escaped. But this place, with its crooked alleys and makeshift homes, is more real than anything I've ever known. The people here—they're my real family. Not by blood, but by something deeper.

Talon, Nyssa, Rowan, Sola—they took me in when I had nothing and shaped me into the person I've become. Gram knew that this place was worth saving, and so do I. I am Ezra, and I'm a Slummer. This place is my home. I'm exactly where I'm meant to be.

END OF
BOOK ONE

ACKNOWLEDGEMENTS

There were times when I thought this book wouldn't get done. As you are reading this, I can only assume you've finished it. So, I think the first thing I'd have to say is, "I'm sorry." That seems to be my go-to response whenever discussing this book. I've apologized to readers, to myself, and even to the characters.

Writing this book was a STRUGGLE. First, it is a deviation from what I've written in the past. Change is scary for anyone, but after Ezariah popped into my head, I knew his story needed to be told and that *HE* needed to be the one to tell it.

Again, if you've read it—you know. Writing a story like this, steeped in so much sadness with very little light, took its toll. I've cried, shut down, cried some more, and grieved. But, something I didn't expect to find in *NOMISMAN* was a level of resilience, even in the darkest of times.

I have to give a special shout-out to my *FAMILY AND FRIENDS.* They saw firsthand what this book did to me. But they were always there, holding me up while *AURA* tried—and failed—to bring me down. They gave me time and grace when I needed it. I know for a fact that this book would not be done if it weren't for them.

This book would not be what it is without the ever-watchful eyes of my amazing—and patient—BETA readers, *DANI* and *KAYLA.* From reading this book piece by piece (as I was drafting it) to your constant words of encouragement, I really could not have done this without you. We went through the wringer on this one, and I cannot thank either of you enough.

ROBIN—my excellent new editor for this book. I learned so much working with you. You really understood Ezariah's voice and how he saw the world. You were the only editor who didn't try to tone him down (even when he got on your nerves). You helped to elevate this story in so many ways. It truly was a pleasure to work with you, and I cannot wait to do it again.

SEMNITZ—my amazing, new cover designer. I had no idea what I wanted this cover to look like. Mostly, I knew the "vibe" I was going for. Not only did you understand what I wanted (without me saying it), but you also added details I never would have thought of.

And finally, *MY READERS*—I want to thank you for taking a chance on this novel! It's not what you've come to expect from me. So, I want to thank you for taking a leap into *NOMISMAN*. I hope you took something from the first chapter of Ezariah's story.

ABOUT THE AUTHOR

LOGAN YOUNG is a young adult author best known for his fantasy series, *THE POWER OF PRINCIRUM*. As a kid, his overactive mind never shut off, filling his head with more stories than he knew what to do with. It didn't take long before those stories found their way onto paper. Now, he shares those fascinating worlds with you.

Hear about LOGAN YOUNG's new releases, cover reveals, publishing news, and much more before anyone else!

WWW.IMLOGANYOUNG.COM

amazon.com/author/imloganyoung
goodreads.com/imloganyoung
instagram.com/imloganyoung
x.com/imloganyoung
facebook.com/imloganyoung

www.ingramcontent.com/pod-product-compliance
Lightning Source LLC
Chambersburg PA
CBHW020233010826

48973CB00006B/1501